# The Mermaid, the Witch, and the Sea

# The Mermaid, the Witch, and the Sea

MAGGIE TOKUDA-HALL

CANDLEWICK PRESS

First edition 2020

Library of Congress Catalog Card Number pending
ISBN 978-1-5362-0431-5

20 21 22 23 24 25 SHD 10 9 8 7 6 5 4 3 2 1

Printed in Chelsea, MI, U.S.A.

This book was typeset in Warnock Pro.

Candlewick Press
99 Dover Street
Somerville, Massachusetts 02144

visit us at www.candlewick.com

MIX
Paper from
responsible sources
FSC
www.fsc.org
FSC® C008955

*Written especially for Clare*

Long after the sun had set, when the passengers were nestled neatly in their cabins, the crew gathered on the deck of the *Dove*. They'd been at sea for a fortnight, playing the role of any passenger vessel crew — all "yes, sirs" and "no, miladys"— seeing to the needs of the stiff-legged landsmen with exaggerated obsequiousness. But no more.

Rake stood at the helm, just below the Nameless Captain, as was his place. The ragged crew below them were the captain's men, chosen for their savagery, their drunkenness, and their predilection for thievery and murder. But it was Rake they answered to at sea.

"It's time," Rake said, and the men scattered belowdecks.

Sleep-fogged passengers were pulled roughly from their bunks and dragged, questioning and sputtering, to the foredeck. The captain scoffed; even their nightwear was finery, silks with careful stitching.

As was ritual, the strongest man was pulled from the ranks of the passengers and forced to his knees. On this particular voyage, he was a spice merchant named Mr. Lam, headed to the Floating Islands without his wife and his children to see about the famous marketplace there. He could be no more than twenty-five.

"Come on, then, Florian," Rake said. "Time to earn your britches."

It had been Rake's idea: The name change. The men's clothes. Being a slip of a girl may have been tenable in Crandon, but it wasn't here on the *Dove*. Not among these men. In taking this man's life, Flora could start a new one. Her life as Florian.

The cost was simple. Rake slipped Florian a dagger.

"Show them," Rake whispered. Not just the passengers, as was Florian's official charge, but the other sailors aboard the *Dove*. They needed to see who this child was, the man this girl had become. Rake could tell from the solemn nod Florian gave that he understood Rake's words exactly.

The child stepped forward, and though he was small-boned and skinny from strict rations, the passengers fell silent. The long, silver dagger in Florian's hand shone like the moon in an otherwise black night.

The Nameless Captain cleared his throat, all theater and cruelty. "It gives me no great pleasure to announce to you fine people that the *Dove* is no passenger vessel. She is a slaver. And all of you aboard are now her chattel."

Sobs and cries of dissent rippled through the passengers. One foolish old man even cursed at the captain. A blow from Rake across the man's chin crumpled his aged and spindly legs for him, and he hit the deck with a crash of bone on wood. The scuffle only caused more shouting and wailing until the captain raised his pistol into the air and fired once.

Silence returned, save for the sound of the sea lapping against the *Dove.*

"If any of you are thinking of mutiny, I can promise you"— he motioned to Florian, who slipped behind the trembling Mr. Lam, dagger poised —"we don't take kindly to mutineers."

Though the man begged for clemency at a whisper, Florian dragged the dagger across his throat. Lam's blood spilled down the front of his nightshirt, and his thick, muscled body fell to the deck. Two of the crewmen hauled the dying man up by the armpits and held him for passengers to witness how the last shudders of life left him. Florian wiped the blood from the blade on his sleeve.

With the passengers now sufficiently terrified, the captain had them locked into the slave quarters, in the hold of the ship. The *Dove's* spacious cabins would be used henceforth by the crew, who until then had been taking turns in the hammocks strung up in the stores.

Belowdecks, the passengers wept.

Abovedeck, the crew chanted, "Florian, Florian, Florian, Florian!"

He was a captain's man now — Rake had seen to that. As safe as he could be among his peers. The child had competently changed stories more than once, and swiftly, too. Rake had seen it happen. What was one more seismic shift? From child to adult. Innocent to murderer. Girl to man.

And Florian, who still had Mr. Lam's blood on his sleeve, smiled into the darkness.

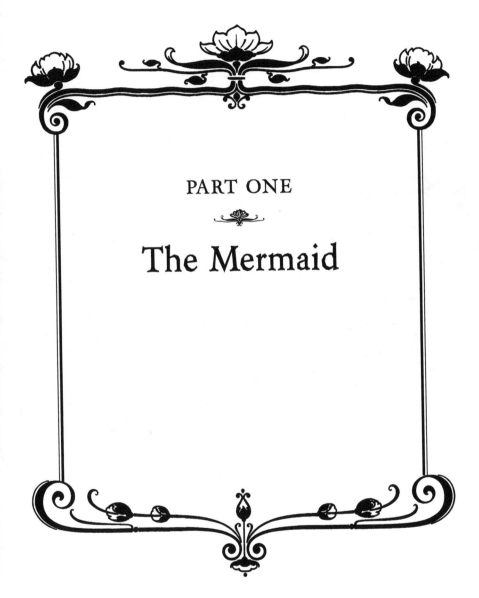

PART ONE

The Mermaid

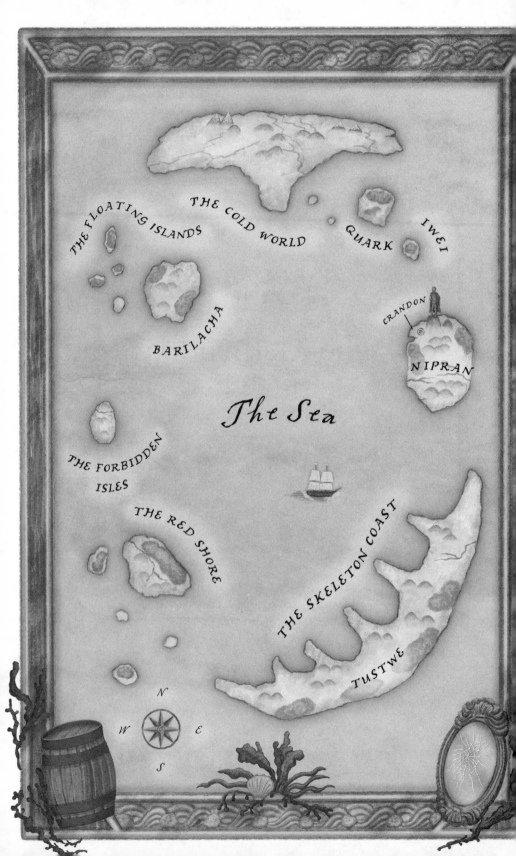

## CHAPTER 1

# *Evelyn*

**E**velyn washed her hands again. The telltale sand under her fingernails stubbornly resisted the fine soap from Quark that her mother, the Lady Hasegawa, had imported especially for her. Her mother claimed that only a foreign soap meant for rice-paddy farmers could possibly conquer Evelyn's dirty fingernails, since her habits were far too coarse for a good Imperial girl.

It was a rude thing to have said, but more so because the Lady said it in front of her lady's maid, who was from Quark.

And sure, maybe digging about the shore near their home looking for shells was not a most ladylike activity. The whole coastline was black from the filth of the Crandon port. Crandon was the capital of the Nipran Empire, and nearly every type of trading vessel passed through her waters. But it was not so dirty that lovely pink and white shells could not be excavated by those with the patience to do it.

Evelyn had convinced her own lady's maid, Keiko, that the Lady Hasegawa would never again find out that she'd been scrounging on the shore. But now Evelyn was carelessly close to breaking that promise, which could lose Keiko her job, not to mention any reference the Lady Hasegawa might give her. But still. Somehow Evelyn could not be called away from her messy hobby. It was as though the sea called to her especially.

"Miss, the Lady has called for you again," Keiko said. She was a little frantic now. As Evelyn's maid, she'd been subjected to all manner of admonishment for Evelyn's many irresponsibilities, but mainly her tardiness. This afternoon's tea would be no exception.

"I'm sorry, Keiko. Truly. But look at this one!" Evelyn held up a whelk shell. A spiral of blue worked its way from tip to door, and only the very point of its apex had been snapped off. "It's practically intact!"

"Hold still." Keiko grabbed Evelyn's hands and, finger by finger, dragged the blunt end of a sewing needle beneath the nail, scraping out the grit. It hurt, and one of her fingers bled, but Evelyn was glad for Keiko's help. She always was.

"Thank goodness for you, Keiko," Evelyn whispered, "or my mother would've disowned me years ago."

Keiko smiled, gave Evelyn a nudge with her shoulder. "Thanks to the Emperor, you mean. Now go, please. Before I'm sacked and you're cut out of the family."

Evelyn gave Keiko a quick kiss on the cheek and ran to the sukiya, where her mother's tea ceremony was held every day.

The Lady Hasegawa and Evelyn had been staying in their Crandon home since Lord Hasegawa had been forced to take a consultancy role in the family's shipping company. The Hasegawas had come upon hard times in recent years, and though the Lady Hasegawa would never admit it, they had all but abandoned their country manor and nearly all of their staff. And though they were still attended to by a handful of footmen, ladies' maids, guards, a cook, and a gardener, one could scarcely ignore the conspicuous lack of service in their household. Hasegawa was an old name, and it was her father's dishonor that they were not better kept.

So many servants gone meant that Evelyn had hardly any family left, either. The servants had been the ones who had raised her, after all. It had been her nanny who'd kissed her skinned knees, the stable boys who'd played chase. She barely knew her parents, and they certainly did not know her.

However, without fail, the Lady Hasegawa still demanded the high tea ceremony each afternoon, and Evelyn's presence was mandatory. Evelyn wasn't exactly sure why. While she liked a good rice ball as much as anyone, tea was invariably boring and painfully tedious, especially in the summer, when there was so much to see and do.

All of which existed outside her mother's sukiya.

"Evelyn, you are late," the Lady Hasegawa said by way of salutation. "Again."

"My apologies." Evelyn bowed low, trying her best to look properly conciliatory. Then she took her seat, accidentally nudging the table with her knees. The preponderance of small dishes clattered.

A quick exhalation through the Lady Hasegawa's flared nostrils was all Evelyn needed to be reminded of her mother's perpetual disappointment in her. How wearying it must be, Evelyn thought, to bear the burden of such ceaseless inadequacy. Still, at least she knew her mother, could recognize the moods — mostly displeasure — that flitted across her face. Her father was as unfathomable to her as the bottom of the sea, and nearly as distant. Once she had asked him if he loved her or not. In response he had drained his drink wordlessly and left the room.

The Lady Hasegawa motioned for the tea to be poured, which

was done in silence. Evelyn did her best to handle her teacup with grace. She'd broken two already and been banned straight out from using the heirloom porcelain, a humiliating rule enforced even in company.

"As has likely become clear—even to you—our family has come upon some hard times," the Lady Hasegawa said.

Evelyn nearly dropped her cup. Her mother never admitted to the financial woes of the Hasegawas, even though they were glaringly obvious. How strange it was to hear their truth so plainly stated. For once.

"Yes, Mother."

"As such, Lord Hasegawa has decided it's time for you to wed. You're nearly sixteen years old. And, thanks to the Emperor, your father has found you a suitable match. One who does not demand too much in the way of dowry."

Evelyn put down her cup gracelessly. Hot tea sloshed over the lip of the cup onto her hand. It burned until it was cold. Evelyn made no effort to brush it away, instead focusing on the gift of distraction it gave her in this terrible moment.

"You should be glad to know," the Lady Hasegawa said loudly—loud enough so that the few servants they still had left in their employ could hear her—"that your father has done quite well for you, despite your many faults, thanks to his high connections within the Emperor's ranks. Your husband may be new money—garnered in the silk trade—but he's achieved something for himself and even served in the Imperial Guard. I hear he was most gallant in the service. He's made quite a name for himself. All of which, let's be frank, is substantially better than I ever dreamed for you." She took a sip of her tea. Her manners were perfect, of course, her hands cupped delicately around her cup just so. "You shall be joining him at his residence."

"Is he . . . is he here?"

"My goodness, no," the Lady Hasegawa said brusquely. She deftly picked up a piece of squash in her chopsticks and elegantly deposited it in her mouth. She chewed thoughtfully, as if imagining the relaxing, daughter-free future this arrangement promised. She was smiling, Evelyn realized. Triumphant. "No, he's in the Floating Islands."

The Emperor had many armies and navies, consulates and ambassadors, all over the Known World. Nearly all of that world was colonized by the Nipranites now, though some colonies were younger, still rough around their edges. Iwei was, of course, the oldest colony. If only she could be sent there! It might be the smallest of the many island nations that made up the Known World, but it boasted famously temperate weather, and all the best wines were imported from there. Even Quark would have been better. It was a new colony, certainly, but it was so close to Crandon, only two weeks' sail on a clinker. Culturally different. Life was a little cheaper there, which lent it a frightening air. But if she were in Quark, she could still come home now and again.

The reach of the Imperial Guard stretched far beyond casual travel, however, and the Floating Islands were proof of this. They were a several-months-long voyage, and an expensive one. With so many days on the open sea, it was risky enough not to be taken casually. If she went to the Floating Islands, Evelyn realized, she'd likely never come home.

"Yes," the Lady Hasegawa said dreamily. "Your father has done quite well."

Like all the children of Crandon, Evelyn had been reared on the tales of the savagery and magic of the Floating Islands. It was said they housed the Known World's last witches. Actual practical witches. It was only thanks to the Emperor that witches were finally all but extinct, and the world was safer for it. And while Crandon, as the capital of the Nipran Empire, was cold and orderly, the Floating Islands were notoriously a nation of vagabonds, baleful merchants, and danger. But then, that was what Imperials said about basically all of the colonies. The ruling classes imported the colonies' goods and prayed that the people who supplied them would stay upon their native shores.

A shiver raked down Evelyn's spine as she tried to imagine herself riding the infamously dangerous wood-and-rope elevators that rose from the Islands' craggy cliffs.

If one thing was for certain, it was that Evelyn's parents had finally found the most expedient and honorable way to be rid of her. What a small cost her dowry must have seemed to them.

She would leave with her belongings packed into her casket, as so many Imperial girls had done before. It was a tradition born of the most calculating kind of practicality, serving the dual purpose of showing the husband that the girl would be truly with him until death did they part, while also providing, at her family's expense, a means for her burial. It was macabre, and Evelyn's skin crawled, thinking of her kimonos and her corsets crammed into the vessel that would one day house her corpse. She had often thought of casket girls with pity — that their parents would be so crass, that their lives would be so transparently close to death, that their futures would be so bindingly arranged.

And now she was one of them.

Evelyn was to depart for the Floating Islands within a fortnight. Without the expense of housing and keeping a daughter, the Lady Hasegawa would be taking on two new kitchen girls and an additional valet. Though it was customary for a lady's maid to accompany her lady, Keiko would not be going with Evelyn. Instead, Keiko had been offered either a demotion to the laundry or a letter of reference.

It was a cruel thing the Hasegawas were doing to Keiko, and it infuriated Evelyn as much as did her own fate. For Keiko's part, she'd held herself together admirably under the circumstances. She padded into the room, her footfalls nearly silent on the tatami mats, in the way that most practiced servants' were.

Keiko was, Evelyn reflected, too good for the Hasegawas. She resolved that she would tell her so before she left.

"Are they asleep?" Evelyn asked.

"Lord Hasegawa has taken his wine for the evening." Keiko hardly met Evelyn's eyes. Instead, she persistently averted her gaze to an imperfectly tied curtain or a speck on the vanity mirror that needed polishing. Keiko had been Evelyn's personal maid since they were both children, and her best friend for nearly as long. Evelyn knew Keiko's face as well as her own; tonight it was wrought with despair.

"Come on." Evelyn pulled the blankets aside, making enough room so that Keiko could lie beside her. Keiko sniffled but obeyed, finding her place in Evelyn's arms.

Evelyn stroked Keiko's hair, which was soft and familiar to the touch, the dark and lovely brown of good soil. Keiko was not Nipranite, though she bore a Nipranite name. Most servants did. The Cold World name her mother had given her had been long and complicated, too much for the Imperial tongue. Evelyn could not remember it. She could remember every freckle on her face, though.

She lifted Keiko's chin with her finger, tipping the girl's face toward hers. Keiko's freckles blurred beneath the tears that converged at her sharp chin. Evelyn stopped to consider Keiko's lips before she kissed her.

Keiko's kisses tasted of salt. Like the sea. It was odd, so unlike Keiko. It was equally unsettling and lovely. With each kiss Evelyn felt further from her new life as a casket girl and closer to Keiko. Closer to home.

But even as she tried to lose herself in the softness of Keiko, of her mouth and her legs and her neck and her cheek, Evelyn couldn't help but wonder if her parents' choice to deprive her of her most beloved lady's maid was not just frugal but calculated.

## CHAPTER 2

*Flora*

It was rare that the crew spent much time ashore. Even more rare that they should do so in Crandon. It had been years since Flora had last seen this cursed city, last witnessed the horrible stone statue of the First Emperor crest over the horizon, to loom, enormous, over everything. She hated that statue nearly as much as she hated Crandon itself. But the captain had paid out all the men so that they could enjoy their stay here. Crandon sprawled with offerings for nearly every appetite, assuming one had coin. There were good times to be had in Crandon for a man with money, and since most of the crew called the city home, they knew just where to find it.

All except Flora, it seemed. Being back in Crandon made her nervous. She felt compressed here, small.

On the other hand, the *Dove* had been to Tustwe's eastern shores twice, and it was not until she had visited there, had been in a place where she looked like everyone else, that she realized the power of blending in. Why her mother had left her native shore only to come to a country where everyone hated her, and her children, was beyond Flora's understanding.

As Nipran's nearest southern neighbor, it was miraculous that Tustwe had not yet been colonized. But it held its own in trade against the Empire. Flora loved it there — loved the heat, loved the way Imperials looked nervous as they walked through the dusty streets and startled at the oryxes.

Someday, she and her brother would live in Tustwe. They talked about it frequently. They'd learn the language — Alfie first, of course; he had a knack for languages, for picking up words and phrases like souvenirs from the different places they visited. Flora would follow. They would blend in. And they'd never return to Crandon again.

That time was nearing, too. They'd been saving. Each voyage on the *Dove* added to Flora's unease that Alfie would do something stupid, that the captain would decide they were no longer worth their weight. Or worse, that they'd become like the rest of the crew, indistinguishable from the murderers and rapists whose ranks they shared. It had not been so long since they started sailing with the *Dove.*

She remembered the ears, severed and cold, handed to the captain as their ticket aboard.

Their ticket away from this place. Crandon. The Empire.

Luckily, shore leave was nearly over now. Unluckily, Alfie was not back on the *Dove.*

So off Flora ran, through the city she hated, through every back alley and dingy pub Sty's End had to offer. They'd grown up in Sty's End, but that didn't mean it was exempt from Flora's hatred. If anything, her ire was inflamed in those narrow gray streets, as if their very dimensions were too small to contain it.

They had been reared on Imperial hate. Rejected from the

16

orphanage. They'd rarely found a roof to sleep under. Amid the desperate and the dying, the funeral homes and the pubs.

This one, the Tipsy Pig, was the last Flora would check. After that, Alfie would be on his own, she vowed.

This was a lie and she knew it. Alfie was the only family she had—she'd never leave without him.

The pub smelled of piss and wine, cheap rum and sweat. Familiar smells, smells she hated. She pushed her way through the bodies, the men bellowing, loud with drink.

Leaning over the bar, propped up on his elbows and nearly passed out, was Alfie. Though he was the elder of the two, Flora felt as though she were his keeper, today especially. Any time he had access to drink, really.

She tried to push down the resentment, hot and red and burning, that flared in her chest. She knew why he drank, knew too well that there were memories he'd rather live without. And that if he hadn't interceded to protect her, he'd not have them. But his burden became hers each time they hit the shore. Any shore.

"You idiot." She tried to shake him awake. "Get up."

He groaned but didn't move.

"Come on," said a woman behind the bar. She was old, the passage of time plain upon her face. Like Flora and Alfie, she was not Imperial-blooded, though she was pink, which was worse, really. There wasn't an uncolonized country left in the Cold World.

Sty's End was full of immigrants from all over the Known World. Hardly anyone there could boast pure Imperial blood.

The barkeep's immense bosom was hardly contained by her yukata, and Flora felt her face flush at the sight of it.

"Let him be," she said warmly. "Have a drink."

She poured a draft of muddy ale into a dirty cup and pushed it forward.

"I've got no silver."

The woman nudged it closer, a wry half smile on her face.

"Or copper."

"You don't look like you do," the woman said. "But then I bet a boy like you has plenty to offer a poor lady like myself as compensation for this here spirit." She gave Flora a long, lascivious look up and down. "You ever been with a woman?"

*Boy.*

Flora took the cup and drained it. It was horrible — flat and stale. It tasted the way a horse smelled.

"If I hadn't," Flora said carefully, "I wouldn't start with you."

The woman laughed a deep belly laugh. "S'too bad!" she said merrily. "Your mate here was much more obliging. My biggest customer all night."

Alfie groaned. It wasn't until then that Flora could see he wasn't just drunk. His stare was focused, but not on anything in the pub. His gray eyes were eclipsed black with dilated pupils. Flora's heart raced. She had not checked their stores, had not seen what he'd taken from them, had not counted their savings before she left the ship.

*Just how much did he spend?*

"What has he been drinking?" She feared she already knew the answer.

The woman smiled, clearly pleased to be the bearer of bad news after Flora's rudeness. "Mermaid's blood. Had it in fresh from the port just this afternoon."

Flora's eyes fell shut.

Mermaid's blood was the oblivion drink. Men drank it to escape the cruelty of their lives. Drink the blood, they said, and you'd see beautiful things. But memories would disappear. Gone,

gone, gone. Which was what most drinkers wanted. It was mermaid's blood that made the Nameless Captain nameless, after all. He'd had enough that he'd forgotten even his own name.

Mermaid's blood changed men. And the cost was high.

How much had Alfie had? Flora wondered. *How much of Alfie is left?*

Flora shoved her shoulder beneath her brother's arm and hoisted him swiftly to his feet. It was a practiced gesture, one she'd made countless times before all around the Known World. With Alfie muttering to himself, she supported him out of the Tipsy Pig and into the gray Crandon sun.

"You're a lucky stupid thing," she said to him. "That you're thin as a skeleton, and that you've got me for a sister."

Alfie twitched in her grasp but managed to find his feet beneath him. He laughed, but it was a distant sound, more like the memory of a laugh than a real one.

"Fish with legs," he said. "Crawling onto the shore."

"Sure. Let's get you home." Her voice was much softer than she might have liked.

As they drew close to the *Dove*, Alfie insisted on walking of his own accord. His legs were shaky, but he pushed her and her help away.

"Oh, save it," Alfie groaned. "Don't let them see you." His voice trailed off, but Flora knew what he hadn't said: *Don't let them see you being a girl.*

The men of the *Dove* knew she was a girl. Or had been one. But after the captain had ordered her to kill — and she had, unflinchingly — she had earned the respect to be something better than a girl. Something safe. From then on, the crew had only ever called her Florian. It was the name that Rake had given her. It was the

19

name of a murderer. It was the name of a survivor. It was a spell that allowed her to blend in with the crew.

Florian was the captain's man now, everyone knew. And so grudgingly, she'd been granted respect.

"I've got no love for you anyway," she shot back. And Alfie's laugh transformed into a retch as his body rejected the black blood he'd paid so dearly for all over the ground.

The question of how much he'd spent dogged her. They always talked about going to Tustwe, about leaving the *Dove.* Just one more voyage, he'd say. There was always one more.

She may as well square herself with it. With the *Dove* and her horrible purpose. With the life she couldn't escape, the brother she loved and hated.

She deposited Alfie in his hammock, and he groaned with relief.

"Just you and me, Florian," he said. "Just us against the world." His voice was hoarse from vomiting.

Beneath the hammock, Flora pulled out their rucksack. In it was a silver dagger, a woven bracelet from Tustwe, and the leather sack they kept their wages in. Years of wages she'd saved. She knew right away, could tell from its weight and the obvious lack of dimension, but she still opened it to be sure.

It was empty.

It smelled of rot on the *Dove,* of decay and mold. But it was home.

At least the *Dove* did not look like a pirate ship, or even a merchant ship. Rather, she looked and felt like a fine passenger vessel, with a vast set of upper decks that befit the wealthy people suckered into paying for passage aboard her.

As Alfie slept off the last clutches of the mermaid's blood, Flora set about her duties to prepare the *Dove* for voyage. She wasn't sure how many voyages of this manner she'd taken with the *Dove*, but this one felt different.

This was probably because it'd be their first time abducting Imperials. From the heart of Nipran.

There was no looking away from what they did — the crew of the *Dove* hoodwinked people into paying for safe passage, then instead sold them into slavery. And as hard as Flora's life in Crandon had been, it was not, she knew, enslavement. That institution was illegal in the Empire — supposedly, though she had seen her fair share of enslaved people in the colonies — but it was fully and actually barred in Tustwe. Not that she'd ever live there now.

While the captain took a great many precautions — he hit new ports each time with his con and did not force the passengers belowdecks until they were far enough from their homeland to preclude any possibility of escape — coming to the Nipran shore, to Crandon itself, not even a day's walk from the Emperor's palace? It seemed like madness.

Despite Flora's small frame, her body was wiry with taut muscle after all her time aboard the *Dove*. It had taken many trips with the crew taunting and teasing her before she'd built the strength to see to tasks like hauling barrels of seawater from the gunwales to the stores on her own. If they were attacked, if the Emperor's fleets found them, these stores would put out the fires that would follow. The stores of water did little to salve her fear, but they were something.

And wasn't it better to do something?

To keep busy?

As she worked, she sang the only song she knew. It was an anthem for pirates, if drinking songs could be anthems. Flora was no great singer, but now in her solitude, she carried the tune quietly:

*Mermaid caught*
*Returned to Sea*
*By witch taught*
*To be free*

*Two souls bound*
*By love, by knife*
*True love found*
*Restored to life*

*Two souls fight*
*For love, to be*
*True love's might*
*To save the Sea*

"That's a good man." Rake's face was split into an uncharacteristic shape. Was that a smile?

He wasn't as big as the captain, not as tall. But the men feared him more. He was tightly wound, always ready. She'd seen him slit more throats than she could count, and not always those of prisoners. He was the hammer the captain brought down. "Just in case, sir," said Flora.

Rake made her nervous. Always had. Not just in the way he frightened the whole crew, but also because she desperately, deeply, wanted to please him. She had not known her father. But she liked to think he might have been something like Rake.

"I know, Florian. And that's a good song for the work." The name rang like a bell. Flora smiled. It was magic, the name, a spell that kept her safe. And when Rake used it, it sent a shiver of something rare through her.

*Pride.*

Florian was never a better man than he was in Rake's regard.

"You ever hear the one about the Pirate Supreme and the Emperor's crown?" Rake asked.

"No." This was a lie. Of course she had heard it. All pirates had. But she loved stories. And she wanted so badly to hear Rake tell it. He motioned for Flora to sit, which she did, ignoring the wet of the barrel through the seat of her pants. It was not every day the first mate offered to tell a crewman a story.

Nor did any prudent sailor speak too highly of the Pirate Supreme in the captain's presence, or even aboard the captain's ship.

The Pirate Supreme may have been the undisputed lord of pirates, but the captain was the captain. He paid his tithes. But the word was that the Pirate Supreme had gotten word of the captain's misdeeds and was angry. That the wrath of the Pirate Supreme would soon find the Nameless Captain. The Supreme had operatives, men and women with secret identities who did the royal bidding. The captain had ordered the deaths of more than one man under the *suspicion* that they were operatives.

This was likely because the captain regularly broke the Supreme's only and most sacred law: never drink the blood of a mermaid.

And now Alfie had broken it, too.

They said the Pirate Supreme and the Supreme's operatives found those who broke the sacred law and saw them dead. There was a time that Flora wished that were true. That justice might even find her captain. But she'd stopped believing in justice years ago.

"When the Emperor's eldest son was to wed, they say the Pirate Supreme came to Crandon. They say this because all could see, even from the shore, the long shadow cast by the *Leviathan*."

Just the sound of the ship's name made Flora's breath catch in her throat. The *Leviathan*. It was the Pirate Supreme's ship — a gift, they said, from the Sea herself.

"Which, of course, sent the Imperials into a madness for security. So the Emperor ordered his entire fleet to ready for battle against that one ship, our Supreme's ship, which they did. Fast as lightning, they took orders — you know how they are. Can't obey fast enough."

Flora listened, rapt. She rarely saw Rake so pleased, his eyes so light.

"They don't catch her, of course. No one's catching the *Leviathan* unless she wants to be caught. They come back to their Emperor with their tails tucked and tell him they've failed.

"But by the time they get back, the Emperor is in a rage. His crown's been stolen, and just before the wedding! He's thundering mad, of course. The ship got away, and somehow with the crown to boot. People say it was magic, but it wasn't.

"I'll tell you what it *was*. It was just smarts. Long before the *Leviathan* was spotted, the Supreme came to Crandon. No Imperial knows what the Supreme looks like, so who'd sound the alarm? Then when the *Leviathan* came as a distraction, the Supreme could slip in and just steal that unguarded crown right from underneath the Emperor." Rake chuckled.

Then he leaned forward and whispered to Flora: "They say the Supreme wears the Emperor's crown." He paused meaningfully. "But only to take a dump."

Flora burst out laughing.

"You know what the moral of that story is?" Rake asked.

"Plan ahead?"

"Sure. But more importantly? If Imperials weren't so hopped up on their own tales of military victories, they wouldn't have

24

been so quick to try to take down the unsinkable ship. It was a fool's errand, and the Imperials were made the fools by their own stories of themselves." He stood and gave Flora what might have been an affectionate pat on the back if it hadn't been quite so firm, knocking the wind out of her. "Know your truth, not your story," he said.

Flora nodded and hopped off the barrel. "I'll keep that in mind. You know, in case I ever command my own ship." She tried to say it with a laugh, but it just came out as pitiful.

"You never know." He examined her, his face inscrutable. "You've the feel of destiny about you."

The word worked through Flora's mind, a rock tossed in the waves. *Destiny.* She felt that, with Rake's belief in her, maybe it could be true. Maybe Florian was worth something, anything, after all.

Rake put his hands behind his back and walked off, the sound of his footsteps silenced by the wind.

◆ CHAPTER 3 ◆

*Evelyn*

T he entire household was to see Evelyn off. All except Keiko, whom the Lady Hasegawa decided should watch over their home in their absence. Evelyn found Keiko in her room, now bare of all the things Evelyn valued, which had been packed neatly into her casket by Keiko herself. Keiko wept freely, and so she didn't hear Evelyn come in.

For a moment, Evelyn was able to watch Keiko in a way she never had before — unimpeded by etiquette or shame. She was small and lovely in her plainness, most beautiful with her hair down.

Evelyn backed out the door as quietly as she could, saying nothing. What good could her comfort possibly do Keiko now? But the floor creaked beneath her step, and Keiko whirled around.

"Hello, Keiko." Stupid.

"You mean goodbye, my lady."

"Don't call me that. Not now."

Keiko looked at her feet and wiped her nose with her sleeve. "What'll I do without you?" Her voice was a whisper.

"You'll keep your hands clean."

Keiko made a noise that may have been a snort of laughter or a sob. She stepped forward and rested her cheek on Evelyn's shoulder, her breath warm against her neck. "I love you."

Evelyn pulled Keiko close, savoring the heat of her body, the familiar curve of her waist. Keiko was lovely, but love? Evelyn wasn't sure.

"I love you, too," Evelyn managed.

She kissed Keiko, gently, on her uneven lips. They were dry and soft, and Evelyn wished she had time to kiss her until she was sure of how she felt.

"You should go," Keiko said. "The carriage is waiting."

Evelyn kissed Keiko between her eyebrows before she stepped away. She could hear the carriage bell ringing below, likely the result of her parents' impatience to have her gone.

"Goodbye, Keiko." She kissed Keiko's fingers and turned to run downstairs.

Evelyn wasn't minding her step, and her flight led her directly into her father. The Lord had come looking for Evelyn when she had not responded to the bell, and he had clearly witnessed more than Evelyn would have liked of her tearful farewell to Keiko.

The Lord Hasegawa dusted himself off, as though the collision with his only daughter had sullied him. His was not a countenance that bore much warmth ever. But now it was full of disdain, disgust, and — as usual — disapproval.

"Oh, don't look so aghast. Your mother has always suspected you were crooked. I've never much cared. Had you been a son, this might have had some importance. You might have been of some importance. Alas for us both, I suppose."

A stab to her chest. The air crushed from her lungs. Too pained to speak, even to cry, Evelyn allowed herself to be led to the carriage by the father who was so indifferent to her and the mother who hated her. They rode in silence to the docks, the cobblestone streets rumbling beneath them. Distantly, Evelyn could hear the plaintive cries of seabirds.

The ship was called the *Dove*, and Evelyn loved it at once. She was grand and fine, with polished wood on her railings that shone in the afternoon light. But most beguilingly, the figurehead of a beautiful woman stood on the prow of the ship, her head bent as though in prayer. She was lovely in her solemnity, if a little sad.

It was real now, her leaving. There was no more denying it. Her casket was on the ship, tucked into her quarters, which, as the Lady Hasegawa had been quick to point out, directly abutted the cabin where the Lady Ayer was staying. The Lady Ayer and the Lady Hasegawa were old friends, and the Lady Ayer had apparently promised to keep a close eye on Evelyn.

While Evelyn was curious and excited to begin her brief life at sea, she found the prospect of constant surveillance unpleasant.

It'd be nearly half a year aboard the ship, and it promised to be the only period of independence Evelyn would have in her life. She'd always gotten along well with strangers, and this ship promised a whole new batch of them. The stories they might have! Men loved to brag, and Evelyn loved a good story. She'd write them all down and send them to Keiko. If she could track Keiko down, once she left her family's employ.

But unfortunately, the Lady Ayer would be there, poised like an owl to watch Evelyn's every move.

The Crandon docks were a faraway thing now, a gray smudge. Only the First Emperor's statue was still distinguishable. They said no matter where in the Known World you went, you were never far from the reach of the Nipran Empire, of Imperial influence. Evelyn had always lived at the heart of that empire, though, safe and warm within the luxurious confines of its bustling and orderly capital. Despite herself, Evelyn felt fear creeping into her mind, warning at a whisper. *You will not be so safe anymore,* it said.

"Lovely, isn't it?" the Lady asked.

Evelyn nodded absently. The Lady Ayer, who was tall, thin, and near the age of her mother, placed a hand on Evelyn's back. She had the unmistakable stiff accent of a true Crandon native and the flawless posture and elocution of the upper class. She was exactly who her mother wished Evelyn was, but Evelyn saw none of herself when she met the Lady's eyes.

"What takes you to the Floating Islands, Lady Ayer?" Polite conversation was low on the list of things Evelyn desired at the moment. But it was good practice politely engaging in tedious chatting. It trained her well for marriage.

"My husband has decided to venture into the world of shipyards. And those in the Floating Islands are without parallel. They're a nautical people, you see." She laughed. "I must admit, the sea makes me a little queasy."

Evelyn could not think of a single thing more dreary than a discussion of shipyards, even those of the Floating Islands. What good, she thought, was a ship in port? But she tried to assemble a smile.

"I hear you're off to meet a husband?" The Lady Ayer was kind enough not to mention the casket that everyone had seen loaded onto the ship. "And if I hear correctly, it's to be Mr. Finn Callum. Good reputation, you know, and word is he's not hurting for wealth, either. You should count yourself very lucky. Thanks to the Emperor, your parents made a fine match by you." The Lady Ayer kissed her fingers and touched her heart. The proper woman's salute. So she was pious, too. Wonderful.

"Yes, my lady." Evelyn could not force the enthusiasm into her voice. She was so tired.

"Well." The Lady Ayer sighed. "Let us hope he's kind, and gentle, and handsome, and that you bear him a hundred sons." She gave what was surely meant to be a reassuring look that provided no salve for Evelyn's pain. The notion of one hundred sons seemed too cruel a punishment for any sin she may have committed in her short life. "I'll be seeing lots of you on this voyage, and I do hope we can become the closest of friends. I'll retire now, but do come by for supper tonight. I promised your mother I'd look after you, and as we both know, it doesn't do to disappoint her, now does it?"

"Of course." Evelyn's voice was colder than she'd intended.

But the Lady Ayer hardly seemed to notice. She left Evelyn to her own dark, self-pitying thoughts.

◆ CHAPTER 4 ◆

*Flora*

Flora and Alfie pulled the casket below the decks of the *Dove*. It was likely laden with riches Flora could only imagine. Probably books. Rich people loved books. Flora had never even held one before.

It was hard work, and halfway down the staircase to where the Imperial nobles would be staying, she and Alfie rested the load precariously between them so that Alfie could wipe his brow. He was just opening his mouth — to say something smart, doubtless — when the captain stepped out from his cabin. Rake tailed him, as he often did, looking impatient.

"Ah, good, Florian. My favorite little man." Rake paused to chuckle at his own joke. Alfie chuckled sycophantically, and Flora forced a smile. They'd been so close to being rid of all this. Fresh anger arose at Alfie, and he seemed to sense it; his chuckling died off precipitously. "I was just going to look for you."

Flora felt her stomach clench with unease. What had she done wrong?

"Alfie, see to the Lady Hasegawa's"— Rake looked at the casket with one eyebrow raised —"things. I trust you can do it on your own."

Alfie looked from the casket to Rake and back again. But even he knew better than to argue, to argue with Rake, to argue with Rake in front of the captain. So he nodded, took a deep breath, and then returned to the thankless task of pulling the heavy load along the narrow corridors. Flora watched him go, wistful for the task that she had only moments ago been cursing.

Once his footsteps had grown quiet, the captain spoke. "There's a young lady joining us on this voyage." His voice was oily. "A lovely, pretty thing I wouldn't want . . ." He let his eyes roll back in his head, as if picking the most respectful word he could think of. Flora knew what he meant. She was to guard the girl against the desire of the crew. The trade of slave-whores on the Red Shore favored virgins for high prices.

"I understand, sir," she said.

"It'll be your role to keep her from wandering," Rake added.

"Yes, sir."

"And to keep men from wandering too close to her," the captain said.

"Yes, sir."

"Especially Fawkes," Rake clarified. He didn't need to. Flora was well aware of Fawkes's crimes. It was his ill-begotten attention that had driven Alfie to the bottle. To the mermaid's blood.

But then, it wasn't as if Flora were in any position to stop Fawkes. Not then, when he'd taken a screaming Alfie behind a locked door, and not now for the sake of some delicate Imperial blossom. Flora was the smallest sailor in the Nameless Captain's employ.

Fawkes, on the other hand, was gigantic, mountainous. He

hardly fit belowdecks, he was so big. And as if that weren't enough, he was a brutal fighter, too. And Flora? Not so much.

But she was not so foolish as to point this out.

"Yes, sir."

"She'll fetch us a fine price," the captain said. "You'll have a piece of that prize, if you guard it well."

Flora's heart leapt. The captain had never once offered her extra compensation of any kind. Maybe she could make up what Alfie had lost. Not entirely, but . . . She pushed her hope down into her belly. It did not do to hope, nor to warn the captain of her desired departure. He'd killed for less.

"Yes, sir."

"Well, that's sorted!" The captain smiled that cold smile of his, an eel's smile. He clapped his hands, then rubbed them together, his best impression of happiness. "Don't let me down, now." He did not say what would happen if she did. He didn't need to.

"Yes, sir."

But the captain wasn't listening. He was already ascending the steps so he might watch his men unfurl the sails, leaving Crandon in their wake.

"You have a pistol?" Rake asked. Flora nodded. "You should not be afraid to use it."

"No, sir."

Rake gave Flora a curt nod, then disappeared abovedeck to join the captain. Already, Flora could hear Rake's voice shouting orders.

Alfie summited the steps behind her, sweating profusely. Flora took one look at him and laughed. She'd almost forgotten the nigh-impossible task he'd just completed.

"Oh, bugger off."

This only made Flora laugh harder.

"What do you think she had in there, even? Bricks? Dead bodies?"

"Books," Flora said. She had not met the Lady Hasegawa, but rich Imperials were of a kind. Flora'd met enough, and she didn't care to meet more.

Alfie smiled. "Rich people love books."

They both laughed.

What books held, neither of them knew.

Flora returned to the Lady Hasegawa's cabin that evening, having been commanded to stand vigil at her door. This seemed excessive to Flora. Surely no one — not even Fawkes — would attempt anything on the first night. But Rake had ordered her just the same, so that the Lady might quickly feel accustomed to her new shadow.

Flora knocked lightly on the wooden door. The wood of the *Dove* was forever damp, even in the fine cabins afforded to nobility and, later in the voyage, to the officers. Still, envy rankled Flora. To sleep in her own private room — to stretch out, even be naked. When had Flora ever been naked to bathe, let alone to sleep?

A girl her own age opened the door. Flora could immediately see why the captain had assigned her a guard. She was beautiful, and not just in the way that all young, rich Imperials were beautiful. She was well groomed like all of them, her long black hair pulled away from her face and arranged in some sort of complicated knot, as was the style in Crandon. She had white teeth, and all of them. Her small waist was nipped in dramatically by a corset beneath a fire-red obi. She looked just as an Imperial woman was meant to look.

But her eyes. They were darkest brown, nearly black. They shone in the dark and the dank of the *Dove*. A single fleck of gold

34

glinted from one, and Flora found it very difficult to look away from it once she'd seen it. Being the same height, they looked eye to eye.

Flora disliked her immediately, in the way she disliked all Imperials. On principle. Sure, they were polite enough when one-on-one, but she knew — because she'd seen it — what Imperial kindness truly looked like.

*Imagine — to be so rich, and to be gifted with beauty, too.* There really was no such thing as justice.

"Yes?" The Lady's voice was friendly but tired. Flora realized she'd stood at the precipice for far too long without saying anything. She stuttered out an awkward introduction, clarifying that she'd be the lady's guard for the duration of the voyage.

"OK," the Lady said peaceably.

Of course, she was likely accustomed to some sort of guard. Most Imperial elites were, especially once they left the confines of Crandon's most wealthy quarters. So Flora leaned against the wall outside the Lady's cabin, listening as she rustled about her things. Occasionally, she shouted questions through the open door, which Flora grudgingly answered.

"Is this your first voyage? To the Floating Islands?"

Flora rolled her eyes. *Surely, she's at least been introduced to the concept of work?* "No, milady. But my first from the Nipran shore."

"It'll take about five months, yes?"

"Yes, milady. At least, depending on the winds."

"That's such a long time."

"Hm."

"Don't you get bored?"

Flora felt her head tip in bemusement. This was, first, the most she'd ever talked with an Imperial noble, and second, the most unusual conversation she'd ever had on the *Dove. Bored?* What'd the Imperial think this was? A pleasure cruise? "I stay busy."

"I'm bored already."

"I'm sorry, milady."

To Flora's shock, the Lady poked her head out of the door to her cabin. She looked about the empty hallway, then cast a blindingly radiant smile at Florian.

"I didn't mean for you to apologize. I just meant let's not be bored separately when we could be entertained together." She beckoned for him to come into her cabin.

Flora only gaped at her. Did she know? Could she tell that Florian was not a man? It would be so deeply inappropriate, so resolutely un-Imperial, for her to open her cabin to *him*. How humiliating, to come so far, to have done such things, only to be called out by a sheltered, idiot Imperial —

"I don't need your help unpacking, and I'm sorry but I'm sure you wouldn't know what to do anyway. Men are useless like that. No offense, I hope — it's not your fault. But I *require* company. You have no idea how monotonous it is on my own in here. I feel like I'm going crazy. If you don't mind?"

She motioned Florian in once more, but it was a gesture of polite entreaty. Not command.

Had an Imperial ever invited her to do anything?

No. Of course not.

"Please?" the Lady added.

And perhaps simply because she was so bewildered, she followed her feet into the Lady's cabin. The casket she and Alfie had carried lay open on the ground. Kimonos and yukatas of various colors and patterns spilled forth from it — the Lady was clearly not unpacking with any kind of care — and a stack of books was piled on the floor. Flora smiled to herself. She'd been right, of course. She was always right about Imperials.

Following Flora's gaze, the Lady smiled down at the books, too. "I couldn't bear to leave them," she said. *Of course you couldn't,* thought Flora. "You're more than welcome to borrow any that catch your eye. I've got some good ones in there. I mean, I think they're all good, but there are a couple that, you know, people *generally* think are good, not just me."

Flora blinked, surprised. The Lady assumed she could read. And also she thought, what, she'd just lend her books out and trust an absolute stranger to return them? Books were expensive. A single one of those stupid things could feed Flora for a week in Tustwe. Flora's consternation must have showed, because the Lady flushed a little, a pleasant pink that bloomed in her ears.

"I know they're just silly novels. I've read them a hundred times, but they're a comfort. Do you like to read, er . . ." She trailed off in a way that was clearly an invitation for Flora to introduce herself.

"Florian," said Flora. She let her voice go deep, let the magic of the name do its work. It felt good, to be so protected, so safe, in the face of the strangeness the Lady stirred in Flora's chest. Wearing Florian could be like that. A spell of strength against the world.

"Evelyn," said the Lady Hasegawa. She reached out a hand expectantly. It was such a polite gesture, a gesture meant for equals, that for a moment, Flora just stared at the hand, at the manicured fingernails, the bright puddles of red lacquer on each. Finally, she remembered herself and shook the Lady's hand. Evelyn's hand.

Her skin was soft, her fingers long and thin. How long had she been shaking the Lady's hand? Flora dropped it, a little abruptly. She would have felt naked except that she could hide behind Florian in this moment, and she was grateful for that.

"Anyway, Florian, do you like to read?"

"I don't know how." She had never been embarrassed by this before. Few aboard the *Dove* knew how to read anything other than their own names. It was, she thought, almost a rude thing to ask. Why would she know how to read? What was this lady getting at? She squared her shoulders. She was Florian. He was a sailor, not a playwright.

The Lady's face fell. Flora braced herself for pity, but it did not come. Instead, the Lady just looked, well, mad. "That won't do," she said. "That won't do at all. If I've understood correctly, we have plenty of time aboard this ship. I'm sure I can teach you the basics in half that. I taught my lady's maid, you know, and it was so much fun, for both of us honestly."

"Teach me . . . ?"

"To read, Florian. It's not hard, I promise, and there are too many good stories in the world to miss out on. This way, neither of us will be bored! You'd be doing me a favor, too, really." All the reticence she'd shown in the doorway was gone. The Lady's cheeks dimpled; her plump lips pulled into a smile. She was a strange Imperial. The gold fleck in her eye flashed.

"Of course, but—"

"That's settled, then! You're supposed to stick near me anyway. Captain Lafayette mentioned something like that. Guard, you said. Whatever. I don't need guarding, but I do love reading, and I feel like—since you must like stories, right?—you would, too, if you give it a shot. Yes?"

Flora's head whirled. She could hardly keep up.

*Who is this lady? What is she doing?*

"Uh—"

"Perfect." The Lady plopped down in an unladylike fashion, her fancy kimono billowing around her. She'd wrinkle it, sitting like that. Flora almost laughed. It was such a careless gesture in such a carefully constructed outfit. The Lady began loosening the strings that bound her — not so much that she'd be indecent, but so that she could breathe more comfortably. It was so casual a gesture, so human, that it hardly seemed right coming from an Imperial.

"Corsets are stupid," she said. Flora coughed a laugh. The Lady smiled appreciatively at her. She'd been testing the waters, Flora realized, to see if they could be honest with each other. Which, of course, they couldn't be. "I'm glad you agree, Florian."

*Florian.* This time the name was less a mask and more a slap. *Snap out of it.*

Flora cleared her throat. "Yes, milady."

## CHAPTER 5

# *Evelyn*

The casket sat, finally emptied, in the middle of Evelyn's cabin. The cabin was small, much smaller than Evelyn might have hoped, so the casket dominated the space.

It was made of fine, deep cherrywood, and her family's crest — a balloon flower — was carved into its lid and inlaid with gold leaf. Her mother was a stickler for maintaining family pride. Even if her daughter had been sold to the highest bidder to cover her husband's debts, the Lady Hasegawa would not have her daughter look like a pauper.

The sight of the casket made Evelyn's skin crawl.

Imperial nobles shipped their casket-laden daughters off daily from Nipran's shore. This was just the way of things. With so many officers in so many colonies, they couldn't be expected to marry the locals. The Emperor conquered, yes, but his men were still meant to marry nice Imperial girls, not any natives, no matter how exotic or beautiful they may be. It was stupid across all measures, so far as Evelyn could figure. She was sure Finn Callum would likely rather marry some pretty Floating Islands girl with curls down to her waist and thick, fisherman's arms, and who could blame him? Evelyn surely didn't.

But then, here she was.

Death and marriage, both so frankly inevitable, both so unavoidable. Mandatory.

She wondered who her parents would have married if they'd had the choice. Certainly not each other. Her father had served the Emperor all over the Known World. There was likely some half sister or brother in Iwei that she'd never meet. Likely in Crandon, too, in all honesty. He was always chasing after other men's maid staff. As for her mother, Evelyn hardly knew. She didn't seem terribly fond of her husband, but then she didn't seem fond of anyone.

Perhaps the dearth of love between them explained their lack of love for their daughter.

Perhaps Evelyn was just trying to make herself feel better.

She'd always told herself that she wouldn't be like them. That she'd find love, like the love she read about in her novels. But then, she didn't love Keiko, not the way Keiko loved her. She loved her, but she wasn't *in* love with her. And Keiko was lovely and perfect, kind and patient. If she couldn't love Keiko, maybe there was something wrong with her, something inherited from her loveless parents. Maybe she was born with a broken heart.

She put aside the letter to Keiko she'd been trying — and failing — to write. What was there to say? Sorry, I'm not in love with you and I never was, but kissing you sure was fun? No. So she instead set about planning an introduction to the syllabaries for Florian. She crossed her legs like a child — how her mother would have hated to see her like that, it was such a crass posture — and used the casket as a makeshift table.

Yes, teaching Florian was a worthy purpose. Maybe the only

worthy thing Evelyn would do in her life. Marriage and death would come and take her. There was no fighting that. But she could teach this boy to read. How it was he'd grown up in Crandon and never learned to read was something Evelyn despised thinking about. She had grown up with access to tutors and teachers so plentiful that she'd resented it. And she wasn't even that smart, if all those tutors were to be believed. But Florian was smart. Evelyn could see it, could see his mind churning unceasingly.

If anything good was to come of her wasted life, it'd be spiriting all the knowledge wasted on her into someone who actually deserved it. The fact that he wasn't Imperial made it all the better. It would rankle her parents to know that after all the money they'd spent on Evelyn's education, she would give it away for free. She smiled at that and set about making the best lessons she could muster. She was not a creature of courage, but she was one of spite. This one little rebellion would sate that, at least.

There was a knock on the door then, which violently startled Evelyn. She knocked over her inkwell. The ink spilled, and she knew immediately that it would stain her casket.

"Yes?" she called. She frantically tried to sop up the ink with — due to her lack of options — a corner of the fine kimono she wore. It was one of her mother's favorites anyway. She was glad it was ruined.

A younger girl — the Lady Ayer's maid, Evelyn was pretty sure — stepped into the cabin and performed a low, respectful bow. The girl's eyes darted to the spilled ink, and a look of superior distaste washed over her face. A spark of annoyance shot through Evelyn. She knew she looked ridiculous; there was no need to goggle.

"Yes?" she said again, a little tartly.

The girl shook herself from judgment, clearly remembering

her place. She bowed again, lower this time — perhaps a little too low, almost sarcastically low — at Evelyn. "My lady, the Lady Ayer wishes to extend her warmest invitation to her cabin tonight, so that, thanks to the Emperor, you may have supper together." She kissed her fingers and touched her heart.

"Ah." Evelyn held her hands aloft, both stained with ink. "Any suggestions here? I'm out of my depth."

The girl looked at her with obvious disdain. "I'll send your *boy* along, my lady."

Evelyn narrowed her eyes at her. "Yes, thank you. Please do send *Florian* along, and please send the Lady Ayer my regrets tonight. I'm just so very busy, as you can see."

The girl bowed, her face sour. She obviously didn't think it was proper for Evelyn to decline the offer. She was right, of course: it wasn't. But the last thing Evelyn could stand at the moment was making more polite conversation with her mother's friend. Not this night, the first night of the voyage. She needed more time to be angry.

"What a little—" Evelyn muttered, but she didn't finish. The girl wasn't Imperial. That much Evelyn could see straight-away from the spattering of freckles across her nose, the point of her chin. She may have lost her accent — Evelyn suspected Quark — but she could never escape her face. She'd done a great job adopting the judgmental nature of Imperials, though. Evelyn's mother would have loved her.

Florian was less impressed with the syllabary lesson than Evelyn might have hoped.

Had she misread him? Not his intelligence — that much was obvious. When she could wrangle his attention, he understood things readily enough. But his interest.

"I just don't see the point," he admitted finally.

They were sitting on either side of Evelyn's casket as the *Dove* groaned beneath them. The sea was a bit choppier that day, so now and again all of Evelyn's belongings slid about the cabin loudly. Florian didn't seem to notice or mind, but it made Evelyn terribly nervous.

"The point?" Evelyn swallowed her indignation. How could he know? She hefted a book into her hand. "I know a book doesn't seem like much, but I promise you, there are worlds in here."

Florian eyed the book dubiously. "You'll forgive me, milady, but it's hard to trust something worth more than a week's supply of food, something that wouldn't keep me warm for a night if I burned it."

Evelyn's eyes went wide. "Don't you dare burn a book."

Florian chuckled. "They'd be terrible kindling anyway."

"Look. I know a book can't feed you, or warm you at night, or, I don't know, wipe your ass —"

"Could do that, actua —"

He stopped himself. As soon as he said it, Evelyn could see he regretted it. It was not proper to joke with Imperial ladies; Evelyn knew this. But he was right. She laughed, and as soon as she did, she could see relief spread over him like a sunrise, his gray eyes alight. She liked him, even if he didn't like her yet.

"My point is not about the physical merits of books. But about what they contain. Master the syllabary and you'll have access to all of it."

"Secrets?"

"No, better. Stories. There's freedom in stories, you know. We read them and we become something else. We imagine different lives, and while we turn the pages, we get to live them. To escape the lot we've been given."

Florian picked up a book and idly flipped through its pages. "My life is fine," he said.

"I'm sure yours is. You live on the open sea! You have the kind of life I read about in my books." Evelyn took the book back from him and flipped to a page where a drawing showed a soldier, his hands to his belly, which bled from a mortal wound. "We don't just read to imagine better lives. We read to be introduced to all kinds of lives. Any kind. Not just for ourselves, but for everyone around us. To understand others better. It's escape, and it's also a way to become more connected to everyone around you. There's power in that, you know. In understanding. It's like magic."

"I'm not sure you'd want to understand the people I know, milady."

Evelyn chuckled, but Florian only looked at her, his eyes serious.

"I'm not sure that's for you to say," she said.

She wondered what kind of men he knew. Maybe he had met pirates on his voyages. Maybe he knew the Pirate Supreme. She thought of the people who surrounded her parents — desperate social climbers, boring officials and their bored wives. No, it wasn't for him to say at all.

Silence spread between them then. Above them, the footsteps of the sailors pounded and the wood of the *Dove* creaked. She wanted so badly to give Florian this gift, this access, but he just didn't want it. Disappointment rose in her throat, and she felt suddenly that she wanted to cry. Which was pathetic, of course. She was pathetic. That she thought she could just mince onto this boat and force a sailor into lessons was so arrogant and foolish. She was as worthless as her parents had so rightly noticed. She took in a breath and tried to steady herself against her own burning humiliation.

Florian watched her, his face impassive.

"I'd be more interested in books if they had secrets," he said finally.

Evelyn laughed, her relief infinite. "Fine. Some of them do. Will you concentrate now?"

## CHAPTER 6

*Flora*

F lora wanted to hate the Lady Hasegawa, but the Lady made it difficult.

Where other Imperials were stiff and proper, she was breezy and — Flora hated to admit it — funny. She seemed to live for startling Flora into laughter, and she was deadly good at it, no matter how stiff an upper lip Flora tried to keep.

Flora was lying in her berth, willing sleep to come, but she couldn't get the sight of the Lady talking with her hands out of her mind. All around her, men of the *Dove* snored and farted in their sleep. Usually at this point in the voyage, Flora couldn't wait until the passengers were moved to the brig so that the men could spread out across the cabins. But somehow, this time, that expectation felt like dread.

A skeleton crew still remained abovedeck, but Flora's new posting had seen her promoted to the day schedule, which was a blessing. Initially, she'd looked forward to all the extra sleep she'd get, but night after night it seemed that sleep would not come.

She was awake still when Alfie came trundling into his own hammock, just below hers. When he saw she was awake, he stood so that his face was uncomfortably close to hers.

"Saw you having a good laugh with her Ladyship today," he whispered.

"I don't know what you're talking about."

She did know what he was talking about. During one of the Lady's supervised walks about the upper deck, she had told Flora a joke so crass it might have offended even Fawkes, and Flora had been so shocked that she'd let out her full laugh, her real laugh, her girl laugh, and had only stopped when she realized at least three men from the *Dove* were watching her. Alfie included.

"You know, you weren't assigned to watch over her so that you could moon about in her skirts." His voice was a hiss, and Flora sat up, angry now.

"You think I don't know that?"

"Remember, we're here for us."

Flora scoffed. "Yeah, all right, brother. I'll remember that the next time I come back to our savings and find them empty."

Alfie's face fell, and Flora knew right away she'd swung hard and aimed low. But she was too mad to care. "I said I was sorry for that," Alfie said. More than that, he'd practically groveled for her forgiveness.

"Doesn't change anything." She glared at him then, and it was as if he shrank beneath her, as if her gaze made him as small as he was inside. "It's me earning the extra coin this go-round, and I don't need you nagging me as I get to it."

Alfie took a deep, steadying breath and held his hands up in surrender. "I'm just saying. I saw you laughing today, and you looked so — happy. And I wanted to remind you what she's here for. What *we're* here for."

*Happy.* As if that were a bad thing. As if that were not allowed — not for Flora, at least.

"You think I could ever forget?" She wanted to hit him, to slap him across his stupid face, that face that looked so much like her own. "I'm the one with blood on my hands, remember."

Alfie glared at her then, and she knew she'd come at that all wrong. "I don't think you want to start playing the suffering contest with me, Florian. It was me that took Fawkes's hazing. Or did you forget?"

Flora could never forget, but worse, she knew Alfie never would either. When they'd first joined the crew of the *Dove,* Fawkes had insisted that some hazing was in order. Alfie, being the elder brother, stepped in and took it so that Flora didn't have to. If he had known what would happen, the extent of the pain Fawkes would deal to him, maybe he wouldn't have, Flora knew. But he had, and now, Flora also knew, it was not for her to judge his need to forget. She wished she could forget, too. She wished they both could.

Flora let her head drop. "I'm sorry, Alfie." She pulled his forehead to hers. "I'm sorry."

"It's just us," Alfie whispered.

Her eyes were closed, but she could still see the Lady Hasegawa, her head tossed back in laughter. But Flora replied in the way that she always did, even if the words tasted sour in her throat.

"Just us against the world."

Once, when Alfie and Flora were still new on the *Dove,* they'd stopped in Tustwe.

They could not stop on the Skeleton Coast, of course. It was called that for a reason — the currents on the western coast of

49

Tustwe were so impossible to navigate that all who tried ended up shipwrecked, their bodies and boats eventually washed up on the shore.

So, like all reasonable sailors, the crew of the *Dove* had sought shore leave on the east coast of Tustwe, where gold was easy to spend. Most of the crew — Alfie included — were drinking in the famous beachside taverns that gave the whole city a festive air. But Flora went wandering.

It was hot, the yellow sun high in the palm fronds that grew everywhere. Flora was delighted. She'd never been anywhere that she felt like she fit — not in Crandon, not on the *Dove*. But as she walked through the sandy streets of the city, she felt powerfully comfortable. The men, the women, and people all manner of genders she didn't recognize strode with their heads held high, their hair in so many different curious arrangements that Flora could hardly keep from staring. And everywhere, people were laughing and dancing and singing and running. It was so unlike the world Flora had known. Vibrant, and noisy, and alive.

She spent most of her coin on a tray of oysters that she sucked straight from the shell, and then to have two elderly women, their fingers gnarled with age, set her hair into a thousand thick twists with beads interspersed in them. She felt full. She felt beautiful. She strode next to the oryxes the locals used to transport their goods to market, feeling like she belonged.

But when she got back to the *Dove*, she was greeted by Rake's cold stare of disapproval. Rake was from Quark, but he was pink, which meant the Tustwe sun was too much for his skin to bear. He had stayed behind while the rest of the men went carousing.

"You look like a girl," he said. This, Flora thought, was not exactly fair. She looked like a person from Tustwe, and all the people in Tustwe seemed to have exciting and different hair, not just the women. But she was a child, and she was afraid, and so she didn't say that.

"I am a girl," she responded. She was not yet Florian then.

Without warning, he pulled her by the arm to the fore-castle, where he stored his things. He pulled out his knife, and for a brief terrible moment, Flora was sure that Rake meant to murder her. But instead, he started methodically cutting off her hair. All around her the twists fell to the deck, like leaves falling from a tree, as Flora watched wordlessly in horror.

"This is for your own good," he told her. But it didn't feel good. It felt like punishment for a crime she did not commit.

"Listen to me," he said. "And listen good. If you want to survive, you're going to have to learn how to blend in. Become invisible. The more visible you are, the more you remind people you exist. And the more people remember you exist, the more likely they are to come for you. Do you understand me?"

Flora nodded, because of course she understood. It was the lesson Crandon had most thoroughly taught her. Rake had left her then, to clean up the remains of her hard-earned hair. As soon as he was gone, Flora let herself cry.

The thing was, she *had* felt like she was blending in. There among the palm trees and the dancing, the oryxes and the sand. That was the great gift the new hair had given her.

She was just blending into the wrong place.

## CHAPTER 7

*Evelyn*

L essons with Florian had been going better than well. Once he mastered his syllabary, he was seemingly unstoppable. He soared through her curriculum, and already he could read sentences aloud, though haltingly. She liked to watch him puzzle out the words, the way his gray eyes narrowed, the way he sometimes bit his lip in concentration.

They had spent the first several weeks of the voyage with the syllabary and Florian's reluctance, but now, now they were already on to books. The days were passing so quickly that Evelyn feared the voyage would be done and she'd be turned over to her husband before she had time to blink.

Florian was reading aloud from Evelyn's favorite book of fantasies, the two sitting elbow to elbow on Evelyn's bed. She liked the warmth of him next to her, and noticed he did not pull away when their skin touched when they were jostled by the ship. His nervousness around her seemed to be fading.

They had just gotten to the part where the princess — afraid and alone — had sunk in her despair to the floor of the dungeon where she was being kept.

"What a ninny," Florian said with a chuckle.

Evelyn looked to the page. She'd always related to the princess, had felt her imprisonment as if it were her own.

"She's been captured." Her voice was defensive, but Florian did not notice.

"Sure, but that's no excuse to be useless."

"Useless," Evelyn echoed quietly. She could feel her ears burning with embarrassment. She made to pull the book away from Florian, but he held tight to it. "You don't have to read this stupid story if you don't want."

"I'm sorry, milady," he said. "I don't mean to . . . I'm not insulting *you*." He pulled in a deep breath. "And for what it's worth — smart lady like you? You'd be out of that dungeon like that." He snapped his fingers.

Evelyn smiled ruefully. "I doubt that," she said. She couldn't wield a sword. She couldn't fire a pistol. "Very sincerely. But thanks. It's a nice thing to say."

An ocean of very uncomfortable silence stretched between them. Florian turned pages, searching out the periodic pictures each story offered. He stopped at one of a mermaid and a sailor. The sailor stretched out his hand toward the mermaid, who reached back for him. All around them the waves crashed against the rock the sailor was perched upon.

"Sad," Evelyn said.

"What is?"

"They're stuck like this forever." She ran a finger over the page, between the mermaid with the long, flowing hair and the sailor in his smart uniform. "Reaching out for each other, but never together, I mean." She blushed. "This picture has always made me sad."

Keiko's face, red and tearstained, surfaced in Evelyn's mind. It was blurred now, as though the memory of Keiko could not withstand their growing distance.

"That's the way of it, though."

Florian shrugged. His hand rested on the opposite page of the book. "But maybe that's focusing on the wrong part."

Evelyn said nothing but looked at Florian. His eyes were still on the page when he spoke.

"They're reaching. Right?"

When Evelyn was eleven, her mother had taken over the duty of her historical education. It was not, the Lady Hasegawa said, for lowly scholars to tell the Hasegawas how to regard the Empire. And so, much to Evelyn's chagrin, her beloved history teacher was sent away, and instead she was forced to suffer daily lessons in her mother's chambers.

Her mother's chambers were as formal as they were stiflingly hot during the summer months. She did not favor open windows, fearing that the pollution from the Crandon port would give her wrinkles, and so it was insufferably stuffy. Yet somehow, Evelyn never once glimpsed a drip of sweat on her mother's brow.

One day, her mother had laid out the architectural plans of the 900th Emperor's palace on the table for the two of them to go over. Evelyn entertained a panicky fantasy about running away, right there and then, but before she could act on it, Keiko had shut the door behind her and left Evelyn alone with her mother. The Lady Hasegawa beckoned for Evelyn to come take a seat on one of the embroidered silk cushions around the table.

"Do you see this?" Her mother's perfectly manicured finger

pointed to a series of secret passages within the walls of the palace.

Evelyn nodded.

"They say that the 945th Empress — Elizabeth — conspired to have her husband assassinated. Thanks to the Emperor, she failed and was executed. Do you know why that is?"

"Because wives are meant to be dutiful," Evelyn recited. The truth was that she didn't care what any Empress did. They had gardens planted and held balls. They rarely had any bearing on history, unless they bore a multitude of sons. But whenever Evelyn recited that wives or daughters were meant to be dutiful, or pious, or meek, it pleased her mother and her lessons were over with sooner, so that was what she said.

But this time, the Lady Hasegawa was not fooled. She took her daughter's hand in hers and gave it a hard smack. Hard enough to sting, but not hard enough to bring tears to Evelyn's eyes.

"Incorrect. Don't be lazy." She released Evelyn's hand. "She failed due to a series of mistakes and miscalculations. First, she thought her servants to be her friends."

Aha.

This was a favorite lesson of her mother's, one she repeated frequently. It was meant mostly as a warning against her friendship with Keiko, Evelyn knew. But what did she expect? That Evelyn wouldn't become best friends with the girl she spent nearly every hour of every day with? That was stupid, so Evelyn ignored it.

"Which, of course," her mother went on, "they were not. Second, she underestimated the great reach of the Emperor's power. From his own palace to every colony in the Known World, his eyes see. Just as there are secret passages in the hallways of his palace, there are secret corridors and channels through which the Emperor is given information from all around the world.

He knows who plans an insurgency in the Graveyard Nation, just as he knows which merchants have been pious in the Floating Islands."

"If an Emperor knows everything, then why did he marry someone who wanted to kill him?" Evelyn knew immediately she'd said precisely the wrong thing. Her mother closed her eyes in silent exasperation. She kissed her fingers and touched her chest, as if in prayer to ward off her own daughter's idiocy. She continued as though Evelyn had not spoken.

"The third reason she failed is the most important." The Lady Hasegawa held her daughter's eyes then, and Evelyn could tell from the way she would not let Evelyn look away that this was serious. "She failed because she overestimated her own power. She may have been the Empress, but she was still a woman. And as such, she was replaceable.

"Hear me, Evelyn. Wives are replaceable. You are replaceable. And if you ever fail to remember that, it will be your undoing."

⬧ CHAPTER 8 ⬧

*Flora*

The Lady Hasegawa stood on the deck with the Lady Ayer, both leaning daintily on the gunwales, chatting. Behind them stood Flora and the Lady Ayer's girl, Genevieve, holding parasols over the two ladies' heads. Flora felt like an idiot. Sporadically, her fellows would walk past, plainly laughing at her. After all she'd done to become Florian, and here she was, holding a delicate yellow parasol.

*Still.*

At least she wasn't burning in the sun. While Flora's complexion could take it, Genevieve's could not. Already her nose was a deep, angry red.

Though Rake's hair was a startling red and Genevieve's was a stark black, their roots in the mountain country of Quark was clear in their skin. While Rake had been burned so much and so often that his skin was more leather than face, Genevieve was still pale as a cherry blossom, and likely as tender. Flora eyed the girl with pity. No doubt she'd soon be burned and peeling. Her lady hardly seemed to notice.

"As I was saying, the porcelain I've brought is the finest. You should settle for no less from Mr. Callum." The Lady Ayer beamed at the Lady Hasegawa. For her part, the Lady Hasegawa seemed brutally bored. She kept catching Flora's eye with a look so obviously exasperated that Flora had to hold her breath to keep from laughing. "It was imported from the Skeleton Coast, you know, but painted by the finest artisans in Crandon. You just can't rival Imperial artistry."

Genevieve's grip on the parasol faltered and she accidentally brushed her lady's head with it, mussing the complicated knot in which her hair had no doubt been painstakingly arranged. The Lady Ayer whirled on her.

"Careful, girl!" she spat.

"Anyway," Evelyn said quickly. "Thanks for the, er, advice. It's all . . . instructive."

"You are your mother's daughter," the Lady Ayer said approvingly. "I am sure you will develop taste as fine as hers in no time."

"Indeed." Evelyn's voice was colder now. "Well, Florian?" She turned to Flora, and the full impact of her attention was startling. "To my cabin, I think. I have so many, um, letters to write."

"Ah, do send your mother my love. And do come by my cabin more often, young lady. If I didn't know any better, I'd say you were trying to avoid me!"

The Lady Ayer gave the Lady Hasegawa a polite bow and a simpering smile to match. The Lady Hasegawa bowed back politely and then hastened with Flora down the great wooden staircase that led to the finer cabins.

"You *are* your mother's daughter," Evelyn mimicked once they were out of earshot. She had, Flora thought, nailed the pompous lilt of the Lady Ayer's accent. It sounded rather like the one Alfie did when the two mocked Imperials. Flora snorted a laugh, then clapped a hand over her mouth, embarrassed.

"Milady."

"I mean, really!" Evelyn went on, though she was smiling at Florian now. "She's everything I've never wanted to be. Blathering. Blithering. And do you see the way she treats her maid? Poor thing was burned to a crisp. She looks like a ham."

She pulled the door to her cabin open and stomped inside. Flora stood at the precipice, ready to stand guard. That was her duty, after all. But the Lady Hasegawa peeked her head out and regarded her with warm annoyance.

"Come on, Florian. I found a story I think you'll really like. It's got pirates and everything! You'll love it."

Flora gulped. The word *love* hung heavy in the air between them. "Milady, I —"

"Evelyn. For the last time, silly, call me Evelyn." She pulled Flora into her cabin by the arm. The reading lessons, the physical contact. It was all too much. Soon all the passengers would be taken down, down, down to the brig, Evelyn among them. The thought of Evelyn behind those steel bars sent an ache through Flora's stomach, her heart.

In her jumble of feelings, Flora forgot to close the door behind them. Perhaps it was an accident. Perhaps not. But the effect was the same.

She had her face buried in the book and was trying to read a big word (*tumultuous*, it turned out, a word Flora thought made perfect sense in a story about the sea) when she heard a deep, ugly chortle from the hallway. It was more like a cough than a laugh.

"What's this, then?" Fawkes boomed. "Learning your letters, Florian? What were you saying? About a pirate's code?"

The blood drained from Flora's face. A quick rejoinder may have saved her, but instead she sat, stuttering like an idiot on the Lady Hasegawa's bed. It was perilous, she knew, to be visible to Fawkes. It was everything Rake had ever warned her against.

"As a matter of fact, he *is.*"

Flora would have given anything in the world — all her fingers, Alfie, the moon — to have kept the Lady Hasegawa quiet then. Fawkes turned his beady eyes to her. He hadn't even noticed her before, not really, but now that she'd gone and called attention to herself, his eyes devoured her.

"Ah. Well. He's a lucky man, then, ain't he? Learning them from a girl as pretty as you."

Evelyn's ears flushed a deep red. Anger burned in Flora's chest. There was nothing his greed would not sully. She shot to her feet, knocking the book to the floor.

"Captain be needing you, then, Fawkes? Maybe Rake?" It was a threat, and they both knew it. Flora let her hand drift casually to the pistol she kept at her back.

Fawkes luxuriated in another long, lascivious leer, then lumbered off, still laughing to himself.

Flora closed the door. "I'm sorry, Evelyn." Her mind was a mess, a messy thing, and she could not seem to bring it to order. She picked up the book from the floor and brushed it off. "He's a monster." She handed the book back to Evelyn and listened after Fawkes to ensure that he was truly gone.

"Thank you, Florian."

"For what, milady?" A strange flame of anger licked at Flora's throat. And oddly, it was directed at Evelyn. *Why had she called attention to herself? Why was she so ignorant of her own peril?* It was just like an Imperial to assume her own safety. Did she not realize what she was risking? If the Lady Hasegawa thought Flora could keep her safe from Fawkes, from anything . . .

"For finally calling me Evelyn."

Flora lay in her hammock, listening to the creaks and moans of the *Dove* as she sailed. All around her, men snored and murmured in their sleep. But rest eluded her, taunting and teasing and just out of reach. She turned over angrily, unable to find anything resembling comfort.

"What's with you?" Alfie hissed. "You're keeping me up," he added a little haughtily.

"Can't sleep."

"Rum?" Alfie raised the bottle he kept in his hammock — he always had a bottle — but Flora shook him off. She fought back the anger that burned in her throat. She had seen what the drink did to him, and it was a road she didn't care to follow him down. She'd tried to love him out of it, nagging and begging and pleading with him. But there was nothing she could do, and she'd long since lost the energy to fight the currents so bent on drowning him. It didn't make it stop hurting to watch, though. It never stopped hurting.

"If you're going to keep tossing, you might as well talk to me, then," Alfie said. She could tell from the blurry edges of his voice that he'd been asleep and she'd woken him. And she could also tell that, before that, he'd been drinking.

"You wouldn't understand." Which was true. He'd never understand why his drinking bothered Flora. To him, it was just a thing that had to happen, like sunrise, or death. And he'd certainly never understand Flora's tempest of contradictory feelings that swirled around the Lady Hasegawa, whose fate — to him — was also another simple inevitability.

"Oh, look who's such a big complicated man, then." He spoke in the silly voice he knew made Flora laugh. It was, secretly, his impression of the captain, though neither would ever say so. Men had been stabbed for less. Alfie went on. "Outgrown me, have you? Suppose I should have seen it coming, now that you're a big important man, taking orders direct from the captain. Think your dumb old brother Alfie can't wrap his simple wee head around your big, profound, existential—?"

"Bugger off." Flora tried her best to keep the laughter from her voice but failed. He was always like that, always able to disarm her. It was infuriating. "Where'd you learn that word?"

"What, *existential*?" Alfie laughed. "Don't actually know what it means."

Flora turned in her hammock so she could look into his eyes. She needed his help. Now that the anger had ebbed, she could see herself as she truly was. She wasn't angry.

She was drowning.

"Alfie," she whispered. She could hear the feeling in her voice, and much as it embarrassed her, she didn't have the fortitude to hide it. Not anymore. "I don't think I can do it. Not this time."

Alfie's smile faded immediately. "Hush. Someone could hear you." They both knew which someone he meant. His eyes darted to where Rake slept, just one hammock over.

Tears welled in Flora's eyes. When had she last cried? She couldn't even remember. "She's not like the others, Alfie."

Their history hung between them, heavy and terrible. Neither needed to reminisce to recall each of the long and hungry days of their childhood in Crandon, begging for food only to be kicked and shooed, the miraculous nature of their survival in the face of Imperial indifference. There was no love lost for those people, the

62

rich and the pure of Crandon, between Flora and Alfie. But still. She wanted to make him understand.

Evelyn was not like them, not like those who had seen them starving and just kept walking. She was sheltered and silly, but she was whip smart, and kind, too, and far too soft for the fate that was coming.

"She is, though." Alfie's voice was quiet but firm. "There's been *good* people on every voyage we take, but they're not *our* people." He reached out a hand, wrapping his fingers through the net of Flora's hammock. "Tell me what I can do to help."

Flora felt tears falling and cursed herself. For her weakness and her foolishness. He was right, of course. What could she do to save Evelyn? *Nothing.* She couldn't save her. And trying would only kill her and Alfie both.

"Trade me shifts? I don't think I can be around her anymore."

Alfie nodded. "'Course, Florian."

*Florian.* She would do well to remember who she was. What she had become. What it took to survive. She lay back in her hammock, and in her mind she said the name over and over again. An incantation against her own weakness.

There was a creak of shifting weight as Rake rolled over in his hammock.

She prayed he was asleep.

## CHAPTER 9

*Evelyn*

When she returned to her cabin, Evelyn noticed that she had a new guard. He was tall and gangly, and not nearly so graceful in his attempts to disappear into the shadows as Florian had been. He nearly tripped over a fellow sailor who was busy knotting nets.

She turned to face him, startled. "Are you my new watchdog?"

"Some kind of dog, miss. At your service. Or milady. My lady. Which is it?"

Evelyn smiled. "My lady, if you want to be proper."

"Oh, totally. Yes. I'm always aiming to be proper. It's just I'm a lousy shot." He offered his arm, which Evelyn took. "Let's take you up to the half deck. The sun's out, but not *too* out, if you know what I mean, and we've seen more than one pod of dolphins swim by."

Evelyn had never seen a dolphin, so she allowed herself to be guided. "Where's Florian?" She was surprised by how much she missed him. They'd become fast friends, after all, and she had a new story she was itching to share with him.

"Traded me duties. He's off cleaning the guns. It's filthy work — you've gotta scrub vinegar all in it, and it makes your hands burn. Me, I'd rather see a fine lady around the ship than smell like pickles, but then I'm just —"

Evelyn felt like she'd been slapped. He'd traded duties? Was this a permanent switch? She let her mind sift through her memories of their time together, frantically scanning for the moment when she had overstepped, when she had offended him. But then, maybe it was *every* time. Maybe she was being too forward. Her mother always warned her of this, hadn't she, of her casual nature with servants. Evelyn certainly hadn't intended to force her friendship on Florian; she'd simply wanted to teach him to read. But that was about her own rebellion, too, wasn't it?

She wanted her mother to be wrong so badly, but then, where was Florian? She tried to push the hurt away, or at the very least, out of her voice.

She let the shield of her politeness come down around her, put on her familiar mask of interest. She could play this game. She'd played this game her whole life.

"There are guns aboard this ship?" she asked. Not so much because she cared — she didn't. But it was something to talk about. Boys liked guns, and she could tell this boy was all boy. Not like Florian.

"Yes, my lady. As a precaution. Pirates in these waters, after all."

"I'm glad to be in safe hands," Evelyn said politely.

The boy laughed far louder than was proper, necessary, or sane. His aim was off, indeed. "Let's take a look at those dolphins!" He was practically shouting.

A few sailors who were busy swabbing the decks looked up, leering at her. Evelyn could see why Captain Lafayette had assigned Florian to her, and she could not help but think that she agreed with his choice. It was not that Florian didn't look at her. He did. But it was not so predatory.

"I remember the first time Florian saw one, I thought he'd shit his pants." He looked as horrified as Evelyn was amused the moment it escaped his lips. "Begging your pardon, my lady. I'm not used to chatting with the upper class. Especially not girls. Women. Ladies. You're a lady. My lady."

Evelyn laughed. "Please, it's fine. Refreshing, honestly." She scanned the horizon for dolphins but saw nothing save the rolling sea and the shimmer of sunlight on water. "You've known Florian for a long time?"

"His whole life. He's my brother. Little brother, that is." The pride in the boy's voice was unmistakable. Now that he said it, Evelyn could see it. For one thing, they were the only two black sailors aboard the *Dove,* that she'd noticed anyway. But they held themselves totally differently. Florian was all square shoulders and chin up. This boy was, well, looser. But their eyes. The light-gray cast of them, the way they shone like gunmetal. Odd eyes.

Florian hadn't mentioned that he had a brother on board. But then, Evelyn thought with a pang, Florian hadn't done much of the talking, had he? Except to comment on a story now and again. Or to tell her she was smart. She turned those memories over in her mind like stones. She knew the exact shape of each of them, each kind word, each comment. But what had she missed, just below them?

Before she could think of something appropriate to say, a weathered hand fell on the boy's shoulder, causing both him and Evelyn to jump.

"Thought the captain ordered Florian to accommodate the Lady Hasegawa," the man said. Evelyn did not like the sound of her name in his mouth, and she could tell from the way he said it that he didn't, either. He was thin but wiry, with a shock of red hair, and the look on Florian's brother's face frightened Evelyn.

The boy gulped. "Yes, sir," he said. "But begging your pardon, Rake, sir, Florian asked to switch duties, sir, and I figured if we stayed abovedeck, sir, there would certainly be no worries of—"

"It's not a problem, really," Evelyn interrupted. But the man's eyes stayed fixed on the boy, who trembled under their gaze. How rude, she thought, to be treated as though she were invisible.

"Arjun!" the man called. A bedraggled man with a patchy beard stepped off the rigging and stood at attention. "Go fetch Florian." Arjun hobbled off, mumbling.

"Stay here until Florian returns," the man commanded. The boy nodded wordlessly, his face pale. "Both of you are to report to me while the Lady has her supper."

"Yes, sir," the boy managed. He sounded as though he were sick to his stomach.

"My lady," the man said coldly to Evelyn. He left, barking more orders to other men as he went. Evelyn watched in amazement.

"Who was that?"

"The first mate. Rake." The boy's voice was still shaky with fear. "Second in command to the captain."

"Lafayette."

"Pardon? Right, yeah." The chattering, laughing boy of only minutes before was gone. Why was the post as her guard of such great importance anyway? She didn't need guarding, even if she longed for company, for a friend. She'd been grateful for that. But then, they weren't friends, were they? They stood in uncomfortable silence.

When Florian did join them, he looked grave. "Alfie, why? How? All you had to do was stand outside her door." His voice was unfamiliar to Evelyn, all sharp edges.

The boy, Alfie, shrank back, visibly abashed. "She called me out straightaway — there wasn't any denying it."

"It's true," Evelyn interjected.

Florian turned to her, his eyes burning. "If you'd pardon us, milady, this is between brothers." His voice was cold, but it sent a flash of heat through Evelyn's chest. She felt herself scowl at Florian, her hurt transmuting to anger.

"It's actually *my* lady," Alfie said, his aim off again. "If you're trying to be proper." He tried a laugh.

"I don't know why I thought I could trust you." Florian shook his head.

Evelyn found that she was actually proud of Alfie when he responded with anger. Good. Now they were united against Florian.

"Listen, don't blame me for your —" He looked at Evelyn, as if trying to decide what could be said in front of her. "Don't ask for my help, then be mad you got it."

"It's not his fault you wanted so badly to get rid of me," Evelyn hissed at Florian. "This is your fault. *You* disobeyed your orders, and now you're just mad you got caught."

"Please, milady. Don't talk about things you don't understand."

Evelyn thought she might actually spontaneously burst into flames, her fury was so great.

"You think the world of men is so complicated? It isn't. You're all the same. Weak, and small, and eager to push your own failure off on others while pretending I couldn't possibly understand the great forces at work that forced your hand. Half of a woman's life is spent pretending she doesn't notice just how stupid and prone to failure you all are!" Her father's face appeared in her mind, and for a moment she wasn't sure whom she was yelling at—and she was yelling—Florian or her father. "I *understand* just fine. *You* failed. And you're mad at everyone besides yourself about it."

Distantly, she was aware of the sailors watching. A couple of them laughed. She didn't care. The insult of Florian's rejection, of his lectures, of his pretension! She left the brothers on the deck and returned to her cabin. She did not need to be escorted.

She slammed the door of her cabin shut behind her. There, on her casket, was a pile of papers meant to be Florian's next lesson. She had been planning to teach him how to write, so that they might stay in touch once the voyage was over.

The sight of it—the papers, the two quills set out expectantly—was too much. Evelyn undid the lacing of her corset as she sank to her knees, crying frankly. She did not know which humiliation was worst. The one-sided friendship. Her dashed hopes. Or knowing that, even here, so far away from her home, her mother had been right.

How stupid she'd been to think she mattered to him at all.

## CHAPTER 10

*Flora*

The walk to the captain's cabin was a long one, which Flora and Alfie made in silence. Flora had not said anything to Alfie since Lady Evelyn had admonished her so aptly. Confusion clung to her like a cloud. What did Evelyn care if either she or Alfie watched over her? Surely, she'd had a long parade of servants in her life.

Flora had never been to the captain's cabin before, but she'd heard that it was the most luxurious on the *Dove.* All gilded details and treasures. Cushions and silks. She hadn't ever wanted to see it — men who had seemed to have a low survival rate — but Alfie did. *Not like this, though.* Men who kept their fingers and throats did not visit the captain. How he could sleep in a room where so many had died was beyond Flora. Surely, he could feel the ghosts that hung like spiderwebs in the air — invisible, but clinging. She hoped she would not soon join them.

She did her best to stow her fear.

The cabin was, in fact, garish from floorboard to ceiling, full of fine objects that Flora couldn't even identify, with windows, actual windows, that looked out onto the sea. Everyone else made do with tiny portholes, pinpricks of light that hinted at the great world beyond the *Dove*. These windows were like standing on a cliff's edge.

Perhaps that explained Flora's vertigo.

A painting of a mermaid, bare-breasted, with an explosion of resplendent ebony hair, loomed enormous on the wall behind the captain. Her face was so happy as to be ludicrous. No one, not even a mermaid, ever looked that stupidly, deliriously happy on the *Dove*.

With a sting of hindsight, Flora kicked herself for speaking so freely in the hammocks. As second in command, surely Rake could have negotiated for a better sleeping berth if he'd wanted it. Likely he chose to sleep close to the men so he could stay aware of their murmurings. How foolish Flora had been. *Rake must have heard everything.*

The captain sat behind a large, dark wooden desk, toying with a quill made from a giant, flamboyantly red feather; Flora wondered for a moment what kind of bird would have such a feather, Rake stood next to him, stiff as ever, with an impatient eye toward the quill.

"Ah, the *Dove*'s most unusual brothers," the captain said, his voice grand. He stood with a flourish, still holding the quill, and pointed it at Flora. "I did not think I'd ever have cause to call you in here, Master Florian."

"Nor I," agreed Rake.

"*You*, on the other hand"— he pointed at Alfie —"I'm neither surprised by nor interested in. You may leave."

Alfie paused, his mouth gaping like a fish's.

"Immediately."

And Alfie was gone. That was fair enough. This was not his fault. Evelyn had been right. And he'd taken enough punishment for them both aboard this cursed ship. *Still.* She felt all the more afraid, left alone with these two men.

"Give me your blade," the captain said.

Puzzled, Flora handed it over. It was the blade Alfie had given her years ago. Short and silver. The blade she had killed Mr. Lam with. The blade that made Florian *Florian.*

*Florian,* she told herself. *Florian, Florian, Florian.* A spell for strength and courage.

The captain examined the blade for a moment, then handed it to Rake, who held it over the flame of the candle that burned on the captain's desk. Flora watched him curiously. Rake kept the blade in the flame, his eyes on her.

The captain lowered himself back into his fine chair, his eyes unmoving from Flora's face. He reminded her of the cats that lived in Crandon's streets, the way they looked while hunting the mice and rats that were ubiquitously available to them. The way he didn't blink. The stillness of him. "Florian, do you know *why* I have let you serve aboard the *Dove*? It wasn't my goodwill or pity. I have very little of either. It certainly wasn't due to Rake's endorsement."

"It certainly wasn't," Rake echoed.

*Thanks.*

"I have plenty of scrappy orphans begging for work, so why you? Why an orphan who'd make things so very, very complicated?" He looked at Flora expectantly, but Flora didn't answer. If the captain was discomfited by her silence, he didn't show it. He smiled placidly and continued. "I thought, here's one just ripe for training. I thought, this one's got potential for true piracy. I can see it! This one'd impress the Pirate Supreme, even. I thought, give this one a chance and I'll have an ally for life." He nudged Rake with his elbow. "Eh? Pretty good idea, right?"

"Yes, sir. But only if you have a true ally." He turned the blade over in his grip. The side that had been in the flame glowed orange. A strange chemical smell, like metal and fire, filled Flora's nostrils. She wanted to spit the smell out of her mouth, it was so strong.

"*Ah*, there's the rub," the captain said. "Due to your unique constraints aboard this vessel, I expected your total and unwavering allegiance could be assumed. And with the Lady Hasegawa aboard, I reveled in the opportunity for unsullied merchandise, being as you lack the tools to disassemble her maidenhood. So I thought, have Florian guard the good lady."

"A reasonable choice," said Rake.

"You would *think* so, wouldn't you? I'm not a betting man, but if I were, I'd have bet on you, Florian, to be her ideal chaperone while on the *Dove*. I'm not a man who puts much faith in anyone, so you can imagine my sincere disappointment in you when it was called to my attention that you had abandoned your post."

He let out a long, dramatic exhale through his nose.

"And let your moron of a brother attend to it." Another pause. "I gave you a direct order. You did not obey it." The captain's voice was hard now, like rigging gone taut. "Give me your hand."

Flora held her left hand across the wooden desk with as much stillness as she could muster. Her fingers trembled mutinously.

The captain stood and took her hand. His skin was shockingly soft for a man of the sea. He pressed his lips against her fingers almost sweetly, then pressed her palm down flat on the desk.

"The blade," he said. As Rake handed it to the captain, the dawning realization of what was about to happen hit Flora.

"Wait," she pleaded.

"*Wait,*" the captain mimicked. He shook his head. "Fire always reveals the true man," he hissed at Flora. Then, to Rake: "Hold her."

Rake's grip was like a vise on Flora. She could not move. The smell of the heated metal was nauseating; the fear was nauseating. Flora thought she might be sick.

As a child, Flora and Alfie had spent enough days in temples bowing before statues of the Emperor, feigning piety in exchange for an hour's warmth. She'd heard the priests' descriptions of the world that awaited sinners and traitors to the Empire. It did not scare her then the way it scared her now.

*This is what death smells like.*

*This is what death smells like.*

In her fear, Flora tried to pull her hand away, but Rake's grip on her arm was too strong, he was too strong, and even when she tried to curl her fingers in, Rake pulled them flat once again, his fingers rough.

"Please," she begged.

But the captain brought down the blade anyway.

In two agonizing cuts, the bulk of Flora's pinky finger was gone, just below the first knuckle. The room swelled and ebbed, but Rake held her. Maybe she heard a voice, his voice, whisper. "You're all right," it might have said, but she could not be sure. Black spots exploded before her eyes. The captain held the blade, wiped clean of her blood, to the flame once more. Then he held it against the wound to stanch the bleeding.

Flora prayed for unconsciousness, but it did not come. Instead, she remained horribly awake, reeling from the pain and nausea that overtook her. There was nothing in the world but her pain, nothing left. She saw a dancing reflection of the captain in the puddle of her blood and was very nearly ill.

"I expect you back at the Lady's side before the moon is high tonight," he said. "Go have Cook bandage your finger. And pray you never disappoint me again."

Rake practically carried Flora to the kitchen. Cook was an old hand at bandaging up pirates. He'd lost a few of his fingers to the Nameless Captain himself. This was no comfort to Flora, though, not while her hand throbbed, her legs weak from the pain of it. And besides, he was out of the kitchen when they arrived, leaving Rake and Flora alone in the smoke from the fire and the steam from the rice.

Rake deposited her on a spare chair and Flora let her head hang over the hand she clutched, still bleeding, to her chest.

"Do you understand why." It was not a question so much as it was a command. To tell him she'd never fail him or the captain ever again.

"I disobeyed an order." Her voice was soft. Rake said nothing, so she repeated herself, louder this time. But Rake shook his head.

"You disobeyed, yes. This happens. You may have received a simple lashing for that, one or two, even."

Rake turned her chin so that she faced him, faced his burning eyes, faced the full brunt of his anger. She'd never seen him so angry, not in all her years aboard the *Dove,* not at her. She'd always been obedient, always did as he said.

"But you disobeyed because your heart has softened. For an Imperial." He practically spat this, his red eyebrows knitted in disgust.

Despite herself, despite the pain that nearly overwhelmed her, Flora felt her own anger grow to match his.

"The Lady Hasegawa is not like the Imperials who took

Quark." It was, she knew, an incredibly foolish thing to say. Rake did not suffer speech about his home country, not even from the captain. She could see Rake's face darken at the mention of it.

"What do you know of Quark?" Rake asked. His voice was deadly calm, but Flora could feel his fury beneath it, churning like a tempest. She was too weak to care, though, her body still in shock from the loss of her finger.

Flora said nothing. She knew Quark had been colonized by the Imperials, just as most of the Known World had. Quark was the last of the Cold World to be conquered. Only a few spare island countries and Tustwe remained free. Battles were fought in Quark and won by the Emperor. She had seen battle in her life, knew its terrible bloody truth. That there were no heroes in battle, only the lucky. But she had never seen a battle rained down upon an entire city. On an entire country.

"Do you know, little Florian, what your mother's intestines look like, spilling out of her belly and being picked apart by dogs?" Rake hissed. "Because I do. I know what it looks like, what it smells like. I know what it sounds like when the dogs start fighting over what little is left. See this?" He drew his finger along a scar that cut down his cheek. Flora had always assumed he'd sustained it during his life at sea. "I got this for trying to take her body. To bury her. I was just a boy, and they whipped me for trying to put my mother to rest. Do not tell me of Imperial kindness. I've seen it."

"But Evelyn . . ." Flora croaked. She tried to catch her breath. She'd lost so much blood, and she could feel the weight of it missing. As if she were untethered from a body that did not want her anymore. Still. Rake *had* to know.

"Oh, it's *Evelyn* now?"

But before more could be said, Cook came back into the

kitchen. Seeing Flora and her bloody hand, he sighed his curmud-geonly sigh.

"What'd you do, then?" he asked. He stuffed some bandages into a pot of boiling water.

"Doesn't matter," Rake said stiffly. "Just see that Florian here is fixed up in time to attend to the Lady Hasegawa by the end of dinner."

And without another word, he left.

# The Sea

In this moment alone, a gray whale has beached itself on the Red Shore.

A fishing ship pulls in more than a thousand haddock in its tightly woven nets.

Off the coast of the Floating Islands, a young boy in his mirth and carelessness as he swims has kicked a tower of golden coral, toppling it and drawing his own blood.

In her depths, in her darkness, a monkfish in search of prey illuminates a lure.

She is aware of all of this, but she is focused on the hollow edges where her mermaid belongs.

She feels the absence like she feels a rock, corporeal and painful as it rubs against her.

It is an ache; it's angry and raw.

She has no special communion with a shark.

No moment of clarity shared between herself and the eels. They are all just denizens in her midst.

*But a mermaid is at once her child and her possession, a piece of herself and something entirely unto herself. She knows each of them by their secret name.*

*Entrusted as only mermaids can be, each holds her memories, for she is too old and too great to hold them all herself. For when a new memory rises and demands to be held by the Sea, a mermaid is born. Rising from her depths, full and whole and beautiful.*

*But one is missing.*

*And though she cannot say what memory she no longer holds, she knows something is gone. What pain it is, to know a memory is gone but not what it is.*

*She reaches out her infinite fingers, grappling in the dark for what she has lost.*

*She howls.*

## CHAPTER 11

*Evelyn*

**W**hen she reached her cabin, Evelyn was not surprised to find Florian at her guard once more.

What did startle her was the wan cast to the boy's face. While typically his face was, if not congenial, at least robust with health and strength, it was now as gray as the mysterious meat chunks Evelyn had just spent the last half hour pushing around her bowl with a spoon. His eyes held a strange and pallid half cast, as though he could just barely keep them open. He cradled his hand, which was freshly bandaged.

"What have they done to you?" Her voice was unrecognizable even to herself, so wrought with strange new fury. Her field of vision narrowed. All she could see was Florian, poor Florian crouching over his mangled hand.

"Just an accident on deck," he murmured, but his voice was blurry with pain and untruth.

"Liar." She helped him to his feet, carefully. He winced anyway. He smelled of the ocean, not unpleasantly. But he also smelled of blood, coppery and unmistakable. Like heated metal and fear.

Gently, she held his wrist in order to see his bandaged hand — and nearly fainted. His pinky finger was gone.

"It'll be fine, milady." His eyes would not meet hers.

"Oh, Florian." Guilt stacked like bricks in her chest. She would never know a life like his, never have to suffer as he did. The sternest punishment she'd ever received was a spanking. It had happened only once and was delivered by her elderly governess. How merciless poor Florian's life had been, how acutely unfair. The awareness hit her again and again, wave after wave, rocking her.

"Please, milady. Don't make a fuss." His voice was so tired.

"OK," Evelyn said. "OK." A wild desire to kiss him came over her. To make him or herself feel better, she did not know or even understand. It wasn't pity. It just seemed like the right thing to do. Evelyn said nothing for fear of saying something silly. Something unhelpful, something burdensome.

Instead, she pulled a stool and a pillow from her messy cabin and arranged Florian upon them so he might stand watch with more comfort. His lips twitched into a momentary smile of gratitude, then fell once more into a grimace. Once she was sure he was as comfortable as was possible in the narrow space outside, she returned to her cabin.

A ridiculous tear fell down Evelyn's cheek, and she brushed it aside angrily. It was not her right to cry. She had not lost a finger. Florian probably hadn't cried, so why should she? Her tears wouldn't help him. There was nothing she *could* do to help. To protect him.

On the floor, her casket lay open, the expensive silks of her various kimonos spilling forth, a cascade of wealth. To think how angry she'd been to be sent away. It seemed at the time like the greatest injustice ever to be thrust on a person. To be taken from home, to be wrenched from the only life she'd ever known and shipped off to a distant shore. Where ... what? Where she'd be the lady of a keep that was famous in Imperial circles for its luxury. To be married to a man she'd never met. And even though she did not want a man, any man, she had all her fingers. She need not fear for her life.

She did not want *any* man, she reminded herself. Not even the boy on the opposite side of the door.

Right?

She lay back in her berth and stared at the whorls of wood in the ceiling that she could just barely see in the dim candlelight of her cabin. The patterns in the wood had no reason, no symmetry, no order.

She slept restlessly.

The *Dove* creaked as she plodded through the sea, and it sounded as though the ship were groaning with discontent. Evelyn abdicated the night to insomnia, extricated herself from her nest of sheets, and snuck out of her cabin.

Florian slept at the door and did not wake when Evelyn opened it. His face was furrowed even in sleep, an almost imperceptible crease between his eyebrows. He was beautiful, she thought, in the way the sea was. The lamp outside her cabin cast shimmers of gold across his dark skin, calling to mind how the sun sometimes cast shimmers of gold across the surface of the sea. She tiptoed past him so he could rest.

Still unused to the rocking of the ship, she stumbled up the stairs to the deck. The sun had only just started to rise, though she'd have never known it in her berth, which was still embraced by darkness. Maybe it was always dark there. On the deck, a handful of the crewmen were circled, yelling and hooting at something Evelyn could not see.

Sidling up to the group, unnoticed in their frenzy, she saw it: a mermaid. The creature gasped for air and thrashed upon the deck, her silver-scaled neck caught in thickly wrought net.

Evelyn had never seen a mermaid before. She'd heard stories about them, of course, knew they were real the way that dragons and magic were real: distant and exotic, denizens of the world outside Imperial reach, outside the bustle of modern colonies. There was a dragon skeleton in the Imperial Palace. She'd seen it. She thought of the drawing in her book of fairy tales, of the mermaid who reached for the sailor. It looked nothing like the one that flopped on the deck before her.

Where the illustrations always showed gloriously beautiful women with clear skin and long, flowing hair, this mermaid was small, stubbed, the size of an infant, with green and silver scales all over her body. Her eyes were awkwardly far apart on her face, more like a fish than a human, and gills flared in her cheeks. Green hair like seaweed wrapped around her neck. Her mouth gaped in silent terror.

A thickset sailor with dense arm hair nudged at the mermaid with his foot and said, "Keep it alive and we can sell it for a fine price." It took a moment before Evelyn recognized him as Fawkes, the man who'd come and harassed Florian as she tutored him. A swell of dislike rose in her throat.

Alfie shook his head. "They never make it."

"Let's just have it now," chimed in another.

"Throw her back," Evelyn said. None of the men heard her, too engulfed in argument as they were. She took a deep breath and shouted, "Throw her back!"

The crewmen turned and regarded Evelyn with equal measures of surprise and amusement, their faces curled into question marks. Fawkes stepped toward Evelyn, his eyes shining. Evelyn took a reflexive step back. Fawkes smiled, baring his broken, tobacco-stained teeth.

"Aw, milady, you wouldn't begrudge seamen like ourselves a bit of extra on the side? Not all of us is so fortunate as to sleep on silks every night." He reached out as though to touch her arm, but Evelyn flinched away. A flash of annoyance burned in his eyes. "If you'll pardon me saying so, miss, but all sailors is desirous men."

The mermaid's tail thrashed against the deck with a wet smack.

"She's scared," Evelyn said.

A wave of chuckles passed through the crewmen. "Yep." The sailor nodded. "So is the pike we meant to pull into this here net, but then, you wouldn't beg clemency for them, would you?"

Tears pricked at Evelyn's eyes and she looked away, embarrassed. How naive she must seem. Distantly, she was aware that several of the crewmen were already working to hoist a barrel full of seawater onto the deck, presumably to keep the mermaid in.

She felt a gentle pull on her elbow and turned to see that Florian had woken up. His eyes were still clouded with sleep and pain, but clearly he would not be caught away from his ward again.

"Come on, milady," he whispered. "There's nothing here that can be done."

The defeat in his voice was like an anchor that held Evelyn fast. She would not let these men, these terrible men, keep or kill or touch this wonderful creature. She squared her shoulders to Fawkes. They may be bigger than she was, may better know the sea, but Evelyn was an Imperial lady. And that had to be good for something. For once.

"Throw. Her. Back."

No one laughed this time. All recognized the tone of command. Evelyn held the sailor's eyes, let him see her fury. She didn't care what he thought of her. Didn't care if she appeared foolish. She would protect this mermaid. At least.

"What's all this, eh?" The voice had the arrogance of privilege. Evelyn whirled to see the man she'd been told was Captain Lafayette. The men immediately straightened. This, she knew, was the man who had taken Florian's finger. She fought the desire to push him overboard.

"Mermaid, on the deck, sir. We pulled it up with the fishing net," said a crewman. "Fawkes has laid his claim to it."

Fawkes nodded. "It'll fetch a fine price."

Captain Lafayette did not respond. Instead, he looked to Evelyn. "Have you ever seen a mermaid before, Lady Hasegawa?"

"No, sir."

"Come." He took her by the elbow and guided her to the barrel filled with seawater where the mermaid now bobbed, looking forlorn. "They're never so lovely as you might hope, the mermaids. Hardly worth the trouble they're said to cause. But Fawkes is right. She'll fetch a good price for him, nonetheless."

"You're going to let them keep her?"

Captain Lafayette smiled in a way that did not touch his eyes. "The sea does not impart many gifts, my lady. A good sailor knows to take what he can get."

The mermaid wrapped her tiny fingers around the edge of the barrel and attempted to pull herself out. Captain Lafayette took a spyglass from his red doublet, pulled it to its full length, and smacked it, hard, against the mermaid's hands. She let go immediately and cradled them to her chest. A splatter of black blood remained. The captain dipped a finger in the blood and, to Evelyn's horror, licked it clean.

Evelyn gasped.

"Florian," called Captain Lafayette.

"Yes, Captain."

"Take Lady Hasegawa to the galley and see that she's well sated. A little midnight snack. Something sweet. Her unease is nothing a treat can't assist."

Florian's eyes flickered to Evelyn, then back to the captain. "Yes, sir."

The captain smiled his beatific smile again and rested his thick hand on Evelyn's shoulder. "Go on, young lady. There's a tin of butter biscuits in there. Tell Cook I said you could have as many as you desire." With a wink and a pat on her back, Captain Lafayette was gone.

The mermaid looked at Evelyn. Evelyn looked at the mermaid.

*You see me.* A whisper in Evelyn's ears, like the echo of waves in a seashell. *You see, you see, you see.* And without a doubt, Evelyn knew it was the mermaid.

"Shall we, milady?" Florian asked.

## CHAPTER 12

*Flora*

**H**er blood is black," Evelyn said. "I didn't know it'd be black."

Evelyn stared off at nothing as she and Flora sat next to each other in the corner of the galley at Cook's table. He'd dropped a cloth full of sweet Cold World biscuits between them, muttering to himself. They were, Flora guessed, from his personal store, and he wasn't pleased to share them. For her part, Evelyn noticed little, her mind clearly still on the mermaid and the mermaid's fate.

"Only while she's alive," Flora said. Her finger throbbed beneath the bandages, and she found she lacked the energy for niceties. She should lie to Evelyn, should tell her the mermaid would be fine. Which, of course, she wouldn't be. "Once she dies, it'll fade to brown and congeal, and it won't be worth anything."

Evelyn put down her cookie. "It's her blood that's valuable?" The disgust in her voice was unmistakable.

"Yes, milady."

"Why?"

"They say drinking the black blood of the mermaid shows a man visions. Beautiful things, strange things. Lets them in on secrets only the Sea knows. They say it's like talking to gods."

"Gods." Her voice was so dubious, Flora nearly laughed despite everything.

"Makes you hallucinate anyway." *And forget.* But she did not say this, not to the Lady Hasegawa. What could she understand about needing to forget?

"That's the foulest thing I've ever heard." Evelyn gave Flora an appraising look, her dark eyes narrowed. "Have you ever drunk the black blood of a mermaid?"

Flora couldn't help it — this time she laughed. As if she could afford it. She shook the memory of Alfie in the pub away. "No, milady."

Evelyn smiled, her pink lips pressed together in a soft line of amusement. "Oh, good. I guess we can still be friends, then."

*Friends.* It was a kind word, but it stuck in Flora's teeth.

"Yes, milady."

Evelyn smiled again, picked up a biscuit, and handed it to Flora. "Really, Florian. Eat. You're so skinny, it hurts *me.*" There was something undeniably flirty in her tone, in the tilt of her head, and Flora felt her cheeks blazing. It felt so hot then, in that small, small space with Evelyn. Their knees touched just barely beneath the shabby wooden table. Did she even realize their knees were touching? *Probably not.*

Flora wiped a droplet of sweat from her brow.

"Don't be ridiculous," Evelyn said, firm now. "It's a biscuit. What's the worst that could happen if you took a —" She stopped herself, her ears coloring a dark, ashamed red. But Flora smiled and lifted her bandaged hand in a mock salute.

"I'm so sorry." Evelyn shook her head at herself. "I didn't mean to. I just —"

"It's OK," Flora cut across her. "It doesn't do to pretend this life isn't what it is."

Instantaneously, she knew she had said too much. She looked away, because Evelyn's eyes were filling with tears.

"No," Evelyn said. "It doesn't."

A thick silence descended between them. To break it, Flora reached out and took a biscuit with her good hand. It tasted of sugar and butter.

"Why do you stay?" Evelyn asked.

Flora choked a little. She thumped herself on the chest. In all the time she'd spent with the Lady in the last month, she had never asked anything quite so pointed. And she asked a lot of questions.

"It's a place to live," Flora said. Which was true. She could not quite bring herself to lie.

Evelyn's eyes scanned Flora's face, and in her gaze Flora could hear the questions the girl did not voice: *Where did you live before that this is better? What have you done to survive?* And what could Flora say that would make sense to someone like Lady Evelyn? Nothing, she knew. *Nothing.* Those weren't even the right questions. The right questions would be: *How can you live this life? How could you let them do this to me? To the passengers before me?*

The fog of silence was practically opaque.

"Have the men caught mermaids before?" Evelyn asked.

"Only one since Alfie and I got here. They're hard to catch." This was not true. They'd caught many. Catching mermaids was one of the captain's great pleasures. It was why the men kept the nets freshly knotted. But Flora had only ever seen one. One had been enough. The sight of it, shriveled and diminished as it was, was more than Flora could bear. After the first time, she took careful steps to avoid the sight of them.

She wasn't alone in this. The mermaids made many of the men leery. *The Pirate Supreme*, they whispered. *The Pirate Supreme will find us, and we'll hang for it.* But the Pirate Supreme never found them, never brought down the hammer of justice upon the men who pulled the mermaids from the sea. The men who either drank their blood or sold it.

"What happened to her?"

"Died before we reached port." Flora fiddled with her bandage, tried to focus on the pain. If she could just focus on that, she could ignore the feel of Evelyn's eyes on hers, the pressure of her concern. "We don't know what they eat, see."

"So she starved to death?"

"Yes, milady."

"Please don't call me that." Evelyn sighed. She lifted the biscuit she meant to eat, but let her hand fall away before it reached her lips. "I thought mermaids were supposed to be beautiful," she mused. "Not like that poor creature flopping around. Nothing is as lovely as I might have believed."

"They are pretty." Flora grinned when Evelyn's eyes met hers once more, narrowed in deep doubt. "Not how she looks now. But in the water. I've seen a couple. It's only once we pull them out of the sea that they look so . . . like that."

"We could care for her, you know. Figure out what she needs. Keep her safe."

"No one ever has."

"So?" Evelyn's eyes glittered in the dim light of the galley, twin stars improbably risen belowdecks. Flora felt her heart as though it had escaped into her throat, drumming a mad and impossible song. "Just because it's never been done doesn't mean it *can't* be."

"Believe me, mil—Evelyn. If there were a way to keep them alive, then men'd have found it. Worth more, you know? Gold's a solid incentive around here."

"But we have an even *better* incentive."

"What's that?"

"To do what's right."

Flora choked back a scoff. When had right and wrong ever had any bearing on anything?

"The right thing would be to toss it back in the sea. But I promise you, Evelyn, you do that and I'll be missing my head instead of my finger. My life is worth less than hers."

To her shock, Evelyn placed a hand on Flora's arm. She felt her skin tingle with heat where their skin met.

"I'll never put you in any danger again, I promise. But you say she'll be worth more alive, yes? Certainly, none of your colleagues will be angry at you for doing them this service. And we'll have done, if not the right thing, at least the thing that's closest to it." There was a pause, but the Lady did not move her hand. "And your life is worth more. To *me*, anyway."

Her hand was so warm on Flora's skin. *Her hand.* Flora gulped. "Fine."

At her words, Evelyn's face erupted into a wide and beautiful smile.

*I'll try.*


It had been only a week, and already the mermaid looked close to death. She hadn't been a lovely thing to start, but now her scales were inflamed and tinged with red, her strange fishy cheeks sunken from hunger. Fawkes kept her barrel with all the other stores, belowdecks, in the stagnant air of the ship.

She bobbed in her barrel, despondent.

Flora looked at the mermaid. The mermaid looked at nothing.

Flora had brought Evelyn to the barrel when she could, and each time the Lady dropped bits of food into it. Always, the mermaid let the nibbles sink to the bottom, and always Flora could see Evelyn's heart break for it. Flora had taken to sneaking off at night to see to the mermaid while the Lady slept, though she could tell the mermaid did not much appreciate the visits. She did, at least, let herself float to the surface when Evelyn came to visit. They had taken to doing their lessons in the stores, so that the mermaid could share in the stories they took turns reading aloud.

A few times the crew had managed to keep a mermaid alive until they reached port. But always those had been the ones caught close to the end of a voyage. A couple of times the captain had bought them off the sailor who hauled them in, on the spot. They were, after all, his favorite treat, and he always gave a more than fair price for them.

Flora remembered the first, who was even uglier than this one, if it were possible. That one had thrashed in her barrel of seawater for more than two weeks before she died. They'd tried to bleed her dry as soon as they realized, but it was too late. Her blood had congealed, rendered undrinkable. They pitched her useless carcass overboard.

*She's just a fish,* Flora told herself. *Just like your dinner.*

She tried not to think of the tales she'd heard, of the Sea and her anger. The mermaids were, according to numerous old sailors who drank too much rum and then shot their mouths off in pubs and taverns, the Sea's own daughters. And that stealing them from the Sea was a crime, punishable by death.

She tried not to think of Evelyn's tears.

But still, the captain sailed on. And still, he caught the mermaids in his cruel nets. No punishment ever came to him. *Much though he may deserve it,* Flora thought, and then shook her head to rid herself of such mutinous ideas. She hated the captain, but it did not do to dwell.

Flora let her fingers trail in the water. The mermaid skittered to the other side of the barrel and watched her with open suspicion.

"No way she survives this voyage," Rake said. It was as though she had conjured him with her mind. She had not heard him coming, had not heard anyone coming. How was it he could be so quiet? It was the second time he'd snuck up on her in a week, and this time she was idle. She braced herself for a tongue-lashing for abandoning her post, but it did not come.

"They say the man who figures out what mermaids eat is a true servant of the Sea." He peered into the barrel. Sensing his shadow, the mermaid stirred and swam closer to the bottom.

"Do you know what they eat?"

"If I did, I'd feed her, wouldn't I?"

"The Lady Hasegawa is bent on solving it."

"Is she."

"Drags me here every day so she can try different things."

Rake said nothing.

"Mermaid likes her. Always comes to the surface when she sees her coming."

"They do prefer women."

This time, Flora said nothing. The spell of safety Florian cast over her life was slipping, and yet she did not seem to be a female anymore, either. The loss stung. She was neither, it seemed. Or at least, she didn't reap the benefit of either.

Silence stretched between them. Flora could feel their strange bond slipping away. Rake hated all Imperials, Evelyn included. But Flora wanted him to tell her that everything would be all right, that he understood her, understood the Lady Hasegawa, that there was justice and that the Pirate Supreme would see to it. Of course, Rake would never make any such claim. Comfort was not in Rake's tool kit. He was, she reflected bitterly, the closest thing to a father she'd ever had. He had taught her to tie knots and had struck her when she was wrong. But she could hardly muster the courage to speak with him.

Rake looked into the barrel and watched the mermaid, who cowered away from them both.

"Have you ever drunk the black blood?" The boldness of her question surprised even Flora.

Rake drummed his fingers along the side of the barrel, as though considering his response.

"Yes," he said finally.

"Did it work?"

Rake smiled his not-quite-smile. "Depends on how you measure it," he said. "I saw things. I forgot things." He said nothing for a moment, watching the mermaid as she lurked in the depths of the barrel.

"Men can't understand what they see when they drink the blood. It's too big for us, I think." He rapped his knuckle against the barrel, startling the mermaid. "What she has to give—we can take it, but we aren't meant to. Not at that price."

Flora repressed a shudder.

"Captain says a good sailor takes any gift the Sea will give him," Flora said.

"True." Rake stepped away from the barrel and held Flora's

gaze unblinkingly. "But I think Florian is man enough now to question what's a gift and what's a curse."

*Florian.* She wished she had his confidence now. His sense of sureness. Flora had never spoken at such length with Rake about the mermaids. He never stopped anyone from bringing them in — but then, he never partook in them, either. Never ordered nets to be knotted for their capture. Never took a cut from their sale. She wondered what Rake believed. Likely, whatever was most sensible. It was his way.

"Why let Fawkes keep her, then?"

Rake laughed, the ugly, barking laugh of a man who has killed. "Men like Fawkes will do as they do. He's not seeking any wisdom from me, nor would I be inclined to give it to him." All the other men aboard the *Dove* loved Fawkes — finding that Rake did not surprised Flora, and emboldened her.

"Why did you let him do that to Alfie?" she asked.

Rake shook his head but did not answer. "Keep your head down, Florian. See to your duties. It's all you can do." He gave her an awkward pat on the shoulder, then left the way he came, his footsteps heavy.

The mermaid, sensing Rake's exit, pulled herself to the edge of the barrel so her strange fishy eyes peered over the edge.

She was looking for someone. For whom was no mystery.

◆ CHAPTER 13 ◆

## *Evelyn*

**E**velyn was at a loss.

   She hated the way the food stores smelled, as though they had gone to rot. She hated the slippery walk down the many staircases that led to them — she had not even realized how tall the *Dove* was, how deep it went, until she'd had to visit its bowels on a regular basis. She hated the grime of wet wood that found its way beneath her fingernails from the railings she had to grip in order not to fall to her death during each descent.

   She hated the hopeful way the mermaid looked at her each time she returned, as though Evelyn would free her. As though Evelyn would care for her. Which, of course, Evelyn didn't and hadn't and couldn't.

   But more than anything, she hated seeing Florian's face as he watched her try, again and again, and then fail again and again. As he watched her, his face would still, like the sea without wind, like a mask of pity.

She'd brought soba noodles with her this time, slippery and sticky in the handkerchief she'd wrapped them in. It seemed unlikely that the mermaid would prefer noodles. But she'd tried fish — raw and cooked — and crabmeat, apples, and nori. A hunk of hard cheese. And the mermaid had eaten none of it.

The mermaid bobbed close to the surface upon recognizing Evelyn, her strange green face turned upward toward her impotent savior. Evelyn extricated a single noodle and dangled it in the water. Annoyed, the mermaid batted it away, then swam sluggishly lower as if to be free of the offensive offering.

"Please eat," Evelyn pleaded. But of course, the mermaid didn't. She looked like she could die at any moment, the way she floated listlessly, the way her eyes had started to go cloudy.

Behind her, Evelyn heard Florian shift from foot to foot nervously. He could clearly sense her growing desperation, and it seemed to frustrate him.

"Please," she said again. She was surprised to hear tears in her own voice.

"Milady," Florian begged, "let's go read, maybe, huh? Go for a stroll on the upper decks? You could use a distraction."

"No!" She whirled on him, angry now. He might be willing to live a life of constant disappointment, but she could show him — she *would* show him. There was more for him. For the mermaid. Something better. "I won't give up on her!"

It was not all she wanted to say, but it was what came out. Florian heaved a sigh. Evelyn could not bear to look at him, could not bear to see his knowing face.

In the barrel, the mermaid watched her closely. Evelyn placed her lantern on the floor. Its flickering light cast eerie shadows around the stores. She could not say what made her submerge her arm, to the elbow, in the mermaid's barrel. Maybe it was her desperation. Maybe it was her fierce desire to prove to Florian, to prove to herself, that the mermaid could be saved. Whatever it was, it drove her to stick her open hand into the water. It was cold.

"Evelyn," Florian hissed. "Don't."

But Evelyn didn't listen. "She needs to eat," she said simply.

And even though some distant part of her was expecting it, Evelyn still had to hold herself firm as the mermaid took her wrist in her small hands.

"She's going to bite you!" Florian nearly shouted.

Which was true. The mermaid pulled her lips back to reveal two rows of tiny, sharp teeth. When she bit down on Evelyn's wrist, it was all Evelyn could do not to cry out from the pain of it. Florian made a noise of disgust and tried to pull Evelyn back, but she silenced him with a withering glare. "I'll be fine," she said. "And so will she."

The mermaid drank her fill, and when she was done, she looked less deathly than even a moment before, her scales flat against her body and her eyes clear. Before releasing Evelyn, she kissed each of the wounds her teeth had made—and to both Evelyn's and Florian's amazement, each cut stitched itself closed. When Evelyn did finally pull her arm from the water, it was as if nothing had happened at all.

*You see me.*

The voice came from nowhere and everywhere, or else from inside Evelyn's own mind.

"Did you hear that?" she asked.

But Florian shook his head. He was examining Evelyn's wrist, his rough hands gentle on her skin. For a moment they stood together in silence, each pretending that it was perfectly normal to dwell like this, a sailor's hands on a lady's bare skin. Florian gulped. His neck, Evelyn realized, did not look like a boy's neck.

*You see me, Evelyn.*

The voice was distant and soft, like the sound of waves caught in a seashell. This time, Evelyn knew Florian had not heard — his eyes were still focused on her skin, where the wounds had disappeared. It was, Evelyn realized, the mermaid. The mermaid who knew her name.

As if in a trance, Evelyn gazed back into the barrel. She looked at the mermaid. The mermaid looked at Evelyn, her strange fishy eyes unblinking.

"You did it," Florian said. Evelyn turned and was surprised to find him smiling. He didn't smile often. A single dimple pressed in on his left cheek. "Men here've seen mermaids a hundred times and never figured it out. But you." He laughed so quietly she could barely hear it. "Blood. No one ever. You're too smart for this ship."

Evelyn's ears flushed red. Something like pride bubbled inside of her, and she found it was most uncomfortable to look directly at him. She looked instead back at the mermaid, who was now gripping the side of her barrel so her head was out of the water.

*Home,* the mermaid said.

"Maybe *I* could set her free," Evelyn replied. "They can't expect you to physically stop me, can they?"

"What do you mean?"

"I'm a Lady of Crandon," she said. "You think these men would dare touch me? It's not their place to lay a hand on me. Why not use that for something good?"

*Let me save her,* Evelyn thought. *Let me save* you. But Florian did not answer.

"Let's get you back to your cabin," he said. "She's well enough for now."

* * *

The Lady Ayer was shocked.

Not that a mermaid was being kept in a barrel aboard the *Dove*, nor that she drank blood, nor even that her kiss had healed Evelyn's wounds. Not that Florian had had his finger chopped off for disobeying orders, not that the captain had menaced Evelyn with his violence toward the mermaid.

Instead, the Lady Ayer was angry that Florian had allowed Evelyn down to the stores in the first place.

"The sea is full of foul and strange creatures," she said. "And I haven't the width of mind to contemplate the many perversions of men. Thanks to the Emperor, it is not my place to. But you must be vigilant here. You're not in Crandon anymore, little miss. Your mother'd break every single one of my porcelain plates if she knew I'd sat by and watched you wandering off into all kinds of dangerous places."

The flame between them flickered, casting shadows across the Lady Ayer's face. The Lady was so like Evelyn's mother. It was no wonder the two were friends. So uncaring, so cruel.

The Lady topped off Evelyn's tea, even though she'd scarcely had a sip. Evelyn had to concede, the Lady Ayer's setup was enviable. Where her mother's style was expensive, it was very plain, prone to whites and ivories. The Lady Ayer, on the other hand, decorated with flair befitting a country estate: tapestries with yellow flowers, ribbons, and whimsical embroideries of sheep. Saccharine though it certainly was, it did brighten the otherwise dingy quarters. She'd even brought a heavy bookshelf along, though it stood half-empty against the wall of her cabin.

"Your doilies certainly are . . . impressive," Evelyn said. She was in want of a change of subject, and doilies would do if they must.

Behind the Lady, her pet dove jumped from rung to rung in

its copper cage. It was a lovely cage, but a cage all the same. Evelyn had the mad notion that she should set the dove free.

"All the trappings of comfort a man would never think of," the Lady Ayer replied. She sounded very pleased with herself. Rightfully so, Evelyn thought grudgingly. While the rest of the *Dove* was wet, drafty, hard, and bore the scent of fish and feet, the Lady Ayer's berth somehow always smelled of freshly laundered blankets and lavender, and boasted an excess of soft fabrics and pillows. It was nothing short of miraculous.

"It didn't occur to me, either." Evelyn had not had the foresight to pack her own tea set, though she found the ritual of its use most reassuring. She thought fleetingly of her mother's insistence upon high tea but shook the thought away. There was nothing comforting about those memories.

The Lady Ayer offered a gentle pat to Evelyn's knee, so light Evelyn hardly felt it. "You'll learn."

The Lady rang a dainty silver bell, and her lady's maid, Genevieve, reappeared. All the judgment Genevieve had passed on Evelyn was cleverly disguised from her face now. She looked for all the world like a simple lady's maid. It took a clever person to pretend to be so dull so convincingly. Evelyn was impressed.

"Yes, my lady?"

"The gelées, please." The Lady Ayer gave Evelyn an uncharacteristically mischievous smile. "They are my most special indulgence. You'll love them, or I'll eat my doilies."

Genevieve returned with a tiny gilded box, which she opened and presented to the ladies. Inside were sugar-coated pink jellies shaped like seashells. The Lady Ayer plucked one with the tiny pair of tongs that were fitted inside the box.

"They're strawberry," she said, and dropped one in Evelyn's palm. "Let it melt on your tongue."

Evelyn obliged and was soon rewarded with a delicious burst of flavor that could only be described as summertime. Even in the dark of the cabin, Evelyn could feel the sun on her skin, the tickle of green grass beneath her feet — her first kiss with Keiko, stolen in the garden.

"It's marvelous," she said.

The Lady Ayer smiled. "They're made by Genevieve's own cousins. I ship them in especially, to remind the dear girl of home, but also just because they're so yummy. The colonies do serve us well, Quark especially. Genevieve here is a shining example of the good labor that's to be found if one looks hard enough." She paused, clearly savoring the gelée, her eyes closed in pleasure. "Men can have their mermaid's blood. I hear it tastes like drowning. But these . . . they're just for our sort."

"Our sort?"

"Women." She motioned for Genevieve to partake as well. "We may be the inglorious sex, but I do think we are better at finding pleasures to which men are not invited."

Evelyn thought of Florian and the biscuits. She fought the urge to request an additional gelée to give to the boy. It seemed unlikely he received much kindness, let alone glory. Certainly he deserved a treat now and again, too. She thought again of his unusual neck.

"I am inclined to agree with you," she said instead.

"I knew your mother long before she was ever wed," the Lady Ayer said. "We were the closest of friends." She motioned to Genevieve, who left them to their privacy once more.

Evelyn nodded. She did not care. When she left Crandon, Evelyn had decided rather pointedly that she left all cares of her mother on the same gray shore where that woman had feigned sadness at her leaving.

"Until her mother married her off to your father, we spent as many of our days together as we could. She was a different person then. Vibrant, impulsive. I was so surprised, I suppose, to see who she'd become in our many years of being parted. So solemn, she is now."

*So terrible,* Evelyn thought. *So hateful.*

"You carry much anger for her," the Lady Ayer said. It was not a question. "I admit, I do, too."

At this, Evelyn looked up, meeting the Lady Ayer's eyes for the first time since she'd mentioned her mother. "May I ask why?"

"What I tell you, I tell you as a close friend," the Lady said. Her face was impassive. Evelyn nodded, her curiosity rising. The Lady rested her teacup in her saucer and looked out the porthole, out at the gray sea beyond. "We knew, when she married your father, that our — particular — friendship must come to an end. I suppose I thought she would still at least speak to me. If only in letters. But she never wrote me back. And after a few years, I stopped trying."

Evelyn suspected she was missing the point entirely. Just a moment before, the Lady's face had been without feeling, but now it was wrought with practically theatrical pain. For several long moments, Evelyn did not know what to say. What was right to say. "Particular?" she asked finally.

"I loved Edith — your mother. And I know, in my heart, she loved me back. In her way. We couldn't be together, we knew that, never pretended otherwise. But those were our feelings just the same."

Evelyn flinched. She'd never heard anyone refer to her mother by her first name before, not even her father, who only ever called her "your mother." It was like a slap, the realization that once, however long ago, however distant it had become, her mother had been a girl, a girl in love.

It seemed improbable. Not only that, but impossible. But why would the Lady Ayer lie?

"But then . . ." Evelyn trailed off.

"Yes. But then. But then she was married and she was gone from my life. And anyway, there are many different kinds of love. She did not contact me, not until now, to ask me to guard you against sin and ruin on this voyage."

"And you said you would."

"Of course." The Lady Ayer sighed. "Love does not work in terms of convenience. Or any kind of sense."

## CHAPTER 14

*Flora*

W hile Lady Evelyn dined with the Lady Ayer, Flora ducked into the stores to check on the mermaid. It was a foolish impulse, and her time would have been much better spent tracking down some hardtack for herself, but neither she nor Evelyn had checked on the creature for days. *I'm just checking to see if it's even still alive,* she told herself. *Nothing more.*

To Flora's horror, the mermaid bobbed at the surface of the filthy, lukewarm water. Flora nudged her with her finger. How many days had it been? Only two? Maybe three?

"Shit!" She poked her once more. The gills fluttered slightly, giving Flora hope. "Come on, you," she begged, desperate. If only she could keep *one* thing safe, *one* thing whole. She drew out her pocketknife and made a deep slit in the pad of her palm. Blood coursed from the wound freely, and, belatedly, Flora wished she had not chosen her dominant hand. Now both her hands were injured. *Oh, well.* As best she could, she aimed her dripping blood at the mermaid's fishy mouth.

The mermaid stirred. She opened her eyes and cast them about wildly, looking for the source of the blood. Flora lowered her hand into the water, and the mermaid was upon it in an instant, drinking deeply with no regard for the pain she caused Flora. It was different, Flora could tell, how the mermaid drank from her as opposed to how she drank from Evelyn — while she was delicate with the Lady, never sipping for too long, she was rough and greedy with Flora. She did not kiss the wound closed.

Her blood, Flora realized, was only a stopgap. The mermaid was dying, regardless of Evelyn's visitations.

She needed the fresh seawater.

She needed the Sea.

As if reading Flora's thoughts, the mermaid caught her eye. *Home,* said a voice. Stupidly, Flora checked around her, but she was alone save for the mermaid. It was not a man's voice anyway, not a human voice. *Home,* the voice said again. It was a plea. *Home home home home home.*

"Shouldn't you be with the Lady?" Alfie's voice was a splash of cold water. He put a tentative hand on Flora's back and peered over her shoulder at the mermaid. Sensing Alfie's shadow, the mermaid darted to the bottom of the barrel.

"She's dying," Flora said. "Even with the blood. It's not enough."

"Death comes to us all," Alfie replied. When he said it, it sounded almost cheery. He gave her shoulder a squeeze. "Remember what Rake told us, about the mermaids?"

She shook her head. Alfie remembered their life before with much more clarity than Flora.

"He said that they're the hinge of nautical justice — the Sea punishes those that punish the mermaids, and rewards those who grant them clemency. I believed him, too."

"You don't anymore?"

"In justice? Nah." He met Flora's eyes and smiled, the empty smile she'd seen so often since they joined the crew of the *Dove*. It was less of a smile and more of a wince. "There's nothing out there to punish evil, no one out there to reward the righteous. We're all just adrift."

The mermaid floated listlessly to the surface of the barrel again, her gills fluttering.

"We'll be putting them belowdecks soon."

"Yep." Alfie smiled. "Better them than us, eh?"

"The Lady Hasegawa, too."

He sighed. "Was losing your finger not enough?" He was angry. That was fine. So was Flora. It had been a long time since she'd contemplated rightness or wrongness, but letting the Lady Hasegawa be sold was wrong.

The whole thing was wrong, and it always had been.

"She does not deserve this, Alfie." *No one had.* Mr. Lam certainly had not.

"There's no such thing as deserving. Only what we get. And for the first time in that girl's life, she's getting the shit end of the deal."

"Alfie," Flora whispered. "I care about her. I —"

He pulled Flora in a tight hug, his skinny arms a vise around her. "No, you don't. You can't. Buck up, now. You can do this, brother. You can because you have to. You can and you will."

*It will do no good to argue.*

"There is no such thing as the right thing," Alfie had told her once, long before they joined the crew on the *Dove*. He had just robbed a pair of children not much younger than they were, a brother and sister, too, of their bread and moldy cheese. Flora was upset by this—the children were even more frail than she and Alfie were, and did not look as though they had even seen bread for days.

"There is only what you must do to survive. Either you do it and you live, or you don't and you die."

Flora had eaten the bread. He was right, after all. Perhaps a week later, when washing herself in the Crandon River— corroded and muddy and full of sewage as it was—she saw two little bodies, frozen stiff, huddled beneath the bridge. They were not moving, nor would they be again. Crandon winters were terrible and fierce always, but that winter especially.

*That could have been me.*

She was glad it was not.

She had returned to her post outside the Lady's cabin and fallen asleep almost immediately. She missed her hammock, which was stiff and uncomfortable but preferable to sleeping sitting up outside Lady Evelyn's door. The storm had been vicious and the work had been hard, so Flora slept more deeply than she had since being assigned as Evelyn's bodyguard.

Her dreams were turbulent, frantic and fragmented. She saw the mermaid and fires, Cook's copper pots, the short silver blade.

She dreamed that Lady Evelyn was a sea turtle.

*Get on my back,* the turtle said.

She pulled Flora through deep black water and into a cave.

*This is where we belong,* the turtle promised. When they reached the shore, Evelyn was human again. But an explosion rang out and blood flared from the Lady's belly, black and thick and viscous. A piece of wood was embedded in her flesh.

*I'm OK,* she insisted, though the blood pooled at her feet, though it stained her dress.

*You are not!* Flora shouted, breathless and panicked. *You are bleeding!*

A gentle nudge to her shoulder pushed Flora from her dream and into waking life. Lady Evelyn stood over her, blessedly intact. Despite herself, Flora felt her shoulders relax with relief. *She's OK.* She was warm and safe, and beautiful in her wholeness. To her horror, Flora felt herself smiling like a lunatic up at the Lady.

Evelyn, though clearly confused, smiled back. "Good morning, Florian," she said.

*Florian.*

The name was less like a spell and more like a shackle. Flora shook what little sleep remained from her mind and stood, with some effort. She offered Evelyn her arm like a gentleman. As she should. "Shall I escort you to breakfast, milady?"

## CHAPTER 15

# *Evelyn*

**W**ith all the visits to the mermaid, Florian's lessons in reading had slowed but not stopped. He did not need as much guidance as he had before, and besides, he seemed as eager to see Evelyn happy as he did to read a new story. He was reading on his own now, borrowing her books as he watched her door at night. He seemed to prefer the ones with a love story, which surprised Evelyn. He wasn't sentimental otherwise.

He never asked for lessons, never asked for anything, really. The lessons only happened when Evelyn offered. So it was with some shock that Evelyn agreed to help Florian with a book he was reading by his request.

It was after dinner, the sun having set hours earlier. The *Dove* rocked and creaked in the waves, but Evelyn was used to the movement now. She'd heard the sailors saying a storm was coming. Selfishly, she was glad she would be safe in her cabin, but doubly glad Florian was charged to stay with her. He'd be safe that way as well. And close.

She invited him into her cabin, and they both took a seat on her bed.

Florian was in an unusual mood. His eyes were pensive and constantly darting toward Evelyn. She wished he would just look at her, just hold her gaze. His eyes warmed Evelyn's skin, and she yearned for that warmth. He opened the book to the story of the Patient Lady.

It was a stupid story, probably Evelyn's least favorite. She did not much care to discuss it, but, it seemed, neither did Florian. He opened his mouth, then closed it again. Evelyn tried not to stare at his lips, but it couldn't be helped when he bit the bottom one in thought.

"Evelyn," he said, "there's something I haven't — You see, I wish to tell you —"

"Your throat," Evelyn said.

Florian blinked. "'Scuse me?"

"You don't have the boy bump." She motioned to her own neck. Then, gently, she touched her fingers to Florian where typically men had a protuberance but where his neck was likewise smooth.

There was a long pause but not an uncomfortable one. Florian's eyes met Evelyn's. They were sitting so close, Evelyn could feel the heat of his skin. The drumming song of her heart played in her ears, as loud and insistent as the winds of the coming storm.

"No," he said. "I don't."

His eyes — her eyes? Did it matter? Evelyn thought not; her feelings were the same whichever way — shone in the lamplight. Footsteps echoed from the decks above them, voices calling.

Florian reached out and gently brushed Evelyn's cheek. Where his fingers had been, Evelyn felt the echo of his touch sparkling.

"May I kiss you?" Evelyn asked. And before her eyes could meet Florian's again, Florian's lips were on hers.

He tasted like the sea.

The world that was not this kiss faded into nothingness. It was an abyss of inconsequentiality, of noises unheard and sensations unfelt. She was unclear if it was one kiss or many as their lips moved softly in concert. She thought of the way the sea stirred against the shore in constant, gentle motion. She thought of nothing.

His lips were not soft, and they were perfect in the way that they shaped around hers.

She felt his heart beating within them.

His fingers found her hair, carefully wrapping themselves in it. The book fell to the floor between them, but neither said anything; neither stopped. Instead, Evelyn pulled Florian over her so that their bodies pressed against each other, warm and right and sure.

It was the sureness that made Evelyn's throat catch. Florian's hand sought her neck, his skin coarse from years of labor. Evelyn heard herself gasp.

And then, as if the captain knew what was happening and would not allow it, the bell that called all sailors to the deck rang. Florian heaved a shuddering sigh and extricated himself from Evelyn's grasp.

"Stay," she whispered. But he shook his head.

"Duty," he said simply. He turned and looked back at her, his eyes still shining. He tried to smile, but the dimple did not appear. "Evelyn," he said. He took her hand, kissed it, and then was gone.

When the knock at her door came later, Evelyn assumed it would be Florian. She flung the door open with unbridled gusto, ready to pick up exactly where they had left off. To her acute shock, it was not Florian. Not him at all. But rather the terrible man she'd heard called Fawkes stood at the precipice. His face was split by a knife's cut of a smile.

"It's time," he said. His voice was all pleasure.

"Time for wh —?" But before Evelyn could finish, he reached out one of his giant hands and grabbed her by her hair. The shock of it, the pain of it, stole the words from Evelyn's mouth. Fear forced the world into a tunnel, where all she could see was Fawkes as he pulled her — sputtering and crying, tripping and stumbling—up the steps to the main deck.

He didn't release his hold on her so much as he flung her to the deck, where she landed with a clatter at the feet of some of the other passengers. The force of her fall split the skin on her knees, on her hands, but she could hardly register the pain. They were gathered, but for what Evelyn had not the faintest clue. There was the merchant man she'd seen loading cartons of silk onto the *Dove*. There was the Lady Wakida, who clutched her kimono closed with an arthritic hand. As Evelyn rose to her feet, she saw that all the other passengers were there, murmuring their confusion and fear. Except the Lady Ayer.

The night air whipped cold around them, and Evelyn shivered against it.

The men were holding pistols. And they were aimed at the passengers.

Captain Lafayette watched. And it was the smile on his face that redoubled Evelyn's already unmanageable fear. He was so pleased with what he saw, so comfortable. This was intended. This was planned. But what *was* this?

He cleared his throat and clapped his hands to catch the passengers' attention.

"It gives me no great pleasure to announce to you fine people that the *Dove* is no passenger vessel," he said. "She is a slaver. And all of you aboard are now her chattel."

Slaver? He was mad. Surely this was some kind of off-color sailor's joke. She looked to the faces of the other passengers, but they mirrored her own. Comprehension creeped at the edges of Evelyn's mind but could not find purchase.

"The hell we are!" one of the passengers called. He was tall, with the posture of a man who'd served in the Emperor's forces. And indeed, there on his chest was the eagle pin that denoted a former officer. He looked sure and unafraid. *Good*, Evelyn thought. *He'll set this right.*

But the captain nodded, and three of the sailors stepped forward. To Evelyn's horror, she saw that one of them was Florian. There was a very brief tussle in which the man tried to stay on his feet, but Florian leveled him with a blow to his gut that knocked his legs out from under him. The sailors of the *Dove* cackled with delight.

"No!" Evelyn shouted. Not Florian; surely he couldn't, he wouldn't, be a part of something so evil.

The men chuckled at her horror.

The two other sailors held the man fast and forced him to stay on his knees.

"Stop!" the man protested. "You will *pay* for this! I was a lieutenant in the Imperial Guard! I—"

"Even better," Rake murmured. For a moment, Evelyn could not understand what she was seeing. There was a glint of metal, a burst of blood. The man sputtered and coughed, his hands at his throat, his hands slick with the red of his own blood. He was dying. That man, Rake, had cut his throat.

"If any of you are thinking of mutiny, I can promise you"— the captain motioned to the man who now lay dying—"we don't take kindly to mutineers."

Evelyn vomited onto the deck. It splattered over her feet.

She was dimly aware as the men stepped forward, pushing and shoving and jeering as they herded the passengers belowdecks, Evelyn among them. As they moved along, she felt a hand at her elbow, oddly delicate in this brutal moment. She turned and saw Florian's face. His eyes were sad and solemn, but he caught hers with them just the same.

"Stay quiet," he whispered. "Stay safe. The more you fight, the worse it will be. Do you understand me, Evelyn." It was more a command than a question. "You must stay still. Invisible."

"How could you?" Evelyn managed. At least he had the good sense to look abashed, his head hanging. Good. The betrayal was more than Evelyn could stand. She felt tears falling down her face, felt them dripping off her chin. Her nose was a river. Florian did not speak again.

They were led into the brig, a tiny room given that nearly twenty passengers were meant to fit in it. There were no beds, no seats or benches, no windows. Just a dank wooden floor that smelled of rot and a wall of iron bars that held them in. They were pushed inside, and the door was locked.

They were trapped. She looked around her. Several of the other passengers were weeping, and the merchant man was trying his strength against the iron bars. Still, though, there were two passengers missing: the Lady Ayer and her maid. But Evelyn did not have the width of mind to process this strangeness. It was all she could do just to stand.

But then, even that failed her. She sank to the floor. What else could she do?

## CHAPTER 16

# Flora

The look of betrayal on Evelyn's face cut Flora like a knife. *So now she knows.*

She was too smart for the ship, too pretty to be safe. Too kind to survive this. She was in the brig with the rest of the Imperials, weeping, likely — and by gods, how that made Flora's heart twist and ache — awaiting her new and horrible life. Flora could barely stand the thought of it.

Meanwhile, the men of the *Dove* bickered and squabbled over the various cabins and the treasures they held. Flora could not muster the will to participate, even though she knew that if she did not assert herself now, this whole voyage would be for naught. All the treasure would be spoken for — and she'd have earned nothing from this.

She did not care.

Alfie had found a store of fine aged whiskey in the dead lieutenant's quarters and was guzzling it gleefully. He'd piss himself in his sleep later, drinking like that. Flora couldn't bear to watch him. So she went out into the night, to lean against the gunwales. For fresh air, she told herself. To get her head back in the game.

The moon was just a sliver in the clear sky, beautiful in the way it nearly wasn't. All around her, stars glittered, winking down at Flora, teasing her. It seemed impossible that the night sky should be so beautiful when the world was so upside down. She had always known her life on the *Dove* came at the terrible price of other people's lives. But then, that was a trade she had been taught to make throughout her life, wasn't it? Better her than them. And if the guilt was sometimes, if it was often, nearly too much to bear, she would think of her brother and the sacrifices he had made to secure this little life for them. This place to live. To be alive.

When she could no longer take the incongruity of the night's beauty, she followed her feet into the stores where the mermaid was kept. Evelyn would not be able to feed her anymore. Surely, she would die now.

The mermaid looked at Flora. Flora looked at the mermaid.

"What should I do?" Flora asked. But the mermaid did not answer. She only watched Flora with those strange fishy eyes of hers. Flora could not save the mermaid, just as she could not save Evelyn. Such a thing had never been done.

Evelyn's words echoed in her mind.

*So? Just because it's never been done doesn't mean it can't be.*

*Perhaps.*

The mermaid would not survive, not without Evelyn's careful ministrations. And what would Flora be doing by escorting the Lady nightly to feed the creature, other than insuring the mermaid's worth? She could claim she wanted a cut. That was believable. That was something Florian would do.

If she could use the mermaid as an excuse to free Evelyn from

117

the brig, she could steal one of the boats. Kill the men on guard, if she must. She could row them to Tustwe. She was no crack navigator, but she knew the stars: she could find south easy enough. If she could just steal some stores first. Some water. She could save Evelyn. And Alfie. And the mermaid, too. Perhaps if she returned the mermaid to the Sea, the Sea would see fit to protect their vessel from wreckage along the way.

She put her hand into the lukewarm water of the barrel so that the mermaid might feed.

"How would you like to go home?" she whispered.

Over the next few days, Flora squirreled away rations. An apple here. A pouch of water there. She hid them in a sack within one of the rowboats, readying herself for the difficult task that was to come.

She could not tell Alfie, of course. Not until the last possible moment. If he knew ahead of time, he would surely try to thwart her. But if she could just surprise him with it, with Evelyn and the mermaid already set to go, then how could he stop her? He'd have to come. He'd risk her death if he tried to stop her then, if he called the attention of any of the other men to her plans.

When she asked the captain for permission to escort the Lady to the stores so that she could feed the mermaid, he casually agreed and did not seem to think this a complicated decision. Of course, of course, he'd said. Flora could hardly contain her glee. As she rushed from the captain's chamber, she nearly ran into Rake, who looked at her suspiciously but did not hinder her.

She found Evelyn in the brig with the rest of the passengers. Her hair was a mess, her eyes hollow from days of crying, her skin gray from fear. Flora had never seen anyone so beautiful in all her life. But she steeled herself, called the Lady Hasegawa to her feet, and grabbed her by the elbow as she walked through the brig door, as though she meant to lead her roughly to the mermaid.

Evelyn let herself be led wordlessly.

As soon as they were at the mermaid's barrel, Flora checked that they were alone. She turned to Evelyn and reached out as gently as she could, but Evelyn flinched away from her. That was fair, but it still stung.

"I know. I know you have every right to be furious, but Evelyn, please, if you'll let me, I'm going to get you out of here."

"What do you mean?"

"I mean to save you. And the mermaid, too."

Evelyn glared at Flora. "Do you mean it?"

"I can't let this happen. To you, I mean. I cannot." She took a cautious step forward, and this time Evelyn did not flinch away. Flora closed the gap so that she could hold Evelyn's face in her hands again, relief flooding her when Evelyn smiled back. *There she is.* "Yes, I mean it."

"Florian," she whispered. And Flora smiled. They would need Florian now more than ever, his strength and the safety he provided. He leaned down and kissed the fear from Evelyn's lips. *Would he really do this out in the open? Or just want to?*

"Come on," Flora said after a little too much time. "We don't have long. The men change guard at midnight. That's when we'll move, and that's soon."

Alfie would be in the midnight guard that night, Flora knew. She could shoot whomever shared his guard and then they'd be on their way. It would be a long journey and a hard one, but with Alfie and Flora to take turns rowing, they'd be there soon enough. They'd be safe.

Admittedly, the plan was a crude one.

Evelyn reached into the barrel and collected the mermaid. She writhed and squirmed in Evelyn's grip as soon as she was out of the water, her gills gasping for air, though in her state she was not able to put up much of a fight. Evelyn held her as she would a baby, cradled.

Flora led Evelyn back abovedeck, her pistol cocked, to near where just a couple of men stood. To Flora's confusion, she did not see Alfie. *Was it not his guard?* As her mind swam with possibilities, she heard Evelyn gasp. She turned, and the world fell out from beneath her.

Rake stood there with his arms crossed.

"You mean to escape, then?" he said. His voice was dangerously low. Flora closed her eyes in despair. She was caught, they were caught, she would die, the Lady would die, the mermaid would die, Alfie would die, this had all been for nothing. Flora was an idiot.

There was no use in lying. "Yes," she whispered back, her voice hoarse with mourning.

Rake looked Flora up and down, registering the pistol with a smile. "Just a little murder, you thought, then you'd be on your way? And you chose a pistol." He shook his head. "I'd have thought I'd taught you better than to choose the loudest murder weapon available to you. You have a perfectly good blade in your belt, you idiot."

For a brief, mad moment, Flora considered shooting Rake. Perhaps sensing this, Rake took the pistol from her grip, right out of her hand.

"Don't be stupid." He checked the bullets and nodded. It was fully loaded. "You're doing this all wrong."

Then he handed the pistol back to Flora.

♦ CHAPTER 17 ♦

# Evelyn

R ake looked at Evelyn then, and though she could tell he
did not like her, he deigned to look her in the eye. "You're
the one who's been feeding the mermaid," he said. It was
not a question, and Evelyn could feel her ears burn under his
frankly appraising gaze.

"Yes." She did her best to look proud, defiant.

"You've done well by her. By the Sea, as well, may she bless
you. And don't worry, that creature has at least another ten minutes before she starts to suffocate up here. So I'll thank you to
keep calm. I need you two to listen to me, and listen well. If you
are going to make it off this cursed ship, you're going to need my
help."

"Wait, but Alfie—"

"Is not coming with you. I'm sorry." He did not look sorry,
though. Florian, on the other hand, looked panicked. "I cannot
keep you all safe. He's drunk mermaid blood now. He made his
own fate."

"I thought you all did —" Evelyn started, but Rake silenced her with a glare.

"Not those of us who serve the Sea," he said.

"The Sea?" Florian's eyes were fixed on Rake. "Or the Pirate Supreme?"

Rake gave a wide grin. "You were always a clever thing."

"An operative. There will be justice on this ship." Florian's voice was dreamy, but Rake's smile faded.

"You, the mermaid, and Lady Evelyn. Those are the only passengers. You didn't pack enough rations for more than two anyway. And the deal was only for you two."

If Florian knew what the deal was, he certainly didn't show it. His mind was still clearly reeling from the news that Rake served the Pirate Supreme, that they would be leaving, that Rake was going to help them leave, but that they would be leaving without his brother. For her part, Evelyn wanted to feel sorry, wanted to have the courage to stand up, too. But the prospect of escape filled her such that she could fit little else.

"I can't leave without him," Florian said. The words clearly pained him. He looked to Evelyn sheepishly. Evelyn looked at the mermaid. Her breathing was slowing. She was running out of time.

"I'm offering you freedom," Rake said. "For the first time in your life."

"You ask too much for it."

"I ask only what is right. You leave now. I'll call the guard away, and you'll have just enough time to lower the boat to the Sea and begone. Dally, and you'll be caught. You'll die, and I won't stand in the way of it. The Lady will, too. And forgive me, my lady, but I've never wept over a dead Imperial and I won't start now. Are we understood, Florian?"

Florian brushed a tear away as if it were a fly. "Yes, sir."

Rake turned to Evelyn then, with his full attention. She flinched under the pressure of it.

"You are not as delicate as you think," he said. "Remember that. What's ahead of you is unpleasant at best, and fatal otherwise."

"I didn't say I was delicate." She held her chin high, defiant.

Rake laughed. "That's the spirit. Leave your casket behind."

Evelyn had never heard such a good suggestion in all her life.

"Why are you helping us?" Florian asked.

"It doesn't do to question the gifts of the Sea, child. You two have a chance at life. Away from the *Dove*, away from Fawkes. Away from the Nameless Captain. And yes, away from your brother. The only question you should be asking me is: What do I need to do to make this sunny future possible?" He checked around them once more to ensure that they were still alone. "Promises are air," he went on, but his voice was softer now. At least, soft compared to his typical growl. "So I will not promise you that Alfie will be safe, or that you will ever see him again. But, for what little it is worth, I give you my word that I will do my best to look after what's yours."

Florian nodded. And in the moonlight, Evelyn could see the tears that crowded his eyes.

"Be free, Florian."

And before either Florian or Evelyn could thank him for what he was doing, Rake stepped clear into the moonlight and started barking orders at the men who stood guard. The men ran belowdecks to see to his command, and Rake followed them, not sparing a glance behind him.

"I don't understand," Florian said. Evelyn was not confident he was speaking to her as much as just speaking.

"I don't, either," she said. She maneuvered so that she held the mermaid with one arm and gave Florian's hand a squeeze. "But we'll have plenty of time to wonder on the boat, right?"

Florian squeezed back, but it was a moment before he turned to face her. It was only when he rested his eyes on hers that she could feel him readying himself.

"Come on," he said. "We'll only get this one chance."

## CHAPTER 18

*Flora*

**F**lora ran to the rowboat she had outfitted with stores and quickly set about loosening the straps that held it fast to the side of the *Dove*. Evelyn was of no help, of course — when would she have learned to undo a sailor's knots? And so she could do nothing but stand there with mounting anxiety as Flora worked.

"Get in," she told her, and Evelyn carefully lifted one leg over the side of the *Dove*, then slid into the rowboat, disappearing into the night. Without a look behind, Flora hoisted herself over and began to let the rowboat down. It made her hand ache acutely, but she hardly noticed for the fear that engulfed her.

It was twenty feet at least until they reached the water, and more than a hundred beyond until they would disappear into the fog and out of sight from the *Dove*. But already Evelyn's face was cracked into a wide grin, as if to say "We've done it!"

Flora's arms worked, warm with the effort it took to lower the boat. She could not afford to be tired, not yet, but typically two men worked the pulleys. Above her, the system of ropes whined with the effort of holding the boat. Flora prayed no one could hear it. She tried not to notice the fresh blood staining the bandage over the stump of her lost finger.

They hit the water with a loud clap that seemed it would echo clear to the Red Shore.

"Almost, almost," Evelyn whispered to the mermaid. They were not to release her until they were safely away, lest she rest in the nets extended from the *Dove* and be caught all over again.

Flora extended the oars and, as quickly and quietly as she could, began to row them to the south, toward Tustwe. Despite herself, she felt a smile tickling at her lips. *Rake is no fool.* With the guard below, this escape was simple and clean. An accident of coincidence, no extra bodies needed. She really had been doing it all wrong.

But then, to her horror, Flora heard a lone cry of "Hey!" from aboard the *Dove.* They were a hundred feet away already, and so the rest of the speech was just inarticulate yelling to her. But she knew the sense of it. They'd been found out. She rowed faster, not looking at Evelyn's face, which she knew was rigid with fear.

The first gunshot rang out, but when no bullet sounded, Flora felt a moment of relief. Perhaps whoever it was had simply fired in the air to alert the rest of the crew. She paddled faster, harder, hoping to clear the fog before they were spotted. It was possible, it had to be possible, she would make it possible.

But when the second shot rang out, she could hear the bullet as it flew past them with a howl. It had missed — the shot was wide — but they had certainly been spotted. She was aware of Evelyn's sob of fear, but she had no time to offer comfort.

Already, the *Dove* was completely obscured in the fog. She could only hope that they were equally difficult to see. A third shot rang out, and a fourth, but none came even close to the boat.

The slap of a second rowboat hitting the water was unmistakable.

*Faster,* Flora told herself. *Faster faster faster.*

"What can I do to help?" Evelyn asked, but Flora didn't answer. There was nothing, nothing to be done except to row as fast as she could.

Perhaps the Lady could pray.

## CHAPTER 19

*Evelyn*

E velyn felt impotent.

She was useless and she knew it.

She could hear the oars of the men pursuing them, and she was sure from the sounds that there was more than one man rowing in their pursuit. Florian had been given an impossible task, to outrow several grown men, and without help. Florian's forehead dripped with sweat. They should have brought extra oars.

Frantically, Evelyn looked around. If they could be lighter? But there was no deadweight on the boat, save herself. The stores they needed, right? Though they'd not need them at all if they were caught. There was a bag of apples and oranges that sat heavy on the deck. With a nod, Florian gave her permission to toss it overboard. Evelyn scrounged, trying to find anything loose. The water Florian would not let her toss. But when she pried loose a seat, he nodded, and over it went with a splash.

And of course. The mermaid was lying still now, but she was not weightless. Evelyn only hoped they were far enough from the

*Dove* to have cleared its nets. With somewhat less care than she would have liked, she extricated the creature and lowered her into the water.

The change was immediate.

As soon as she touched the sea, the mermaid began to change. She stretched longer, her fins firming with strength returned. Evelyn dropped the mermaid entirely, and she disappeared beneath the black water for a moment. When she resurfaced, she was entirely transformed, her wide eyes set now on a face that fit them, her skin the healthy and tawny gold of the sun, high cheekbones illuminated in the scarce moonlight. Black hair cascaded behind her, and she regarded Evelyn for a moment through thick black eyelashes.

Evelyn felt the breath catch in her throat. She was beautiful.

Then, silently, she ducked under the water once more and was gone.

At least, Evelyn thought, at least she had done this one good thing in her life.

Behind them, the men were closer. Evelyn could hear their voices.

The crack of a gun rang out, and Evelyn could hear the bullet strike the water not far from where the mermaid had been.

"Damn it all," Florian muttered. More shots rang out. Though they could not see the boat that pursued them, they could hear it growing ever closer. The only reason they still lived, they both knew, was the thick fog.

Under her seat, Evelyn found it. The pistol. She had never held one before, let alone shot one. She looked at Florian hopefully.

"Do you think I could—?"

"No." There was no time for explanations, Evelyn knew. She felt herself deflate.

But before she could let resignation settle into her completely, the boat shuddered and picked up speed. It was not Florian's doing; that much was made abundantly clear by the look of utmost bemusement on the boy's face. He'd all but stopped rowing and yet forward the boat moved, at a faster pace.

"The mermaid," Evelyn whispered, as Florian shook his head in wonder. It did not do to question the gifts of the Sea.

"Give me that pistol." Florian traded spots with Evelyn, an awkward affair that nearly tipped the boat. "Stay down and keep your eye on the water."

Evelyn did as she was bidden. Even with the borrowed speed from the mermaid, the men gained on them and bullets screamed past them. When one hit the side of their boat, cracking the wood, she could hear the voices of the men rise in collective victory. They had placed them now. Florian cursed again, and with a deep sigh of what emotion Evelyn could hardly even imagine, he opened fire back upon them. He took his shots slowly, pausing thoughtfully between them, and with the sound of a pained shout, Evelyn knew at least one of his shots had hit home.

They could make it, Evelyn thought wildly. They could make it. With one less man to row, the other vessel had slowed, and still the mermaid propelled their boat from below.

But then two shots rang out at once, both with catastrophic effect.

One hit the boat just below the water, creating a hole through which seawater poured mercilessly.

The other hit Florian.

He let out a cry of pain. For one terrible moment, Evelyn thought it had hit him in the heart. That all was lost. But then he reached up to clutch himself in the shoulder and crumpled forward. And before Evelyn could reach him, before she could try to stanch the bleeding, the boat started to sink, too much weight for the mermaid to bear. The water was cold and ghastly, first around her ankles, then her waist. Evelyn did not know how to swim well, but she also knew she could not let them be recaptured. Florian would be killed; that was certain. And so, praying that perhaps swimming in the ocean was not all that dissimilar from swimming in a pond, and that there would be something to alight upon and rest soon, she took Florian in her arms. He'd passed out, from the shock or from the pain. She kissed his forehead lightly, whispered her apologies, and tipped them both under the water.

It was a foolish choice.

The sea was not like the ponds she'd grown up swimming in; it had been stupid to think it might be. It fell endlessly below her, and she frantically tried both to keep Florian's face above water and to fight the pull down, down, down, on her, on her skirts, and on her shoes — why had she kept her shoes on? The salt water stung her eyes and nose, and in her panic and fear she inhaled a great gulp of it, burning her throat and lungs.

Water pressed in. Into Evelyn's ears, her nose, down her throat. She kicked wildly, but still, down she went. If she freed Florian, would he float to the top or simply drown even faster? Not knowing, Evelyn held him close, fighting for the surface for them both. For surely, she may have deserved to die — she'd been an indolent youth, and had done little to nothing to improve the lives of those around her at any stage.

But Florian.

Florian had been given no chances, no kindness, and no mercy, and yet he still risked himself for her, whom he hardly knew and who had done nothing but cause him pain. She would not be the death of him, not if she could help it.

She swam.

Gunshots on the water.

The Lady Ayer straightened in her hiding place, heart racing. It did not bode well — she knew, of course, of the many dangers on the sea, and she was prepared. But gunshots? Now? Deep within her trunk, wrapped in corsets, several ornate pistols waited for her.

Obedient Imperial noblewoman though she may have seemed, the Lady was no fool. She whispered to Genevieve, bade her ready her blade, small and silver and strapped to her ankle with a leather thong for the entirety of the trip.

She ordered Genevieve to stay close and to stay silent.

Gunshots on the water.

Rake feigned ignorance for as long as he could, before ordering the men in pursuit of the runaways. He prayed silently to the Sea that they would find freedom, but the alarm had been sounded so early, too early. Their safety was not his ultimate goal, however, and so he could not sacrifice his mission for their sake, nor even for the mermaid's.

The captain emerged from belowdecks, his eyes still bleary with drunken sleep. His breath smelled of rum and sick as he pulled Rake in close and gave a mess of orders, of which only several made any sense.

Rake thought of his many commands from the captain, the man he hated. Someday, he told himself, he would no longer take orders. Not from him. Someday soon he would know justice. Someday soon Rake would hand him to the Pirate Supreme and see his true duty done.

But this night, Rake only nodded and did as he was told.

* * *

Gunshots on the water.

Alfie woke with a start in his hammock.

He looked wildly about for Flora, but she wasn't there.

He steadied himself, his legs wobbling mutinously beneath him, as he went abovedeck, joining his fellows. Rake was barking orders to secure the remaining prisoners, to find the Lady Ayer, who was still — somehow — missing. *Someday,* he told himself, *we'll live in Tustwe and these days will just be a blur of memories we never visit. Someday, we will be free of this ship.*

But when he looked about for Flora, she was nowhere to be seen.

He was alone.

# *The Sea*

*The mermaid is home.*

*The Sea knows at once from the warmth that gathers like a pinprick in her midst. She knows the mermaid as she knows herself, and she is home. Her daughter is home.*

*With her the mermaid brings the memories she was entrusted to hold: Of an island long since drowned. Of mountains moved, and of a continent shifted.*

*Relief spreads through the Sea, spreads over her surface, and she is anchored in her happiness.*

*Men and women stand upon her shore and remark,* Have you ever seen the sea so still? *And they have not, for never has a mermaid been taken and then returned. If ever a mermaid is brought home, it is only her shell, empty and lifeless. How many daughters, dead and gone, has she buried in her depths? How much despair still lingers?*

*Ah, but this time.*

*What kindness is this? Unprecedented.*

It was Evelyn, *the mermaid says.* She fed me and she freed me and I am home, Mother. I am home.

And the other? *the Sea asks.*

Freed us both.

Then they shall both be saved.

*With care, the Sea lifts them both, cradles them to her breasts as she carries them, so that they might feel the beating of her many hearts.*

*A small pod of dolphins jumps in her wake, playing in the rolling waves created by her elation. They're wise enough to know that it will be long beyond their years before the Sea will show such joy again.*

*She is as gentle as the Sea can be, as gentle as she is enormous.*

*She leaves them where humans belong, on the soft sand of the shore.*

*And still, as they sleep, she sends lapping waves against their feet to remind them of her gratitude.*

Thank you, *she says.* Thank you.

PART TWO

The Witch

## CHAPTER 20

## *Flora*

The salt of the Sea licked her wound, burned it, sent pain through her whole being. Flora felt her body convulse, and she was sick into the sand that was in her mouth, on her face, everywhere.

*Where am I?*

She tried to move but found that she could not, not without being sick again. The pain was everything, it was everywhere, it was Flora's whole world. She was adrift in a body that did not want her anymore, a body that was no more. Another wave hit her, and the pain doubled. Flora cried out.

*Let me die.*

Distantly, she was aware of voices. A shadow cast over her face, the beating of the sun mitigated, if only for a moment. She tried to look about her, but all she could see was light and darkness, both blinding, both infuriatingly disorienting.

A hand, gruff and without grace, shoved something against the wound in Flora's shoulder, and even though she knew that it was to stanch the bleeding, she cried out and tried to free herself from the pain.

*Let me die!* she cried, though she was unsure if she had spoken or screamed. The hand pressed on, and Flora was sick again. This time the vomit stuck in her mouth and in her nose until she was tipped onto her side once more.

Vaguely, she was aware of being lifted by many hands.

In a far-off place, she heard her own moans, echoing, terrible, into a world she could not see.

She called for her release from life over and over again, but either no one heard or no one cared to listen. The result was the same. She remained, despite her wishes, despite her better judgment, despite the pain.

And as she faded back into a black sleep, she saw Evelyn's face, tears streaming. And she wondered if the Lady Hasegawa was real or a taunt from her own cruel mind.

## CHAPTER 21

*Evelyn*

A bove her, the cliffs towered. They rose straight into the heavens. From the narrow strip of beach where she stood, Evelyn could see the many rope-and-wood elevators that allowed for ascension along the stark side of the cliffs where homes had been carved out of sheer rock, could hear the creaks and groans of the many pulleys. She could not see the top of the cliffs, though, as they disappeared into clouds.

Florian lay on the sand. He was breathing again, at least; a fisherman had seen to that. Florian would make it, she told herself. He'd be just fine. The fisherman had promised in broken Imperial to send for an elevator to be brought down to the shore, which he said would take Florian and Evelyn to the witch for healing.

Evelyn had not argued. Witches, she knew, had been eradicated by the Imperial Guard, found and burned and gone. They were tricksters, hucksters, and worse. They'd preyed upon the weak and had not survived the colonization of the Floating Islands. They'd worshipped the sea, and could not, like so many others, be converted to the Imperial Faith. These things were for the best, she'd been told. There were no more witches. The fisherman just meant healer. Perhaps the truth of where he took her was lost in translation. Perhaps *witch* was the closest word he had to *doctor.*

So she waited for the elevator.

They were called the Floating Islands by Imperials, and for the first time Evelyn could understand why. They were not actually suspended above the water as legend had it, but the cliffs were so tall that they rose above the clouds. From far away, they likely did appear to be floating. From where Evelyn sat, they seemed equally impossible. It was as if the sea had eaten all except the apple core of the land. They were beautiful in the way that gallows were beautiful.

Finally, the fisherman returned. Sweat dripped down his wrinkled brow, and Evelyn could see from the deep lines carved by the sun that he'd spent his entire life outside. Probably coming up and down these elevators, carrying fish from the sea to the market. He motioned for Evelyn to come and to bring Florian, which she did with no small effort. He seemed reluctant to touch Florian, and he left Evelyn to drag him by his feet through the sand until she, too, was drenched with sweat.

"Look," he said. He pointed to a flat wooden pallet resting on the ground that was connected to four thick ropes. "Elevator. Yes? You get on."

Evelyn looked from the man to the elevator and back again. She did not trust it, but she could not afford to be choosy. She didn't speak the language of the Floating Islands, and gesturing wildly and crying for a doctor had not gotten her terribly far with most people on the shore. If this elevator would take Florian to a doctor, then this elevator would have to do.

Evelyn turned to check on Florian once again. His face was

pallid and drawn. He needed food and water and warmth and care, and Evelyn did not have the means to give him any of that, not until they reached the market. Hidden beneath her sleeves was a gold bracelet with a ruby clasp. She would trade it for all the things Florian needed.

And if she couldn't?

Then Florian would die. Florian would die saving her. Florian would die without his brother. Aboard the *Dove*, Evelyn knew, Alfie remained. As did the Lady Ayer. And her girl, Genevieve. She hadn't even stopped to think of them, not once, as she made her own escape. What a selfish thing she was, so in need of saving, without a second's thought to those she'd left behind. To be sold into slavery. Punished by death, perhaps. That's where their friends would be. On the Red Shore.

But then, when had she ever spared a thought for those who were left, wrecked in her wake? Keiko's face came to her mind with startling clarity. She had not secured work before Evelyn had left.

She would save Florian. She had saved the mermaid; she could do this. She could master her fear. And so she pulled Florian onto the elevator and thanked the man with a kiss on the cheek. He smiled at this but left hastily.

With a shudder, the elevator began to rise. It was a little rocky at first, and Evelyn had to hold fast to a rope while trying her best to hold on to Florian. But once the ascent started in earnest, it was a remarkably smooth journey up and up and up, away from the sea.

How it was they'd survived, Evelyn didn't know. The current had been swift and, fight as she had, Evelyn had only been able to catch a breath sporadically. She'd vomited as soon as they'd hit the shore, again and again, the salt of the sea burning her throat and her nose, her body exhausted from her fight. The only luck, so far as Evelyn could see it, was that Florian had washed up alongside her.

As they rose, the air grew colder. Evelyn shivered against it and tried her best to keep Florian's fingers warm by blowing on them. Once they reached a great height, they began to pass the little houses, each with its own elevator stop along the many lines that punctuated the cliff sides.

The houses were in varying stages of disrepair, and it was evident the people who lived in them made do with what they had. Old barrels repurposed as seats on porches. Doors built of weatherworn wood that looked as though it had likely once been part of a ship. If she had not been so fearful for Florian, for herself, she might have stopped to remark on the genius of their ingenuity and the beauty that resulted from it.

"You'll be all right, Florian," Evelyn whispered. Being unconscious, he didn't answer, of course. But speaking to him reminded Evelyn of her purpose. "I promise."

The elevator stopped in front of a small house.

The house was like so many they'd passed, carved straight into the side of the cliff. It was small and white, with purple shutters. The spindly vines of out-of-bloom bougainvillea spread like veins over the white plaster walls, giving the whole building the feeling of sickness. Evelyn wondered how her guide had recognized it — it looked so much like all the others, save for the golden hand that served as a door knocker, an incongruous signal of wealth amid so much evident poverty.

Evelyn knocked on the door with the golden hand.

It was several long moments before a woman, perhaps her mother's age, stood before them. Her hair was stacked tall atop her head in a messy bun, equal parts black and white, with a red spurt of cloth that Evelyn could only assume kept it in place. She was black like Florian, her skin darker than his. She certainly did not look like the people on the shore. She was bigger, for one thing, taller. Her lips were full and her hair had tight curls. Her dress was gray and spattered with something Evelyn hoped was not blood. A long string of pearls hung loosely around her neck and dipped — improperly — into her cleavage.

Without speaking, she eyed Evelyn and looked beyond her to Florian's prone body on the elevator.

"Well," she said. Her voice, too, had a thick accent, but unlike the fisherman, her Imperial was clean and clear. "You'd best come in, then." And she turned on her bare foot and padded off into the darkness of her home, leaving Evelyn to drag Florian inside unassisted.

She led them by a dripping candelabra into a small kitchen. The ceilings were low, and the room was night-dark compared to the bright of outside.

Evelyn hoisted Florian onto the low kitchen table. His legs hung off the edge limply.

"Please. Florian needs your help." She paused as the woman looked at Florian appraisingly. "I'm Evelyn," she added, rather stupidly. The woman had not asked.

"Been expecting you," the woman replied. "I'll take that bracelet, Evelyn," she said curtly. Evelyn had not realized she'd shown it. Hastily, she undid the clasp and handed it to the woman. She took it without looking at it and stuffed it in her cleavage.

"Can you help him?"

"What. This child?" She lifted Florian's arm and then dropped it unceremoniously. "That was a better question for *before* you handed over your jewelry."

"They said you were a healer?"

"They say I am a witch," the woman corrected. Evelyn did not reply. Apparently the success of their eradication had been exaggerated. Perhaps, Evelyn hoped, the tales of their untrustworthiness had been, too.

"And yes," the woman said, "I can help this person you've put on my kitchen table, and I can do it before dinner."

She rolled her head in a circle, stretching her neck, and sighed. In the strange and wavering light of the candelabra, she was not beautiful. But she fit. The cruel cut of her lips and the sharpness of her eyes. Her traits seemed perfectly suited for her kitchen, seemed so appropriate within it. In the darkness, surrounded by seemingly innumerable potted herbs that cast ghostly shadows upon the walls. A woodstove piped warmth in, and finally Evelyn could feel her muscles unclench, just a little, in the comfort it offered.

"You can call me Xenobia." It was an odd way to phrase it. Was that not her name?

"My name is Evelyn Hasegawa and—"

"I don't care who you are," the witch interrupted. "There are a thousand girls just like you in this world, and I haven't the patience, fortitude, or, frankly, the time left in my life to know you each."

Evelyn felt her mouth go slack. It was like the witch had punched her. "I—I paid you—"

"Yes, indeed. And I'll help your friend here. But you." She eyed Evelyn up and then down, her lips pursed into a thin, cruel line. "You must go. Your friend and I have much work to do, and from the stories the wind tells me, it sounds as though we have precious little time to do it."

"Florian?"

"Is that what you call this person? Yes, then. Florian."

"What makes you think you have anything to do with him?"

Xenobia rolled her eyes. "Because I am older than you and wiser. And because I do magic and I know things. That's what I do. What *you* do is sit around and brush your hair and read romance novels, if I have you pegged right."

Evelyn's eyebrows rose, completely of their own affronted accord. "You're just a crazy old lady. And a rude one at that." She looked about the kitchen for any obvious signs of madness. "And I'm not leaving, not until you help Florian."

"Fine."

Xenobia examined Florian's wound once more and, to Evelyn's absolute horror, stuck her finger in it. She rubbed the blood her finger came away with between her forefinger and thumb thoughtfully and then spat in the wound. Blessedly, Florian was still unconscious and did not feel the pain or the disgust this would have certainly caused. But before Evelyn could yell out in protest — which she fully intended to do — the witch slammed her elbow into a small, wood-framed looking glass that hung on the wall behind her. It shattered immediately, and one long shard fell to the ground.

Evelyn made a noise of exclamation that was more shout than words, but Xenobia waved her hand dismissively.

"Your friend is not whole," she said, as though that explained anything. "And until I can teach this Florian to be whole, nothing will be accomplished and destiny will be delayed."

"Destiny?" Evelyn asked, but the witch either did not hear her or simply ignored her. Evelyn imagined it was likely the latter.

With some effort, the witch reached down to the floor and

picked up the long shard from the looking glass. She held it in her fists over Florian's wound and began to murmur words Evelyn could not hear.

The evidence of Xenobia's madness, it seemed, was unfolding before her eyes.

Florian was dying. She had no time to fuddle about with charlatans who believed in magic. She was just taking a deep breath so that she might impart her fury on the so-called witch when Xenobia looked up.

Her eyes were foggy with what looked like storm clouds that had not, just moments ago, been there.

She smiled.

Evelyn stepped toward the table where Florian lay and saw why.

His wound was healed. All that remained of what had been bleeding was a small brown pucker of skin. Like a scar, but from years and years ago, a scar whose origin was all but forgotten.

Xenobia put the shard down on the table next to Florian and pointed with one long finger toward the door. "I have proved myself. Now you must do the same. Go, and do not return for a month. I need all that time and more with Florian here, if I should serve my purpose well in this world."

"But —" Evelyn interjected. She did not speak the language of the Floating Islands. She did not have anywhere to go. And she'd just given away her only belonging of any value. Her eyes filled with tears. "I'm not leaving without Florian."

Xenobia's lips pursed once more, and she looked at Evelyn dubiously. "Evelyn Hasegawa, you say. Is that Lady Hasegawa?" Evelyn nodded, hopeful that her rank might help in this moment of dire need. Finally, Xenobia smiled a strange crooked smile. "If you can make yourself useful, you may stay."

Evelyn nearly passed out from relief. "Of course." She had no idea how to be of any use in any home, let alone the home of a witch. She'd never washed a dish or cleaned a floor or cooked a meal in her life. Her few attempts to help Keiko over the years had varied from annoying to disastrous. Xenobia didn't need to know that. This was a fresh start. She would do her best.

For Florian.

## CHAPTER 22

*Rake*

The Imperial girl had been an unforeseen complication.

Just the thought of it — an Imperial who served the Sea? — made Rake's mind twist into strange, indecipherable shapes. It just couldn't be. The Emperor sought to own the Sea, just as he owned nearly all of the Known World. Just as he now owned Quark. And yet, here was this girl, this stupid girl, who'd somehow improbably — impossibly! — solved a mystery that had bedeviled sailors for centuries.

Had it been anyone else in the crew to point this out to Rake, he would never have believed it. But Flora. If you had told Rake years ago, when he'd first met that feral little girl, that he would come to care for her, he would have laughed. But now that little girl had grown into a fine man. An excellent sailor. He deserved better than life aboard the *Dove*. He deserved better than to serve the captain. Someday, Rake believed, Florian would serve the Pirate Supreme, too.

As Rake had done. As Rake still did.

Rake had never served the Nameless Captain, not truly. His orders came from the Pirate Supreme, and those orders had been clear: Infiltrate the crew of the *Dove*. Direct the derelict captain to the arms of the Pirate Supreme so that he might stand trial. Justice waited. Justice had waited for years.

But now, the girl and her blood. The mermaid.

He sent a message to the Supreme and awaited command.

Not a night later, an albatross flew over the deck of the *Dove*.

It was the dead of night, so Rake knew it was not some lost bird. It was a messenger.

It landed on the gunwale and waited patiently for Rake. The note was tied to the bird's spindly leg, and as soon as Rake freed it, the bird took flight.

*The two souls and the mermaid must be saved,* the note said. *But all other crewmen must pay their fair price to the Sea.*

The note did not mention the brother, or any clemency he could expect. Rake nodded. Fair was fair. And if the Pirate Supreme was expected do the Sea's bidding, well, then blood would have to be paid.

So it was. So it had always been.

*I will come with the* Leviathan. *This time, we will have him.*

The Pirate Supreme. The regent of the Sea would be there, in person, to see the Nameless Captain caught. In their best and biggest ship. Something like pride lifted its head in Rake's heart.

Florian would escape. The mermaid would be returned.

The Nameless Captain would know justice. Finally.

Rake crumpled the note and dropped it overboard. The wind carried it back and away until it was invisible in the night.

Silently, he stepped to the mast, where he could see Florian and the Imperial girl already bent on escape. Rake tried not to smile.

Any word to Alfie's protection had been a lie. Rake had known it. He'd known it when he'd said it, and he knew it now as he watched Fawkes lash him at the captain's command. Alfie's narrow hands were strapped to the mizzenmast, and though he had taken the first strike without noise, by the third he howled with piteous pain.

Fawkes relished his work. Rake could see it in the ugly glint in his eye. He'd rolled up his sleeves, revealing his thick forearms to the sun. As if Fawkes hadn't already punished the boy enough. As if his cruelty didn't already scar the boy. Between lashes he cracked wise with the men, who laughed and ignored Alfie's cries. Rake did not. Could not. Despite himself, despite his awareness of the boy's near uselessness, a prickle of guilt rankled him. Would Florian have left if he knew this fate awaited his brother?

The captain had not even stayed abovedeck to watch. Bored, maybe. Indifferent to the pain he caused. The passengers, now prisoners, watched in horror. One of the ladies wept openly, a strangely incongruous sound amid the open laughter of the men.

Somehow, the Lady Ayer and her maid were among the missing, presumed by the captain and crew to have escaped with Florian and the Lady Hasegawa. It was a sensible thing to assume. The *Dove* was not an enormous ship, not like an Imperial galleon, but she had her nooks and crannies. She was a proper passenger vessel, after all. They were hiding somewhere. Rake didn't know where, nor did he have time to find them. They were on their own. Just like poor Alfie.

The whip cracked against his back with a wet smack. Alfie's body had gone limp, hanging by his hands. He'd passed out. That was good, Rake thought. Better to receive the rest of his whipping from the vantage point of unconsciousness. His back was a bloody mess, and his pants were filthy with the evidence of his pain. Blood and piss. The life of a pirate.

If they had known, if they had truly understood, would Alfie and Flora have come aboard the *Dove*? They were only children in search of a bed. In search of food. Though Rake had known, and yet here he was. What would his life be had he not been cruel in his youth? Where would he be today had he not willingly sought criminality and mermaid's blood? His debt was a great one to the Pirate Supreme. Without the Supreme's mercy, his bones would likely still be hanging, picked clean by gulls, off the ramparts of the Supreme's stronghold.

"That'll do, Fawkes," he boomed. It had been fifty lashes. That was all the captain had demanded.

Fawkes flashed an ugly look at Rake just shy of insubordination. But he stopped.

A couple of the men helped take the boy down and carried him off to Cook for bandages. He'd be lucky if the wounds didn't get infected. Cook would treat them with boiling water, meaning the boy was in for a second round of nauseating pain. All this before his short life was over.

For the captain had not believed Alfie when he'd claimed, truthfully, to have had no idea about the escape.

"You helped them," the captain had hissed. And Alfie had protested and cried and wept, but it was to no avail.

He would be the one killed, Rake knew. The captain had not yet ordered it, but Rake knew, the same way he knew the wind would pick up in the afternoon.

The noose had already been around Rake's neck when he'd seen the Pirate Supreme for the first time. It was not the Supreme's role to attend trials. This everyone knew. So why the Supreme was there for the executions was a mystery.

Yet there the Pirate Supreme was.

The Pirate Supreme had the lean build of a knife fighter, and the scars of one, too. They were from Tustwe, likely, judging from their black skin and their accent, which was round and rhythmic. The Supreme was not dressed as Rake might have guessed a Supreme would dress. No finery. No useless frippery. Just the clothes of a sailor, albeit free of stains, and innumerable thin dreadlocks, neatly pulled back with a thin rope. They were not a man, nor were they a woman, but rather something else entirely.

Rake was of a crew that had been captured just beyond the Red Shore. They were headed to land, to drink their mermaid's blood, to reap the benefit of it. She was the fourth mermaid his crew had caught, and whatever they did not drink they would sell. There was always a high price to be had for mermaid's blood.

Instead, they had been caught.

The Pirate Supreme's fleet flew flags of black, with a white mermaid emblazoned upon them. As soon as he'd seen the flags, Rake knew he was as good as dead. They all were.

Killing, robbing, and capturing of merchant ships and people were permitted by the Supreme. As long as the captains paid their tithes, of course. But mermaids. Mermaids were off-limits, lest the Sea rescind her kindness to all pirates. It was the law — the only law — not to capture mermaids. The Sea's favor was the only thing that kept pirates safe from Imperials. The Imperials were stronger, after all. There were more of them, with more money, more boats, more men. But the Sea favored pirates, thanks to the Pirate Supreme, and their dedication to enforcing the one and only law.

And though Rake had only actually participated once — just

to see, just to taste — he was just as guilty as everyone else aboard. He had not protested. He had seen things he had no right to see. Strange, terrible fish that glowed in the depths of the Sea. A shark that moved like an eel. And he had lost memories, though which ones he'd never know.

Rake felt the sting of seawater on his face, the wind whipping his hair about his ears. The gallows of the Pirate Supreme's stronghold faced the Sea, at least. His last sight would be that of the sun rising over the Sea, casting golden, glinting light across the horizon that stretched endlessly before him.

A small mercy, which he surely did not deserve.

Already, half the crew had been summarily executed, their listless bodies dangling.

The rope about his neck itched, but he could not scratch, not with his hands bound. Useless hands on a useless body, put to a useless death after a useless life. At least he could see the Sea.

"You," the Supreme called. "The ginger one."

Rake nearly laughed. When was the last time he'd even seen himself in a looking glass? But still, he knew. His hair was red and ridiculous. The Pirate Supreme had addressed him.

"Yes, Your Majesty."

"You don't look afraid."

"I've always been a fine actor," Rake said. It was true that he did not fear Death, or the pain of Death at least, as much as he feared whatever punishment likely awaited him in the afterlife. Fear of any kind, he knew, was useless now. And more than anything, Rake hated uselessness.

The Pirate Supreme laughed, white teeth flashing.

"You amuse me. What is your name?"

"Rake."

"I have an offer for you," the Supreme said. Around them,

people hummed and murmured. The Supreme's presence at an execution was not the only unusual thing to happen that day. "Be an actor for me, red-haired Rake, for the rest of your days. And I'll spare you on this one."

Rake blinked. "You'd trust me?"

Again, the Supreme laughed, and their laughter was one with the sound of the waves that crashed beneath them. They were beautiful the way the Sea was beautiful — for both the Sea and the Supreme dealt in death. Power was beauty as embodied by them.

"Of course not. But you could spend your life proving your trustworthiness to me. And should your usefulness run out, I will see you right back to these gallows."

Rake agreed to these terms. They cut his rope. Rake was not hanged that day. But he was cut with the tattoo of a mermaid upon the sensitive flesh of his ribs, so that he might remember his crimes and his promise.

## CHAPTER 23

*Flora*

**F**lora awoke to a face only a breath away from her own. The face belonged to a woman and bore the cracked remains of rouged cheeks and coal-black eyeliner. It was impossible to see what she looked like, her face was so close, but Flora felt sure she'd never seen her before.

The next thing Flora realized was that she was naked. That was strange all on its own, but was doubly so since Flora was *never* naked. It was very cold.

"Good," the woman said. "You're up." But she did not move her face away.

"Yes." There was a long pause, in which Flora hoped the meaning of what she saw would in any way become clear. It did not. "Think you could give me a little space?"

The woman blinked once, then did as Flora asked. She sat down, with some effort, on a small wooden chair in the corner of the room. "You were shot," she said. "But I fixed you."

*Shot.* Flora's drowsiness evaporated. She put her hand to her shoulder reflexively but found nothing. Just a scar. The memories poured back into Flora, and with a start she remembered everything. She and Evelyn had fled the *Dove.* They had freed the mermaid. They had been pursued, and the mermaid had helped. But then Flora had been shot. And then, in flashes, the sting of seawater, and she was on a beach? How had she lived? How long had she been asleep? Where was Evelyn?

Flora practically fell out of the bed in her haste to get moving. "Where is the Lady Hasegawa?" she demanded as she tried to jump back into her britches. It was a graceless affair, and she fell over more than once. But the old woman did not seem bothered in the least. "Evelyn?" she called, but no answer came. "EVELYN?"

"You're welcome, by the way. It was a handy piece of work I did there. Your finger, too."

And then, all at once, Flora was hit with a terrible notion.

"Oh, no. Oh, shit. Milady. Miss? I don't know what to call you—"

"Xenobia."

"Did she see me? Did Evelyn see me naked?" The thought was more horrifying than Flora could put words to.

The lady laughed, and it was a dry sound, like a knife being sharpened. "Oh, child." She wiped a tear from the laughter that would not cease. "If you could have seen her face."

"Evelyn!" Flora called again, her voice desperate now. Evelyn had figured it out, of course, had seen Flora for what she truly was. Right? Or had Flora misunderstood entirely? They hadn't exactly talked about it, hadn't had a chance to talk about it, really. And there was so much to talk about.

But Xenobia leveled Flora with a sobering look. "She's gone."

"Where?"

"Off with her husband. Richest man on the Islands these days. Fitting story for a girl like that."

"She didn't . . . want me to join her?" It seemed impossible that Evelyn would abandon her now, and even more impossible that she'd wed some faceless, nameless man. But then, hadn't Flora known that all along? That was what beautiful Imperial girls did. They wed rich men. Just because they had kissed, just because Flora had rescued her, just because they had escaped — together — did not mean that Evelyn wanted her for real, or forever.

And anyway, the man Flora had pretended to be was a lie. And Evelyn knew it, didn't she? No wonder she'd left. To be with a real man.

Of course the Lady Hasegawa did not want her.

Flora was a liar. A liar, and a criminal, and, worst, a girl.

And Flora had abandoned Alfie for this Imperial. He could be dead by now, and it would have been Flora's fault. She wanted to cry, could feel the need for release cresting like a wave. But no tears came. Instead she sat, her hands hanging stupidly at her sides. Confusion and self-loathing, hopelessness and self-pity, all battled in Flora's heart. It was a cacophony. It was a tempest. It made no sense. Nothing made sense.

"You have a lot of feelings," Xenobia said.

"It's been a strange morning," Flora said, then realized that she was not entirely sure that it *was* morning. She had so many questions, though the clues to some, at least, were coming into focus. She was in the Floating Islands, that much was clear from the walls of the room she was in — stone and windowless, carved directly into the side of the cliffs. From Xenobia's accent, she could tell she was in Barilacha, the biggest of the Floating Islands and home to the marketplace where most imports and exports were made. And from the look of Xenobia, and her claim that she had healed Flora of a bullet wound, she could guess the woman was a witch.

"Lot of conclusions, too." Xenobia smiled at Flora, and it wasn't warm as much as it was an impression of warmth. Her eyes were not friendly, either. They were calculating. "You don't trust me."

It was unwise, Rake had told her, to trust anyone. But it was doubly unwise to trust a witch.

Flora did not argue. Witches, they said, could hear your thoughts, could listen to the words you did not say and learn your story. From the way Xenobia looked at her, she guessed this was likely true. The witch's eyes stared straight into her, through the fortress of the many lies she told to keep herself safe, and alive.

There was a long pause, in which Flora tried to get a better sense of the witch but was unable.

"I want to know where Evelyn is," Flora said finally.

"I told you: she's with Mr. Callum. Her fiancé. Her betrothed." Xenobia tilted her head and looked at Flora with mock quizzicality. "Surely, the story of a rich Imperial girl marrying a rich Imperial man is one you've heard before?"

"Yes," Flora admitted. Of course it was.

"If you'd like, I could tell you a story," Xenobia said. Her voice was all invitation, all entreaty, but Flora could still hear the knife's edge in it. It was a voice for cutting.

Flora shook her head. She was in no mood for stories, no mood for nonsense. She wanted to curl back into a ball, but then what? She'd still be in Xenobia's home, still stranded on the Floating Islands.

"Go ahead. Curl up, then." Impatience rang loud in the witch's voice. "Give up. Your story could end here, if you like. You could jump from my balcony, let your body come apart on the cliffs below. Or you could take that knife you have in your pocket and be done with it. You'd not be the first, nor the last, to go that way. In this house, even."

She stood and walked to the door, leaving Flora sitting on the bed, still miserable and confused.

"Or," Xenobia said. She was clearly trying her hardest to keep her calm. "You could be greater than your misery. And if you pull yourself together, I can show you how." She gave Flora a hard look with her steely black eyes. From the pocket of her dress, Xenobia pulled a shard of looking glass. She put it down on the rickety bedside table.

"This is yours," she told Flora. "See that you earn it."

Then she shut the door so that Flora was alone with her thoughts.

It was night when Flora finally extricated herself from her room, from her misery.

The only way Flora could tell it was night was that Xenobia wore a nightgown now, a brown, scratchy-looking, ratty thing that hung just past her knees. Her kitchen, a small room with a hearth, was uncomfortably warm. Xenobia sat at a carved wooden table, which boasted many cracks and only two chairs. Before her on the table, a lopsided clay cup steamed, filling the room with a strange, herbaceous scent.

Without invitation, Flora took the other seat at the table. She did not want to trust the witch — better judgment told her this was a grave mistake. But she could not bear to be alone with the truth. That Evelyn had left her. For a real man, a man who could provide. These things made sense, but still they beat against the ramparts of Flora's heart mercilessly.

And so Flora, in her desperation, in her sadness and her

disappointment, turned, as so many had done before her, to the witch.

*Witches,* Rake had said, *could give you respite.*

*But the cost,* he'd said. *You must always mind the cost.*

Xenobia named no price. Instead, she pushed the mug to Flora, as though she had been expecting her.

"You have already been doing magic of a sort, haven't you? But accidentally. Do you wish to learn to control it?"

Flora had no idea what she meant, but nodded. Anything to feel less useless. Less alone.

"We'll start with a story, then," Xenobia said. "It can be a salve for your pain. But you must build a house for this story in your heart, and keep it. It will be yours then. If you listen. Will you do this?"

"Yes," said Flora.

And so Xenobia shared her tale.

Long ago, there lived a queen whose love died, suddenly and in the night.

They had only just been wed, and the queen's wife had been a good and kind woman. The queen's grief was a terrible thing, black and enormous, and it loomed in the sky of her land for all to see. This saddened her people, and from the peasants to the nobility, all tried to alleviate their queen's suffering to no avail. Her sadness was too great. The night would not break into day.

In her desperation—to be whole, and to be happy once more—the queen went to the witch.

"Help me," she begged, "and mend my broken heart."

The witch said that she would do this thing that the queen

asked, but in order for her to cast the spell, there was something the queen needed to do.

"I, too, have loved and lost," the witch said. "And so I will help you. But in order for me to do so, you must fetch me what I need and you must pay me a fair price."

"Of course," the queen said.

And so the witch gave the queen her task: collect a thousand mustard seeds and return to the witch with them in a glass jar.

Her people loved her, and they would be more than willing to share their meager seeds with her. The queen knew this, and so she smiled.

"But," the witch added, "know this: A thousand mustard seeds are easy to find. However, should a single one of them come from the hands of a person who has known heartbreak, the spell will fail."

"And your price?"

"We will arrange upon your return."

Reluctantly, the queen agreed. Off she went, into the countryside to gather the seeds. It had been so long since she had walked the roads of her own land, and she was surprised to find that the walking was difficult, the roads uneven and cold.

At long last, she came to a farm owned by an old man. He did not recognize his queen, but he offered her respite from the cold anyway, with a warm bed and a cup of hot steaming tea.

"Please," she asked him, "can you spare me any mustard seeds?"

"Of course," the man said, "of course." And he went to his kitchen to gather them. He returned with far more than the queen needed and handed them to her with a kind smile. "Take them all," he said, for he was generous and took pity on the bedraggled woman before him.

The queen took the jar, but before she tucked it into her skirts, she asked if the man had ever had his heart broken. The man's smile dissolved, and he took a seat next to the queen.

"Do I seem like it?" he asked.

"No," the queen said. "No, but all the same I need to know. Have you?"

The man sighed heavily. "Yes," he said. "Yes." He had been married once, long ago, and though he and his wife were perhaps not the greatest love story of their generation, they had borne a child into the world, a daughter. The man loved his daughter fiercely, and she was in turn a good child, sweet and earnest, with kindness in her heart.

But then one winter, the cold came. And with it, terrible snowstorms that battered the windows and froze the doors shut. The family hunkered down as best they could, keeping the fire alive in the hearth. But while the fire lived, the girl did not. In the night, sickness came and stole the daughter from under the loving care of her parents. She was gone, irrevocably and forever.

"I'm sorry," the queen said, and she meant it. She could recognize the pain in the man's face as if it were her own. She knew what it was to dwell in sadness, to be swallowed by it. And she could see the man trapped in it, just as she was, like a room with no doors.

She did not take his mustard seeds, but she did stay the night. In the morning, she left a large gold coin in her wake, more money, she knew, than a man like him had likely seen in his life. It would not assuage his sadness, but it would keep him warm.

Next, the queen visited a tavern. It was empty, save for the proprietor, who was as impatient as she was cold. She did not recognize the queen, but she served her cider regardless.

"Please," the queen asked, "do you have any mustard seeds?"

The woman looked at her suspiciously but bade her wait as she retrieved them.

"Here," the woman said as she thrust a small woven bag at the queen. She was eager to be rid of her, and the queen knew it. Still, she had to know.

"Have you ever had your heart broken?" the queen asked.

The woman did not like the question. Annoyed, she said no, she was never so foolish as to give her heart away. Love did not last, the woman said, and so she protected her heart jealously. The queen could not understand what she meant. And so, in her anger the woman showed the queen her heart—which she kept, locked and hidden and safe, in a steel box.

It was cold. And it did not beat.

"It is broken," the queen said. She had never seen a heart so pink with life yet cold with death. "I am sorry," she said, because she meant it.

But the woman did not want to be told that her unbeating heart was broken, so she cast the queen out, into the night and into the cold.

The queen traveled her land, from the north to the south, from the east to the west. And though her people were gener-ous and were willing, none could share the mustard seeds she

165

needed. The queen's feet were callused and sore from walking, her heart heavy with the tales of grief she heard.

"He left me," they said.

Or "She did not love me back."

And "We grew distant, even as we lay side by side in our bed."

After a year, the queen returned to the witch empty-handed.

"You lied," the queen said. "You gave me an impossible task and told me you could take my grief away. Why did you tell me you could fix my heart when all hearts are broken? Why?"

And the queen wept and wept. She wept for herself and her love who was stolen by death. She wept for the farmer and his lost daughter. She wept for the woman who had broken her own heart. She wept for all her people, destined for heartbreak and with heartbreak in their wake.

And all the while, the witch crooned, and she sang: "Cry, my lady, cry, cry, cry."

Soon the queen's weeping was so great, so full of all the pain in the world, that it fell from the ceiling of the witch's hut. It fell on their heads, wetting the hair of the queen and the witch both. And outside, it rained, too — and the plants that had shriveled in the perpetual night, once brown and withering, stiffened, green with vibrancy once more.

Several days later, when the queen was done crying, the witch smiled. She refilled the queen's teacup.

"Your tears," she said, "were the price of my spell. Pain begets life, Your Majesty, and life begets pain."

The queen left then and saw her land anew.

Everywhere flowers bloomed and crops thrived.

And still, the queen's heart beat. 

◆ CHAPTER 24 ◆

# Evelyn

The men had come in the night.

Evelyn was brushing the edges of sleep when she heard the sound of boots on the wooden floors. The low murmur of men's voices, then the knock at her door. It was a strangely polite gesture given what was to follow.

She'd gone to bed in her own kimono, though it was sticky and dirty and too formal for sleep. But she barely had time to wrap it more tightly about her own body before the men came pouring through the door, bent at the neck under the low ceilings.

They were Imperial soldiers, that much Evelyn could see right away from their neat uniforms, their shaved faces. Each carried a blade in an ornate scabbard on his back, a pistol strapped to his side.

"Lady Hasegawa?" the commanding officer asked. He was a young man, just older than Evelyn herself. But he had the straight back of discipline and training, the eagle pin of a lieutenant on his chest.

Evelyn's mind whirred. How did they know she was there? She hardly knew where she was.

Evelyn confirmed her identity with a curt nod. "What is this about?" she asked. What could she have done wrong? She had done nothing wrong, not by Imperial law, that she could even dimly imagine. But none of the men replied.

Instead, they spilled forth and took her — rather roughly — by her arms. Her memory flashed to the moment Fawkes had pulled her from her cabin, and it set her heart racing. Her knees were still stiff and raw from being thrown to the ground, her arms still tender from being grabbed and led.

"You will come with us," the lieutenant said.

In the doorway, the witch watched, impassive.

And though she protested, howling and crying out, Evelyn was taken. She called out to Florian, but there came no reply. Florian was likely still passed out, only just healed from the bullet wound so his — her? — their? — silence was reasonable. She pleaded to Xenobia, but the witch kept her mouth closed, her lips pressed into a line. Florian did not rescue her, and, overpowered by the soldiers, she was unable to save herself.

"What did I do?" Evelyn asked, but no reply came.

As they passed Xenobia, the young lieutenant pressed a thick gold coin into her hand.

The soldiers escorted Evelyn to one of the rickety platform elevators, the wood creaking under their weight as they were pulled, slowly and inexorably, to the top of the cliffs. The cold night air nipped at her skin, for her kimono was not nearly enough to guard against the fog that rendered all but what was directly in front of her invisible. She'd not even had time to properly bind it.

No one spoke. Evelyn, because she did not dare.

As the elevator slowly rose, so did Evelyn's fear. She had never broken the law. She had been raised—as all Imperials of good breeding are — with an utter disdain for criminality and an utmost respect for Imperial soldiers. Their laws were ironclad. That was what made the Empire function. Reason. Law. Order. Justice. And those who did not obey paid dearly.

She could not bear to look at the lieutenant, who stood closest to her, though she could feel his eyes on her. She had been betrayed by Xenobia, and now she had been arrested. A waking nightmare — a week in the stocks — rose in her mind, and she shuddered against it, against the cold. Imperial punishment was so public, so humiliating.

"I will speak to your commanding officer," she hissed. But he did not respond to this.

"Are you warm enough, my lady?" the lieutenant asked. When Evelyn did not reply, he shook his own jacket from his shoulders and wrapped it loosely around her. The jacket was warming, but it hung uncomfortably around Evelyn's body. "The fog is thick," he said, as if this explained everything.

The soldiers led Evelyn through the dark streets, past an open-air market whose stalls were closed with cloths of all different colors. The night was cold, but at least as they walked some of the warmth came back to Evelyn and her shivering ceased. Still, the silence of the soldiers unnerved her, the sound of their boots hitting the streets in concert frightening in its uniformity.

She was led past an enormous white church built in the Imperial style, but with enormous stones the likes of which did not exist in Crandon. From the parapets, the First Emperor looked down on them, his frowning face full of disdain. Despite his perpetual marble judgment, the angels who flocked around him looked to him lovingly, and stone lions were frozen forever in midroar beneath him.

Evelyn had always hated church, but she especially despised it now, as the soldiers marched her past it. The First Emperor was a cruel god, prone to punishment. Evelyn did not worship him, not in her heart, not ever and not truly. And frankly, the notion that the Emperors were each a god in their own right was a preposterous idea. If that was true, then why did they die?

Perhaps the pirates and the witches were right to worship the sea. The sea did not die. The sea was no man.

Each of the Imperial Guard saluted the Emperor's visage as they passed. Evelyn's fear leaned into her, and though she regarded it as a silly tradition, she kissed her fingers and touched her heart, the proper salute of women.

And that was when one crucial detail made itself obvious — her hands were free.

If she were under arrest, then why would they leave her hands unbound? She looked to the men around her and saw that at least two of them carried shackles.

The relief she felt then was immediate and profound. Her heartbeat settled into its normal pattern, a metronome rather than an explosion. Even the way the soldiers flanked her was not that of arrest — it was that of protection.

Still, then. Why the rough treatment? She was a lady, and this was not proper treatment of a lady.

As if hearing her thoughts, the young lieutenant caught Evelyn's eye and gave her what she could tell he meant to be a reassuring smile. "Don't worry, my lady," he said. "We're almost there."

Though etiquette dictated that she should return the soldier's smile—for who was more revered in the Empire than instruments of the Emperor?—she could not bring herself to do it. She had never been thus treated in her whole life, and the indignity of it rankled her. She wanted to yell at this young lieutenant, shame him for the fear he had caused her. But when she turned to glare at him, she found he was already looking at her, his face still split into that smile of his, nearly as discomfiting as the events of the night themselves.

She knew that smile. It was the smile many young men gave her. When she walked by, or when they met her. It was that smile she was always expected to return. It was that smile that had nothing to do with her but was—somehow—her burden to bear.

The urge to roll her eyes was enormous, and the effort required to ignore it was gargantuan. She would need to play the proper lady, at least until she sorted out what was happening to her. After that, she wondered, how improper was it—really—to slap a man in the face for staring?

She wished she hadn't saluted the First Emperor and his stupid, scowling face.

Evelyn could tell where they were headed the moment she saw it. While most of the homes on the Floating Islands' topside were built similarly to those carved into the sides of the cliffs—small and white, plaster with red-tiled roofs, colorful doors and windowpanes—one building loomed, enormous, over them all.

It was built in the style of the 900th Emperor, with eaves that curved heavenward and stone lions prowling the parapets, and was easily two or three stories tall. Several towers flanked the main building, which looked for all the world like a palace, or a prison, amid the otherwise small and modest homes.

Around it, a tall stone wall stood guard against all who might seek entrance, save for the gate, which was iron, spiked, and surrounded by even more soldiers. And everywhere it was gray stone, as unyielding and cold as Emperor Henry himself. The keep loomed like a giant.

The guards at the gate saluted the young lieutenant and opened the doors without question. And though the discipline of the men was as uniform as their posture, Evelyn could feel their eyes pass over her with curiosity and interest. It made her skin crawl.

"Please notify Commander Callum that we have arrived," the lieutenant barked, and one of the younger men scurried off to see his orders done.

Commander Callum. It was a moment before the name's full significance hit Evelyn. First, the realization that she was on her way to meet her fiancé. A new horror washed over her. She'd thought that in escaping with a pirate in the middle of the night, she was somehow absolved from this whole terrible arrangement. Florian had only rescued her from slavery, what, a day ago? And already she would bear new shackles.

Second, hadn't he retired from the Imperial Guard? And she'd heard no mention of his being a commander. He certainly kept himself well guarded. Suspicion washed over her like a cold wind, chilling her.

The lieutenant turned then to Evelyn and bowed a curt, polite bow. "Please see that you are as gracious with the commander as you have been with me, and hopefully we shall see each other again under happier circumstances." He smiled broadly, the easily confident smile of a young man entitled to the world.

What a slappable face he had. She would enjoy that. Or, better, waking him up in the middle of the night, marching him for an hour in the cold with no shoes on, and then reminding him to be polite.

Evelyn said nothing, and the lieutenant nodded at his men, who led Evelyn into her future husband's keep.

## CHAPTER 25

# *Rake*

T he captain slurped his soup, splattering the fine ivory silk of his absurdly enormous cravat. Why he had called Rake into his cabin while he was eating was a fine mystery Rake did not wish to solve.

Everything about the captain reeked of excess. Excess fabric, excess food, excess cruelty, excess drink, excess theatricality.

Rake hated it. Hated him.

He sat as he was bidden to do in the seat across from the captain's wide wooden desk. The captain, for his part, made no effort to hurry through his meal. Or to tell Rake the purpose of calling him. Aside from his disgust in watching the captain eat, there was also the issue of the smell. Cook was really scraping the barrel these days if even the captain was eating the foul gray soup Cook claimed was fish. Rake ate only hardtack and apples. Once they got to the Forbidden Isles, there would be tortoise meat, fresh and filling. But until then — until the Pirate Supreme found them — well, hardtack and apples it was.

Finished, the captain smacked his lips once and then licked them with his fat pink tongue.

"I should think you would know why I have called you into this, my fine cabin, on this most excellent day."

Excess words.

Rake said nothing.

"You don't have a guess? A hypothesis? An estimate of what your beloved captain may want?" The captain shook his head at Rake condescendingly. "You know, they say the very best help anticipates the needs of their superiors, Rake. And as my most loyal and competent subordinate, I had hoped you would have anticipated my need on this occasion."

Rake said nothing.

"Ah, you are efficient with your words, my man, I will give you that!" He shook a finger at Rake and chuckled. It was clear from the maddening grin on his face that he laughed at Rake's expense. "Well. Perhaps you have not heard the rumors."

He waited, looking at Rake expectantly. The *Dove* was always rife with rumors. Which one the captain could possibly mean eluded Rake.

"Do you mean the one that you're crooked?" Rake asked. "Because I've already told the men to stop with all that nonsense, per your wishes last time that circulated."

The captain shook his head. "No. Try again."

Rake did his best to contain an exasperated sigh. His duties aboard the ship may have amounted to a sham, but he still wished to attend to them. "OK. The one that Cook slips bilge rats into the soup and tells us it's fish?"

Captain coughed into his hand. He looked, Rake thought, a little green. He had not heard that one, apparently.

"No. Although do check on that."

"As you wish, sir."

"No, I mean the one about the Pirate Supreme."

Rake said nothing. This time, it was not out of annoyance. Silently, he accounted for every moment he'd attended to the Supreme's business aboard the *Dove*. Who could have seen anything? Who could have discerned it for what it actually was? The creaking of the ship seemed extraordinarily loud, as did the sound of blood pumping in his ears, as did the whoosh of his own breath in and out of his nose.

But Rake was a fine actor. Externally, he knew, he looked the same as he had the moment before.

"I have not heard that one, sir."

"Oh, do strap in, it's an exciting one," the captain said. His voice was less genial now. Rake could sense his fear or his anger — he could not tell which — bubbling beneath his calm veneer. "It seems the Pirate Supreme has taken to punishing those who capture mermaids."

"They always have."

"Yes, not very effectively, right? But Cook heard a rumor in Crandon, that our noble regent has adopted a new tack in this quest. Namely, the planting of operatives within the midst of crews known to pull mermaids ashore."

Rake said nothing.

"It is no great secret that I have tasted mermaid's blood." This was a gross understatement. The captain had drunk so much of it, killed so many, that his own memory was nearly as eroded as the Sea's. His name had been lost years ago. Not that it mattered. Being the Nameless Captain had its benefits.

"And so," the captain continued, "I am, of course, lightly concerned. Surely, the Pirate Supreme would miss my ample tithes. But our *majesty* has a mind to chase down those who would indulge in the Sea's finest treat . . ." He drummed his fingers absently, lost in the memories of his own debauchery, Rake guessed. "Well, that cannot stand. We will need a new Pirate Supreme if that's the case."

Rake snorted. "You mean to depose the Supreme?" This was a curious turn of events, and fortunate, too. If the captain sought to make war, Rake could lead the *Dove* right to the Supreme and their fleet. All his years of subterfuge now seemed incredibly complex for so simple an operation.

"Perhaps. But first, we need to vet the ship for operatives."

Rake's heart sank. There was no love lost between Rake and the crew, but still, he did not wish to question or torture them purposelessly. And that was exactly what he'd need to do. With the passengers turned prisoners, the sailors were likely to take out any frustrations they had upon them. There would be blood on the *Dove.*

"As you wish, sir."

After being cut down from the noose, Rake had been given a day to collect his thoughts in the drafty prison of the stronghold, before being called in front of the Supreme once more.

The Supreme's court was a seemingly makeshift one. The treasures that served as tithes — golden cups and silver diadems, infinite coins and jewels — were piled against the walls without any discernible sense or organization. The Supreme's throne, however, was just a chair. Just a plain chair, made of driftwood. Yet it was surrounded by unimaginable wealth. Rake could not tell if this was laziness or profundity.

He stood before the Supreme, his hands no longer bound.

"I have heard about you, red-haired Rake," the Supreme said. Their voice boomed through the court. They seemed more royal today than they had the day before. They were dressed better, for one thing. And even sitting upon the absurdly plain chair, upon the dais, over their crews and their captains, their wealth and their finery, they carried the nobility of royalty well.

Rake, for his part, could not imagine how the Supreme had ever heard about him. He was just a sailor. The Pirate Supreme, on the other hand, was one of the only forces standing between Imperials and outright world domination. Tustwe was — and probably would always be — independent. And sure, small nations did their best to resist colonization. But those little countries were no match for Imperial might. Quark was evidence of that.

But the Emperor's fleet had only so many ships, and the Known World was big. The Pirate Supreme had used this truth to their benefit for years now, upsetting trading routes and altogether blocking the conquest of the Red Shore and — of course — the Forbidden Isles.

The Pirate Supreme was responsible for the continued freedom of the Sea.

"When it became apparent that your captain not only allowed but sought mermaids for capture, your crew was infiltrated." The Supreme motioned and Manuel, the gunner, stepped forward. Rake almost laughed out loud. Manuel was older than most of the men, and quiet, often teased for his introversion. He never partook, Rake realized, of the blood. But neither had he ever protested. He had simply watched the men, as he watched Rake now, from the right-hand side of the Supreme.

"You," Rake said. Stupid.

Manuel tipped his head to Rake. "At your service," he said.

"He has written to me, as all my operatives do, to keep me abreast of his mission. But also to bring sailors of value to my attention."

Rake looked at Manuel, who smiled back at him. They'd always gotten along. Not only because Rake valued silence and Manuel was willing to share it. But also because they had both, quietly and efficiently, gone about their duties next to each other. Privately, Rake had believed Manuel to be the only good man in the crew. Certainly the most competent.

"As you said, you are a fine actor. And I have need of your skills." The Supreme stood and took a step toward Rake. "Would you pledge your life to me as an operative, to exercise my will, for the good of pirates and for the good of the Sea?"

Manuel nodded his encouragement. "Let your life have purpose, boy," he whispered.

Rake did not have to think about it. No better offer could have been made.

"Yes," Rake said.

The Supreme smiled. "So eager. You should know, this life offers little reward."

"And a high likelihood of an early demise," Manuel added.

Rake bit back a smile. Death did not scare him. Death was his constant companion, dogging him since the day his mother fell. So far as he could see, he had nothing to lose. Everything that mattered to him had already been taken at the end of an Imperial sword, all those years ago in Quark.

"It seems to me," Rake said slowly, "that all lives worth living bear those risks."

The Supreme laughed, large and loud, filling the room with their mirth. "I see what you mean, Manuel," they said. "This one's got the right attitude."

## CHAPTER 26

## Flora

Flora pushed the wet rag across the stone floor of the witch's kitchen, but she paid no mind to her work. The cost of her stay was to do chores as Xenobia assigned them, and it was a price Flora was more than willing to pay. She had nowhere else to go — she'd abandoned her brother and had in turn been abandoned by Evelyn. She was not capable of love, apparently, and so she could not receive it. So staying with Xenobia made as much sense as anything. She was no stranger to chores, and frankly, these ones were easy.

Grit from the floor caught in her fingernails, and she felt her fingers prune from the water. Still, it was the cleanest she'd been, maybe in her whole life. Xenobia had a wooden tub that she filled, improbably, from hot water delivered via the elevator outside her door. It was as luxurious a life as Flora had ever known. She was clean and warm and well fed.

She did not care.

For her part, Xenobia was content to cook at the hearth, and the smells she produced made Flora's mouth water, despite her lack of appetite. She'd never been less hungry in her life, but the smell — of meat and lime and onion — was too enticing to be ignored.

"That's some shoddy work," Xenobia said. Flora looked about her. The floor was wet in the exact arc of her arm span around her, nowhere else. The witch was right.

*Useless.*

"I'm sorry," Flora said. She made to scrub more diligently, but the witch motioned for her to sit at the table, which Flora did. Xenobia ladled out some stew from the hearth into a wooden bowl. Flora's mouth watered. She was more hungry than she'd realized.

"Have you thought more on the story I told you?"

Flora did not respond. It had been, she thought, more like advice than a story, and she was in no mood to receive wisdom. Her heart ached. What did Xenobia know of her heart? Only that it was not unique. Only that pain was universal. It was not, Flora thought, advice she cared to hear at the moment.

She took a spoonful of the soup, which was too hot. It burned her tongue. But it was delicious, and it warmed her belly like a hug. She nodded her enjoyment to Xenobia, who stared back at her appraisingly.

"Powerful things, stories. If you care to listen to them."

"I have no patience for stories," Flora said. She had not meant to say it quite so bluntly, but she had not the fortitude for pretense, not anymore. When the walls of Florian had come crumbling down around her, she'd found she had little strength left in the rubble. She could not bear the thought of more lessons, more tales. Not after Evelyn.

Xenobia laughed her cutting laugh. "What a little shit you are," she said. "Come into my house, tell me you have no time for my craft." She lifted an eyebrow at Flora, all challenge and vinegar. "Do you know how long I have had to wait for you to get here?"

Flora put down her spoon. "Excuse me?"

"What would you give?" Xenobia asked. Her voice was a whisper, a breeze of promises too impossible to keep. "To have agency in this world? To see your will done, to control your own story? To be powerful? Free?"

*Anything.*

"I have nothing to give," Flora said finally. It was true.

"A lie," Xenobia replied tartly. "You could give me your patience. Or your respect. Your belief. Or your love." Her eyes burned into Flora, and she could feel the heat of it, the fire of the witch's gaze on her skin.

"What's in it for you?" Flora asked. She knew enough of witches to know they were not selfless.

Xenobia's eyes softened, and for one strange moment Flora feared she might cry. But the emotion was there and then gone so quickly Flora could not possibly name it. "I have nothing to lose and everything to gain from your power. That is all you need know."

Flora's heart beat in her mouth, the distant drumming of unease, of nausea.

In her mind, the song echoed:

*Two souls fight*
*For love, to be*

Perhaps, she thought, she could use the power to get Evelyn back. To win her. To show her that she was as powerful as any rich man who sold silks, who bent his knee to the Emperor.

"How do I — how can I do as you say?"

Xenobia smiled and put her hand over Flora's. It was a motherly gesture, a comforting gesture, a gesture of love. It did not fit Xenobia, and Flora did her best to ignore what it stirred in her. "You'll listen to my stories. You will keep them in your heart."

"What does that *mean*?"

"To believe." Xenobia squeezed her hand reassuringly. "Can you do this? Can you open the gates of your mind and welcome these stories into your truth?"

What she did not say was that as soon as Flora had made her choice, but even before she had spoken it aloud, the witch had taken her price from Flora. Flora could feel it, feel something loosen inside of her and disappear. But she could not say what it was, and could not remember it.

And just as she felt it leave, she forgot that it had existed at all.

All she could think of was the witch's promise.

*To be powerful.*

*Free.*

"Yes," Flora said.

"Good." Xenobia's eyes glittered in the candlelight. She leaned forward so that her long pearl necklace draped forward, dangling. "Then sit quietly, and I will tell you the first story every witch should know. Of the First Witch and her power, and the price she paid for us all."

A thousand years ago, the First Witch stole the moon.

Without it, men lost their way in the night and were gone. The tide all but disappeared, angering the Sea. And everywhere, babies howled for mother's milk that would not come.

Everyone cried out against the chaos the First Witch had

caused. They begged their queen to stand up to this wicked woman.

"Get us back the moon!" the people howled, and the queen listened.

She was a fair queen, and she was young. She had only recently bled for her first time, only just sat upon the throne in Barilacha. She was beautiful, with long black hair and skin like the Sea at twilight—smooth and perfect. And so her people loved her, for youth and beauty and fairness was all they had ever wanted in a queen.

"I will get you the moon!" she promised. And her people believed her.

The queen ordered all her best men out into her streets, to find the First Witch and to bring her before the court. And so the men turned over the country, lifted every rock, opened every door. They stormed every home, entered every stable, but to no avail. They could not find the witch.

They told the queen, and she despaired.

"I would give anything to retrieve the moon!" she cried. The queen sat alone at her chamber window, brushing her long black hair. Above her, the night sky listened, bleak, black, and lonesome without the moon.

But that night, the sky was not the only one listening. So, too, was the First Witch.

She appeared to the queen in her chambers. On seeing her, the queen was greatly angered.

"How dare you steal the moon!" she shouted. "I command you to put it back where it belongs!"

The First Witch was an old woman, much older than the queen. Her back was stooped with the weight of her many years, her eyes lined with the passage of her many days.

"For a price," the First Witch said, for this was her way and is the way of all witches.

"I would give you whatever you like," the queen said. "Gold. Goats. A ship. Name your price."

The First Witch thought long into the night. As she waited, the queen brushed her hair until it shone, as smooth and perfect as her skin.

Finally, the First Witch decided. "I shall take your hair," she said. The queen agreed, and the First Witch cut the queen's hair, which was lovely and long.

She cut it until there was nothing left. Then the First Witch ate the queen's hair.

As she did, the moon rose into the sky. And as she did, the First Witch became beautiful. The wrinkles fell from her skin. Her back straightened.

When she was done, it was morning, and the First Witch was young again, and beautiful.

More beautiful than the queen, who was bald.

The queen greeted her people, to tell them the good news. She had gotten them the moon!

But her people recoiled at her bald head.

"But you are ugly now!" they cried. They saw the wrinkles she had formed in her worry, saw the way she hunched under the pressure of her rule, and they recoiled from her. She looked as the First Witch had looked, bent with age and burden.

"But I have gotten you the moon!" she cried.

The people ignored her.

Instead, they bowed at the First Witch's feet. They crowed of her beauty and her fairness. For she had given them back the moon. She was as kind and fair as she was beautiful, they said.

"But she *stole* the moon!" the queen cried.

No one listened.

"They have forgotten," the First Witch told her. "They prefer a story of beauty. And we have traded stories, my queen. This was my price."

In her rage, the queen ordered the First Witch to be burned. And though the people wept and they protested, the queen still saw this punishment done.

And forevermore, the queen was remembered as she was the day the witch was burned: cruel and ugly. Unjust and covetous of the beautiful young witch whose power the queen could not match, even in ordering her dead.

And forevermore, the First Witch's sacrifice and cleverness, her trickery and her wisdom, was both the price and the gift of all witches.

The more they gave, the higher the price. That was their power, but it was their burden as well. ✎

## CHAPTER 27

# *Evelyn*

It was not hard to spot him. With a retinue of servants surrounding him, Commander Callum had the bearing to match his title. He was handsome in the way that Evelyn could appreciate in an objective sense — a hard-cut jaw and a strong chin, his black hair generously streaked with gray at the temples and tied neatly at the nape of his neck. He was older than Evelyn, with well-carved lines in the corners of his eyes, but he wasn't old. He sat at a great wooden table in the center of a great round room. It was just like the 900th Emperor's great hall. If she turned left and followed the long corridor to its conclusion, she'd likely find the calligrapher's library.

Through the skylight, the moonlight shone down on him, and he looked the way Imperial Guardsmen were supposed to look: cold, impassive, and imposing.

He looked up as Evelyn walked in. Though she could tell he looked at her, their eyes did not connect. He looked instead to the young lieutenant, who saluted him.

"Commander Callum, sir. We have brought the Lady Hasegawa." His voice was different now, less sure than when he had been the commanding officer. He was scared of Callum; that much Evelyn could see.

"That remains to be seen." Callum's voice was deep, reverberant. Though he spoke quietly, the sound of him cut across the room, and the various soldiers and servants — all before attending to this task or that — fell silent.

"Mr. Callum," Evelyn said. She swallowed her despair. She could not return to Florian if she were dead. "Commander. It is a pleasure to meet you." She bowed, the low and proper bow of a lady meeting her fiancé. And even without her shoes, without a good night's rest, she knew she had done it gracefully, correctly. Her mother may have hated her, but she had taught her etiquette well.

But Callum only grunted. "Where'd you find her, Inouye?"

The young lieutenant stood straighter. "On the cliffs, Commander. We received a tip from a citizen there that the Lady Hasegawa was in her care."

"Leave."

It was unclear to Evelyn who the command was meant for, but every servant and soldier in the room cleared as though there had been a fire. But when Inouye made to leave, Callum raised his hand, bidding him stay. The young man did, and soon only he, Callum, and Evelyn were left in the enormous room, under the soft silver light of the moon.

Callum stood. He was tall, taller than he had seemed sitting down, his posture stiff as that of a soldier. He stepped purposefully toward Evelyn, looking her up and down. She looked a mess, and she knew it. Her cold, bare feet ached under her. A good man might have offered her tea. Or a warm bed. But Callum only walked a slow circle around her, judging her.

"The citizen," Inouye said, "had a bracelet she'd received in payment for lodging from the Lady. It bears the crest of the Hasegawa family on its clasp." He was talking too fast, talking as a boy talks to a man. Who was this Finn Callum her parents had sent her to?

"Did you steal that bracelet?" Callum hissed in Evelyn's ear. She had not realized he'd gotten so close to her. Much to her embarrassment, she felt herself flinch at his breath against her skin.

"No!" Anger flared inside her, the flames of it licking her cheeks, burning red circles into them. "That was my bracelet, and my mother's bracelet before me. I am Evelyn Hasegawa, sir." She let her voice carry loud and clear in the cavernous room, let it echo off the walls. Let her fury penetrate the stones. "And I have never been thus treated in my whole life. You and your men should be ashamed."

Inouye visibly cowered at her speech. *Good*, Evelyn thought.

But Callum only stepped around so that he faced Evelyn head-on, too close. She had to crane her neck to meet his eyes, which burned down on her with indifference.

"I believe you are an interloper." He enunciated each word carefully, slowly. And in turn, each word felt like a punch to Evelyn's gut. "The Lady Hasegawa was not meant to arrive for another month. And yet, here you are, a dirty little girl who is both too early and too crass." He reached down, lifted Evelyn's chin with his thumb. His skin was cold and dry, and his touch sent shivers of fear through her whole body. "Do you know what the punishment is for pretending to be Imperial nobility, child?"

"Sir, if I may—" Inouye interjected, but Callum shot him a disapproving glare, silencing the young man immediately.

Evelyn did know the punishment.

Death.

"Please. We are meant to be wed. An arrangement made by my father, the Lord Kazuo Hasegawa, just after my sixteenth birthday. Your consent to his offered dowry came in the spring. He offered you two thousand gold pieces, along with the right of inheritance of his name and his rank in his passing."

Callum narrowed his eyes at Evelyn.

"Clever. But that does not prove anything. You could just be a lady's maid with a fine ear for detail."

"My father," she said hurriedly. "He does not seal his letters with the balloon-flower crest of *his* father. He uses, instead, the Imperial lion, befitting his former rank in the Guard."

At this, Callum blinked just once. It was, she realized, the most she'd seen his face move without speech.

"How did you get here." It was less a question, more a command, which Evelyn fractionally obeyed. She told him of the *Dove*, and of its true purpose. Told him that, among others, the Lady Ayer was still aboard the *Dove*, still at risk. Told him that she had escaped, but did not tell him with whom. Told him she had washed upon the shore of Barilacha and been taken to the witch for care.

"Witch?" Callum interjected.

"There are no more witches," Inouye said, the anger in his voice unmasked.

But Evelyn could not tell the men of her evidence, not without compromising Florian. "It was only what she said, sir, and I think she only said it to frighten me." Evelyn bowed her head, doing her best to look like a chastised child. "It worked, sir."

"You mean to tell me," Callum said after a long, terrifying pause, "that you lowered a rowboat from a galleon into the sea, then rowed and swam your way to the Floating Islands. On. Your. Own." His voice was venom.

"A sailor aboard the *Dove* helped me lower the boat. Otherwise, yes." She knew how improbable her story sounded, how silly. But if this was how she was treated — a lady of Imperial nobility — then what would Callum do to Florian? Florian was, at best, an urchin. At worst, a pirate. And the Imperial Guard did not take kindly to either, even if they had proven helpful to nobility.

She would not lead Callum — cold, cruel Callum — to Florian. Not now, not ever.

So she held herself straight and looked into Callum's eyes. She would not let him see her fear. She would not give him Florian.

"Take her to the east wing," Callum told Inouye. "Her tale is impossible; no one could survive the voyage from the middle of the sea to Barilacha in a rowboat. Her evidence is interesting but is not enough. See her barred in her chambers, and guard the door yourself."

He looked then to Evelyn. In one smooth movement, he wrapped his hand about her neck so that his thumb pressed against her windpipe with just enough pressure to send chills of panic through her.

"You will stay in those chambers, miss. Until I say otherwise."

Then he released her, turned on his heel, and was gone, his footsteps echoing down a stone corridor.

Inouye led Evelyn through the serpentine halls. They seemed unending, echoing infinitely, the sound of their footfalls lonely in the otherwise silent night. There had been so many servants and soldiers, but they had all but disappeared.

191

The keep was most certainly built in the style of the 900th Emperor. Evelyn could see the traces of it everywhere, from the tidy way the sconces were bound to the walls to the gray tiled floors. Each of the innumerable tiles was painted with intricate gray vines, to represent the 900th Emperor's vast network of spies. She wondered if, like the Emperor's temple, Commander Callum's keep also boasted the secret passages the Emperor had used for spying.

If she was any judge of character, she imagined it did.

"You'll be comfortable here," Inouye said.

His voice was quiet, a low, secretive whisper. Evelyn looked into the young man's face and was a little surprised by the earnestness she found. He quirked one side of his lips, a hint of a smile, and then was the good soldier once more.

"My feet are cold," Evelyn replied. Which was true. They ached from the long walk, not helped now by the chilly route to her room. It seemed colder inside the keep than outside.

"Of course, my lady. We'll see that you're well outfitted posthaste."

"And they ache." It was not in her nature to complain so, but she wanted to make Inouye feel bad, wanted to see the sting of guilt on his face. It would not make her feel better, not really, but it'd at least spread her discontent so that she did not bear the burden of it alone.

He looked at Evelyn, and she could practically hear the creaking gears of his mind churning. It was cruel to complain to him, she knew. He only followed orders. He was only a cog in a much larger machine. But she had not the patience for empathy after her long night. After Callum's interrogation.

Still, the spot where Callum had touched her neck echoed with the fear he'd caused her.

"It's been a terrible night," she added. And she was shocked to hear the tinge of tears in her voice. She tried her best to push them down entirely, but it seemed the harder she tried to keep the feeling at bay, the more insistently she felt it.

"For what it's worth," Inouye said, "I believe you."

"It's not worth anything, clearly. He did not ask you."

And Inouye had not tried to defend her. Not while Callum berated her. Not when he grabbed her neck. Callum could have killed Evelyn right in front of Inouye, and he would have let it happen.

Inouye looked stung. Good.

"Here," he said. And suddenly, without asking, he scooped Evelyn into his arms so that he carried her, like a child, like a *thing*, like some lopsided sack of grain. It was so inappropriate, so uncomfortable, so intrusive that for several paces she was simply too shocked to react. Inouye clearly took her silence for appreciation and smiled his stupid, earnest smile at her. "There. That better?"

The ice in Evelyn's voice was painful even to her. "I prefer to walk."

Inouye slowed but did not put her down.

"Please. Put. Me. Down."

She did not relish confrontation. But he had not even given her a chance to say no. And his presumption was the last stone on the pile that broke her. She could not take it, not anymore.

Inouye put her down, but he did not dare meet her eyes again.

"I thought — your feet?"

Evelyn did not reply. She did not trust herself. It would not do to berate the man who was to guard her. If she was to prove herself a fine Imperial lady, she needed to start acting the part.

But one did not simply lift an Imperial lady. Not without permission. Inouye should have known better.

They walked on in silence.

When they got to Evelyn's chambers, Inouye gave a polite bow and then wordlessly locked her inside.

## CHAPTER 28

# Rake

With the passengers all stowed tightly in the brig, Rake had a cabin to himself. Usually, he rejected this luxury, choosing instead to remain among the men. It didn't do to lead from afar. But this time, he surprised everyone by accepting the offer.

He did enjoy silence. And anyway, these were not his men, not truly. Though there were more than a couple of competent sailors aboard the ship, their impending doom didn't sadden him, exactly, so much as irritate him. They were useful men. Men of use were hard to find.

But then. So it goes. So it went. So it always was, that good men should pay the price for the bad.

He'd claimed the Lady Ayer's cabin as his own. Not because it was stuffed to the gills with pillows. He'd thrown most of them to the men to use in their hammocks.

No one in the world required more than one pillow, as far as Rake was concerned. Let alone a bookcase.

No, he'd chosen the Lady's cabin in the hope that she might return.

She'd evaded capture for nearly a week now. She was no normal noblewoman. He'd heard, long ago, that noble Imperial ladies were trained in swordplay. He had doubted the verity of it. He'd met an awful lot of Imperial ladies who died at the end of a sword, begging for their knees to be bound. That hideous Imperial tradition. As though the humiliation of spread legs was worse than death.

If he could turn her in to the captain, though. He could remind him of his purported loyalty. He could be of use, and as such above suspicion. The captain did not seem terribly bothered by the Lady's absence, but then he never took women seriously. This one was trained; Rake would bet his life on it.

Rake lay back in her bedding and allowed himself to enjoy the clean smell of it. Not much aboard the *Dove* was clean. And not much aboard the *Dove* was enjoyable. The Lady Ayer's sheets smelled of lavender, and of something else. Something earthy. Women, Rake guessed. It'd been a long time since he'd smelled a woman. That must have been the smell he could not trace.

He tried in vain to remember when last he'd been close enough to a woman to smell her. Years, easily. After drinking the mermaid's blood, he'd rather lost the taste for intimacy.

What good did it do to dwell? It was a useless pastime.

It was as he measured the various gains and losses of sex that he started to notice his eyes closing. This of itself was not odd, except that Rake was not tired. So why was it he could not seem to keep his eyes open? Why was it that sleep overtook him, even as he struggled furiously against it?

* * *

Rake woke with a blade pressed to his neck. It was pitch-black in the cabin, but he could still make out two female forms. One grown, one still a child. Ah. The smell had not just been the smell of woman. How stupid he'd been. It was the smell of Kiyohime powder, the favored poison of the Imperial elite. Rubbed into fabric and touched by bare skin, it caused a deep, immediate sleep. Inhaled or eaten: death.

It was a coward's weapon, but a clever one.

She was no fool, this noblewoman. Rake bit back a smile of approval.

"Where is she?" demanded the Lady Ayer.

"Safe," Rake croaked. Safer, anyway. The blade was pushed harder than was, he thought, strictly necessary. Still, he could understand the Lady's enthusiasm.

"Tell me or I'll slit your throat."

"She and the boy, Florian. Escaped in the night."

The Lady Ayer made a sound that could have been a scoff or a laugh. She pushed the blade harder into his flesh, and Rake felt the warm slide of blood trickle down his neck.

"Take me to them," she ordered.

"Would that I could." Rake did his best to push his head back and away from the Lady's blade. "But they are long gone. To the Floating Islands, if luck held fast. On one of the rowboats."

"There is one less abovedeck than when we boarded," the girl chimed in. Her voice was not nearly so confident as the Lady's, but still she held a pistol trained on Rake's heart.

"Them — and the mermaid, too."

"I told you she's gone," the girl said triumphantly. "We've looked everywhere, and —"

"Quiet." The Lady's voice was hushed but held the undeniable assurance of command. So. The girl was trained, too. Or training.

"They're in love, you know," Rake said. Florian had not admitted as much, but he could see it. He was different with Evelyn. But caring for these two young people — it was the only thing he and the Lady Ayer had in common. "The Hasegawa girl more assuredly than Florian, but only because she has known more love in her life."

The Lady Ayer held Rake's gaze, and it seemed to him that she did not blink. It was not often that Rake felt anyone truly looked at him. He had the talent of slipping into the periphery. But the Lady Ayer regarded him with such intensity that he could not deny it. She saw him, all right.

"Go on." Her voice was ice.

"Florian came to this crew along with his brother. And no matter how the boy suffers for his brother's incompetence, he never leaves him — and he could have left a dozen times. Slipped off in the night. But then the Lady Hasegawa came aboard and everything changed."

"Anyone could have seen that. Him mooning about after her."

"He was assigned to her, milady. He wasn't mooning. Not at first anyway. But he grew to love her, and when I offered him freedom, for him and for her, he took it."

The Lady laughed openly at Rake now. "And you'd have me believe it was you who offered them freedom? How very gallant of you. Though . . ." And here, she pressed the knife to his neck with more pressure. It was not the first time Rake had a blade held to his throat; however, it was one of the more effectively held ones. He could not move for fear of being cut. "You don't seem the gallant type. Does he, Genevieve?"

"I'm afraid not, my lady." Rake felt a flash of hatred for the girl, this Genevieve. She was a traitor to Quark, one of those who chose Imperial rule over freedom. She disgusted him, just as much as he clearly disgusted her. She regarded her lady with simpering pride.

That — perhaps — he could understand.

The placement of her blade. The confidence of her interrogation. This was indeed no normal Imperial lady. Too expert, too smooth. Rake would have to tread carefully with her.

"I could ensure your freedom, too, milady," Rake gasped. He wished she would not hold the blade just so. "I chose your berth in the hope that you might return. I see the bookcase has been moved slightly; you've been hiding behind it?" He paused, watched to see if her face betrayed anything. It did not. But her girl looked from the bookcase to him with worry. Rake smiled.

"You're most astute, madam," he continued. "I am not, in fact, the least bit gallant. But I am also not a part of this crew — as you know it, anyway. And if you would join me, not only could I keep you safe for the remainder of our voyage, but I could also ensure your release once it is complete."

"I know what you are," the Lady Ayer said at a whisper. "And if you think the word of a Pirate Supreme's operative means anything to me, you're wrong." She reached around and held Rake by the back of his neck menacingly. "Why should I trust you?"

How did she know? Rake's mind whirred with fear. If this woman knew, what was known among the crew? A thousand questions screamed in his mind. If he turned her over to the captain to maintain his facade, she would spill his secrets.

He would have to make an ally of her now. It was his only hope.

"For one, do I seem surprised to find your blade at my throat? As I've said, I came here looking for you. Second, you could surely kill me now. But the slit neck of the first mate would certainly tip the crew off to a danger on board, and they would not stop looking until you were found, gutted, and strung up on the rigging for all the other passengers to see. Currently, they believe you escaped with the young miss and Florian. So, as it stands, you have no choice but to trust me."

"Is that so? I think that, should I be so inclined to tell him, your Nameless Captain would be very pleased to receive confirmation of the Pirate Supreme's operative on board his ship."

"Here's what I think. I think you can hide here, under my protection. No more skulking about the *Dove*, in constant risk of being caught. You may sleep during the day so you make as little noise as possible. I will bring you food with as much frequency as I can. At night, you and I shall plan. We will work together. Can we agree to these terms?"

Genevieve looked to the Lady hopefully. Likely the offer of food would have been sufficient for her needs. Rake had some idea of what limited stores they'd been able to steal, and it certainly couldn't have been filling.

"We have an accord," the Lady said. She pulled the blade from his throat, but not gently. The tip nicked the sensitive skin just above his collarbone. A drop of blood disappeared beneath his shirt.

He'd have to be very careful with her.


The Nameless Captain had become a grave nuisance. Whereas before he had focused his passenger-ship con upon small outpost towns, far from Imperial rule, he was now becoming brazen. He brushed liberally against the Imperial shores, which endangered all pirates. It was known, of course, that Imperial merchant ships could and should be robbed on the open seas. But only the Pirate Supreme sailed on Crandon.

Even more grievously, the Nameless Captain not only allowed but encouraged his men to trap mermaids. The colonies had seen a boom of them, both in supply and, since more had tasted the blood, demand.

Rake was more than happy to chase down a rumor on behalf of the Pirate Supreme.

Word was, the captain had gone to an artisan in Quark to weave ropes, invisible when wet, made especially for trapping mermaids. It was a rumor that Rake assumed to be true, since when he found the home of the purported artisan to verify the story, he discovered that the man had been murdered not long ago.

Rake did not dally in Gia Dinh. It was the capital city of Quark, and also home for a childhood that was long since gone. Being there only served to make Rake's skin crawl with recognition of past terrors. *Here is the town square where they hanged the resistance fighters. Here it was they put Mother's head on a pike.*

Since the Imperial Guard had taken Quark, nothing was the same. Everything that had made Quark Quark had been sacrificed at the altar of Imperial rule. It was an orderly place now. Orderly and dead inside, just like Crandon.

So it was not long before he was back in the Pirate Supreme's stronghold to report what he had found.

For their part, the Supreme had bad news. Manuel was dead.

They sat, as the Supreme preferred, on the steps of the stronghold that led directly into the Sea. As was their way, the Supreme had picked up two chalices from the floor of the throne room, mismatched, and had bidden Rake to join them for some rum.

When Rake heard of the death, he did not cry. But he and the Supreme did raise their chalices to Manuel, in silence and before the Sea. It was a blue day, but the Sea was alight with whitecaps from the wind that howled across the waters. It seemed a worthy tribute.

"He was a good man," said the Supreme after some silence.

"Truly." Rake turned his chalice in his hand. It was gold, encrusted with sapphires cut like teardrops. He'd never held anything so beautiful, or valuable, in his life. It was odd to drink from it, to see it in his own hand. Inappropriate, somehow. That he should be holding it. That Manuel should be dead.

The Supreme stretched their hands to the sky and cracked their back. They seemed almost like a normal person in that moment, just another sailor enjoying the view of the Sea. "I am sad to lose him, but I am especially sad to lose him to the Nameless Captain."

"Ah." Rake had wondered what Manuel's mission was. He'd been gone for nearly two years already.

"With the majority of our fleet fighting off the Imperial forces along the Red Shore, I hardly have the ships and men it would require to simply take the *Dove* by force." The Supreme paused, took a long, thoughtful sip from their chalice. "So. Red-haired Rake."

"You want me to bring you the Nameless Captain." Manuel had not been the first operative sent to take the man down. At least one other that Rake had heard of had gone and was presumed dead. Being assigned to the Nameless Captain was not something Rake took lightly. If Manuel had been caught — and Manuel was easily the most competent man he knew — then how was Rake to succeed where he had failed?

He took a swig, somewhat larger than he'd meant to, and sputtered.

The Supreme slapped him on the back and laughed. "And that is precisely what you shall do."

"I'll try."

"You will. He will stand trial, of course, but we both know his blood must return to the Sea."

They raised their chalices once more.

## CHAPTER 29

*Flora*

B ut she died. In a *fire.*"

Flora had not been taking to her lessons easily, and Xenobia was clearly frustrated with her lack of progress, which was fair. Flora knew she wasn't the smartest, knew that Evelyn had been overly patient with her. The memory of it now itched, humiliating for a variety of reasons, not least of which was the witch's look of annoyance now. They sat across the table from each other, as they did every night, and discussed the stories Xenobia told.

Flora, for her part, still did not understand the story of the First Witch.

"It was the price she paid," Xenobia said. Again. "All power comes at a price."

"Then why use spells at all?" Flora asked. She did not like the idea of making trades, the consequences of which she did not understand. She was no gambler, not like Alfie. She'd watched him lose at dice enough to know that gambling was a foolish endeavor.

And if she understood Xenobia correctly, then all witchcraft was — at its core — a kind of high-stakes gambling.

"That's a simple way of looking at it," she said.

Flora glared at her. "Well, I'm simple."

Xenobia sighed. "Are you hungry?" she asked finally.

"Always."

The witch chuckled. "Make me some soup, then."

Flora stood. Usually Xenobia cooked, and cooked well, but fair was fair. She was willing to earn her keep. She looked about the kitchen and at the empty shelves. "Should I go out and get something to cook with?"

"Everything you need is here."

Flora looked around more carefully now. There was the hearth, with the empty cauldron. Fresh drinking water in a wooden barrel, lowered down from the flats by the pulleys only that afternoon. But nothing edible, nothing of substance.

"Do you have stores elsewhere?"

"No."

"Then I can't make you soup." Flora sat once more. Her mind was tired from the many lessons Xenobia had been trying — and failing — to teach her. And still, the fact that Evelyn had abandoned her at the first chance weighed on Flora's heart, a burden too large to ignore. She did not have the strength for this newest riddle, did not have the patience for learning. Education, it seemed, led only to folly.

Xenobia stood and pulled a stone down from her shelves. It was unremarkable, one of the lined black stones that made up the cliffs of the Floating Islands, of Barilacha's streets.

"This stone," Xenobia said, "was once a part of the mountain in which this house is built." She held it to her ear, as though listening to it. "It was knocked loose by an elevator that rocked in the wind, carrying a heavy load. And so it fell, down and down, until it hit the soft sand of the beach. And then it was alone, a small thing that had once been part of something great. Until a young boy picked it up and chucked it at a stubborn goat who would not move. He missed the goat — the rock was too big for him — but the rock shattered into two pieces from his efforts. Then the rock was trodden under the feet and hooves of people and goats until it was small enough for me to pick up and tuck into my skirts."

"Uh-huh . . ." Flora said. It was, she could tell, another riddle. Another story. It did her no good, did not ease the ache of her hunger, nor the ache of her heart.

"Then I found it. And I held it to my chest, and I listened to its story. I let that story into my heart and I kept it there, safe and sound, and honored. And now" — Xenobia dropped the stone into the cauldron with a loud clunk — "I will help it tell the next chapter of its story."

Flora laughed. "I've heard this story before. A traveler asks for food in a village and everyone says no. So the traveler says they will make soup with only a stone, and, entranced, everyone gathers to watch this miracle. As he cooks, he calls out for the ingredients he needs — onion, garlic, carrots, meat — and the villagers, so invested in seeing stone soup become real, contribute each ingredient in turn. Right?"

"A nice story, but not a likely one. People are stupid, but not *that* stupid. No, that is not the story I'll tell today." Xenobia lifted the barrel and splashed some of the water into the cauldron, over the stone, then lit a fire underneath it. "Today, I will tell this stone: Once you were a part of something great. Once you were part of a mountain, and you were happy, and you were important. When you fell, you thought that you would never be happy, not ever again, never be important, not ever again. But you were wrong,

205

sweet stone, for now you are a part of a great pot of nourishing stew. Like the mountain, you will give life. Like the mountain, you will be great. Like the mountain, you will have purpose. You will give sustenance to those who had none, and that will make you great again."

Xenobia's voice was almost like a song, the way the words rolled from her tongue, soft and melodious. At first, Flora thought she only imagined it. That it was simply an olfactory hallucination caused by her hunger. For as the witch spoke, the smells of a rich stew — of lime and cilantro, of onion, of fatty meat — began to fill the kitchen.

Flora's mouth watered.

Xenobia took a ladle, spooned out a great steaming serving of meat stew into one of her wooden bowls, and pushed it before Flora. It looked as delicious as it smelled, and Flora could hardly contain her wonder.

"If you would listen," Xenobia said. "If you would let these stories into your heart, you could guard yourself against hunger. Forever."

Flora took a bite of the stew. It tasted, if possible, even better than it looked, even better than it smelled. Delicious. Delectable. Like a warm, dry blanket on a cold, wet night. Like relief, not only for her hunger, but for her worry, for every day that she'd had to fear for her life. As though in one bite, the stew had cured her of a lifetime of hunger. As though she would never be hungry ever again.

What price would she have paid, in those days of stolen moldy bread, to know she could be free of that fear? To be free of that constant, terrible worry?

*Anything.*

She would have paid anything.

"Do you see?" Xenobia asked. "Do you hear me now?"

"Yes," Flora said solemnly. "I do."

She finished the bowl of stew, then another. Then another. She let it fill her belly until she felt slow and sleepy from it. Had she ever felt so relaxed in her whole life? Had she ever felt so full?

*This is what wealth must feel like,* she thought. *Like a warm belly full of food, and knowing that still there is more should you desire it.*

Likely, this was how Evelyn had lived her whole life. And if Flora wanted her back, that was the life she needed to be prepared to provide. Of course this was the life Evelyn wanted. Flora wanted it, too. Xenobia could teach her how to take it. Maybe. *Maybe if I can do this, then . . .*

It was as she sat back in the small wooden chair that she realized she'd been eating alone. Xenobia had only been watching. When she saw Flora looking at her quizzically, she smiled a thin, papery smile.

"Not hungry," she said simply.

And without being told, Flora knew. That was the price of the stew. It was appetizing and perfect. But Xenobia had given up her appetite for it.

Xenobia nodded at Flora. "Are you ready to listen?"

Once there was a lonesome man who went to a witch so that she might grant him a wife.

"Please," he said. "My brothers laugh at me, and my mother worries. I need a wife so that I might have family and tend my father's farm."

But the witch told him: "I do not deal in the magic of love. Go comb your hair and leave me be."

"I have tried everything," he said. "And I need a wife."

The witch sighed. "You must know, loneliness is power, too," she told him. "On your own, you can accomplish great things, unencumbered by the many webs and nets love weaves."

The man would not listen, would not be dissuaded. "Please," he begged, and he begged, and he begged.

Day turned into night, turned into day. But the man would not leave.

And he wept and he wept until his tears became so dense, so thick with his feeling, with his despair, that they turned into pearls. All around their feet, the pearls rolled.

"Fine," the witch said. "I shall do this thing you ask. But it comes at a price."

"Anything," the man said.

"I will take your loneliness," she said. "But you must never introduce this wife I grant you to your family nor your friends, and you must never speak of her to anyone, so long as you both shall live."

The man blinked, confused. "But then, how will she work upon my father's farm?"

"This is the price," the witch said, and she would say no more.

The man agreed, and the witch smiled.

"I shall take your loneliness, then," she said. "And within the week, you shall meet a beautiful woman who wants nothing else but to be your wife."

"Yes!" the man cried. "Thank you, thank you!" And he left the witch's home with a lively step. To be free of his loneliness would be a great relief.

Every day, the man woke up hoping to meet his wife.

On the seventh day, he did.

She was even more beautiful than he could have ever dreamed. Her black hair flowed, long and perfect, curling into the wind. She had smooth brown skin and wide hips. Her legs were strong; her lips were full. And in her eyes, the man could see the Sea in summer, cool and calm.

He wed her on the shore of the Sea. It was, she said, where she was from, but the man did not care. All he cared about was the ebb of his unending loneliness, of the warmth in his bed night after night.

Together, they had many children, who worked the farm just as the man had desired.

"Where do all these children come from?" his brothers asked again and again. But the man could not say.

Soon, the brothers grew suspicious. "They are slaves," they told the townspeople. Not long after, word came back to the man that his children were to be taken away.

"No!" he cried. "They are my children!"

But no one believed him, for none had ever met or even heard of his wife.

When the people came, with their blades and their guns, to take the children, the man fell to his knees.

"Please!" he begged them. "They are my children! Mine and my wife's!"

And he flung open the door to his home so that they might look upon his wife in all her beauty.

But all that remained there was a small black fish, gasping for breath and flopping on the ground. As the people watched, the fish died, lying still upon the floor.

So they took his children. Later, the man realized that the fish had been his wife. Now just as dead and gone as his children from his life. He would never see any of them again.

Angry and desperate, he returned to the witch.

"My wife is dead!" he raged.

The witch shrugged. "You did not do as I told you. This is the price you pay."

In his anger and in his sorrow, the man made to strike the witch. But he found the blows would not fall. He could not touch her.

"You gave me your loneliness," the witch said. "It could have been your power. Instead, it is mine."

And she turned the man into a pearl and wore him — along with his sorrow — around her neck. ❧

◆ CHAPTER 30 ◆

*Evelyn*

For days, Evelyn was kept to the confines of her assigned
chambers. It was a beautiful set of rooms, appointed with
the mahogany furniture and tatami mats Evelyn had grown
up with—but it was still a prison. The servants had been told
to keep her there under all circumstances other than a fire, and
Inouye stood at her door day and night. And so Evelyn had little to
do save stare out the window into Commander Callum's rock garden or chat with the various servants that came in to tend to her.
She swapped stories with those that were willing, learned what
life was like on the Floating Islands. Or Barilacha, as they called it.
It was not nearly so exotic as she'd been led to believe.

As prisons went, Evelyn could accept that she was lucky, if
frustrated.

She thought of the last time a young man had been assigned
to be her keeper and wondered where Florian was now. What
Florian was doing.

Surely, Florian would be looking for her.

Surely, Florian would come to rescue her. Just as he had before.

Surely, Florian of all people would know how.

She thought of the princess that despaired and felt a swell of empathy for her. Likely, that princess had suffered an education of art and architecture, of etiquette and elocution as well. Of beautiful and useless things. The despair wasn't self-pity. It was a deep disappointment in her teachers.

She had been marinating in the bath Callum's servant had drawn for her. The steaming water left her skin red and tingling, and she relished the cleanliness of it, the way her skin felt soft and familiar once again. She hadn't realized what a great gift a hot bath was until she'd been without one for so long. The water had gone cold some time ago, but still she sat, to feel anything other than the constant, itching anxiety to return to Florian. She was still in the tub when Commander Callum came into her room. Without knocking.

Evelyn nearly splashed all the water out of the tub in her shock. She held an arm across her chest protectively and glared at Commander Callum, who seemed wholly unperturbed by the consternation he had caused.

"It seems you were telling the truth about at least two things," he said by way of greeting. "The ship carrying the true Evelyn Hasegawa has not made port, and rumor is that pirates have taken it."

"Sir, I'm naked," she said, hoping that somehow maybe he hadn't noticed and would be properly chastened once it was called to his attention.

"You are either my future wife or an interloper," he said calmly.

"Either I would see you in this condition shortly, or else you are a criminal and have renounced your right to privacy. So your honor is hardly at stake here."

Evelyn folded her knees to her chest. If he was determined to talk to her while she was nude, she could at least make herself comfortable.

"At any rate, it's still highly suspicious that you would have escaped on your own, and much more so that you would have made it to your intended port as well."

He looked briefly toward her chest without any self-consciousness that Evelyn could discern.

"I will need you to give me more information." He pulled a chair toward the tub so that he sat uncomfortably close. The lines in his face were visible in the daylight. She had not seen him, not once since their first meeting, and had not been able to get any sort of read on him. He looked as stern as the stone Emperor Henry who loomed over the church.

"We are alone now."

Evelyn suppressed an impatient roll of the eyes. Obviously, they were alone. She had rather been enjoying the solitude of a bath until he'd come charging in.

"You can tell me the whole truth. How did you escape?"

"I told you," Evelyn said. Her voice was peevish; she hated the sound of it. As if she were whining to her parents. "A sailor aboard the *Dove* helped lower me."

"Why."

"Because . . ." She tried to think of what Rake's motivation could possibly have been but came up short. She knew nothing of his mind, knew nothing of his life. "I don't know. But he did not seem to like the captain?"

"Captain—"

"Lafayette."

Callum nodded, and she could see his eyes alight with something that must have been recognition. When he saw her looking at him, his face hardened into an impassive shape once more.

"So you think one lone pirate, seeking to sow revenge, decided the best way to do this was to free only one of the captain's purportedly many prisoners?"

"I—"

"Listen. Do you think you are the first young woman I have ever interrogated? Did you think that your Imperial blood, or your youth, or your sex would grant you any clemency from me?" He leaned so that he could peer directly into Evelyn's eyes. "I have broken grown men trained in stoicism. Breaking you will take little effort from me. But I promise, it *will* elicit great suffering from you."

Evelyn could taste her heart in her throat, the heft of it, the flesh. She could feel herself trembling before this man, knew her fear was likewise naked.

Callum leaned back and pulled a small glass vial from a pocket in his coat. It was only the length of his pinky finger and narrow, half-full with a white powder. He rattled it before her face.

"Do you know what this is?"

"No."

"This is Kiyohime powder." He opened the vial and took a sniff of it, his eyes closed in evident pleasure. "It is my favorite poison. Do you know of it?"

Of course she knew of Kiyohime powder. It was reviled and respected among the Imperial elites, who saw it as both deeply powerful and unspeakably cruel. It was the chosen poison of the

Imperial Guard, and it was known that any who died of Kiyohime poisoning died by the Emperor's leave.

Callum tipped the vial so that the powder hung precariously close to the vial's mouth. "Do you know what would happen if I, say, emptied this vial into your bathwater?"

All she could see was Callum and the poison. All she could feel was terror.

"Death," Evelyn managed.

"True. But not immediately." He held the vial over the tub, toying with her. "First, you would feel a burning. Not everywhere. Only in the parts of your body I am too proper to mention. I am a gentleman, after all. Though this is not a gentle poison. And it would not be a gentle burning, mind you; it would be a burning like fire. It would spread from down there through your veins. You'd feel its passage, too. From those tender hidden corners to the tip of each finger and the end of each toe." He ran a finger along her bare knee softly, just barely touching her, as if to show her, to mimic the flow of death through her body. "And as the burning passed through you, your body would try to reject the poison, convulsing and vomiting. Emptying your bowels. But it would be to no avail. Once Kiyohime powder enters the bloodstream, it cannot be stopped. It is an ugly death, miss. One I should not think you would relish."

Tears rolled down Evelyn's cheeks. She was too afraid even to be ashamed. The shame would come later. In that moment, all she could think of was the vial tipping into the water. Of the burning that would follow. Of her body, cold and useless and twisted in the ignominy of death. And she knew, with all the certainty that she knew her own name, that he would kill her. And he would not regret it.

"There were two," she admitted. Her voice cracked.

Callum corked the vial. "That's better." But he did not put the vial away. He rolled it between his fingers restlessly, never once looking away from Evelyn. "Tell me everything."

## CHAPTER 31

# *Rake*

I t was not that he cared for the boy. But he had given Flora his
word, and however little that was worth, it could at least be
worth checking that Alfie hadn't died of infection.

Alfie was laid out on his stomach in a cabin also being used
to store the various treasures stolen off the passengers. It was an
odd sight. Silk kimonos were draped over luggage trunks, and one
delicate ivory sculpture of a dragon teetered with the motion of
the *Dove*. Alfie lay, wheezing more than breathing, next to piles
and piles of treasures all kept together in one of the *Dove*'s finest
cabins. A tansu chest stood ajar, and in it Rake could see the glim-
mer of gold likely packed for trade on the Floating Islands.

It was a testament to how badly Alfie was injured that he
could be trusted in such close proximity to the treasure. Anyone
could tell just from looking at him that thievery was the last thing
on his mind.

Alfie's back was — Well, it was ruined. Fawkes's lashings had
wrought deep wounds. In one horrible spot, Rake thought he
could see the white of bone.

"Who'sit," the boy mumbled. He couldn't even muster the strength to lift his head.

"It's me, Alfie. It's Rake." Rake took a seat on a spare trunk that wobbled under his weight. He thought about reaching out, touching the boy. But it would likely cause more pain than comfort.

"When'll death come?" Alfie sounded drunk. For an idiot, it was at least a realistic question. Rake did not have the heart to tell him Death was already there. Death was always there.

Rake looked around. A bottle of rum lay empty next to Alfie. Fair enough. Rake knew Alfie to be an incurable drunk, though he hardly blamed the boy.

"Not yet."

"H'will, though."

"You're drunk."

"Mmm'yep. Yep. Sure is." Alfie made like he was going to roll over but then seemed to think the better of it and stayed as he was. "Cook. G'man. Dun. Dun get 'em in trouble."

"Hardly seems worth it," Rake said, and he meant it. Giving the boy rum had been a rare act of kindness aboard the *Dove*. "I came to see that you're all right."

"Ohhh, m'great," said Alfie. "'Bandoned. Whipped. *Great.*"

"You know . . ." The boy was drunk. Drunker than drunk, he was nearly gone. He'd not remember anything come morning, not even, likely, that Rake had paid him a visit. "She's free now. Better off. You should be happy."

This time, Alfie did turn, if only fractionally, so that he could look Rake in the eyes. "Yeah?"

"So."

"Ah, that's. Thasomethin'." Alfie's eyes filled with tears, and Rake looked away. He wasn't sure who he was embarrassed for, the boy or himself.

"Anyway." Rake pulled his flask out of his coat and took a swig. It was the unpalatable rice liquor favored by Imperial peasants, but it was still booze. He didn't need it. "Take it," he said, proffering the bottle to Alfie. "This here's the only comfort I'll be giving you. Next time I see you, I'll likely be here to kill you."

Alfie let out an unmanly sob but took the bottle. He took a long, ineffective swig, dribbling most of it down his chin. "Thanks, I guess," he said.

"You're welcome."

Rake left him with his tears and the bottle.

The captain hadn't made the order yet. But he would. Rake was sure of it.

And when it came to the captain's acts of cruelty, Rake was not often wrong.

As he stepped out of the cabin, he nearly ran bodily into Fawkes. Internally, Rake sighed. The last thing he wanted was to interact with Fawkes. With all the care he could find, he tried to erect the shields he held around his heart.

"Checking on little Alfie, then?" Everything Fawkes said sounded cruel. It didn't matter what it was; he could ask what was for breakfast and he'd still sound evil. Rake wanted to slap Alfie's name out of Fawkes's mouth.

"Just seeing that he's alive," Rake replied. "And that there was no treasure in his pockets."

Fawkes grunted his approval but did not move to let Rake pass. He smelled of stale sweat, stale booze. Rake hated him. Why did anyone so malevolent need to be so gigantic? His body alone seemed proof there were no gods, save for Death.

"Seeing as the mermaid is gone," Fawkes said finally, "I was thinking it'd be fair to let me have a bit of that treasure."

"The captain's treasure?" Rake raised an eyebrow. He had little patience for impertinence.

"Well. Since Florian absconded with my best and most valuable treasure, it seems only right."

"And you're asking me because . . . ?"

"Because you can get in a good word with the captain."

"And I'd do that for you because . . . ?"

"Aww." Fawkes made a sound that Rake supposed was meant to be jocular laughter. "C'mon, then."

"I won't. I won't because that is the captain's treasure and it is not my place, just as it is most certainly not yours to decide what he does with it. And besides, if he wanted you to have some as recompense for being on watch during an escape, I'm sure you'd know by now."

Fawkes glared at Rake but still did not let him pass. He stood, boulder-like and terrible, on the spot. But he did not mention the truth that hung between them — that it'd been Rake's orders that led him out of Florian's way, clearing the path for escape.

"It's not right," Fawkes said.

"Take it to the captain, then." Rake gave him an impatient nod to signify the conversation's end. For a moment, he thought Fawkes might try to fight him. It was not a favorable matchup. But after some time, Fawkes stepped aside, allowing Rake to pass.

Soon, Rake thought. Soon, all these men would know the hangman's noose.

For Alfie, it would be a mercy.

Rake had only been aboard the *Dove* a year, maybe less, when the two orphans had come along. Pirate ships were always stacked with orphans, though not typically from the Imperial shores. But these two were no Imperial-blooded youth — their black skin and gray eyes did away with that notion right off.

Several of the men had caught the pair trying to pickpocket them, but were impressed by their seeming lack of fear once they were caught. They had argued and thrashed until they were set free. The captain, amused by his sailors' account of them, had invited them aboard the *Dove* so that they might beg for a place on the ship directly to him. He had them meet him in the galley, which was at the time full of treasures plundered on the previous voyage, ready for sale in Crandon.

Rake could see it right away—the boy wanted the treasures for himself. He could see already the dreams of wealth forming in his little mind.

The girl, on the other hand, hardly seemed to notice. She kept her eyes on Rake and the captain, as if expecting them to attack at any moment.

One would make a far better sailor than the other; that much was clear.

Both the boy and his sister had their hair shorn to the quick, as urchins, lice-infested and starving, often did. Some would buy hair off the destitute to stuff pillows. And if they couldn't sell it, well, no hair meant no lice. The boy was about the age Rake had been when he'd begun his career as a criminal — maybe thirteen. The girl, though, was smaller, maybe ten or eleven. Too young for the rusted knife she carried in her fist.

The boy did all the talking.

"And anyway, sir, as you can see, we ain't afraid of hard work nor violence."

"An easy thing to promise," Rake said.

"Aye, but sirs, even Flora here's got grave digging under her belt. I mean, lookit her! She seem unprepared for a life o' hardship?"

The girl said nothing.

"She's a girl," Rake said. Again. He'd been making this point ever since the two had stepped aboard. The boy was all bluster. And the girl was a girl. Why the captain had allowed them on the *Dove* at all was completely beyond him. A ship was no place for a little girl, and a pirate ship doubly so.

"Tell me," the captain said. "Would you promise me your undying devotion and loyalty?"

"Aw, yes, sir, of course, sir, for our whole lives, sir," the boy replied hastily.

"And you would never shirk your duties to me?"

"No, sir, never, sir. We'd work so hard you'd have to dream up more jobs for us," said the boy.

"Tell me, girl," the captain said, turning his full attention to her. The girl, Flora, did not move, did not blink. "If I told you to, would you kill?"

Say no, Rake urged silently. Say never.

"Yes," Flora said.

The captain laughed. The sound of it, ugly and empty, echoed in his cabin. "You're just a chit of a thing!" He could hardly contain himself, he was laughing so hard. "And you're ready to kill?"

"I seen dead bodies before," she said, as if that were all it took.

"It's true!" the boy cried. "We seen loads of 'em in the street. We saw old Peeves take a knife to the eye! One minute he was shooting the shit, and the next, bam! Blood everywhere, an —"

"Tell me," the captain interrupted. He was still looking at Flora. "Would you kill Rake here if I asked you to?"

Rake rolled his eyes.

"Yes," Flora said.

The captain clapped his hands, laughing again. "Oh, marvelous, marvelous. What a little sprite you are, what a little demon." He looked at the girl approvingly. "I think I may have room aboard for the likes of you."

Rake wanted to hit him, the idea was so stupid. Who would let a child aboard a pirate ship? She'd be dead in a week, if not sooner. He supposed that since the captain could no longer remember his own childhood, he hardly had respect for the sanctity of anyone else's.

"Oh, thank you, thank you!" The boy was beaming — already, Rake guessed, imagining himself the next captain of the crew. "You won't regret it, and we —"

"Not you." The captain waved his hand at him. "You must go."

He and Flora looked at each other, clearly panicked. "What?" the boy asked, his voice quiet.

But Flora stared right back at the captain. "I don't go nowhere without Alfie," she said decisively.

"You say that, but what if I told you you'd have meals for the rest of your life, hm? What if I told you you'd have a place to sleep every night until you're old and gray or until you die?"

But the girl held strong. "Not without Alfie."

"Girls don't belong on ships anyway," Rake said, more to the captain than to her. But Flora glared at him all the same. "They're bad luck, it isn't safe for them, and they can't carry their load."

"Aw, too bad. You seemed like you'd make a fine sailor." The captain gave Flora a pitying look.

"She would. She will! And so will I!" Alfie sputtered.

"You, boy," the captain said, "are all talk."

"No, sir! Please, sir, give me a chance! We won't survive another winter here, please!"

"What would he have to do," Flora asked, still calm, "to prove that we're *both* worth it?"

The captain smiled his true smile. Rake saw it infrequently, but when it showed itself, it sent shivers through his body. It wasn't right. It looked like a skeleton's smile, toothy and morbid.

"Go back into Crandon," the captain said. "And bring me the ears of a man you killed."

The children left, practically sprinting into their life sentence. Not even a moment of pause. Rake had met rough children in his life, but murder was a step above the robberies and beatings the hard kids of his own youth had doled out. The captain was a cruel man.

"What if they actually do it?" Rake asked. He couldn't imagine the captain truly meant to hire them on; it was foolhardy. They were hardly seasoned murderers — there was no way they'd get away with it, even if they did muster the guts. And besides. A girl? It was mad even by the Nameless Captain's standards.

"Then I'll always have at least two sailors in my pocket," the captain said. He steepled his fingers thoughtfully. "They will always owe me, Rake. They will always know they are here by my goodwill, and my goodwill alone. You cannot force that kind of loyalty."

"Their highest loyalty will always be to each other."

The captain laughed. "Familial bonds mean less and less with every day aboard this ship, Rake. We sail. We rob. Have you ever seen a crewman of mine write a letter home? All that matters in a life like that is survival. We'll make solid men out of them both. You'll see."

Internally, Rake sighed. Of course family meant nothing to the captain.

The captain couldn't remember his.

Later, when the children returned, Rake could tell from the bloodlessness of the ears they toted that they had not killed anyone. Found a corpse, rather, and from the looks of it, a child. Cut off the ears and left the body. But the captain did not notice, and so Rake did not say anything.

## CHAPTER 32

# *Flora*

"W ell, try again."

Xenobia, Flora had found, had even less patience than usual for her these days. So when she found Flora in her kitchen again, holding a stone to her ear with a peeved look on her face again, and asked if Flora could tell the stone's story again, and was told that in fact, no, Flora could not tell the stone's story again, Xenobia's face crumpled into a deeply disapproving shape.

*Useless.*

"I'm no good at this," Flora spat. *I'm no good at anything.* She had been trying off and on again for weeks now, it felt. Day in and day out to listen to a goddamn rock tell a goddamn story, and all she ever heard was the sound of her own breath. And occasional cussing. "I have no magic in me." She sat down at Xenobia's small table, defeated. It was not like Flora to pout. She was no stranger to hard work. It had been her most steadfast companion. But to see it thwarted—so consistently—shook her.

Xenobia did her best to rearrange her face, strode over to Flora calmly, and took a seat at the table across from her.

"Have you told the stone any of your story?"

Flora nodded. And never in her life had she felt so foolish as she did when whispering to a rock. She passed her fingers over it again. It was warm from her touch, and Flora felt like the longer she held it, the more the pale pink of the quartz dulled, the more its edges softened.

"What story did you tell?"

Flora's face flushed. "I — I told it the story of when the Lady Hasegawa kissed me. Or kissed Florian, I guess."

Xenobia sighed and gave Flora what could only be described as a look of profound disappointment.

"There's your problem," the witch said. "Try a story from your life you actually understand. Something you hold in your heart. Something that is a part of you."

Flora held her tongue. That kiss was a part of her now. But Xenobia was right — she hardly understood it. Evelyn had abandoned her, after all. So that kiss could not have meant all that Flora had hoped it had meant, and besides, it had been meant for Florian, not her.

"Think."

Flora racked her mind. What story was a part of her?

"I have one," she said finally.

There was a moment when Flora expected Xenobia to leave, but instead Xenobia sat expectantly.

"No time like the present."

Flora inhaled deeply, trying her best to master herself and ignore her pride. If she wanted to do this, she would need the witch's help. She held the stone to her chest.

"Listen," she said, as the witch had told her to. "Once I was a child, starving and scared, and I was told by a cruel man that I'd never be hungry again if I brought him the ears of a person I killed. I didn't want to kill anyone because I never had. But I knew where there were two dead bodies. My brother and I ran to that place. The bodies were there, two children not so different in age from us. Not a week earlier, we had stolen their bread. And now they were stiff with death. My brother, the coward, could not muster the will to cut the ears off either of them. He vomited and sputtered. So I took his knife. I said, let me do it. And I did. I chose the older brother, not the little sister, because he had not protected her, just as my brother did not protect me.

"I held his head in my lap as I worked. When people say something smells like death, it is because the smell is inescapable, because it's undeniably what it is. There is no other smell like it. And I sat there with that dead boy's head in my lap, the smell of his death around me, and I cut off his ears. First his right and then his left. My brother did not want the knife back. It is yours, he told me. Consider it a gift, he said. As his thanks. I still have that knife."

All the while, as Flora spoke, Xenobia nodded, smiling. "Yes," she whispered. "Like this."

Flora took a deep, shaky breath. She was not sure she had ever said these things aloud, ever, in her life. She felt oddly free in the wake of her words, which still seemed to echo around her.

*My brother, the coward.* How good it felt, to tell that truth. How light she felt, to be rid of him.

And in her pocket, the knife felt cold.

"Now," Flora said. She held the stone to her ear. It was small and smooth and black, and cold against her skin. "Tell me your story."

Flora nearly dropped the stone when it started to speak. But

Xenobia's eyes widened with victory and motioned for her to keep it close to her, to listen. And so Flora did.

The stone's voice was small and soft in her ear.

"Once," the stone said, "I was under the Sea. Ages and ages I was, until in her rage, the Sea created a great storm that battered the shore. I broke away. I was alone. I was adrift, caught in the current, which beat me against that which I had been a part of, the island and the mountain, again and again. Then the Sea carried me to a soft beach, where I rolled in the waves.

"I rolled back and forth, inland and back out again, for even more ages than I had been a part of the mountain. I rolled until I was nearly flat, all my edges smoothed, and I became the small thing you hold now. And then I was picked up by a girl so that she might throw me into a stream to see how many times I would skip before sinking.

"But in her youth and in her inattention, she forgot she was holding me, and she dropped me on the beach, far from the Sea and her merciless currents. And that is when I was picked up again. So that you could learn my story."

When the stone finished its tale, Flora sat still, her eyes wide. The stone had spoken. The stone had spoken to her. She knew the stone's story.

"You heard," Xenobia said, smiling. It was a true smile, a smile Flora realized she had not seen yet.

"Yes," Flora said, too stunned to be excited, too nonplussed to recognize her own triumph.

"It is for you to tell that stone the next part of its story." The witch held Flora's eyes, her own now serious. "This is real magic, child. Do not take it lightly."

"I don't," Flora said.

"Go on, then." Xenobia's eyes shifted so that they shone now with her evident pleasure. "Tell that stone its story."

And so Flora did. She tried to think of a story that the stone would like, a nice story. A kind story.

"Listen, stone, and listen well: you will go back to the Sea," Flora whispered. "But you will not dwell upon her shore, being tossed and rocked so violently. No, you will sink to her depths, to her most secret quiet and her tranquility, where the waves do not roll and the currents do not reach. Deep, deep in the Sea, where you will rest upon the soft sand, only ever to be touched with kindness. This is the next chapter of your story. See that it begins now."

Nearly as soon as she had uttered the last words, the stone shot from her hand. Only when she heard the crash of Xenobia's only window did Flora realize the stone had flown straight to the Sea, and the shock of it wrenched a laugh from somewhere deep in her belly. How eager the stone was, how pleased it must have been! She leaned back in her chair and shook her head at the curiosity of it.

"What on earth did you say to that stone?"

"I told it to go back to the Sea," Flora said. She just barely kept her lips from curling into a smile.

Xenobia closed her eyes and took a deep, steadying breath, as if she were mastering pain. "The Sea?" she asked. But before Flora could answer, her eyes shot open and she stared at Flora as though seeing her for the first time. Or at least, seeing her idiocy for the first time. She held out her hands as though she were either going to cup Flora's cheeks or strangle her. "Why. Would. You. Give. Your. Story. To. The. Sea?"

"I did not give my story to the Sea. I gave it to the stone."

"Oh, you precious, stupid thing. Do you think the Sea does

not know each stone in her midst? Do you think anything passes in her depths that she does not see?"

Flora said nothing. She had only ever heard one other person speak of the Sea as they would a god, and that was Rake. And he, too, had only ever spoken of the Sea as a dangerous thing.

"Pray," Xenobia commanded. "Pray that you never run afoul of the Sea, pray she never sees reason to punish you. For she already has more than enough to make it so."

Flora gulped.

"Pray!" Xenobia shouted.

So Flora hung her head. She did not know how to pray — she never had. But what was prayer except the request for a better story? And so she prayed.

For she had already served aboard the *Dove* — had already seen mermaids caught and killed.

If punishment was due to anyone, certainly it was already due to her.

Once there was a mermaid who fell in love with a woman.

The mermaid saw the woman twice every day: once when she came to set traps for crabs in the morning, and then again in the evening when she checked the traps. While the woman checked the traps, she hummed a song. While she set the traps, she sang. Her voice was a panacea for the mermaid, and she waited every morning and every evening so that she might catch even a note of the woman's beautiful voice as she worked.

It is known among mermaids that humans cannot be trusted. They are told this by the Sea from the time that they are born, because it is true, and because humans have always proved themselves poor friends to all others. So the mermaid did not show herself. But still, she pined for this woman and her sweet voice and her strong hands. She thought of nothing else all day and all night. Because mermaids do not sleep, this meant she thought of the woman constantly.

And because she could not tell the Sea of her desire, she sought out a witch.

She found the witch as she stepped along the tide pools, searching out urchins for a stew.

"Please," she said. "Make me a human so that I might court the woman I love."

The witch did not want to — for witches are no fools, and only fools run afoul of the Sea. "I cannot," she told the mermaid, "for your mother."

But the mermaid begged so ardently and described the woman so lovingly that the witch felt she could not resist her. For the witch knew love well. She thought of her own love, and the pain she would feel if she could not have them. So she bent under the pressure of the mermaid's words. She told the mermaid of the love in her life and of her willingness to help.

"Tonight, you must tell the Sea that you wish to leave her," the witch conceded. "And then I will help you."

The mermaid vowed that she would do this.

The mermaid lied.

For the Sea is a jealous mother, protective and selfish. The mermaid knew that if she told her mother what she wished to do, the Sea would only stand in her way. And so she did not tell. But still, the mermaid returned the next morning so that she might be turned into a human.

The witch gave the mermaid a looking glass. "Look into

this," the witch commanded, "and listen to my tale. When it is done, you shall be human and free to court the woman you love."

The witch began her spell.

The Sea could tell that magic was being done, magic that would take her daughter from her, and willingly so. For the Sea has magic, too, far more powerful than any witch's. And in her anger at her daughter's betrayal, at the witch's impertinence, the Sea cast her own spell.

The looking glass she cast into the desert, where it became a small green oasis. There, the Sea exiled her daughter, still a mermaid. There she would live, adrift in the sand and alone, without her mother or her sisters or her love, known to no one.

The witch she cursed, too. The Sea took her love and called them her ally. And though the witch still loved them, they did not love her back, not anymore, their heart too full with their new love for the Sea.

To this day, the mermaid lives alone in the oasis.

To this day, the witch lives alone. ⌒

"The witch is you," Flora said. It wasn't a question. She looked at the pearls that hung loose around Xenobia's neck. The stories. All but the tale of the First Witch had been her own.

Xenobia did not reply. She did not need to.

"This is why you should never deal in the magic of love. And why you should never deal in the magic that touches the Sea."

"But you didn't know."

"That doesn't matter," she said. She breathed deeply, and for a moment Flora wondered if she might cry. She didn't. "I only sought to help her daughter."

"Do you still love them?"

Xenobia smiled then, but it looked like a flinch.

"Yes," she said simply.

"Who are they?"

"I knew them as Xoan," she said. "But they took up the mantle of Pirate Supreme, and they've been known by that since."

"You're kidding."

"Has my sense of humor been so broad?" She touched the pearls at her neck, running each through her fingers. "I thought they would love me as I loved them. Forever. But I was wrong."

"I'm sorry," Flora said, because she meant it.

"Ah, then." Xenobia smiled her false smile. "It doesn't do to dwell, does it. Xoan is gone; I am alone. These are the ways of things. Sing me a song. I could use a little music."

"I only know the one, and —"

"I know which. Please. Sing."

Flora did. And though she knew her singing voice was rough and strained, she sang as best she could. And though it seemed cruel to sing of true love and the Sea to Xenobia, the witch smiled with her eyes closed as Flora sang, mouthing the words in silence to the broken melody.

## CHAPTER 33

# Evelyn

Today's servant was a girl named Lida. Normally, she was Evelyn's favorite. She was crass and candid and made Evelyn laugh. But not today. They sat at the table where Evelyn's food was going cold, each with their ankles tucked under them, the formal Imperial posture. Lida was trying to learn, she said, and was eager to take any etiquette cues Evelyn would give her.

"Aren't you hungry?" Lida asked. She pushed the plate of fish toward her.

Evelyn was not hungry, had not been hungry since her interrogation by Commander Callum. Unable to eat since she'd been cowed under his pressure and realized that she was, categorically, a coward.

"No," she said. She tried her best to make a smile. "Thank you."

Her hope that Florian was coming to rescue her dwindled by the minute. It had been too long. And likely she had, in her fear, tipped Callum and his men off to where Florian was. Though she'd claimed he'd died at sea, she had to assume Callum didn't believe her. He was too smart to believe her. But then, all he'd really wanted to know about was Rake. Who was he? What did he want? But of course, Evelyn did not know.

"Do you not eat to be ladylike?" Lida looked at her quizzically. Everything Evelyn did was fodder for Lida's curiosity. But how could she explain the truth?

"No. Imperial ladies eat." She willed herself to take a bite of the fish — it was served in the traditional Imperial method, with its glassy eyes still staring — but she could not do it. With all of her extra time to sit around, alone with her thoughts, flashes of her parents had been popping into her memory with frightening regularity. Had they known what kind of man Callum was? They must have. And still they'd sent her.

"You know" — Lida leaned in conspiratorially — "all the men around here, they say how beautiful you are."

Evelyn knew that Lida was only trying to comfort her. But knowing that her prison guards thought her comely only made her more angry. Good enough to look at, not good enough to listen to. What a pretty sight she'd make for them as she walked to the gallows. She pushed her plate away.

"You must eat," Lida said after some time. Evelyn did not reply.

There was a knock at the door, and Inouye slipped in. Upon seeing him, Lida excused herself, despite Evelyn's silent pleading that she stay.

"My lady," he said. And his voice was sad, all dripping, useless unsaid apologies. Evelyn shook him off and looked out the window so that she wouldn't have to look at him.

"You do not like me," Inouye said. His voice was matter-of-fact. And what he said was true. Evelyn violently disliked him, and

236

often, in moments of solitude, she comforted herself with little fantasies about his bloody demise.

"That's fair," he went on. "You're being held prisoner, and you're scared. I understand. But I'm on your side, Lady Hasegawa. You have to know that, and —"

"So you admit I am the Lady Hasegawa?"

Inouye flushed. "My lady, I —"

"You are just as afraid as I am, and as such can do me no good."

Silence was a funny thing. Before she'd left home, it had, as a rule, made her deeply uncomfortable. She'd long recognized her own tendency to fill silences with useless chatter. Then, aboard the *Dove,* she'd experienced it as something new as it stretched out affectionately between her and Florian. And now she was coming to know a third kind of silence altogether. It was blunt and uncomfortable, but she relished it. At least this way, Inouye was suspended in it with her, momentarily sharing in the burden of her unhappiness.

"If I could —"

But Evelyn waved him off. "You could, but you won't," she said. "Because you're a coward."

Evelyn could tell the blow had hit its target. His attraction to her was obvious and did nothing to soothe her anger for him. If anything, it exacerbated it. How could he, on one hand, moon about after her and try to ply her good favor while still seeing to her imprisonment? It was baffling.

She thought again of Florian, who had saved her. Who had tossed his whole life overboard in order to see her safe. She had not deserved his bravery, but at least she could love him for it.

"We're not so different, you know," Inouye said. "Our parents sent us here, without a thought for our happiness and —"

"No." She stared him down until, in his shame, he looked away. "We are nothing alike."

For a while, neither said anything. Evelyn felt Inouye's presence like a stone in her stomach, the kind that preceded her monthly bleeding. She wanted him gone.

"So," he said. "You are not hungry."

"No."

He lifted her plates and carried them to the door. Then, looking back at her, he added, "I am just doing my duty, my lady. If you could open your heart to me, I think you would see that. That's all. And we all must do our duty."

When Evelyn did not respond, he left her alone once more.

She had to get out. She could no longer count on Florian to come rescue her, and she certainly couldn't count on any help from Inouye. The time for despairing was over.

She needed a plan.

Any plan.

To free herself.

## CHAPTER 34

*Rake*

The Lady Ayer was proving to be a difficult ally.
It was not that she was foolish or ignorant. Quite the opposite. Her questions were plentiful and pointed and connoted a level of expertise Rake had not expected. And any time he tried to elude or misdirect her attentions from information that was more than he cared to share, she noticed and simply asked her question again.

It did not help that he was hardly able to sleep anymore. With the Lady and the girl Genevieve hiding in his cabin, he was lucky to get a few hours in between interrogations by the Lady Ayer. And so he felt slow.

The question was: Who was she?

They were in the middle of yet another interrogation. Genevieve was taking the time to sharpen and polish the numerous blades she and the Lady Ayer typically strapped all over their bodies. He did not like the girl. She smiled at the wrong times. And besides, she was from Quark — and yet here she was, a lady's maid to the worst kind of Imperial.

Rake lay on the bed with his arm thrown over his eyes, trying to ignore them. His body language had done nothing to dissuade the lady, who sat primly on the tansu, barking questions.

"For the hundredth time," Rake said, "I cannot tell you why the Pirate Supreme has sent me rather than the armada. It's not for me to know, and so I was not told."

"But it hardly seems the most efficient use of resources," the Lady said, more to herself than to Rake. "Are orders from the Supreme often that way? Without apparent sense or motive?"

Rake sat up, annoyed. "Madam." He tried his best to keep his voice measured, but even he could tell his anger was obvious. "It is not for me to judge the Supreme's orders. The Supreme is a wise and good leader. I am not. I simply do as I am told and trust that it is for the best."

"Pirates," the Lady scoffed. "For the life of me, I'll never understand—" She stopped herself midsentence and raised a finger, calling for silence. Her entire bearing changed, her posture taut, her eyes pointed at the door. Rake heard it then, too. Someone was trying to step away from the door. Someone had been listening.

Before he could stand, the Lady was on her feet. In a swift movement, she swiped a long, sharpened blade from Genevieve and opened the door.

Not one step away stood Cook. He froze, in shock at being caught.

Rake's stomach flipped. Cook was a good man, but loyal to the captain.

The Lady grabbed Cook by the scruff of his neck and, despite his considerable size, hauled the man into the cabin and shut the door behind him. Before Rake could even fully comprehend what had happened, her blade was at Cook's throat.

"Is he one of yours?" the Lady demanded.

Cook's round eyes found Rake's pleadingly. Rake could do him no good.

"No, milady. Unfortunately, he is not."

"Rake —" Cook pleaded, but Rake did not reply.

"Genevieve," the Lady said calmly. "Look away."

The girl did as she was told.

The Lady Ayer handed Rake her knife, guessing correctly that he would prefer to undertake the task himself. He did his best. It was an expert cut, efficient. The life was gone from Cook's eyes before, Rake hoped, he had felt the pain of his own impending death. Genevieve handed the Lady Ayer a woven blanket off the bed so that she might at least contain some of the bleeding, which the Lady did.

"A dead body," Rake said coolly. "A big one."

The Lady nodded. "You'll need to carry him abovedeck on your own, I'm afraid. Obviously, we can be of no assistance."

"Yes." He tried not to think of every little kindness Cook had afforded him through the years. There had been many. Silently, he made a prayer for the man, that his soul might find peace. He was a good man, even if he was the captain's.

"Will he be missed?" the Lady asked.

"Oh, yeah. That's Cook."

"That's not ideal."

Rake rubbed his face with his hands and tried his best to clear his mind. He'd need to do some expert lying, and soon. He'd need a very tall tale to justify the execution of the *Dove*'s only cook, and he'd need to have a replacement in mind before he told the captain.

Whatever happened, Rake knew, he'd need to be even more careful of his new and tenuous ally than he'd originally imagined. She was quick to kill, and competent. The fact that she was not the simple wife she'd purported to be was glaringly obvious. He handed her back the blade, which she wiped on a cloth.

On it was the insignia of the Imperial Guard.

The Lady saw him look and stuffed the blade into her skirts. "My husband's," she said.

But Rake did not believe her.

When the captain announced they would, on their next mission, be kidnapping Imperials, Rake wanted to shake some sense into him. Not only Imperials, the captain went on, but the nobility. Rake's stomach dropped. If the Imperials guarded anything, it was their wealthy. And anyway, it did not do to unnecessarily court the Emperor's ire. They often stopped in Crandon for stores and for shore leave, but they had never launched a proper voyage from there. They did not collect from there.

"This is folly," he told the captain.

They were in the captain's cabin, and Rake was watching him eat, as he so often did. The crew was ashore, making mischief. Usually a man or two would be lost each shore leave, to violence or arrest. But Rake typically stayed with the captain, who did not enjoy leaving the *Dove*. It was stuffy in his cabin, and Rake could feel a droplet of sweat snaking its way down his back.

The captain took a generous mouthful of pork chop and chewed it loudly. He shrugged.

"If you've got us a plan that'll earn us ten thousand a head for each of the men while wasting zero ammunition, I'd love to hear it."

Rake said nothing.

"The brilliance of this operation," the captain went on, "is that the Imperials never expect us to come to them. Think about it.

They send thousands of ships to track the likes of us down, but they never think to search their own port." The captain cackled, delighted by his own strategy. "They walk right onto our ship! Just step right up. And the best part is, their people will bring the best prices!"

He took a long slug of drink. Some dribbled into his beard, but he did not notice. Rake did.

How he hated the captain.

If the Imperial Guard caught them, not only would his mission be thwarted, the Sea unappeased, and the Supreme at higher risk for not appeasing the Sea, but Rake would also die. And while Rake was more than willing to die for the Supreme, he did not wish to die at the hands of scum like the Imperial Guard. Their training was in brutality, and their desire to rule the world under their fist made Rake want to set their vast swaths of land on fire.

He hated the captain for his cruelty and his myopia. But he hated the Imperial Guard more.

"Sir," Rake said, "we cannot do this. When noblemen do not appear where they are meant to, people notice. These are not plebes. These are men and women of power and wealth."

"Exactly!" The captain smirked. "Which is why their trunks will be so ripe for the picking."

"But we put ourselves and our men right into the gloved hand of the Imperialists if we stay. We should not be here." It was more of a plea than Rake had meant it to be.

"Tell you what," the captain said, his voice uncharacteristically kind. "If we catch more than one mermaid on this voyage, we will have enough gold to buy ourselves some time. If you can think of a new operation as lucrative as this one, I will consider it."

Rake said nothing, which the captain took to be his consent.

"You're a good man, Rake. I'm happy to have your help aboard my ship. But if you come to me to question my judgment, you'd best come with suggestions for clear alternatives." He belched and wiped his mouth with the back of his sleeve. "You know what the best part of the mermaid's blood is?"

Rake shook his head. The captain had often chided him for not partaking.

"It's not the trip, not the wonders you see. It's that the memories you lose, they're not the ones you need." He looked off into the distance thoughtfully. "It frees you from your past, you see. It even frees you from all the made-up rules of good and bad you were taught as a child. Memories are a burden. They're shackles. Just foolish stories we tell ourselves so that we can feel as though life has meaning. See, I remember what I am, but not where I came from, so I don't have any irrational fondness for any random plot of land, any random group of people. I remember that luck favors the bold, and that kindness is a lie taught by weak people. I remember that I like to rut and to eat and to kill. And that's all I need to know."

He paused and looked at Rake with a pointed silence. "The gift of the blood is oblivion. You should try it. You'll like it."

Rake thought of the Sea, the promises the Supreme had made to her. The agreement that kept pirate ships safe, even as the Imperial Armada plodded through the seas, searching them out. To be on the side of killing mermaids was, in its complicity, to be on the side of the Emperor.

The Pirate Supreme's forces were the only thing standing in the way of complete Imperial rule on the open sea. If pirates could still disrupt the merchants, still stymie the trade routes, then the Imperialists could not claim full control. Every robbery, every kidnapping, every galleon destroyed was a protest against the Emperor. They may have taken Quark, may have taken the Floating Islands, may have had their greedy eyes on the Red Shore — but they could not have the Sea.

He remembered what it was like when they took Quark.

It had been bloody. It had been terrible. The Imperial Guard had descended swiftly and dispatched of all those who stood in their way. They beat the country into submission and then made the people say thanks for the privilege of being beaten.

Rake had been thirteen at the time. And he knew, right then, he could no longer live by the law of the land.

"The problem with you is that you hold on to too many of these memories. You let what you've seen in the past scare you into being a coward in the present. You fear the Imperialists too much. That's your past talking. Forget the past. Let go of all that, my good man, and we could accomplish whatever we wanted!"

"Yes, sir," Rake said.

But Rake would not forget. Rake would not let himself forget.

# ✦ CHAPTER 35 ✦

## *Flora*

As the days passed, Flora started to tell Xenobia her own stories.

It was odd at first, for several reasons. For one, Flora was not given much to speaking. In general, she was tight-lipped, and, to a fault, she did not divulge secrets. There was the added strangeness of speaking to inanimate objects, but that had quickly passed after the first stone spoke back to her.

But the hardest reason, the one Flora struggled with the most, was the malleability of reality.

For that was what magic was — it was understanding the truth of something, and then changing it. Reality, Xenobia said, was created by belief, and as such even its most fundamental trappings could be altered. Magic was at its core, she said, a kind of madness. It was a willingness to look at the corporeal world and to see it only as the story *up to* that point. That everything that followed could be changed. Rocks fell because the belief that they would fall was so strong. But that belief wasn't binding. It didn't have to be binding anyway. For a price.

And while Flora could, by now, easily make soup from stones, she could do little else.

"The problem," Xenobia told her, "is the stories you tell. Nothing will believe you if you do not fully believe them yourself. You cannot make a new reality if you do not even understand your own."

Which, of course, sounded like good advice. Flora had come to accept that Xenobia was no fool. But it was not advice she knew how to follow.

Most curiously, Xenobia had ordered Flora to fix a broken looking glass. It had been hanging in Flora's room for the entirety of her stay with the witch, and Flora—who was no stranger to disrepair—had simply figured that a broken looking glass, which had been split in two by a crack, with one long shard missing, was still better than no looking glass at all. She could still see herself within it, in clouded fragments.

"You will fix it," Xenobia told her. And it was less of a command than a statement of fact.

There was the added bonus that, in concentrating on the myriad seemingly impossible tasks Xenobia put forth, Flora was able to distract herself—for moments at a time—from the horrible thrum in her chest where Evelyn's rejection lay. And though the pain remained, constant and hollow and aching, any distraction from it was sweet respite, the likes of which Flora had not known in her life. Pain, she knew. Relief was new. And so her study—though burdensome and frustrating—was essential. Without it she could not sleep, could not eat. So she worked.

Still, the looking glass hung broken on the wall.

Seeing Flora's exhaustion, Xenobia made dinner that night. A hunk of goat leg, delivered along the elevators, and two round, juicy onions that she had cooked with it. Flora had long since realized that even the witch could not use magic for every meal — the loss of appetite it cost to do so would starve the witch to death if she were not careful. And Flora relished the meals they ate together. Quietly and in companionable silence. Like family.

How long had it been, how many years, since Flora had seen her mother? She'd been so small, but still she could remember the warmth of her body, the tight grip of her hugs. The food stirred those memories in her, and it was, she realized, the fullness of her belly that did it. The only other time she'd felt that way was when her mother had been there to care for her, and for Alfie.

When they were done, Flora stood to attend to the dishes, but Xenobia stopped her and bade that she remain where she sat. Xenobia rose and picked up one of the many carnivorous plants that she kept in her kitchen. Flora did not much like the plants, with their strange mouths like eyes. She did not trust them and did her best to ignore them.

"This plant is called witch's mouth. Do you know why?"

"Because people are afraid of witches?"

Xenobia smiled. "No, child. Because they share our nature. They take, but they can also give. The leaves of the witch's mouth can be used to heal all manner of ailments, if the plants are raised correctly. But one must feed them a steady diet of flies and spiders for them to be of use. And they are hungry little plants, and difficult to maintain if not fed. Their hunger defines them.

"If one knows the nature of this plant, and its truth, then one can harness its power."

Flora looked at the eerie little plant. Its mouth hung open, wanting and hungry.

"You do not know your own nature," Xenobia said. "That's why you can't fix the looking glass."

Flora blinked, confused. Of course she knew her own nature.

"You said it was because I did not understand my reality," Flora said.

"Same same, but different. You may not completely understand all the forces that made your life the way it's been — that much is true. But then, most don't. Most can't. There are simply too many factors in any given life for any person to possibly parse without devoting their life only to understanding their life. And what good would that do anyone? None, even to the person who pursued it."

Flora's head ached. Frustration boiled in her belly. Xenobia was wise. But her tendency to speak in circles made Flora's skin itch with irritation.

"Your problem," Xenobia went on, "is that you have never reckoned with yourself. Or rather, any time you have tried, you have only ever taken on pieces of yourself. Tell me, Florian. Who are you?"

*Florian.* The name startled her: she had not heard it in so long. She had introduced herself to Xenobia as Flora and had been thus addressed for the entirety of their time together. Hearing *Florian* aloud dragged her back to the *Dove,* back to her life on the sea with the Nameless Captain and Rake.

*And Alfie.*

"That's not my name," she said finally.

"Isn't it?" Xenobia held Flora's eyes, unblinking. The room behind her swayed into darkness and was gone. All Flora could see was the witch and the terrible truth she bore. "There are those who are neither a man nor a woman. Those who were born and called the wrong gender and must reshape their story for those around them. But you. You're something else. You're whatever is safe. Both, maybe, but not neither. Or interchangeable. Names are funny things, because they can feel like lies but tell our truths."

249

It was true that Florian was Flora's spell of choice. Casting him felt like a ward of protection. It had been Florian that Evelyn had kissed. But where did Florian end and Flora begin? For the first time, she felt she could hold both in her heart. That both might be true.

Xenobia pushed the plant to the side and pulled from her pocket the missing shard of the looking glass. Flora recognized it right away. Now that she had spent hours staring into the space where it belonged, she knew its contours perfectly. In it, her own gray eye peered back at her.

"Tell me," Xenobia said, her voice hard. "Who. Are. You?"

Flora held the shard of mirror in her fingers. It was warm now from her touch, from the rising morning sun, and from the thin blankets Flora and the shard shared on her bed. In her mind, Xenobia's question echoed.

The answer, Xenobia said, would mend the mirror. And so Flora had been starting and then restarting, over and again, to tell the story of her life to the shard.

*Orphan.*

The abandoned child of a man she'd never met and a mother who left. Those adults who should have been the guard against danger in her life were long gone, probably dead.

*Sister.*

To Alfie. Distantly, she knew she should be worried about him, the only family she had. But where her love for him usually lived, there was only ash. One does not choose their family, and she would not, if given the chance again, choose Alfie. He was weak. He was a coward. And his nature had forged hers, for better and certainly for worse.

*Pirate.*

A life of tasks and duties and shame. Of blood and of eyes averted. And though she had revered Rake, in a way, as the distant father she'd never had—for gruffly teaching her to tie knots and fire straight—she had hated her life aboard the *Dove*. Had hated the captain, and Fawkes, and the men who drank and told untrue stories of their own grandeur. They were liars, all of them, drunkards and liars and killers. And they'd made a murderer of her.

Still the shard remained, broken and jagged, in her hand. She looked into the shard, at her own gray eye, which blinked back at her.

"Come on," she pleaded at a whisper. "Show me who I am."

For a moment after she spoke, her breath fogged the glass.

When it cleared, the eye that looked back at Flora had changed.

It was brown, with black eyelashes that pointed skyward, as though they had been painstakingly curled daily for years. The heavy lid of the Imperial-blooded. Tears pooled in the eye, around the minute pink veins that told Flora the eye had been crying for some time.

It was not her eye.

But before Flora could even make sense of what she was seeing, she heard voices coming from Xenobia's kitchen. At least two of them. In her time at the witch's house, there had not been a single visitor. Her curiosity piqued, she pushed the shard into her pocket and went to see who had come.

"Of course I remember you," Xenobia said. Her voice was curt and, if Flora was not mistaken, a little scared. She held back instinctively at the sound of it, hiding in the hallway so that she might still eavesdrop upon the witch and her visitor.

There was the sound of a man clearing his throat, and then,

"Well, I need your help once more, my lady." He was a younger man, Flora guessed, perhaps Alfie's age or just older. His voice bore the affected accent of the Imperial elite, that theatrical enunciation.

"I'm no lady," Xenobia spat.

"Well, the Lady Hasegawa is."

For a moment, Flora's heartbeat lurched to a halt. *Evelyn.*

"Your point?"

"My point is that she is a gentle creature, one who requires my aid. She does not love her betrothed, and he does not love her back."

*She does not love him.* The news lifted Flora, a gust of wind beneath a flapping sail. *She does not love him.*

"I was not under the impression that love was a matter much considered in the marital arrangements of the Imperial nobility."

The man laughed, a low, mirthless chuckle. "Perhaps not. But she is such a lovely thing, and—"

*Thing.* Flora felt her fists clench.

"You want her for yourself."

A silence stretched out between the man and the witch, long and, even from Flora's vantage, uncomfortable. She heard the scrape of a ceramic cup being lifted off the table and then the clunk as it was returned.

"She does not love me, nor want me, either."

*Of course she doesn't.*

*She loves me.*

A smile spread across Flora's face, her first true smile in ages. She had not been wrong all this time. Evelyn did not want any of these men. Because Evelyn wanted *her.* The truth of it filled Flora; it was the only thing she was in that moment.

In her pocket, the shard flashed hot. Flora pulled it out and

252

regarded it, hoping to see the eye once more. It had been Evelyn's eye. It had to have been. But the eye was gone — all that was reflected back now were the cobwebbed wooden beams of the ceiling.

Flora heard Xenobia stand, pushing her chair back from the table. "Then I am sorry, Lieutenant. There's nothing I can do to help you. Go comb your hair and try harder. Perhaps your charm can be conveyed to her over time."

"Please," the man begged. "I can pay you."

*No,* Flora pleaded. *She does not want you.*

"What is it, exactly, that you think I can do for you? There is nothing, I assure you."

The man sighed. "You should know, under interrogation the girl admitted you were a witch. To Commander Callum. Commander Callum of the Imperial Guard," he said meaningfully. "Officially, I am here to ensure that you are not one, or else to bring you to him if you are."

"Ah." Xenobia's voice was a knife, cutting and derisive. "Blackmail, then, is it?"

"Are you a witch?" the man asked.

"Are you a sniveling coward?"

"Mutually beneficial assistance, I should say. You help me, and I help you."

"I have already helped," Xenobia said. "I gave you the girl, I have done my duty by the Emperor. If you men can't wrangle her feelings, that's your problem. Not mine."

The floor dropped from beneath Flora, and she was falling through the infinite darkness of Xenobia's betrayal. Evelyn had not left her at all. Evelyn had been sold out. By the witch.

All this time, Xenobia had let Flora wander her home, heartbroken. All this time had been a lie.

Evelyn had not left her. Evelyn had *not* left her. The truth of it beat a drumming song in Flora's chest.

Flora had to rescue her. From this man, from Commander Callum. From interrogation and cruelty.

And as soon as the thought crystallized in her mind, the shard burned hot in her pocket once more, so hot that it burned Flora's skin. It was all she could do not to cry out from the pain of it. It was like all the pain she'd ever known, all the pain that had ever been. It started where the shard touched her skin, and then in a breath it was her whole body, alight with the fire of her own truth.

*Lies.*

She was a liar. She saw Evelyn's face, saw her as she did when she first met her. Naive, so willing to stand for what she thought to be good, to be right. Flora had seen that goodness in her heart and still she led her knowingly to torture, to humiliation, to death. She had been willing — even for a moment — to lead this kind and silly creature to a terrible fate in return for her own safety. Worse, Evelyn had been told where they were headed. And it was not Flora who had told her. She saw through the other lies, though, didn't she? She thought of Evelyn's fingers on her neck, the kisses that confirmed she did not care.

And Alfie. She had left him. Without so much as a look back or a note to explain. She had jumped at the chance to be rid of him and the difficulty he made in her life. She saw Alfie's face, saw him as he peered up at her from his hammock. They'd always stick together. That much she had sworn time and time again, not only to Alfie but also to herself. All lies. He was her blood, her kin, her only family left. And all she'd felt, all she'd had room to feel, when she left him was relief. But now the guilt of it, of her love for him and her acute awareness of her inexcusable betrayal, bore down upon her, threatening to break her.

And Mr. Lam. The sailors of the *Dove* had not made her into a murderer. She had made herself into one. In her desperation to be recognized as worthy by them, Flora had eagerly become a murderer, too, so that she might earn their respect, might be granted power finally among the men who scared her so. The cost of it was her respect for herself. Like a spell running its natural course. Blaming them had been the lie she told herself to guard against the horrible shame that swelled in her chest now, incendiary and burning.

The knife was what Florian had made it; it had not made Florian.

*Power.*

Her life as a pirate, the murder, even now her time with Xenobia. All of it was just a desperate grab for any kind of power, to see herself lifted above the wretchedness of her birth, to know that she might be worthy of something more, to know that maybe she could have something more. And she was willing to kill for it.

*But — oh.*

*Love.*

She was love as much as she was lies and a hope for power. For in her lying, terrible heart was the love for her brother, dormant these many weeks. The brother too gentle to kill, too fragile for life aboard the *Dove,* but who lived that life anyway so that he might ensure a home for Flora. How had she lived for this time not seeing it, not feeling it? And yet, even as she wondered, she knew the answer. It was what Xenobia had taken. She'd felt it leave, but she had not known what it was.

It was not the only thing the witch had taken from Flora.

*Evelyn.*

She thought of the warm press of her hand in Evelyn's, the gentle press of her lips. Evelyn had understood. Evelyn could see that Flora was many things, some contradictory, and that did not matter. Evelyn loved Florian *and* Flora. If Florian was the wall that guarded Flora, then Evelyn had scaled his heights. Evelyn had loved her before Flora could have loved herself, had guided Flora to a life worth living with her affection. Because what had her life been before Evelyn? What was her life without Alfie? Their love defined her life; it was the part of the story that had been missing, the most important part. Yes, she was an orphan, a sister, a pirate, a girl, and also a boy. But more importantly, she was a person who sought power to protect those she loved.

Including herself. Or himself. Both were equally true to her. Neither told the whole story.

For what was any of it, the lying and the shame, the desperation and the desire, other than a devotion to protecting herself? To surviving?

Distantly, Flora was aware of the sound of glass shattering, of cries of surprise, of chairs being pushed away from a table and footsteps on the earthen floor. But those noises meant nothing, were nothing to her. She felt Xenobia's cool hands on her cheeks, heard the sound of the man's frantic voice but not the content of his words.

She lay on the ground of the hallway, drenched in sweat, her mind and body both too exhausted to move or care or do anything other than to weep and to breathe and to hear the pounding of her heart in her ears.

And though she could not see it, she knew the same way she knew she could hold two identities in her heart at once, the way she knew she could be a murderer and beloved, complicit and brave, that the looking glass was mended.

## CHAPTER 36

*Evelyn*

It was a point of great irony to Evelyn that her mother's excruciatingly boring education of Imperial architecture might save her from the terrible arrangement her parents had made for her marriage. Just the thought of it brought a smile to her lips.

For Commander Callum's keep was, indeed, modeled exactly after that of the 900th Emperor's. From close examination of her own quarters, she could find more than ample evidence to support it. The carved details in the beams of the ceiling. The eastward-facing windows. The two doors, one to the west and one to the north, each built of heavy mahogany. It was a replica of the palace. Which meant there were secret passages that wound all throughout the keep, and even, if Evelyn navigated carefully, out of it.

Claiming boredom, Evelyn requested some needles, thread, fabric, and a pair of scissors so that she might begin work on sewing her bridal kimono. It was, she thought, an admirably proper Imperial lie. Lida had brought her the requested materials without question, and even offered to help as she could, but Evelyn declined. She did not want Lida to be blamed for her escape. *Just the supplies,* she'd said, and brought right to her quarters was nearly everything she might need to escape.

Staring out the barred window of her chambers had proven to be valuable use of her time, after all. First, since it faced the east, her view pointed directly to the servants' quarters, which allowed her to learn the patterns of the servants — when they rose, when they ate, when they washed. Where they gathered, where they went, where they did their laundry. And second, it gave Evelyn the unlikely vantage point of seeing Commander Callum's guests — who invariably were Imperial soldiers. But in the last day, she had noted a strange and dramatic uptick in officers, each attended to by their own men as befitting their ranks.

The servants, distracted by their many new guests, were frantic. And with the arrival of so many new servants, there was a massive influx of new faces in the keep, and nobody seemed to recognize one another, and no one had time to care.

Last, it had given her time to pick off all the bright-red polish from her fingernails so they now looked torn and plain.

When her lunch was delivered, Evelyn focused on the servant who had brought it, a new girl she'd never seen before — likely temporary help to see to the influx of nobility at the keep. She was a young and timid thing, too, which was perfect.

"Oh, pardon me!" Evelyn called after her as soon as she had stepped clear of the door.

The girl peeped her head back in, and Evelyn met her uncomfortably close to the door so that the girl retreated slightly into the hall, granting Evelyn a rare glimpse of the hallway. It was empty. No servants. And more importantly, no Inouye, who had been absent for nearly a day now. "If you please," Evelyn said, trying her

258

best to hide the distraction from her voice. "I'd love some extra salt."

The girl bowed low as was polite, and was gone.

But she did not see how the door did not quite close behind her.

Evelyn grabbed the sack she'd made of the white wedding-kimono fabric, which held the scissors, and hastily stuffed the bread from her lunch in it as well. After checking the hallway once more, she stepped out into it and made for the yard where the servants hung their clothes, taking care to go steadily, never to look as though she were worried.

There on the lines, as always, were the newly cleaned clothes of the myriad people who lived in the keep. Evelyn hastily grabbed some boys' clothes — a white shirt, some wool trousers, a blue vest — and stuffed them into her sack with the bread and the scissors. Then, taking care that still no one watched, she scurried southeast, where — if Callum's keep was indeed a replica of the 900th Emperor's — there would be an entrance to a secret passageway.

And so off to the wine cellar Evelyn went.

It was a small, cool, dimly lit room with innumerable bottles of wine stacked from floor to ceiling on bamboo shelves. But in it, she knew, would be the entrance to the passageways.

She just had to find it.

She scanned the shelves, hunting for a break in the woodwork, but could not discern any. She shoved the tatami mats aside and felt along the wooden planks of the floor in vain for one that was loose. And then she began her examination of the wine bottles.

Most, she could see, were rice wine from the Imperial shore. No surprise there. Obviously, despite his location, Callum had done everything he could to afford himself the comforts of home.

But it did not seem that he touched his stores often, for there was a thick layer of dust over the bottles that Evelyn tried her best not to disturb, lest the evidence of her snooping be noticed.

It was as she was taking care not to molest the dust that she saw it. One bottle that shone, free of dust in the spattering of fingerprints that dotted its neck.

She reached out and pulled at the bottle. But it did not come free of the shelf.

Instead, the entire shelf swung silently open, revealing the passage that would lead Evelyn between the walls. She removed her shoes and stepped inside. The shelf swung closed behind her.

In the darkness and the solitude of the passageway, Evelyn started to furiously tear off her clothing. The dress would not do for her escape, marking as it did her identity as nobility far too clearly. It crumpled at her feet as she hastily pulled on the boys' clothing she had swiped.

She had done a poor job selecting it — the shirt was far too large. The vest accentuated her breasts, which would not do. And so she did her best to tuck the shirt into the pants, and left the vest on the ground with her dress. She'd have to go barefoot, but that was not unheard of among the peasant class. The dust and the grit from the floor of the secret passageway would serve to obscure her coddled, clean feet.

All that was left was her hair.

Evelyn pulled the scissors from her sack. They were cold to the touch and not the right kind of scissors, much too small for hair. She hoped they would do, hoped desperately that this plan would work.

It was a foolish moment to feel sentimental, but Evelyn loved her hair. She'd cared for it daily her entire life, painstakingly brushing every knot and snag from it, sifting her fingers through the silk of it. When she pictured herself, her hair was the only part she truly found beautiful.

But what price was beauty for freedom? From Callum and his cruelty. From Inouye and his burdensome desire. From captivity.

And so Evelyn cut. She cut and she cut, felt as her long locks drifted to her feet. Gulping back sobs, she did her best to keep silent as she cut away every tress. She kept cutting until she could feel her scalp prickle to the touch. Without a looking glass, Evelyn had no way of knowing what she looked like. Probably like a crazy person. But she ran her fingers over the soft stubble of her scalp and knew her hair, her long black hair, was gone.

Her transformation from Imperial noblewoman to servant boy was as complete as it could be. And while she knew she must leave with as much haste as possible, one thing still rankled her.

What was Callum up to?

If she did not find out now, she would never know. So Evelyn set off into the secret passages, in search of the meeting of Imperial officers she knew must be taking place.

It did not take long to locate the room where the meeting was being held—Commander Callum had ordered his entire wing emptied, so it was the only room with any voices in it at all. It was made especially easy by all the yelling.

"She operates on the Emperor's orders."

"The fact is the girl is *here*." It was Commander Callum's voice, just as terse as usual. "And by that mere fact, we can know that the Lady Ayer, no matter her competence, is not in control of this mission!"

"She's the Emperor's finest operative," another man's voice said. "You dare to interfere with her?"

The Lady Ayer? An operative? Evelyn's mind tumbled over itself. But she was so boring. So domestic. She'd brought along so many doilies.

"I interfere because the Hasegawa girl has not been sold upon the Red Shore as was planned," Callum said. "Without her, our excuse to invade the Red Shore is gone. Surely, the Guard will not be granted permission in this current congress. But if we want the Shore, we will have to let the *Dove* take an entirely new batch of our nobles, *our nobility,* sir, and frankly I will not abide it. The Hasegawa girl was perfect—young, beautiful, from an old and respected family. Even her parents agreed. All the Lady Ayer had to do was stick close to her and then report her death to all who could listen. She'd be the perfect corpse."

*Her parents had agreed.*

They had sold her into certain death. What better way to rid themselves of their shameful, crooked daughter than in service to the Emperor? No wonder her mother had been so pleased with the arrangement.

Pain like the Kiyohime poison beat through Evelyn's heart. She knew her parents had not approved of her, but they had been more than willing to trade her life for better standing in the court. She caught her breath and did her best to stifle the cry of agony.

"Well, then what do you suggest, sir? It seems the chicken has already flown the coop."

"We take the Hasegawa girl to the Red Shore!" Callum shouted. "She can do us no good here!"

They were never to be wed at all, Evelyn realized. She was always meant to be a sacrifice made for the benefit of Imperial greed. No wonder his greeting had been so cold. A martyr for the Empire. Surely her parents' "sacrifice" would have been rewarded. Perhaps her father's debts would have been paid.

"Commander Callum. No." The man who spoke now had a deep voice, with the unhalting manner of authority. "That makes little to no sense, and logistically, how do you suppose we explain it if the rest of the *Dove* does not make it there? Without the Lady Ayer to report her deceased, that whole mission is dead in the water. The fact is, our war with the Red Shore will have to wait. The priority now is the Pirate Supreme."

"Air," Commander Callum spat. "Air and lies. We do not even know that he exists."

"We do, Callum. The Lady's mission was not just to abet our claim to the Red Shore. It was, most importantly, to lead us to the Pirate Supreme. We have reason to believe that he, too, has an operative aboard the *Dove,* who could lead us to him. She's done some fine work forming an allegiance on that ship, and though I'm loath to say it, that woman is cunning. We cannot endanger her mission."

"But surely the Emperor must know there are great treasures to be had if we take the Shore!" Callum shouted. He sounded desperate.

"Won't matter if our merchant ships keep getting sacked by pirates. That's the real issue here, isn't it? Always has been. Without safe trade routes, no conquest will matter."

"True! And with the Supreme gone, it'll only be a matter of a few short years before we take the Red Shore," said another voice. "The Lady Ayer is no fool. She'll send word. Our ships are faster, stronger, and bigger than any fleet on the open sea. Don't you fret."

"I should say, sir," said another voice jocularly, "you ought to be happy. You have a young woman to wed now, and her family's name to go along with it."

"Word is she's not ugly."

"Yes, so her mother said. But her father told me the truth of it. She's crooked," Callum spat. The disgust in his voice was apparent.

"That's never stopped a man from taking his husbandly rights," one of the men chuckled. "It could be worse."

Evelyn was not sure how.

## CHAPTER 37

# *Rake*

Rake hauled Cook up the main staircase by his armpits. It was no easy task. Cook was a large man, and being dead, he was of little help. How Rake wished Cook had been killed in his kitchen — it could have been pinned on anyone then. But he had not been in the galley; he'd been in the officers' cabins. And only he, Alfie, and the captain could claim cabins there these days. No one would believe Alfie had done it, and Rake certainly couldn't accuse the captain.

Which raised the question: Why had Cook been on the upper deck at all?

The treasure?

Rake would have to claim that he caught Cook trying to steal the treasure. But it would have been ruthless to kill him for such a crime, and rather unlike Rake. Cook was useful, after all. And everyone knew that he was no thief.

If only there were a better story. But Rake could not conjure one. He'd have to rely on the crew's fear of him, their trust that he was the captain's man.

At least it was night. Rake hoped against all odds that the night crew was shirking their watch.

But when he reached the half deck, he was seen. Of course he was seen. The alarm was sounded — likely, Rake thought, by men trying to be of assistance to him. He was first mate, after all. It was time to act the part.

"Cook?"

"Captain find out about the bilge rats?"

"What'll we eat?"

Rake lay Cook down and clutched his sides, still panting from effort. "Get the captain," he ordered. The captain had, by some miracle, not been in the great cabin, so he was likely in the brig, availing himself upon one of the prisoners. Rake tried not to imagine who was the unfortunate soul this time.

As the men ran to do as he'd commanded, Rake closed Cook's eyes. He would have been dead soon anyway, Rake reminded himself. Most of these men would be. Several of the Supreme's ships would be along any day now, flying the mermaid flag. The captain had been less vigilant this time while plotting his course. They'd catch him — Rake was sure of it.

All he needed to do was live until then. Then he would be safe. Safe, and free of the burden of his awful pretense. Days had become weeks, had become months, had become years under the command of this man, this man Rake hated. Every day, Rake had contemplated simply slitting the man's throat and pushing his body into the Sea. But that was not the Pirate Supreme's way, and Rake was the Pirate Supreme's man. Justice was so close, finally, to the Nameless Captain.

For the first time since taking the mission, Rake wondered what might happen to the *Dove* once the captain was removed. She was a fine ship, well built. The wooden woman figurehead had long since been worn down, so that the curls of her hair were only suggestions thereof. Time had rendered her face indiscernible. She could be anyone, and who'd remember otherwise?

When the captain came, he hardly looked surprised. The itch of worry spread through Rake's body, but he held himself as though he were simply angry.

"Found this louse digging about in your maps, sir," Rake said. "He drew a knife on me when I caught him."

The men murmured among themselves. No one had been fool enough to draw on Rake in years. He'd long since proven himself deadly to the crew. But the captain only nodded.

"And why do you suppose he was in my maps?" the captain asked. His voice was calm, almost disinterested, as if there were nothing Rake could tell him that he had not already known or guessed.

"I think, sir"—Rake leaned closer so that he would not be overheard—"I think he was the rat we'd been looking for."

It was a ballsy lie. Cook was one of the captain's most loyal men. He had been for more years than Rake had been on board certainly, perhaps for more than he'd been alive.

"Is that what you think? You think Cook here, this fat, silly slob, was an operative of the Pirate Supreme?" The captain hardly made an effort to keep his voice down, as Rake had. The crewmen hushed, their bodies like a wall around Rake. One did not speak of the Pirate Supreme lightly.

"I do," Rake said. He kept his voice even, thankfully.

"Then why did you not keep him alive, hm? I should have liked to question him, if he were the traitor we seek."

"As I said, sir. He pulled a knife on me."

"In my cabin."

"Yes, sir."

"And so you slew him, right then and there?"

"Yes, sir."

"So his blood stains the floor of my cabin?"

Shit.

Rake said nothing.

He could feel the men around him, could feel their eyes and their breath. It seemed no one blinked.

"The thing is, Rake," the captain went on, "I sent dear old Cook to look after you."

It was a beautiful night, Rake thought. Clear. He took a deep breath and let the cool sea air fill his lungs, let his eyes drift to the multitude of stars that shone above. He thought of the day he stood on the Supreme's gallows. For Rake, Death was always near. He felt the brush of its long fingers daily aboard the *Dove*, felt it in the shadow he cast. But on the gallows, and now, he could feel Death as though it stood just next to him.

His lifelong companion. His only friend.

The captain nodded and several of the men stepped forward, toward Rake. "It seems we have found our rat, after all." Rake shivered at the cold of the cuffs that were snapped into place around his wrists.

He turned and saw Fawkes. Of course it was Fawkes. Fawkes smiled his terrible smile back at Rake.

"Now, then," Fawkes hissed. "Times, they are a-changing, eh?" And he laughed.

Rake breathed in deeply, steadying himself for the pain he knew was to come. He was caught. The worst was only just beginning.

But though the captain did not see it, an albatross flew overhead at that moment. It was unnoticed by all except Rake.

268

## CHAPTER 38

## *Flora*

lora slapped Xenobia's hand away from her face.

"You lied to me." She tried her best to sit up, but still exhaustion racked her body. She settled onto her elbows so that at least she met the witch's eyes, which were as cold as the floor beneath her.

"I have never," Xenobia retorted. "I didn't need to," she added when Flora only glared at her dubiously.

The man, whom Flora had never seen before, still stood in the doorway, looking simultaneously puzzled and angry. "Who is this?" he asked, motioning wildly at Flora, but both she and Xenobia ignored him.

"You could be so much stronger." Xenobia's voice still held its knife's edge, but Flora found it no longer cut through her as it once had.

She had trusted her.

Just as Rake had told her not to.

She had believed her.

Even as she stole her love for Alfie away.

She had listened.

Even as Evelyn was held captive by Imperial swine.

"Why?" Flora asked.

"Think of the song," Xenobia said, and there was a note of pleading in her voice that Flora had not heard before. "The only one you know."

"You speak nonsense."

"It is you. The song is you, if you would just —"

But before Xenobia could finish, the man pulled her to her feet and pushed her roughly out of the way. He stood before Flora and stared down at her imposingly. She could see now that he was an Imperial officer, and it was all she could do not to sneer at him.

"Who are you?" he asked in an official tone.

Flora looked him up and down. Despite the tone of his voice, she could sense the unease that lurked, knew his story without him telling it. His story was a tale of fear. Scratch the surface of most Imperials and that's what lay beneath. For all their bluster, that's what they were. Afraid. That the Emperor's influence was not so great as they believed. That they were not so safe from the colonies. That they'd have to share. That criminals would get them. That witches would. That was why they killed. That was why they burned. And this one. He was among witches and he knew it.

*He should not have come alone.*

"You say you want help with the Lady Hasegawa?" Flora shot back.

"Flora, no —" Xenobia tried to interject.

"Be still, woman!" the man shouted, and just like that — like the fall of one foot after the other, easy, inevitable, and immediate — he struck Xenobia. The back of his hand collided with her face, and the witch stumbled back, clasping her cheek where his blow had landed.

Flora felt her heart harden against him.

"I will help you," Flora told him through gritted teeth. "Even if she will not."

"Who are you?" the man asked.

"The witch you came looking for."

Behind him, Xenobia slumped to the floor, her back against the wall, shaking her head.

*Good.*

## CHAPTER 39

*Evelyn*

The notion of revenge was not something that struck Evelyn as a purpose. She had her petty moments, small rebellions. But now fury built in Evelyn's chest, brick by brick, until it formed a fortress against these men, her parents, and their cruel plans. How casually they discussed her demise. How thirsty they were for more power, more land, more trade routes. Already, the Nipran Empire was spread across nearly every nation. With the sack of Quark, what more could they possibly need? What resource was not already available to them in abundance?

Their greed sickened her. These men of power, these men who had raised her. Who taught them such cruelty? Who allowed them such means?

She would not abide them any longer.

And still, aboard the *Dove* remained one of their operatives, bent on catching the Pirate Supreme's man.

Evelyn could not let these men win. Not that she bore the crew of the *Dove* much affection — she had been but chattel to them, a prize yet to be realized. But instinct told her that she knew who the Pirate Supreme's man was. And she owed him her life. If she could save him, if she could thwart these men, then her life would have finally had use.

She had to find Florian.

If she wanted to make her escape, she'd need to do it when the servants were most distracted. So when one of the men mentioned that dinner should be along shortly, Evelyn knew it was time to leave the passages and make her break. It was slow going — in the dark, which was complete, through the spiderwebs. But, keeping her left hand to the wall, she followed the passages until she could smell fresh air.

She promised herself that when she breathed free once more, she would see these men ruined.

When she breathed free once more, she would fight back.

She waited by the end of the passage for some time, trying her best to gauge the location. Footsteps passed by, then echoed away, and from the sound of them she could guess the passage opened into a stone hallway. When no more footsteps came, Evelyn cautiously pushed against the dead end of the passage. For a moment, it did not budge, and Evelyn feared it was, in fact, only a dead end and not a door. But with more effort, she heard first the grind of grit beneath stone and then felt the shudder of the passage opening.

The light was, after so many hours in the passageway, too much to bear. But she could not be caught emerging, so she hurried into it even as it burned through her eyelids. Hastily, she shut the door behind her and blinked furiously, trying to gain her bearings.

It was indeed a stone hallway, though Evelyn had not realized it had opened outside, directly into the evening. The sun had begun its descent, but she could still see the bleeding red orb just over the stone perimeter walls of the keep. With the sunset, she'd have an even better chance — darkness could act as a mask over her face.

Doing her best with her bare feet, she spread the dust kicked loose by the passage in the hall. When she heard another set of footsteps from around the corner, she made the quick decision to simply walk toward it, head bowed, playing the part of a lowly servant boy simply passing between his many duties.

To Evelyn's horror, Lida turned the corner and gave Evelyn a double take, which Evelyn clocked as recognition. The servant girl was holding a basket full of laundry and flanked by a couple of new faces Evelyn didn't recognize. For a moment, they simply stared at each other.

What could she say? There was nothing. They stood in silence for what felt like too long of a time.

"Carlos, you are so silly," Lida said. "You are not needed here — you're needed at the gates to help unload the carts." She held Evelyn's eyes, her lips curled into a flirtatious smile. "Yes?"

Relief and gratitude washed over Evelyn, and she hoped that if she felt it strongly enough, Lida would feel it, too. Evelyn coughed, dropped her voice low. "'Course." She bowed in the stiff-legged way men were supposed to.

"Get on, then." Lida moved past Evelyn, and the two new girls trailed after her, giggling. They clearly thought they had witnessed a simple flirtation rather than the escape of a prisoner. "It's over there, you silly boy, or did you already forget?" She pointed lazily to the south and kept moving. "The pretty ones are always the dumbest," Evelyn heard Lida say to the girls, who cackled their agreement.

What Evelyn had done to deserve Lida's kindness, she did not know. She prayed for a moment that she might be able to repay her, then took off at a run in the direction the servant girl had pointed.

When she reached the gate, a guard stood in her way, his arms crossed over his chest. She could tell right away that he was of Nipranite blood, probably from an old family, judging by his perfectly erect posture. Probably resentful of his low station, probably bored.

"Where d'you think you're going, boy?"

"On an errand for the cook," Evelyn replied quickly. Not too quickly, she hoped. "He needs more eggs for the morning meal tomorrow, what with all the fine men visiting."

"Market's closed."

"That's true," Evelyn said. "But word is there's a lady who lives in the cliffs and stays open all night." When the guard looked at her dubiously, she added, "Please, sir. I can't imagine how angry Cook'll be if we're short provisions."

"We've got orders to keep everyone in for the night."

"Yeah, I know. But there's Imperial officers in our estate tonight, sir. We'll all look like backwater bumpkins if we can't feed 'em. And when that happens, I don't want to be on the brunt of Commander Callum's rancor." She leaned in conspiratorially to the guard and whispered: "You know what they say about him. New money and all."

The guard chuckled. Evelyn had pegged him correctly. "Right you are. On your way, but be quick. We change shifts in two hours, and if I'm not here, you'll have to explain yourself all over again."

"Right!" Evelyn practically shouted. At least now she had an excuse to run. "I'll be back before you know it!"

So off she ran, into the night.

But she'd hardly made it a hundred strides before someone grabbed her by the wrist. Before she could even yell out, a hand clamped over her mouth and she was held, one hand behind her back, barely able to breathe in the tight embrace of a person she could not see.

"Shhhh," the man hissed in her ear, hot and wet.

Evelyn screamed into his hand and fought against his hold. But neither her voice nor her body had the strength to see her will done. She'd been caught.

## CHAPTER 40

*Flora*

"Y ou will regret this," Xenobia said.

But Flora ignored her.

Instead, she led Inouye out of the witch's home. The sun was just beginning to set, just now becoming heavy, dipping on the horizon. Inouye bounced from one foot to the other nervously once they were outside. Being seen with Flora was, she guessed, incriminating all on its own. What would an Imperial soldier be doing with an urchin like her? And if that weren't enough, being seen cavorting with a witch was, by Imperial law, a capital offense.

Still, he stayed by her side, if several comfortable feet from her.

"Let's just do this here," Flora said. The witch's porch was as good a place as any. Inouye nodded eagerly.

The spell would be an easy one. For the man whose name she'd learned was Inouye was more impressionable than even the stone had been. He wanted so badly to have Evelyn, was so desperate in his longing, that he would accept Flora's story without even a blink.

She took Inouye's hand, and though the feeling of his skin on hers disgusted her, she held it and his eye contact firmly. She could feel his reluctance in his touch, could feel his fear.

"Do you love her?" Flora asked him.

Inouye paused, shuffled his feet a little uncomfortably. "Yes?" he said, but it was more of a question.

His indecision disgusted Flora. It was all she could do not to roll her eyes. Only an Imperial man would go to such lengths for something he wasn't even sure he wanted. Only an Imperial man would be so confounded by not having gotten what he wanted with ease. How upset he must be, that this one time the world did not grant him his heart's desire on his first request.

"Listen," she said. "But listen well, for this spell has a cost. If you should dishonor this spell or speak of it to anyone, it will break and you will never love again. The mechanisms that turn in your heart shall rust and erode; they will dissolve into dust in your chest. You will never know the softness of a lover's lips nor share a cry of pleasure or the quiet shelter of a lover's arms. Do you understand?"

"Yes," he said. His eyes were alight with desire. But he was not listening, not really. He simply waited expectantly in that way men sometimes did when waiting for their chance to talk.

"Then listen to me, Tomas Inouye, and hear these words: You will find your heart's desire, and you will hold her close. You will feel the press of her against you, will take her hand in yours, and you will lead her to love. Your love will make your love's love a reality. Your love will lead her to love; your affection will see her free. And neither of you will ever return to Commander Callum's keep. This is the next chapter of your story. See that it begins now."

Again and again she said the words. As she spoke, Flora could feel the wind in her lungs, the Sea in her belly. She gripped his hand and felt how easily he'd accepted her tale, his grip tightening on hers. He was so hungry, despite the feast that had been his whole life. His eyes were clouded with his greed, and he did not see.

"Yes," he said. "Yes."

"Come, then," Flora said. "Let's go get the Lady Hasegawa."

## CHAPTER 41

## *Evelyn*

The man pulled Evelyn several steps before finally letting go. She whirled on him and sucked in a breath.

"Inouye?"

His face was drawn with pain, his eyes strangely distant. His mouth opened and closed like a fish's, seemingly unable to speak. Evelyn took a step away from him experimentally, but he shifted toward her, mirroring her movement. He was bigger than her, and stronger. She doubted she could simply make a run for it.

"Your hair," he said faintly.

Evelyn opened her mouth to respond, but he took her by the hand once more. And try as she did to shake her fingers from his grasp, he held fast, pulling her along the cobblestone streets.

"Where are you taking me?" she demanded.

Inouye did not respond.

If he was leading her to Callum, he was leading her in the wrong direction. As they hustled down the streets, the keep grew smaller and smaller behind them until all Evelyn could see of it was the torch of the tallest parapet, a tiny speck of light nearly indistinguishable from the stars.

They passed the Imperial church, passed the marketplace where merchants were hurriedly shutting down shop, all the way to the cliff's edge. The elevators still ran, though not as frequently. The donkeys that powered the pulleys looked as tired as Evelyn felt. And though Evelyn asked, again and again, what they were waiting for, Inouye did not or could not answer. Again and again he opened his mouth, but no sound was ever produced. He filled the silences he created by staring at her scalp, his mouth twisted in an obvious display of disgust.

Evelyn shivered, but this time Inouye did not offer her his coat.

There was a shudder of gears, and then one of the donkeys grunted. Soon all three were walking in their steady circle, slow and plodding. Below, Evelyn could hear an elevator rising.

Inouye looked down and grimaced.

When the elevator crested the cliff, Evelyn gasped.

There stood Florian, wearing a smile, wide and warm. Inouye released Evelyn from his grasp, and before she could think in words, before she could audit her new reality, before she could question why Inouye — of all people — had brought her here, she was running to Florian, she was in Florian's arms, she was kissing Florian and Florian was kissing her back.

She was unaware of Inouye as he slunk away into the night.

She was unaware of the stares their embrace brought.

All that mattered was that Florian was there.

Tears filled her eyes, spilling onto her cheeks, onto Florian's. But she did not care.

"Florian," she whispered. And how at home she felt, how right.

As though the crook of Florian's neck had been constructed with the purpose of cradling Evelyn's face.

But Florian pulled back and held Evelyn's eyes in his own. "Flora. Also."

"All right." Evelyn smiled. The name suited Florian, felt right on Evelyn's lips. What it meant, Evelyn didn't care. All that mattered was Florian — Flora — and the closeness of their bodies.

## CHAPTER 42

*Flora*

How she loved the way Evelyn's lips curled around her name.

"Flora."

The spell had worked. The truth of it kept Flora's face pulled into a perpetual smile. It had worked. And it had only worked because Evelyn loved her, truly, bindingly. If it were not so, she would not have found her with that fool soldier, simply waiting for her.

Xenobia's warning seemed a silly thing. How could she ever regret this, the feeling of Evelyn in her arms, of their reunion at long last, of her lips covering her own?

"Do you . . . ? Should I call you by he or she? Or they?" Evelyn asked. She didn't seem to care which, and for that, Flora was more grateful than she could say. After all of the time spent worrying, fretting, over the lie that was Florian, and now she could be anything. She could be herself. Florian smiled.

"I guess it doesn't really matter. Any of them feel true."

"All right, then," said Evelyn. And she kissed Flora's fingers.

They rode the elevators down to the shore so that they might be away from the eyes that seemed to stare from all directions. Evelyn may not have known it, but Flora was well aware that the Floating Islands did not boast a particularly elastic culture of acceptance when it came to love. And with Evelyn's hair shorn and Flora's questionable appearance, they certainly did not look like a man and woman the Islanders — or Imperials for that matter — would expect to be romantically entangled.

For hours, it seemed, neither could find words, let alone use them. In the quiet of the cove they found, their shared happiness could not be expressed with speech. Spoken words were useless then, just noise, air. Flora folded into Evelyn's arms, let herself be enveloped in her kiss. And with a sureness she had never known before, she knew she was loved.

Flora. Florian.

The pirate.

The liar.

She was loved and she was safe in Evelyn's arms and she was warm in her embrace. Evelyn's lips traced a burning line from her neck to the jut of her collarbone, and Flora understood the strange communion of simultaneous hunger and satisfaction of love. How full she felt, with Evelyn's flesh beneath her fingers. How ravenous she felt from the scrape of Evelyn's teeth on her lower lip, the press of Evelyn between her legs.

Immune to the chill of the night air. Immune to the crash of the Sea. And though exhaustion nipped at them both, neither could close their eyes. Neither could look away from the other.

"I thought you left me," Florian said.

"Never," Evelyn said. And she kissed the fear from Flora's voice.

"I wonder if Rake knew," Flora mused between kisses. "If that was why he let us go."

To her acute disappointment, Evelyn pulled away from her. "Rake," she whispered. And Flora could see from the way her face fell that whatever news was to come, it was bad. Evelyn took Flora's hands in hers and sighed deeply. "We have to save him," she said.

"Rake doesn't need saving," Florian said immediately.

"He does, though. And Alfie, too."

At the mention of her brother's name, Flora froze. That Alfie needed saving was certainly something she could believe.

As Evelyn spoke, Flora felt dread building in her chest. The joy of their reunion dissipated into the cool of the predawn air. Evelyn was right. They had to return to the *Dove*. Go back to the life Flora had wanted so desperately to escape. For Rake. And for Alfie.

And, loath though she was to admit it, for the other Imperial prisoners. She may have fallen in love with only one of them, but that did not mean the others weren't human as well, as deserving of life as Evelyn. She could not separate people like this anymore, not even Imperials.

"They were willing to see us all dead," Evelyn said. "All of us were expendable."

Flora had magic now, but what could she do? She'd have to return to the *Dove*. *And then what?* She gritted her teeth against the growing realization that she was the only one who could help.

*Well, not the only one.*

"We have to do what's right," Evelyn said.

*Save the prisoners. Save Rake. Save Alfie. Protect the Pirate Supreme. Protect the Sea. Thwart the Lady Ayer.*

"I know," Flora said. "I know."

# The Sea

There are countless ships in her waters, but only one is hers.

It only sails to serve the Sea.

She feels the Leviathan more than she sees it. Her eyes are not what they used to be, so many of her waters clouded and murky now, polluted. But she feels the Leviathan as it pushes away from port like the farewell kiss of a lover.

In her shallows, she feels the many schools of fish part, making way.

Eels slip back into the safety of their coral homes.

In her depths, an anglerfish douses her light.

First one shark, long and cold, follows in the Leviathan's wake. Then many.

*And all the while, above, the seagulls circle and call.*

*Blood is coming.*

*The Sea knows this, and she swells in anticipation. The* Leviathan *is her ship, her gift to humanity. She made it herself, from the bones of ships she'd swallowed before, cannons stolen from sunken decks. It is kissed by mermaids. It bears her blessing. It rose from her depths, and it was a gift of her as much as it was a gift from her.*

*A promise was made: to protect the mermaids from man.*

*A deal was struck: a ship to see it done, and blood to pay its price.*

*A treaty was made: protection for protection.*

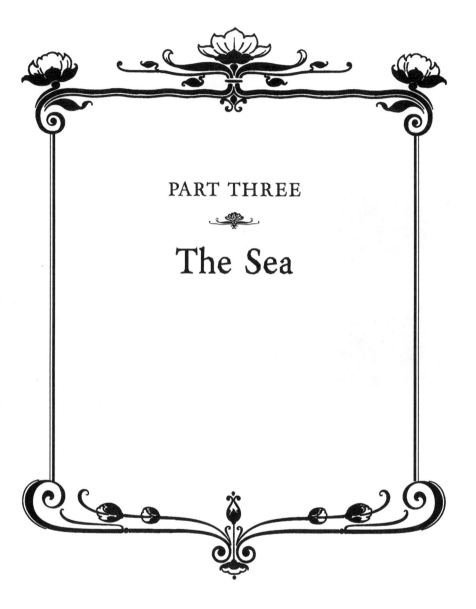

PART THREE

The Sea

◆ CHAPTER 43 ◆

*Evelyn*

Flora purchased a small boat with the money she'd taken as payment from Inouye. The vendor had laughed at her, at them both, when he realized they meant to take it past the bay.

"Idiots!" he'd said, laughing. "You boys never find anything out there, and you die." Neither Flora nor Evelyn made to correct him on either count, and ultimately, he'd accepted their money.

After they rowed out past the break, Flora told Evelyn they'd need to sit still for a while, and so — if she could — to stay silent. It was, Evelyn thought, a clever way to ask. Of course she could, but making it a challenge made it something Evelyn would relish. And so she sat, silently, as Flora tried her best at her second spell cast without Xenobia's careful supervision.

The revelation that Flora was now a witch had been a lot to take in the abstract. It was even stranger to accept now that Flora was attempting a spell in front of Evelyn.

She had never had a moment to appreciate the Floating Islands from afar, and now she could see where their name came from — mostly obscured by the fog, it looked as though they were suspended impossibly in the air. On those islands in the distance, Lida pretended not to know where Evelyn had gone. On those islands, Commander Callum seethed with rage. The witch waited. The markets would be open and loud with commerce. They were beautiful.

Evelyn never wanted to see them again.

Flora's face was screwed tight in fierce concentration as she murmured words Evelyn could not quite decipher. Her eyes did not waver from the small knife she clutched in her fist so tightly that her knuckles shone white from the effort. It was, Flora had told her, a knife Alfie had given her. It would lead them to the *Dove*, she said. If she could do the spell.

It did not appear to be working. Part of Evelyn was nearly thankful for that. She knew, of course, that basically everything she'd been taught as a child had been a lie. But it was hard to shake the notion that witches were evil, especially since one had just sold her out so coldly. It seemed impossible that her beloved Flora would be one.

"Listen," Flora said. "You are a knife that binds, and you bind me to my brother. You will take me to him. You will put me where I belong, at his side, together again as we are meant to be."

But nothing happened. They were not, in fact, close to Alfie, nor the *Dove* for that matter. They sat in the boat, Evelyn playing her game of silence, as the sun beat down on them, the winds picked up and then died again, and the sun set.

But still, Flora chanted.

"You do not cut anymore; you will never cut again. You bind me to Alfie, and Alfie to me."

It was just as Evelyn thought it may be time to gracefully break the bad news that Flora was not, in fact, a practical witch when it happened.

"I can't believe it!" Evelyn cried. Which was true. She couldn't.

"Neither can I." Flora looked around, bemused.

It seemed she had only blinked, and when she'd opened her eyes once more, the Floating Islands were gone. Instead, on the horizon, she could see a ship. The air, which had been warm and without wind just a moment ago, whipped Evelyn's skin with freezing seawater. It gusted with the power of the open sea, and their little boat rocked.

Flora had some new talents, indeed.

So much of what Evelyn understood and knew about the world had changed since leaving Crandon. Florian was Flora, and Flora was a witch. Magic was real. The Emperor's forces were cruel and unjust. Her parents were happy to see her dead if it meant a settlement of their debt. The Pirate Supreme was not just a myth made up by superstitious sailors. Witchcraft was just a skill, like reading or dancing, capable of being taught.

"The *Dove*," Flora said, whispering at first. "The *Dove*!" she cried.

It should have been harder to accept. And yet. Somehow, this new reality, Evelyn knew, was as right as her life had ever felt. Magic was real, and she was in love. These truths held hands in Evelyn's mind, entwined.

They each picked up an oar and made to paddle to the boat. It was night, at least, and they prayed they would not be immediately spotted. Flora thought if they could sidle up along the starboard side, she would be able to reach the rigging and climb aboard the *Dove* undetected. Evelyn would have to do the same, a task that Flora had full confidence in Evelyn accomplishing. Evelyn was not quite so sure of herself, but she did not wish to hinder their mission.

"You're going to do well," Flora said. She gripped Evelyn's hand and squeezed reassuringly.

"I wish I shared your confidence." Evelyn tried to smile, but it didn't take.

"You just escaped an Imperial commander to come find me. And you doubt yourself now?"

"I'll just say you're somewhat more equipped for this than I am." This time the smile did take.

"You're the smartest person I know, and I need you if we're going to pull this off."

"Do you need some flowers arranged, or —?"

But Flora cut her off with a stern look. She took Evelyn's hands in her own and held her eyes meaningfully.

"You are my love and my equal, and we will see each other through this. If you had not been here to remind me of my conscience, we would not even be here. We're in this together. Yes?"

"Yes," Evelyn said. She kissed Flora's hand.

Then up they climbed.

The rigging was taut, and it hurt Evelyn's hands even sooner than she'd expected. The combination of the wetness and the texture of the coarse rope tore at her soft skin. *Good,* she thought. *Who needs soft hands, anyway?*

Flora was nearly a body's length ahead of her, and she looked back periodically to check on Evelyn. In her periphery, Evelyn was aware of their boat floating away.

There was no escape now.

◆ CHAPTER 44 ◆

# *Genevieve*

Genevieve tried not to look at the blood. Not directly, at least. She was aware of it, of course. She could smell it so strongly that she could nearly taste it. But she did not want to look at it, if at all possible. She knew blood was a part of her life, but she did not like it.

The Lady Ayer was a flurry of activity. As soon as Rake had stepped from the room, she'd started strapping her various pistols and blades to their particular hiding places around her body. The dagger at her ankle. The pistol at her thigh. But Genevieve knew the time had come when she pulled the samurai sword — earned in years of service to the Emperor — and strapped it visibly across her back.

Genevieve felt her face crack into a grin. How lucky she had been to be blessed with the Lady Ayer as her mentor. How lucky she'd been to be selected for training as an operative at all. She was young, but not as young as she looked; she was told she could pass for twelve. But she was fifteen, and she was being trained by the Emperor's finest female operative, his *only* female operative, a fact that left Genevieve suspended in a nearly constant state of heart-thundering pride.

Because if she was worthy of being trained by the best, Genevieve reasoned, it was likely that she, too, was thought to be the best of her generation. And Genevieve had no intention of proving anyone wrong on that count.

"Thanks to the Emperor, we have delivered the captain his operative," the Lady said. "Now it is his turn to deliver."

"The Pirate Supreme." Genevieve's voice was a whisper. The Supreme had evaded more than one of the Emperor's finest operatives. But he'd never sent his best.

The Lady Ayer smiled. "We shall have the scum in shackles by morning. I'm afraid poor Rake is in for a tough night."

Genevieve nodded. Of course he was. What did he expect? For an operative of the Pirate Supreme, he was not nearly as smart as Genevieve had assumed he would be. When the Lady Ayer had briefed her, she'd come aboard the *Dove* expecting the operative to be nigh impossible to spot, like smoke. But there he was, with his bright-red hair, his eyes ever watching the captain.

She liked Rake, in the way any law-abiding citizen could like a criminal — which was to say, she appreciated his utility in this short window but was not terribly sad to know their time as enforced allies was over. Besides, his animosity for the Imperial Guard had been clear, and Genevieve could not and would not abide his irrationality. She was not of Imperial blood, either, but that did not cloud her judgment. She'd been eager to leave Quark for just this reason. She could not stand being surrounded by those who acted against their own self-interest.

"You've done fine work here, my lady."

The Lady Ayer turned and regarded Genevieve warmly. Genevieve knew her comment did not demand any response, knew she could never demand anything of the Lady. But all the same, the Lady reached out a hand and ran it down Genevieve's cheek affectionately.

"Thank you, sweet girl. You know how disappointed I was when that Hasegawa girl managed to bungle her role. Alas, Callum will have to find another excuse for war, won't he?" She rolled her eyes. "Men. Always thinking about conquest, never about logistics. If you can't get shipments to and from a colony, what's the point in having it? But I dare say you're not wrong. The Pirate Supreme. Quite the prize."

"Quite the prize," Genevieve echoed proudly. "Thanks to the Emperor." She kissed her fingers, and the Lady Ayer beamed at her.

"Well. Let's not celebrate before the fight's won. Have you all the weapons you require?"

Genevieve patted her sides, accounting for each of the blades and pistols she carried beneath her kimono. "Yes, my lady."

"Good girl. Let's go make the Empire proud, shall we?" She opened the door to the cabin and stepped daintily over Cook's blood.

Abovedeck, the men of the *Dove* seemed stymied. Certainly, none had ever imagined that their first mate was anything short of the captain's man, through and through. And yet there was Rake, shackled at the wrists and tied to a mast.

When he saw the Lady Ayer, saw the sword across her back, he swore loudly.

Even in the night, Genevieve could see that Rake was glaring not at the Lady Ayer but at *her*, his eyes aflame against the dark sky. She was hardly surprised. She could sense him, always, sizing her up, trying to see the Quark in her, smell the rice paddy on her, though she'd all but trained it away. He could hate her all he wanted now. He wouldn't be alive for much longer.

The captain reached for the Lady's hand and gave it an audibly wet kiss across the knuckles. "I trust your hidey-hole has been lavishly comfortable?" he asked.

If she did not know the Lady so well, she would not have recognized the distaste that furrowed her brow for only a fraction of a second. In fact, the tiny space where the Lady and Genevieve had been hiding — a cupboard-size secret hold behind the bookshelf the Lady had installed in her cabin — was anything but comfortable. It was cramped and wet and smelled like feet. Surely, the captain knew that. Surely, he'd known that when he made his deal with the Lady all those months ago. Surely, he'd had a good laugh at their expense, imagining them with their knees to their chins for hours on end.

The Lady held her composure well, though, and her chin high. "Absolutely not, sir. I am glad to be abovedeck, and I'll thank one of your men for bringing as fresh of food as you can muster for my girl and for me. Those apples you left for us were hardly adequate."

She snatched her hand back from the captain and pulled a spyglass from her sleeve. She scanned the horizon briefly, then stowed it away once more. "Our ships are but an hour away."

"Great," the captain said. He sounded, Genevieve realized, a little drunk. "Fantastic."

"Food?" the Lady reminded him, a little irritably.

"We'll do what we can. What with the cook bein' dead." The captain bowed with facetious theatricality, then clapped his hands. A sailor stepped forward, and the captain ordered him to fetch something good from the kitchens for the Lady and for Genevieve.

"You'll all die, you know," Rake shouted. "Imperials are coming! Do you think they will spare you? Do you think they'll consider honoring a treaty with crim—" But before he could finish, the man standing next to him, a huge man with the build of a wall, punched him across his jaw, silencing him. There was some murmuring from the men, but none stepped forward. Surely, they must have heard the truth in Rake's words. Yet all were too cowardly to speak to it.

"There now, Fawkes, that'll do. I imagine the Lady here would like our Rake intact."

"Quite right."

The man called Fawkes shook out his fist and smiled. "You just let me know if you'd like him punched again, milady. I'd be happy to do it."

The Lady regarded him coolly but did not deign to respond. Instead, she turned to the captain once more. "I have done my part," she said. Her voice was like steel. "I am sure I need not remind you what shall happen if you do not do yours."

The smile fell from the captain's face. "Indeed not, ma'am."

"My lady," Genevieve corrected, and the captain had the propriety to at least appear abashed.

"Apologies. My lady." He barked some orders at the men to prepare the ship to be boarded. As they scurried about seeing his orders done, he turned to the Lady with an uncharacteristically worried look upon his face. "The deal is the same, then? I can keep my ship and —"

"But not your crew, I'm afraid. They've all seen too much."

The captain waved this away, as though their lives hardly mattered. They didn't, Genevieve supposed, but it was still a cruel gesture. "Yes, right, but the mermaids?"

The Lady gave him a patronizing smile. Genevieve knew, of

course, that pirates enjoyed the hallucinogenic effects of the mermaid's blood, but she hardly respected the tradition. Not because she disapproved of killing mermaids; on the contrary, according to the Lady Ayer, the Empire had nothing to lose and everything to gain from their demise. The capture of mermaids was hardly a credible pursuit for Imperial operatives such as the Lady, but it did serve the Empire's interests. The more the Sea forgot, the more memories stolen from her, the more egalitarian her waters would become. Finally, they would be free of the scourge of pirates. Their trade routes safe. Their control absolute.

The Emperor could not make the sea favor his ships. But he could rob her of her will to see them harmed.

"Yes, of course, man, you can still hunt your quarry of choice. When I return with reports of your good behavior, the Emperor will surely legalize the hunt of mermaids, and you'll do so on an Imperial stipend. So long as you deliver us your Supreme."

## CHAPTER 45

## Rake

The he albatross circled and left.

The wind had changed. Not just because Imperial sailors were boarding the *Dove*, though that certainly did not portend well for him. It changed in the way it always did as the Forbidden Isles grew near. He'd been so close to completing his mission, and to be thwarted in such tantalizing proximity to the end set his hands shaking with fury.

The Lady Ayer stood next to Rake proudly, as though he were an animal she had hunted, shot, and trussed. It served him right to trust an Imperial, even only by half. They were a cruel people, and if he ever freed his hands from his bindings, he'd see them wrapped around her thin, pale throat until the life faded from her eyes.

For his part, the captain stood at his helm, as though he couldn't be less concerned about all the Imperials now boarding his ship. And though he played the part well, Rake was an experienced enough actor to see that his vague smile did not touch his eyes, and that his hand fiddled absently with his spyglass, stretching it out and then closing it again.

Good. He should be nervous. He should be unhappy. His life was about to become Imperial property. And whatever the captain had said—on many occasions—about the Pirate Supreme, at least he respected them. All pirates did. And with this deal, the captain had committed the greatest and most irredeemable treason of all.

There were some stiff introductions between the Lady Ayer and the ranking Imperial officer before the officer bowed to her in that strange, formal way the Imperials did. So she outranked him. She wasn't just any Imperial; she was an important one, higher in regard than the commander of a fleet.

Rake wanted to kick himself. How had he not realized immediately that she was an Imperial operative? The leading questions. Her skill with the knife. The goddamn insignia on the blade, and he'd only distantly wondered if she was who she said she was. He was going to die, and he deserved it.

"Thanks to the Emperor," the Lady said. "Here's the Pirate Supreme's operative. It is my belief that he meant to lead this ship into the Supreme's grasp."

The officer nodded. Rake wanted to spit at him but didn't. No reason to court a beating right off the bat.

"Thanks to the Emperor. We'll interrogate him immediately," the officer said, but the Lady Ayer shook her head.

"I will. You may bear witness." She motioned to the Imperial sailors, who set about making Rake ready for transport belowdecks. He did not struggle. It would do no good to struggle.

Instead, he stared forward, looking over the deck of the *Dove*. She was a beautiful ship.

A flutter of movement, and Rake saw a foot as it slipped beneath one of the upturned spare boats. It was a bare foot, shining with recent wet. As though it had only just touched the Sea, perhaps, before climbing up the rigging. Onto the *Dove*. Not from the Imperial galleons. But from below.

A wet footprint remained in its wake.

He looked away, studiously fixing his eyes elsewhere so as not to draw attention to the foot and its owner.

"C'mon, then." One of the Imperial sailors hoisted Rake roughly away from the mizzenmast. Rake's hands were bound behind his back, and he was led down the great staircase to the captain's cabin.

He took care to keep his chin high as he walked. He would have the men of the *Dove* know that, even facing torture and death, Rake was still their first mate. And he did not fear any of that. No true pirate did. As he passed, several of the men nodded their farewells to him. Rake did not nod back.

He wondered what torture they had in store for him, and how long they would make it last before they killed him. He wondered what it would be like to die, and what awaited him on the other side.

He wondered what would happen when the *Leviathan* arrived — for it was already on its way, the Pirate Supreme themself aboard.

He wondered who the foot belonged to, and why it was there.

Hours later — surely, it must have been hours, it had to have been — the Lady Ayer washed her hands in a tub as Rake lay weeping on the table. She was calm in her demeanor, and efficient. She did not waste movement, did not waste words. And there was nothing Rake could do to stop her.

303

As soon as Rake had been properly bound to a chair in the captain's cabin, she'd gotten right to the point.

"Where is the Pirate Supreme's stronghold?"

But Rake had only shook his head. He did not wish to hear his voice betray the fear he knew was swelling in his chest. He would not have Imperial scum know the terror they wrought. He thought of Quark, thought of the flames. He did not forget. He would not make this easy for them.

The Lady had nodded then, and one of the Imperial officers stepped forward, the sleeves of his stupid, posh little uniform rolled up to his elbows. They were stupid uniforms, impractical for life on the Sea. Too much white in them.

He punched Rake in the gut. There was no air anymore, not for Rake. He gasped but said nothing. The Lady nodded again, and again the officer punched him, this time in the face. The man shook out his fist. Rake could see where he had skinned his knuckles on Rake's teeth. It had to sting, Rake knew. He spat a mouthful of blood onto the floor.

He'd smiled at the Lady Ayer then, a wide grin, knowing his teeth were red and disgusting.

"I see you're hoping to be difficult," she said. "Which is your prerogative, of course. But unfortunately, we're somewhat pressed for time. And so if you do not wish to cooperate?"

Rake kept on smiling his morbid smile.

"Then we'll have to go about this the quick way." She reached to the table and lifted a pitcher of water that stood there. It was an oddly hospitable gesture, as though she meant to pour him a glass so he could clean the blood from his teeth.

Instead, two of the sailors picked up the chair to which Rake was tied and slammed it down on the captain's table, so that Rake's head dangled off the edge of it. He stared up at the room, strange and upside down.

The Lady pulled a handkerchief from her breast and placed it carefully over Rake's face. It smelled just as a piece of silk tucked into an Imperial woman's cleavage would smell. Expensive.

"Now, Rake," the Lady said, her voice tinged with condescension, "we know who you are. What we want to know is where you were leading the Nameless Captain. Where is the Pirate Supreme's stronghold?"

But Rake did not reply.

"Remember, you were given a chance to answer under much more comfortable circumstances."

And then she started to pour.

It felt pleasant at first — Rake had not been able to wash in weeks. But the pleasantness subsided almost immediately once the water began to trickle sickly into his nose. He tried to open his mouth so that he could breathe but found that it, too, was filling with the wet cloth of the Lady's kerchief. He sputtered against it, but still the water came, insistent and terrible.

Soon, he was sure he was drowning.

Distantly, he was aware of his hands and feet thrashing against their constraints as he tried to right himself, tried to rip the cloth away from his face. He was dying; he was dying slowly and painfully, drowning on a table. His body fought and screamed against it.

The blackness of Death crowded in on him, and he welcomed it, for it was preferable to the unwavering pain of fighting for breath, feeling it elude him. His lungs howled, and he writhed in pain.

She pulled the kerchief from his face and smiled down at him beatifically. Rake gasped for breath, the joy of it filling his lungs more than he could bear.

"You can suffocate like this, you know," the Lady said coolly. "It's happened many times in interrogations. We call it dry drowning. A humiliating end for a sailor, don't you think? To spend your whole life tangling with the sea only to drown in a cupful of water?"

Rake said nothing but shook his head violently. He had no words anymore, no more breath for them. All he could think about, all he could hope for, was to stall another dose of torture.

"Let's try this again, shall we?" She smiled, and it touched her eyes; Rake could see it, her true joy in her work. She liked it, and she was good at it, and she was eager to get on with it. "Where is the Pirate Supreme's stronghold?"

Rake tried to keep the Supreme's face in his eye, to see them, the person who had granted him a life worth living. The person who had toasted to Manuel with him, the only person in the world, it seemed, who could hold strong against the Emperor and his many tentacles of influence and power. In his mind's eye, they watched solemnly. Their men had seen worse than this.

And, knowing more pain would come to him, he shook his head.

"Right, then." The Lady covered his face once more. "Thanks to the Emperor," she whispered. Rake could hear the smile in her voice.

Immediately, he regretted his choice, and he fought, his wrists and ankles burning against the ropes that he could not break.

But the water came just the same.

Again and again the Lady asked. Again and again she drowned him, let Death bring him close and whisper its secrets into his ear.

Everyone dies alone, Death told him, and Rake did not argue.

And Rake—he could not stand it, could not stand the pain.

So he told her. He told the Lady the Pirate Supreme's truth. They were headed for the Forbidden Isles. Where the Forbidden Isles were.

But—and it was such minor consolation in the face of his own weakness—he had not told her about the *Leviathan*. And so at least the Imperials sailed without knowing they would be met head-on by the Sea's own galleon. Perhaps he would be killed in cannon fire. If he'd had more of his wits about him, the thought may have been comforting.

The Lady Ayer washed her hands in the tub of water her men had brought into the cabin and barked some orders Rake could not hear. He was gone now, adrift in the sea of his own suffering.

Death had come, but it had not taken him.

And for that, he wept.

## ◆ CHAPTER 46 ◆

# *Flora*

The first gunshot was a surprise.

For a breath, it stopped all other noise, save for that of a body hitting the water a moment later. There had been murmuring before, a spattering of voices raised in argument. And then the shot. From the yelling that followed, Flora knew more shots would be fired.

Huddled beneath the spare boat, Flora and Evelyn clung to each other, taking up as little space as they possibly could. Flora had not expected quite so many men abovedeck — it was the middle of the night, after all. Typically, the night watch was sparse and most of the men would be belowdecks, drinking or eating or sleeping. Nor had she expected the *Dove* to shortly be boarded by Imperial forces. Evelyn had pointed out their uniform boots, and they'd stared at each other wide-eyed in fear and confusion. At least the captives would be safe, but that said nothing of Alfie, nor Rake. Nothing about this *Dove* resembled the *Dove* Flora knew like the back of her hand.

Then men shouted, and even through the cacophony of their voices Flora heard the wet smack of knuckle on flesh. And before she could tell Evelyn to hold fast, to be ready, as their moment for potential escape belowdecks could soon be upon them, the sound of an Imperial officer's voice pierced the night.

"Thanks to the Emperor, your captain has seen fit to hand you over to our control," he yelled. "And the Emperor does not look kindly upon pirates." There was the sound of men being pushed into position, their backs against the starboard gunwale. Flora could see their feet, could recognize some of them. This was the crew she had sailed with, the crew who had shaped Florian. She searched them furiously for Alfie but did not see him.

There was a terrible moment when Flora realized what would happen just before it did. But there was nothing she could do.

She forced her eyes to stay open.

The Imperial sailors opened fire. And the men, the men who had raised Florian, the men whom she'd seen nearly every day for the last few years, whose cries of defiance were cut forever short, either fell overboard from the force of the bullets that tore through them or crumpled where they stood, their arms and legs folded gracelessly in death.

Beside her, Evelyn clamped her hand over her mouth in mute horror.

The Imperials set about pushing the rest of the bodies overboard, two men to lift and toss each life they'd taken into the sea.

"Sharks'll eat well tonight," one quipped, and several others laughed.

Flora had known Imperial cruelty in her time. She had witnessed it in the streets of Crandon, seen indifference more deadly than murder. She had seen battle, witnessed the frantic actions of men cut down without reason. But still, her stomach roiled.

In anger and in horror. The Imperials promised order when they colonized, swore that their rule was the only just rule in the world. But there had been no trial here. No justice. Just men before the firing squad, no more official than the bloody business of one street gang eliminating another.

Everywhere, the copper smell of blood, the unmistakable earthen odor of opened guts.

"We have to find him," Evelyn said.

What she did not say, what she did not need to say, was: before they do.

There was a call, and all the men stood in erect salute.

"We will be sailing for the Forbidden Isles," the officer's voice declared. "We sail to destroy the Pirate Supreme. For the Emperor. For glory. For justice."

There were cheers from the men, hooting and hollering. Their forces were split back upon their original boats, with only a skeleton crew remaining aboard the *Dove* to lead the sail. The *Dove* was only a decoy to lure the *Leviathan,* Flora realized, to distract the Supreme before the true threat was realized.

But at least one thing was true: a skeleton crew would be much easier to avoid than a full one. She clutched her knife in her fist.

*This knife binds.*

She would find Alfie.

It was nearly dawn by the time Flora and Evelyn were able to slip out from underneath the spare boat. They made immediately for the lower decks, where the brig and the stores and some of the lower-ranking sailors' cabins were, scrambling across the deck, which was still sticky and wet with the blood of the crew.

But the lower decks were where Alfie's berth was. Perhaps

he'd just slept through the call to assemble? It wouldn't be the first time. He was a viciously deep sleeper, especially when he'd been drinking. Flora had not seen him, his feet easily identified by his black skin and the tattoo of a pelican that wrapped his ankle.

*He's still alive.*

She did not spare a look behind as she scurried, and simply trusted that Evelyn had followed. When Evelyn tumbled down the stairs after her, landing on her bottom with a thud, Flora smiled. She may have a bruised ass, but she was safe. She grabbed Evelyn's hand, and they ran to the brig, with Flora's pistol drawn and cocked.

As they turned a corner to head down the next staircase, though, Flora nearly ran headlong into Fawkes. His arms were full with pistols and ammunition, and in his surprise he dropped much of his load. For one crazed moment, it seemed he did not even see Flora, what with his mind on the task at hand. But it was only a moment. A horrible, wide grin spread across his face.

She was just out of his reach, but she knew a man like Fawkes could close that distance quickly.

"Well, I'll be damned," he said. "If it isn't little Florian." He looked beyond Flora to regard Evelyn, whom he apparently did not recognize. "And you brought a friend."

It was as though her mind had stopped entirely. Flora stalled, frozen to the spot. Of all the men to survive the firing squad — Fawkes was big, and cruel. She'd never stand up to him in a hand-to-hand fight. He'd kill her. He stared the way hungry dogs stare. She was scared of him, and he knew it. She tried to think of anything useful to do, anything clever —

There was an explosion just next to Flora's ear. Before she could understand what had happened, Fawkes sank to the ground and curled in on himself, around a wound in his thigh that blossomed red. Dumbly, she turned to look behind her and saw Evelyn with one of Fawkes's dropped pistols still pointed.

"You little bitch," Fawkes spat. But he could do nothing but try to stanch the blood that pooled beneath him. Evelyn had accidentally shot well. A puddle spread, too fast to be stopped, under the enormous man. He'd bleed out in minutes, Flora could tell. And from the way Fawkes's face lost its color, she imagined he must know as well.

"I was aiming for his heart," Evelyn admitted a little sheepishly.

*Evelyn. Evelyn with a pistol!* Flora felt a strange pride billowing in her heart. She wanted to take Evelyn in her arms and kiss her the way a pirate ought to be kissed.

But now was not the time. Surely, someone would have heard the shot. "Let's pick up the rest of those guns," she said, and Evelyn did.

They made to leave Fawkes where he lay, cursing and moaning, but Flora paused. She wondered if she should kill him where he sat, if she could bring herself to do it. She'd not killed since Mr. Lam, always seeming to find an excuse not to pull the trigger. Her fist was just as fine a weapon as a blade at this point, her tolerance for pain as high as it was.

*But this is Fawkes.* He was a liability, an unknown variable she was adding to an equation already dense with the uncontrollable, the unknowable.

She tried to think of what Rake would do.

She pulled her pistol and pointed it at Fawkes.

"Why'd you not face the firing squad?" she demanded, though she hardly needed to. The captain had not died. He must have made a deal for them both. The two worst men of the *Dove.*

Still clutching his wound, his face going paler by the minute, Fawkes managed the energy for a throaty chortle. "You going to shoot me, little man?"

Flora cocked the pistol. Beside her, she could hear Evelyn draw in her breath and hold it.

"It'd be a kindness if I did." She did her best to keep her voice calm and reasonable. She was talking to a dead man, after all, and it did not do to taunt the dead. "You're going to bleed out on this floor, so you might as well make yourself useful before you pass. Where is Alfie?"

"Wish they'd let me at him again. The captain. Rake. He was punished, you know, after you ran off, fifty lashes I delivered myself. Squealed like a right piggy, he did." Even close to death, bleeding out, he was a monster.

"You're disgusting," Evelyn spat. She didn't even know the half of it, and Fawkes knew it. He smiled his hideous toothy grin.

"You think that was the first time I made him squeal?"

Flora tried not to think of Alfie, of the terrible day the other sailors had left him and Fawkes alone, of the screams. She'd known, of course, what was happening just as well as she'd known there was nothing she could do about it. The rest of the men were bent on holding her back, or laughing at her, laughing at Alfie. *It's all part of being in a man's world,* they'd said. It was the price they'd have to pay if they wanted to live among them. And besides, Fawkes had been riled up on drink, and under those circumstances his actions were hardly surprising. They said this, and Flora accepted it, because she could not imagine how they'd survive another Crandon winter. She'd accepted it because she didn't know better.

But she did now.

She did not know if Alfie was alive or dead. But she knew he had not deserved what Fawkes had given him. She and Alfie were bound in love and in betrayal, bound as family. And she knew that if Fawkes lived, he'd do it again.

"Tell me where he is." It would be the last time she asked.

Fawkes grinned up at her defiantly. "No," he said. But his voice was less confident now; a touch of fear seeped in around the edges.

Flora leveled her pistol at him and took slow, careful aim.

"You're on the wrong side of the *Dove* entirely," Fawkes added hastily. So he feared death. Flora should have known he would.

"Say your last," she told him.

"Don't shoot!" he called, frantic now. "He's in the officer's cab —" But before he could finish, Flora pulled the trigger.

She did not need to hear the end of the sentence. She knew where Alfie was now, and she knew how to get there.

She did not even hear the explosion as the gunpowder ignited, propelling the bullet from her pistol straight into Fawkes's broad, lined forehead. It was as though all sound evaporated in that moment of justice. Fawkes's head snapped back with the force of the shot, a spray of blood painting the wall behind him.

It was the second time Flora had killed. And though it would haunt her, as taking a life always does, she felt sure of her own righteousness.

Men like Fawkes were too cruel to live. He was a disease. And she had cured the world of him.

Beside her, Evelyn clutched her stomach, fighting the nausea that comes when one witnesses death straight on for the first time.

"You're OK," Flora told her. "Breathe."

Evelyn nodded, looking away from the thing that had been Fawkes. She took a deep, steadying breath.

"We killed him," Evelyn said finally.

*We.* Flora kissed Evelyn's knuckles.

"We had to." She did not tell her that they were bound now, both of them, to Fawkes. She did not mention the weight of his life that would stay with them forever. It was not the time. And besides, Evelyn was strong. Much stronger than she realized.

Instead, she pulled Evelyn by the hand down the stairs. They'd have to go through the stores to get to Alfie. With the *Dove* crewed by men who did not know her, it was possible they could do it. It was what they had come back to do.

*This knife binds.*

## CHAPTER 47

# Genevieve

**W**hy not just kill him?"

Rake was still tied to a rickety wooden chair, his head hanging despondently. He was positioned in the corner of the captain's cabin so that he was out of the way of the officers now using the table to discuss and debate their plans.

Genevieve almost felt sorry for Rake. He wept freely. She knew the dry drowning was a cruel but efficient technique, well chosen by the Lady for the circumstances. Time was of the essence, after all. What she didn't understand was why the Lady had not simply had him shot and tossed overboard along with the rest of the criminals.

The Lady Ayer smiled, the same patient smile she often used when Genevieve was slightly more bloodthirsty than was strictly necessary. Which was, the Lady had chided her, rather too often for someone who had witnessed so little death.

"We have not faced the Forbidden Isles yet," the Lady said. "We do not know if we are yet done with him."

Genevieve nodded. Of course. Why hadn't she thought of that? The Lady Ayer was so wise.

"And he could prove a useful bartering tool," the Lady added.

Genevieve had not thought of that, either.

Rake was — arguably — the worst among them, since his whole role in life was to support the Pirate Supreme and thwart Imperial plans and forces. How was it that someone would come to make so many wrongheaded decisions in so little time? She pitied him. He wasn't stupid, exactly. He could have made something of himself if he'd been willing to do a little hard work. She shook her head at him.

"He's a strong man," the Lady said. "Most men can't stand the dry drowning for nearly as long as he did." She looked at him with something like respect upon her countenance. "It'd be a pity to waste a life like his."

Rake coughed and snuffled his snot loudly.

Genevieve was not so sure she agreed, but said nothing.

"And now we sail for the Forbidden Isles?"

The Lady Ayer nodded solemnly. She had been on the Pirate Supreme's trail for years now, and Genevieve could feel the Lady's growing anticipation. She could see it in the way she drummed her fingertips, how uncharacteristically fidgety she was. They would use the *Dove* as a decoy and a trap, the Imperial galleons sailing in her wake. When the Pirate Supreme's men spotted the *Dove*, they would, according to Rake, sail the mermaid flags that would render the stronghold visible at a distance. The *Dove* would lead the Imperial forces right in, cannons blazing.

When they returned to Crandon, the Lady would have finally earned the respect she deserved from the Emperor. Though she was widely regarded as his best operative, the Emperor himself had never deigned to comment on the Lady Ayer's fine work in front of his court. He never hesitated to comment upon the many deeds of his male operatives, however, a fact that Genevieve was keenly aware of. The injustice of it rankled her, though the Lady had never once mentioned it. This was, Genevieve knew, a side effect of the Lady's good training, her honor, and her ability to always place her duty before her own needs.

There was a holler from abovedeck, and the Lady Ayer snapped to attention. She was a fearsome thing at her full height, with her eyes glowing and hungry, her shoulders square. Genevieve did her best to mimic the Lady, standing at attention as though she herself had been called.

Another ship had been spotted. Perhaps. The men were unclear.

The Lady walked with a quick, purposeful clip abovedeck. There, a handful of the crewmen huddled around a spyglass, taking turns looking through it. With the morning sun starting to peek through the clouds, it was difficult to see, they said, but there could be something. There?

They pointed, and the Lady Ayer took the spyglass from them and looked.

Genevieve knew something was horribly wrong when the Lady gasped. The Lady never gasped, not in earnest, not as an operative of the Emperor. And yet the sound had been as unmistakable as a black ink stain on white robes.

"Get me the Nameless Captain," the Lady barked, and two of the sailors ran off to see her bidding done.

"What is it?" Genevieve asked. But either her voice was whisked away by the wind or the Lady Ayer ignored her, for there was no answer.

One of the men returned holding on to the captain's sleeve.

The captain looked drunk. He swayed a little where he stood. Genevieve wanted to punch him.

"Look through this spyglass and tell me what you see." The Lady handed him the device, and the captain snatched it gracelessly from her. The Lady wiped her hand on her robe where the captain had inadvertently touched her. The wind carried the scent of his nasty rum to Genevieve's nostrils.

"Oh, bugger." He seemed unable to take the spyglass down from his eye. The stupid drunk smile was gone now.

"I feared as much." The Lady called to the men then, her voice strong with the power of command. She kissed her fingers in silent prayer. "It seems the Pirate Supreme has sent the *Leviathan* to us."

There was murmuring, undeniable apprehension among the men. Genevieve knew now why the Lady had gasped. No one had faced the *Leviathan* and won. Not with ten ships, and certainly not four. Their assured victory looked like nothing of the sort now. She looked to the Lady to see how she might better comport herself and was pleased to find she stood just as tall as she had even before receiving the bad news. Perhaps even taller.

"Ready the cannons. Just because the *Leviathan* has not been defeated does not mean she cannot be," the Lady Ayer said. Genevieve could see the Lady's pride as she looked at the men, her men, and reminded herself of their skill. Their power. The men looked back at her with admiration. Of course they did. She had commanded their commanders, and now she was leading them to the Pirate Supreme. She was unstoppable, like death itself.

The Lady Ayer stepped up to the foredeck and faced her men, her face alight with a smile of assured victory. "The only reason the *Leviathan* has not been defeated is because she has never faced Imperial men, Imperial might, Imperial majesty," she shouted to them. "We will blast that abomination from these waters. Whose glory do we fight for?"

"THE EMPEROR'S!" the men called back in unison. Genevieve could see the effect of the Lady's rallying cry immediately. The Emperor's men stood with their chins high.

"Whose flags do we sail?"

"THE EMPEROR'S!" Some of the men raised their fists now, their voices rising together like flames that would burn the sky.

"WHO OWNS THE SEA?" the Lady Ayer bellowed.

"THE EMPEROR!" the men called back.

Genevieve could feel the pride swelling in her heart. The Lady looked for all the world like the warriors of old, her eyes afire, her hair whipping about madly in the wind. If anyone could take down the *Leviathan*, it was she.

"Genevieve," the Lady said, "have the men bring me Rake."

There were no men left in the captain's cabin. Only Rake on his chair, looking pitiful.

They were both from Quark; this Rake had acknowledged the moment he and Genevieve met. When she had told him her name, he'd cocked his eyebrow judgmentally. She'd seen it. He knew it wasn't her true name, since it was not a name from Quark. But she had grown past her roots, unlike him. And now look at them. She stood, the student of the Emperor's finest operative. And he sat, the broken man of the Pirate Supreme.

"Your Supreme will die, you know," she said. She resented how impetuous her voice sounded. One of the many curses of being young was lacking the proper gravitas. Rake did not reply.

Genevieve grabbed the shackles from the captain's desk, pulled the captain's chair from it, and dragged the chair across the room so that she could sit face-to-face with Rake. He lifted his chin almost imperceptibly as she sat down, but not so high that they saw each other eye to eye. Pathetic.

"The Lady has called for you. The *Leviathan* has been spotted."

Again, Rake said nothing but only sniffled, as he had been doing for hours. How wearisome his suffering was to watch. It was like a long act he put on just to remind the Imperials that their treatment had been rough. And of course it had been! What did he expect, cavorting with pirates? With the Pirate Supreme?

"Look at you," Genevieve spat. "You're an embarrassment to Quark."

At this, Rake did lift his chin. His face was swollen from being punched, or the dry drowning. Whichever. He looked terrible. Strings of snot hung from his nose.

"Do not speak of Quark," he murmured. His voice was firm, and for one ridiculous moment Genevieve felt chastised. As though he commanded any respect, as if he had that kind of power.

"People like you — you give us all a bad name." She was more angry than she'd realized. She could feel the heat of it burning red in her cheeks. How hard she'd worked to distance herself from men just like him. "You're the reason people think we're all thieves."

Rake did not say anything, but Genevieve could see his hatred for her; she could actually *see* it, like a storm gathering behind his eyes. He was old enough, she guessed, to have been alive when Quark first became an Imperial colony. And though that should have been a happy occasion — for soon after there were paved roads and constables — she was not so naive to think there had not been a handful of misled rabble who'd kicked and screamed the whole way through. Rake, she guessed, had been one of them.

"And anyway," she continued, "you got what you deserve. And now I'm to take you abovedeck."

This was not strictly true. She had been told to get the men to escort him. But she was not weak. She had been trained by the Lady Ayer. How impressed the Lady would be when Genevieve came with their prisoner on her own. And besides, Rake was only a shadow of a man now. Men were always diminished after the dry drowning.

With her knife on his throat, Genevieve undid the knot that held Rake to the chair easily with her other hand. The moment the ropes loosened, he rolled his wrists experimentally, and Genevieve could see the burning red rashes from where he'd fought against them.

"Stand, with your hands above your head."

He did, his hands held up in supplication. Genevieve smiled. Though she knew duty was not meant to inspire pleasure, she could not help but be pleased. Here he was, the Pirate Supreme's own man. And he was helpless against her as she had her blade to his throat.

She pulled the shackles from her skirt. "Put one hand down, behind your back."

Rake did.

Genevieve fumbled with the shackles. Why hadn't she checked to make sure they were open first? The key still rested in the lock, and she tried to hold the shackles against her side and turn the key all while holding the blade to Rake's throat. She'd have him cuffed and ready to go in just a moment, as long as she could —

A knock to the side of her head sent the shackles spinning to the ground. She could hear the pain just as well as she felt it. She hadn't even seen him move. But Rake was no longer under her blade, his eyes like the black coals of a raging fire. He stood before her as she clutched her head foolishly.

Another punch sent her reeling to her hands and knees. She'd seen his fist just before it connected with her jaw. The blade, too, fell to the ground with a clatter, beyond Genevieve's reach.

Rake pulled his foot back and kicked Genevieve savagely in her side. Nausea roiled up in her belly, and she coughed for breath.

"You will never speak of Quark again," Rake hissed. He kicked her again, and this time the sick did come, involuntarily and suddenly, burning Genevieve's throat. "You may kiss Imperial feet. You may take Imperial names. But you" — he kicked her once more — "don't speak" — again — "OF QUARK."

The last kick caught Genevieve in the side of the head. She felt herself falling backward, as if through molasses, slowly and strangely, until her head hit the deck with a smack.

"You will never be one of them. Not truly."

Distantly, she was aware of Rake picking up her blade, but try as she might, she could not make her limbs obey her bidding. They were like rags, lifeless things, not so much a part of her as simply attached. She wanted to scream; she wanted to stop him. But she could not.

And as the black embrace of unconsciousness took her, she saw him step cautiously from the cabin and slip out freely into the *Dove*.

◆ CHAPTER 48 ◆

# *Rake*

It had been foolhardy to let him live, arrogant to leave him in the room as they drew up their plans. Idiocy to send that slip of a girl to handle him. If there was anything predictable about the Imperials, it was their ridiculous pride. The moronic notion that they were somehow better than other people, less vulnerable.

Rake would make them pay for that mistake.

Belowdecks, there were stores upon stores of explosives. All he'd have to do to keep the Pirate Supreme safe would be to blow them up. He would just have to hope that the other Imperial galleons were still close by—perhaps the explosion would do some damage to them, too. But at the very least, a skeleton crew of Imperials, including a high-ranking Imperial operative and the captain, would all be killed. Best of all, the Pirate Supreme would know something was wrong and steer the *Leviathan* away.

Death had not left his side. Not since the captain had named him the traitor in the ranks. Rake could feel it clinging to him like dried blood.

"Soon," Rake said aloud. It did not do to fear Death, only to welcome it.

He grabbed his pistol from the Lady Ayer's cabin and then slipped below the decks. It was a narrow fit, but Rake was a narrow man, and he'd made the slimy, rat-ridden trip more than once in his years aboard the *Dove*.

He made it to the gun stores before someone found him. He'd been coming down the ladder and hadn't seen anyone as he descended. But there was someone there.

"Stop." He knew the voice. He heard the unmistakable click of a pistol being cocked.

He turned slowly, his hands up, and looked into the face of the captain once again.

"So they let you live," Rake said.

"Indeed they did!" the captain said cheerily. "Me and Fawkes, so we might help their efforts."

"The other men —"

"Already gone."

Rake shook his head. "You have no honor."

"Nope." The captain smiled his awful smile, all yellowed teeth and cruelty. There was no joy to the captain's smile, only amusement. "Honor is a scam perpetuated by cowards. But I tell you what: you come with me without a fight, and I won't shoot you here and now even though you so coldly betrayed me, and for *years* no less. Sound like a plan?"

"How could you bend to them?" Rake was stalling for time, but he hoped the captain could not tell. He was a vain man, after all, and there was nothing he loved more than a good bout of bloviation. Rake readied his patience for it, tried his best to ignore Death, though it lurked in the shadows.

"Who, the Imperials?" The captain laughed. "They're uptight, sure, but at least they don't want me dead."

"Surely they do," Rake said coolly. "You can't imagine you'll survive this."

"Oh, I'm sure I've survived worse. And anyway, I don't much care for my crew being infiltrated." Here he paused and gave Rake a condescending look of rebuke.

Behind the captain, Rake saw something stir. Not a rat. Something big. A foot, perhaps. He remembered then, in a flash, the wet foot he'd seen slip beneath the spare boat. But before he could see who it was, they had ducked behind a tall stack of cases.

"I must say, that is something that makes me very angry indeed," the captain continued, motioning with his pistol impatiently. "Now, I think we've stalled enough, my good man. Come with me and you live, for now. Don't, and I get the pleasure of shooting you right this second. You must know I am eager to see you dead. I did nothing but treat you well in your years with me, and yet you still saw fit to betray me to that idiot Supreme. Now. Ready?"

Rake tried to think of a reply, but none came.

Instead, two figures slipped out from behind the stores.

Florian, he recognized immediately. Though what he was doing there baffled Rake entirely. He'd worked so hard to see the boy safely away; why was he back? The other one — Rake could hardly tell. They had Imperial features, but none of the Imperial trappings of wealth. The two of them held pistols, aimed squarely at the captain's back.

The captain whirled to see what Rake was looking at behind him. In his shock, he let his pistol hand droop, giving them the drop on him. When he saw whom he faced, the Nameless Captain burst into boisterous laughter.

"Florian!" he exclaimed. "And who's this? Is this the Lady

Hasegawa, then? You've gotten matching haircuts! How absolutely charming of you." He was practically doubled over, he was laughing so hard. "Rake!" he gasped. "Look at 'em!"

Rake looked at them. The Lady Hasegawa. He'd have never guessed. She was not the same girl who'd left the *Dove* so recently.

"What say you, Rake?" Florian asked. "What should we do with the captain?"

The captain's laughter subsided into the echoes of a giggle, irritation visibly washing over him. "You think I'd let you little worms decide my fate?"

The Lady Hasegawa pointed her pistol at the captain, her hand unwavering. "I have already shot one of your men today. You would do well to respect Florian."

"You must be joking," the captain said. "You must be joking!"

"Have you anything to bind him?" Rake asked.

Florian produced a pair of shackles. So he'd already been by the brig, looking for Alfie, Rake assumed. Florian tossed them to Rake.

"Drop your weapon," the Lady Hasegawa commanded.

Several moments passed as the captain looked around him, clearly trying to understand not only what *had* happened, but what *was* happening, and also if he had any means for recourse. Even a fool could see that he did not. His pistol hit the deck with a clatter.

"Kick it to me," Florian said, and the captain obliged. Florian scooped up the pistol with a smooth motion, the motion Rake himself had taught him. "Hands behind your back."

Rake snapped the shackles into place, relishing the deep metallic click as the locking mechanism shifted into place.

"We cannot escape with you," Rake told the captain. "Nor can I abide your survival. So you will stay in these stores."

The captain snorted. "They'll find me, you know. After they've killed your fool Supreme."

Rake smiled. It felt so strange to smile. It had been so long. "Floria — Flora. You know where the barrels of gunpowder are."

"Yes, sir," Flora said.

The captain's face paled — clearly he understood. From the look of shock on Flora's face, she did, too. It was, Rake knew, a dicey plan. But it'd do the trick.

"You can't destroy the *Dove*," the captain interjected angrily, but Rake ignored him.

"We need to ensure we have enough time to make our escape. Can you see to this?"

Flora's face crumpled with worry. "But Alfie, sir —"

"Is on our way out."

The Lady Hasegawa caught Flora's eye and smiled at her. Trust passed as clearly as words. Flora nodded her consent, and the two of them set off to create the trail of gunpowder that would lead to the many stores of it. To blow up the *Dove*. To kill the Imperials. To end the Nameless Captain.

"You." Rake turned his full attention to the captain. For once, he would allow the full brunt of his hatred free. "You we will leave down here, among the rats and the rot and the bilge water where you belong. And while my Supreme no doubt would have preferred to have presided over your trial, they'll no doubt be pleased to hear that you have been blown into dust, into nothingness, into a form more befitting your character."

"You should have killed me years ago," the captain said.

"I could not agree more."

Rake wanted nothing more than to cock a fist, punch the captain in his gut, hear the grunt of his pain. But he knew the dry drowning had left him diminished and weak. He'd already wasted so much energy on his escape. He could afford no more frivolous expenditures of strength.

He would not make the same mistake as the Imperials, though. He would not underestimate his enemy. "Sit," he told the captain, and the captain did as he was told. How refreshing it was, Rake reflected, to give him orders for once.

The Lady Hasegawa returned before Flora, but she said nothing and Rake bid her tie the captain's legs together. Rake watched as she struggled with the knots. If she wanted to be a pirate, she'd need to learn.

"You'll die here, nameless, unloved, and unremembered. Your body will be given to the Sea, and if she wills it, she will forgive us for your many crimes against her."

"I didn't see it coming. I'll give you that," the captain said almost wistfully.

"Have you any last words?" Rake asked. Because it was the right thing to do. Because it was tradition. But only for those reasons.

"The Sea is not your ally, son. She'll see what's best for her, and that's all."

"I am not your son," Rake replied tartly. "You have no family. Remember?"

And with that, Rake left the captain to his fate. With Death, who, for once, did not follow.

## CHAPTER 49

# *Evelyn*

Flora was all impatience. She said nothing, but Evelyn could see it. The way her eyes darted constantly. The strange, tight way she held her fists closed.

They passed by the cabin that had once been Evelyn's. It felt odd to run right by it, that place where her life had, in a sense, both ended and begun. Inside, she knew, likely remained her things, her dresses, vestiges of a life all but gone now. An empty casket waited for a body that would not come. Not today. And how marvelous it was to pass those things by, knowing how soon they would be gone.

Rake had caught them up on everything as they ran, and even though she already knew, it had been startling to hear of the Lady Ayer's ruthlessness, of her high rank. The Lady Ayer and her girl Genevieve, too. How foolish Evelyn had been to trust them, to assume they were bonded in womanhood, as Imperials. Some niggling little part of her, the part where she kept her pride, ached to confront them both one last time. To flaunt her escape, to punish them. As if somehow in confronting them she would be confronting her whole family, and by extension the whole Empire, the Emperor himself. But this moment would not come and Evelyn knew it.

Flora flung open the door to the cabin Alfie now rested in and gasped. Evelyn could see why — the boy had clearly been whipped, though the wounds had the soft pink edges of healing. She swept to her brother immediately, and even though Evelyn could not see her face, she knew Flora was crying.

"Come, brother," Flora said. She made to lift him from his bed. But Alfie did not move.

"Florian?" he murmured. His voice was blurry. He must have been sleeping, or drinking. Or sleeping off his drinking. Evelyn felt a pang of sympathy for him, his broken body, his pain. He did not deserve the life he had been given.

"We don't have time for sweet reunions," Flora whispered, but she kissed his forehead anyway before handing him his tattered, bloody shirt. "We have to move."

She turned to Evelyn, who stepped forward and helped to lift the injured boy as carefully as she could. She and Flora each inserted a shoulder beneath an arm, and soon Alfie was on his feet. They helped him loosely pull on his shirt.

"I thought you'd left me," Alfie said. His voice was thick.

"I did," Flora said.

"But she came back," Rake added quickly. "We can discuss all the various logistics once we are well and safe, but right now we have about three more minutes until this boat is blown into sawdust."

"The *Dove*?" Alfie asked. But no one answered. Instead, they hustled him out of the cabin. There would be time for answers later.

Assuming they survived.

"Do you hear that?" Rake whispered. Flora nodded.

Then, the unmistakable sounds of men shouting, fear obvious in their voices. Panic.

Rake caught Flora's eye meaningfully. "Battle's started."

Evelyn's heart raced. She'd read of battles. The Empire's history was full of them. But it was one thing to read of violence, another to witness it. Fawkes's death had been proof enough of that. She could feel her stomach turning with anxiety, and she wondered if she might be sick again. Flora squeezed her hand.

"OK," Flora said. She looked to Evelyn. "Keep your head down. Move with purpose. We'll go in a straight line, as best as we can, straight for the gunwales. Got it?"

"Yes," Evelyn said. Then, "What are gunwales?"

Flora smiled. "Just follow me."

# ◆ CHAPTER 50 ◆

## *Genevieve*

Genevieve woke slowly. She knew she should not be lying down. Why was she lying down?

Then the memory of what had happened came back in a rush.

Rake.

She had to tell the Lady Ayer. But first she had to stand. It was difficult. Her legs shook with effort. She rested on her hands and knees, trying desperately to work the worthless appendages she needed to get abovedeck.

But Genevieve could hear the telltale sounds of battle already. Cannons blared from the gun deck below, and the *Dove* shuddered and shook with every explosion. She had to find the Lady Ayer. To confess her terrible mistake.

She pushed herself to her feet, grunting in a way that made her glad for her solitude. She wondered if the Lady Ayer had ever made such a foolish tactical error, but doubted it. She'd likely lose her post as the Lady's student, sacrificing any chance she ever had of becoming an operative. Shame pulsed through her, hot and fast, setting her heart racing in her ears. She could hardly lift her head from the burden of it.

None of that meant she could give up now, though, Genevieve knew. And though she'd already failed so pitifully, she would not yet abdicate the day. She had her honor to tend to, at least.

The crawl up the stairs was slow going, and Genevieve had to use the handrail to haul herself up, step by awful step, the pain in her sides and in her head blaring. Still, as she went, she could hear the cannons, could hear the men that screamed for reinforcement here or bullets there. But curiously, she could not hear any return fire.

As she finally poked her head abovedeck, she saw it. The *Leviathan* undulated in the water just beyond the *Dove,* its cannons pointed to the Imperial fleet. It was huge the way a sunrise is huge. It was like the horizon, spreading infinite. Bigger than the *Dove,* of course, but also bigger than all three of the Imperial galleons. Its name was well earned. It loomed, enormous, like some horrible sea monster of tales, its mermaid flags snapping in the wind.

Genevieve was jostled back into awareness when a man ran by her, easily knocking her aside. The pain of it tore through her, through the bruises she'd already sustained from Rake's beating. And the reminder of that brought her back to her purpose.

The Lady Ayer.

Genevieve ran about the deck of the *Dove* calling her name, but everywhere there was only chaos. Men called and they ran and they fired uselessly on the *Leviathan,* which did not seem to take any damage despite the constant fire, from all four ships now.

But then.

There she was — not the Lady Ayer, but, looking bizarre with her head shaved and her peasant's clothing, the Lady Hasegawa, of all people. Genevieve's head whirred; perhaps Rake had hit her harder than she'd realized. But no, there she was, the Lady Hasegawa, along with the missing sailor, toting a boy Genevieve scarcely recognized.

And Rake.

Fury boiled in Genevieve and she pointed a finger, screaming like a ghost from one of her mother's stories. *"There!"* she called. *"Rake!"*

It was as she sprinted toward Rake that she spotted the Lady Ayer. Her hair streamed behind her like some ancient goddess of war as she ran through the tumult and the madness. She was Imperial power embodied.

The Lady Ayer had also spotted the Pirate Supreme's operative and was running at him, too, her pistol outstretched. She fired, but Genevieve could see from the explosion of splinters in the gunwale just beyond him that she had missed, if only by inches.

Rake turned, and it was then that many terrible things happened at once:

The Lady Hasegawa and the two pirate boys jumped clear over the gunwale, directly into the sea.

Rake raised and fired his pistol. Genevieve saw the instantaneous fiery blossom of ignited powder, and then, to her absolute horror, she saw the Lady Ayer buckle, her hand to her neck.

The *Leviathan* fired its cannons for the first time that day, and Genevieve learned why tales of that ship did not die. The crack of the explosion was deafening — like death itself, it was so loud. Her ears rang.

And then, nearly as loud as the *Leviathan*'s cannons, the *Dove* itself exploded from underneath her.

# The Sea

She tastes the blood in the water and she knows — her bidding is done.

Traces of the memories she'd lost, sipped in the blood he'd stolen from her mermaids, sift back into her mind.

Of a legged fish, crawling from her grasp for the first time.

Of the volcano that erupted and formed the Forbidden Isles, though the memory is faint and she cannot tell when it was, only where.

Of daughters long since gone, their faces vague.

Memories the Nameless Captain had stolen from her returned, if only in fragments.

Men fight against her currents, fight against the force of the explosions that sent them kicking and screaming into her midst.

There, one still wears his uniform, though the trickle of blood that comes from the back of his head tells her that he is already gone. She does not know him, and so she does not care. Already, a shark circles beneath him, ever ready, ever hungry.

Here, this one has bright-red hair. She watches as he struggles upward, his eyes bulging against the pressure of her depth. On his ribs, a tattoo of a mermaid flashes beneath his shirt and then *is obscured once more. He kicks furiously, but his progress to the surface is slow.*

*She reaches with her great arms and topples another ship, crushing its wooden bones beneath her.*

*More men fall, more bodies to be lost in her depths.*

*They will tell tales of this battle, of the Sea and her might. They will say sea monsters emerged from her depths and reached up their long tentacles. They will say this because they cannot comprehend her truth, that she can pick and choose, that vengeance burns deep within her.*

*And all the while, the* Leviathan *fires her cannons, sending splinters and shrapnel flying.*

*But there —*

*She knows these two.*

*They have shared their blood with her mermaid; she has saved them once before. They have found her surface, and so with as gentle a push as she can muster, she guides the floating piece of wood they cling to toward the closest land.*

*Her daughter follows.*

◆ CHAPTER 51 ◆

## Flora

S he's bleeding," Alfie said. And though the siblings had only just been reunited, and though she'd risked her life to accomplish it, annoyance flared in Flora, fast and brilliant, like a piece of paper suddenly engulfed in flame.

Yes, Evelyn was bleeding. Flora could see that. *How could I not see that?* She could see the blood that spilled from her gut more clearly than she'd ever seen anything in her life. It was black from volume. Alfie was bleeding, too, though only a trickle from his forehead.

They'd managed, somehow, to float upon a wooden door into a shallow volcanic rock cave in what was, Flora guessed, the Forbidden Isles. Despite her better judgment, she felt sure she'd been here before, more than once. There was some cool, black sand, which the waves only kissed, where Alfie and Flora had pulled Evelyn, who could neither stand nor speak much with any clarity.

She hadn't been hit by a bullet, but rather by a large, splintered piece of wood. Flora had heard the shot go off, had seen the explosion as they'd tipped overboard into the sea. But she had not seen a piece of it embed itself in her love's belly.

"Do we pull it out?" Alfie asked. He sounded nauseated at the thought of it.

"I — I don't know." Flora pressed the palm of her hand gently to Evelyn's forehead. It was clammy to the touch, her face pale from blood loss. "It may only cause her to bleed faster."

Evelyn blinked, as if only just realizing where she was. "Florian?" she croaked.

The weakness of her voice was a blow. Florian felt it — the first rock thrown in a stoning, a punch to his gut. He squeezed Evelyn's hand, his mind reeling with his terrible new reality.

"What do we do?" Alfie asked. He looked wildly about the cave, as if there'd be a clue. There was nothing, though, save for the sand, the drip of cool water from stalactites. The gentle caress of the Sea.

"I don't know, Alfie!" Florian shouted. Alfie recoiled, but Florian could not care.

*The flies are always the first to know.*

It was a truth Flora had learned on the streets in Crandon. Even before a body fell, the flies would come, circling the wounds, the eyes, and the nose. And here, even in this cave, so far away from her life in Crandon, the flies came, and Evelyn was too weak to bat them away.

Their buzzing turned Flora's stomach, sent angry shivers through her limbs.

She thought furiously of what Xenobia had taught her — surely she could bind the wound with her knife. But she'd have to pull out the wooden stake first, have to risk Evelyn bleeding out there in the cave, gambling her life against Flora's dubious competence as a practical witch. It had taken the best part of a day to get to the *Dove* with her magic. It was hardly trustworthy.

"I'll be all right," Evelyn said.

She was, Flora knew, categorically not all right, but she forced a smile anyway.

"I know, my love, I know." It would be impossible in their short time left to tell Evelyn how much she loved her. To tell her what she had meant to her — that love was even possible in her life had been a revelation, never mind that she should receive it from someone as pure and kind as Evelyn. Tears dripped from her nose, unceasing. Her fear was a tangible thing, heavy in her chest.

Alfie sprang to his feet with an exclamation that was either fear or surprise; Flora could not tell which. He pointed toward the entrance of the cave, his finger shaking. She whirled to see what had startled him so, only to see the mermaid.

Her head protruded from the water as she swam, slowly and deliberately, for the shore.

"You," Evelyn said. Her voice was like a breeze, barely there.

The mermaid pulled herself onto the shore so that she lay at Evelyn's other side. She was beautiful, like the illustrations from Evelyn's books. The golden scales of her tail shone even in the dim light of the cave. She held Flora's eyes, then opened her fist.

She revealed in her hand the stone, that small plain stone, which Flora had sent into the Sea. At the sight of it, Flora knew. The Sea had seen Flora, had seen her love for Evelyn, and had sent the mermaid to their side. Hope floated.

Alfie gaped at the mermaid openly, his mouth slightly ajar, for once at a loss for words.

"Can you help her?" Flora asked, unable to keep the desperation from her voice. *Why else would the Sea have sent her?*

But the mermaid only shook her head sadly. She reached out her hand and ran one long finger down Evelyn's cheek affectionately.

Fury rose in Flora's chest, a beast she'd never known dwelled within her raising its horrible head for the first time. It roared.

"Then why are you here?" Flora demanded. "She saved you! Now you save her!" She could feel Evelyn's entreaty to silence more than she saw it, but she could not control the beast that was her rage.

The mermaid blinked back at Flora. But she said nothing.

Instead, in her silence, more mermaids surfaced. First one with her hair the improbable green of sprouting grass. Another, whose eyes sat strangely far apart on her face, her skin iridescent. A third, who still had the face of a child. More and more, until the black water of the cave was stippled with their faces. One looked, Flora thought, very much like her own mother, her lips pulled into a solemn line of concern. They rose from the Sea, though no other came upon the shore, to watch Evelyn in silence. There were so many of them, too many to count. An impossibility of them.

When had Flora ever seen so many female faces? Never, never. Her life had been full of men, had been made safer by her invisibility among them. And in that way, she was rather like these creatures, wasn't she? Her eyes passed over them, over the great diversity of them, drowning in the unreality of this whole situation.

It would have been beautiful if Evelyn did not lie bleeding. It would have been the most marvelous thing Flora had ever seen in her life. But instead, she could only look to Evelyn, whose face was pallid.

"Flora." Evelyn squeezed her hand with what little strength she had left. "I'm all right."

"No," Flora admitted. She brought Evelyn's hand to her lips and kissed it, holding her close, holding her dear as though her love alone could save her. "You're not. You're bleeding."

"I have loved you." Evelyn smiled, a quirk of her tremulous lips. "That is enough."

*How could that be enough?*

For someone so young. Someone so vibrant. Flora felt her eyes cloud with tears, with the inevitability of what was to come.

Evelyn lifted her chin then, an entreaty for a kiss, which Flora met. Her lips were cold to the touch, so much that they hardly even felt like Evelyn's lips at all. Everything that made Evelyn Evelyn seemed to slip away. Flora held her there, in that kiss, praying that if she could just kiss her long enough, if she could just kiss her like the prince from the stories her mother told, then maybe, maybe everything would be OK. Maybe Evelyn would live.

But when Flora pulled her head back, Evelyn's eyes stared up into nothingness.

The mermaid who lay beside her bowed her head. Her sisters followed suit. It was this show of respect, this obvious and universal signal of mourning, that made the truth evident to Flora, though still not acceptable.

Evelyn was gone.


"Listen," Flora whispered. "Listen, Evelyn Hasegawa, and listen well: You are not dead. You cannot be. That is not your story. You will live, and you will be safe and happy. Love will sustain you: my love, the love of these mermaids, the love of the Sea. You will breathe, and you will smile, and you will open your eyes."

But Evelyn did not stir.

Flora chanted for hours and still Evelyn did not stir. The mermaids watched, their heads bowed in mourning. Her knees ached from kneeling, her eyes ached from crying, and her heart ached from loss; she was nothing but ache. *Nothing.*

Finally, Alfie pulled at Flora. "Come," he said quietly. "We have to find a way to a proper shore."

He had said this many times over the last hours, but this time Flora could see that he was right. She met her brother's eyes and saw her own sadness mirrored there. She had saved him. She had lost Evelyn. And now Alfie would save her. He took her hand in his and nodded once.

"We have to go," he said. "The tide." Already the water had crept inexorably toward them. Soon, there would be no dry sand left.

Flora kissed Evelyn one last time on her cold forehead. Alfie lifted Evelyn gently from his sister's lap so that she might stand once more. Flora's legs shook beneath her, from misery and from exhaustion, but still she stood. Alfie lay Evelyn gently on the black sand of the cove. And as he did, the mermaid that Evelyn had saved reached for her.

"Let us," she said. Her voice sounded like the Sea as heard in a seashell. Distant and soft. More echo than voice. She looked to Flora for permission, and when Flora nodded, a wave lifted her and three other mermaids forward to serve as Evelyn's bizarre but beautiful pallbearers. With utmost care, they lifted her and carried her to the water's edge.

"She will be safe," the mermaid vowed, and Flora believed her.

The mermaid bowed her head once at Flora. Then she and her sisters pulled Evelyn under the Sea.

As she disappeared beneath the glassy surface, the reality of her absence hit Flora, knocking her to her knees, and she wept.

## CHAPTER 52

# Rake

The sting of seawater burned Rake's throat as he coughed. He'd been turned on his side, blessedly, mercifully, so that he could evacuate his lungs more efficiently. It was a while before he could think of anything besides air, and when he did, he realized he was on a ship.

Not just a ship.

The *Leviathan*. He'd recognize her trappings anywhere: The complicated metal filigree that covered the gunwales but never rusted. The dark, almost black wood that never creaked, even as the ship rocked. She was just as enormous and beautiful and silent as Rake had always been told.

Relief washed over him in a tidal wave. He lay on his back and barked out a laugh.

The Nameless Captain was gone. The *Dove* was blown to dust. And from the absolute lack of cannon fire, he could guess that the Imperials had been defeated. He lay with his hands over his eyes, not sure if he was laughing or crying anymore. It didn't matter. He was alive. The day was won.

A shadow came over Rake's prone body and blocked the sun. "I see you've finally pulled yourself together," a voice said.

Rake laughed. "I still feel a wreck."

He pulled his hands away and blinked. There stood the Pirate Supreme, in all their glory. Though their words had been cold, their face was cracked into a wide, warm smile. They reached out a hand and pulled Rake to his feet. The Supreme's hands were rough from life at sea, just as a proper captain's hands should be.

"You're not the only prize we've found afloat today." The Supreme motioned behind them. There, huddled together on the decks, were Florian and Alfie. Rake grinned at the good fortune of it until he saw the grimace of pain on Florian's face.

The Lady Hasegawa was not with them.

"Where —?" he started, but Alfie shook his question away and held his brother closer to his side.

"Found them trying to paddle their way to the shore on a bit of wood," the Supreme said. Their voice was serious now, thick with empathy for Florian. "Seems your boy has lost someone very precious."

Rake had never once mourned an Imperial. And though he could not quite force himself to mourn this one, he did at least feel the sharp point of loss he could see in Florian's face as if it were his own. He had never known his own father, did not know how that arrangement might look. But seeing Florian there, on board the *Leviathan* — the *Leviathan*! What better place was there for a pirate? — with the weight of the world's every injustice on his shoulders, Rake felt the desire to do something, anything, to make him feel better. To be his father, to protect him. He was free now to do that.

He knelt before Florian, took the boy's chin in his hand, and lifted it so that they could see eye to eye.

"There is no comfort except for time," Rake said. "But I'll stand by you until you ask me to leave."

"He's got me," Alfie said, a little tartly. Clearly, he had not forgotten or forgiven that Rake had overseen his lashing. Rake narrowed his eyes.

"I see you're back on your feet. Haven't found the rum here yet, have you?"

Alfie flinched, but Rake could see that his blow had struck true. Florian looked away, wiped his nose with the back of his hand roughly. Rake had never seen him cry before.

"Wouldn't need to drink," Alfie said, his voice was quiet, but sure, "if it weren't for you."

"Weren't for Fawkes, you mean," said Rake. It had not been Rake who dragged Alfie away, after all. "I'll not take the blame for his deeds."

"If it weren't for your indifference. You could have stopped it, you know."

Rake blinked at Alfie, stunned. Something like guilt, hot and dripping, clogged his throat, and words would not come. Alfie held his gaze until Rake could not bear it, and looked away.

"Rake." The Pirate Supreme's voice called him away from his shame.

All around him, the Supreme's crew scuttled about, tending to their business. Unlike the crew of the *Dove*, this crew was made up of all kinds of people, men and women and those who were neither or both or something else altogether. Rake felt a little dizzy seeing them all, or else he was still a little dizzy from nearly drowning. It was hard to say.

"I think these two need some rest," the Supreme said, and put their arm around Rake congenially.

"Suppose you're right."

"'Course I am. Now, come on. We've caught a good wind, we'll be back to the keep soon enough, and we can see this all sorted. In the meantime, I need you to catch me up on all that's happened."

"Yeah," Rake said. But his eyes were still on Florian, who was now weeping openly in his brother's arms. "Yes, I will."

*The Sea*

*A new daughter.*

*A new memory.*

*Of the girl, and her life. Of her kindness.*

*Her daughters return to her, their minds abuzz with her, this girl they loved. They hold the girl's blood and her memories together, but they cannot possibly keep them.*

Help us, Mother, *her daughters cry.* Help us remember her.

*And so she is born.*

*So that the Sea may remember.*

*She is born full of the memories she is meant to keep, just as all her daughters are born. She is touched by magic, and she gasps with her first breath.*

Hello, Evelyn, *the Sea says.*

*Evelyn stretches her arms and opens her eyes. She looks as her memory thinks she should look, with long black hair and skin smooth like a crescent moon. She is lovely. She belongs to the Sea.*

Hello, Mother, *she says. She reaches up, to the light of the sun, to the surface.*

Where is Flora?

Close, *says the Sea.*

*Her daughter smiles, and how pleased the Sea is to see her baby smile. To feel her joy as if it is her own.*

*Let us find her.*

## CHAPTER 53

## *Flora*

Night came, but Flora could not bring herself to leave the deck. It was as if going to sleep would only confirm what she wanted so desperately to be untrue. Seeing that his words meant nothing to her, Alfie stopped talking, though he still refused to leave her side. So they sat in silence, their backs against the mainmast, Flora's eyes up at the stars, the moon.

She was aware of the other sailors, the night watch, knew that now and again they spoke. But she could not focus on their words nor their faces. All she could do was watch the stars as they performed their slow and inexorable dance across the sky, tiny pricks of light, cold and remote. There were so many more stars over the open Sea than there were above Crandon. Usually that was Flora's favorite part of a voyage — the night, when they grew distant enough from civilization that the stars could reveal themselves, in their multitudes and in their density.

Had it only been a single day, the sun up once and down once, since she had held Evelyn in her arms?

*Impossible.*

It was strange. How something could feel like it had happened a hundred years ago, but also was still happening, or just finished happening a moment earlier. Still, she could feel Evelyn's lips on hers. But what did her voice sound like with her full health? Some details indelible. Others only coming in tiny fragments, obscured by the memory of the cave.

*I'll be all right,* Evelyn had said. And Flora knew then that wasn't true. Not for either of them. Evelyn was gone. And Flora would not be OK. Their stories had converged forever, and there was nothing — no magic, no power, no spell — that could undo that.

As Flora watched, the sail above her began to deflate. She looked to Alfie, who saw it, too. The wind had died down, and suddenly. The *Leviathan* slowed, the wood creaking in protest. The crew called to one another, words Flora did not understand. And despite herself, despite any logic or better reason she had access to, an unfamiliar feeling billowed in her chest.

She dared not name it. Instead, wordless, she stood. She walked to the gunwale and peered over the edge, down at the water below. It was black and shining in the moonlight, and some-how — even next to the giant *Leviathan* — impossibly still.

Behind her, she heard Rake's low voice and Alfie's. But she could not take her eyes off the water. She could not say why. She just felt that she had to keep watching. That if she could just focus on the Sea, then maybe, maybe. *Maybe.*

"Evelyn?" Flora whispered.

As if in answer, the Sea moved. Flora watched in disbelief as the water shot up, and up, and up. It formed a shimmering and undulating wall before her. It reminded Flora distantly of Crandon's city wall, if the wall had been made entirely of water, and reflected her face back to her when she looked into it.

"Florian!" Alfie called, his voice thick with warning. "Step back!" She felt his hands on her, trying to pull her away. But Flora would not let herself be moved. Instead, she reached out a hand, her palm flat, and touched the wall.

It rippled at her touch, cool and wet. She pulled her hand back and watched as its mirror image did the same. But when she put her hand back at her side, the image stayed. With her eyes squinted, Flora tried to focus on the form that was beginning to materialize behind the hand, the hand that was not her hand at all, the hand that remained.

A face, an impossible face, formed behind the hand.

The hand reached out to Flora, out past the barrier of the wall, the palm turned up in entreaty. Long, elegant fingers beckoned.

"The Lady Hasegawa," Rake said to no one, to himself, to the air.

Evelyn smiled behind the shimmering wall, her eyes soft with love and invitation.

Someone put a hand on Flora's shoulder, and she turned to see the Pirate Supreme smiling down at her.

"Go on, child," they said. They held Flora's eyes for a moment. "The Sea does not make this kind of an offer often."

"I don't understand," she said.

"She's reaching for you," Rake said simply.

Flora's eyes darted to Alfie, whose face was contorted in a way she did not recognize. He did his best to smile through his tears. If she went, she would be leaving him. Again. And they had only just been reunited.

"Who'll take care of you?" Flora asked.

"I will," he said. Neither of them were convinced.

"You're the only family I have left."

"Nah." He smiled, his real smile, wide and toothy. "You've never had a hard time finding family. Go," he said.

Flora nodded. But before she could turn to face Evelyn again, she met her brother in two quick steps and pulled him in a close, tight hug. Tears slid down her cheeks.

"Don't let me hold you back," he whispered. "Not this time."

There was nothing she could say, and so she didn't. When she finally loosened her grip on him, he had mustered a smile. She met his eyes and smiled back.

"I love you, Flora." He pressed a kiss into her forehead and nudged her gently toward her impossible future.

She turned back to the wall of water, to Evelyn, to the love of her life. She did not know what would happen. But she knew she was done with reaching. It was time.

She took Evelyn's hand. It was warm in hers, exactly as it had been only a day before. And with one last deep breath of air, she plunged into the Sea.

## CHAPTER 54

*Evelyn*

How strange it was to have a mother who loved her. How astonishing her mother's power.

Flora followed Evelyn into the Sea and within moments, she was as Evelyn was. Where once she'd had two legs, now she had a long graceful tail, glimmering with tiny scales that shone in the moonlight. Her mouth, which had only a moment ago been clamped against the pressure of holding her breath, was open, grinning, delighted, her laughter ringing all around Evelyn as she realized she could breathe.

That they were together.

It was her mother's gift to them both. The Sea knew their hearts and had decided in her infinite wisdom that she would break every natural rule of the world and see them together. That she would give them the space to love each other. They had earned it. Together.

"How?" Flora asked. But she did not wait for an answer, instead covering Evelyn's lips with her own before a reply could be formed.

There was no gravity anymore, no down, no up. There was no Empire, not here, no rule of man. Instead, the two let themselves be suspended in the miracle of open Sea. Distantly, Evelyn was aware of the *Leviathan* moving away, but only because soon the full light of the moon shone down upon them, no shadows to hide beneath any longer. Stars glimmered on the surface of their new sky.

Flora was always beautiful, as Florian and as Flora, as a sailor aboard the *Dove,* and as a witch's apprentice on the shore. But now. Now. Where Evelyn's tail was the stark red of the last rays of a bleeding sunset, Flora's was black, black like the night, black like the cave they had found each other in, black like the inside. When she moved, the scales of her new tail shifted in color, opalescent. She was beautiful this way, impossibly beautiful.

"You're home now," Evelyn said.

She did not need to say: You're home because you're with me.

She did not need to say: I will be your home.

She only needed to kiss Flora, to let every part of them entwine. To give herself over to the love they had found together, extricated from circumstance and saved from tragedy.

And that is exactly what they did.

# Genevieve

G enevieve lay on the piece of wood, letting the sun beat down on her face as she floated. For a while, she had tried to paddle, but had quickly learned that it was only a quick way to feel hungrier, thirstier, and more desperate. And so now she just lay down, letting the seawater lap against her stinging, sunburned skin like the piece of shipwrecked refuse that she was.

The Lady Ayer was certainly dead. The Imperial ships destroyed.

All her life, Genevieve believed there was no fight the Imperials could not win. They were the strongest, smartest, and best in the world. And the only reason they'd lost this battle, she knew, was her own incompetence.

She'd seen a man pulled underwater by what was, she assumed from the blood that surfaced, a shark. How she'd survived was not a miracle. A miracle would have been a quick death. Not this long, terrible drift into the unknown that she was currently undertaking.

Just more time to contend with her overwhelming, nauseating guilt.

The Lady Ayer was dead. The finest of the Emperor's operatives. And it was all Genevieve's fault. For thinking she could handle Rake on her own. For her arrogance. For her foolishness.

If she was honorable, like the Lady, she'd simply tip over into the water and let herself drown. And though she thought this with metronomic regularity, she still could not muster the courage to do it.

The Imperials had lost.

A wave pushed her, then another. The wind picked up. All around her she could see the whitecaps of churning seawater. She sat up to scan the horizon.

There. In the distance.

Land.

Genevieve squinted against the sun and could not believe she had not seen it earlier. There, and not so far, not so far that she might never make it, land! Land! And even better than that, it seemed that the current was pushing her toward it.

As she drifted closer, she peered harder and could even make out the shape of the land. Then the color, which was red. Genevieve gulped. The Red Shore.

The Red Shore was not safe for Imperials, that much she knew. It was a savage and cruel country, full of cutthroats who dealt in slaves and blood magic.

But she also knew she could not survive on this piece of wood. No one was coming to save her.

And so she paddled as best she could toward land. Toward survival.

# ACKNOWLEDGMENTS

This book was written for Clare Sabry. Without her and her expansive imagination, I never would have been inspired to write it. I'm sorry it took so long. I hope it was worth the wait.

The book was finished thanks to the persistent and often bossy support of Adam Wolf. I had all but given up on writing, and it was only his unwavering belief that gave me the confidence to try again. He was with me every day as the first and second drafts were completed and suffered having many sections read aloud to him, whether he wanted to hear them or not, sometimes multiple times with only minute edits. On a related note, I'm not allowed to do that to him anymore.

Joe Wadlington was the first person other than Adam to read a completed draft and even hopped on a several-hours-long video call from San Francisco to Ecuador to discuss it and hammer out its many, many issues. I eagerly await his impending meteoric rise to fame.

Jennifer Laughran, my agent, who could have easily been a full-time editor in another life — or a hit woman — provided invaluable feedback and support. She likes to pretend she's cranky, but she's an expert hand-holder. And frankly, I required a lot of hand-holding.

My editor, Karen Lotz, pushed me to make the questions more complicated and the plot simpler, which I think is always perfect advice. She's an excellent editor, and I felt so much more assured under her guidance. I have been very lucky to have such kind people to work with at Candlewick, particularly Jamie Tan in publicity and editorial liaison Lydia Abel.

I am also incredibly grateful for all the great early readers of this project: Na'amen Tilahun, Meg Elison, Ryan Boyd, Martha White, Melissa Manlove, Rachel Chalmers, Clare Light, Charlie Jane Anders, Annalee Newitz, Mel Hilario, Liz Henry, Audrey T. Williams, Sasha Hom, John Talaga, Carolyn Hart, Debby Bloch, and Justine Larbestelier.

A special added thank-you to Charlie Jane Anders, who has really thrown the ladder back down for me. She is a role model of what success should look like. The San Francisco writing community owes her a great debt.

This manuscript was edited almost entirely within the walls of The Ruby coworking space in San Francisco, and the first draft was finally completed during National Novel Writing Month 2016.

The very early, very weird, and mostly scrapped versions of this story were written during my time with Books Inc., the West's oldest independent bookseller and my forever store. Not all communities are lucky enough to have an indie bookseller, but if you do, please support them. Without them, the literary community would be much the poorer.